K. B. PELLEGRINO

BERYL KENT AND THE BLEEDING MAN

A CAPTAIN BEAUREGARD MYSTERY

©2021

Livres-Ici
PUBLISHING™

Livres-Ici Publishing™ of WMASS OPM, LLC
265 State Street
Springfield, MA 01103
1-413-788-0652
Livres-Ici Publishing is a registered trademark of WMASS OPM, LLC.
Livres-Ici Publishing books may be ordered through booksellers.

Because of the dynamic nature of the Internet, any web addresses or
Links contained in this book may have changes since publication and
May no longer be valid.

The views expressed in this work are solely those of the author and do
Not necessarily reflect the views of the publisher, and the publisher
Hereby disclaims any responsibility for them.

ISBN: (HC) 978-1-951012-18-2
ISBN: (SC) 978-1-951012-19-9
ISBN: (EB) 978-1-951012-20-5
Library of Congress Control Number: 2021921277

MAIN CHARACTERS

West Side Major Crimes Unit Detectives
Captain Rudy Beauregard
Lieutenant Mason Smith
Lieutenant Petra Aylewood-Locke
Lieutenant Ashton Lent
Sergeant Ted Torrington
Sergeant Lilly Tagliano
Sergeant Juan Flores
Sergeant Bill Border
Sergeant Bobby Barr

Other Recurring Characters
Chief Coyne
Attorney Norberto Cull
Sheri Cull
Mona Beauregard
Mayor Fischler
Jim Locke
Luis Vargas
Roland and Lizette Beauregard
Monique Smith
Charlotte Torrington
Martina McKay
Lavender James

Introducing
Beryl Roisin Arabella Kent

Beryl Roisin Arabella Kent's Favorite Quote:

In any moment of decision, the best thing you can do is the right thing, the next best thing is the wrong thing, and the worst thing you can do is nothing.

THEODORE ROOSEVELT

CONTENTS

1

The Bleeding Man

A quick movement caught by her eye caused Beryl Roisin Arabella Kent to focus on her back yard and glance out her kitchen French doors. She expected to see the doe that lately had frequented the woods disappearing into the trees, but it was not an animal moving. A man was running from the direction of her neighbor Mr. D'allasandro's extravagant ranch home back area. She watched as he entered her space, giving her a more complete vision. Beryl's brain balked and her body registered a stunning impression of fear at the sight of blood on the man's chest. She quickly scanned the area but saw no one following the man. Grabbing her cell, she hurried through the French doors while dialing 911 and yelling into the phone, "24 Yellow Brook Dingle, West Side, man hurt and bleeding." Downing the three steps to the grassy area almost resulted in her tipping sideways. When she reached level turf and felt grounded, the bleeding man grabbed her, falling and pulling her down with him landing partly on top of Beryl, insisting, "Help me. I don't deserve to die so soon…."

Momentarily immobile, Beryl struggled to get up from under what she thought must have been two hundred pounds of weight. She was on her back and her head had just missed the large landscape rock she had stolen from a Vermont mountain trail. She thought, *I deserve to have died here, after all I stole the rock. Thank you, God. You've saved me again.* She found herself wedged tightly beneath the man.

Beryl tried several times to push him off, but he was too heavy. Finally, using the strength of her thighs she was able to push enough to allow herself to slide out from her wedged position. Yoga breathing helped her calm down, at least enough to evaluate the situation. She thought, *check the carotids to see if he's alive. That's what's done on television. There is a pulse. Oh God, help me, I've never taken a CPR course. I've wanted to, just never got around to it. Probably I thought I had too many other important things to do. What's more important now than this man's life? There's no blood on his back, but there is blood all over me. And there is a smell. I've read blood has an odor, it does and it's also sticky. How can I do CPR on his back when he might have a bullet or knife piece or something in his gut? He's bled a lot. I'd do more damage. I absolutely hate it when I don't have a solution or even a plausible idea for one.*

The voice on her cell was repeating, "Is this an emergency?"

"Man is dying in my yard with blood all over him. That, in my mind, is an emergency."

"Do you know who he is?"

"No."

The 911 operator asked, "Who are you?"

Identifying herself, she explained the situation and that she could not lift him to press on his chest to help him breathe if he stopped breathing. She was told to wait for the ambulance and the police. They had already been directed to the site. Waiting, Beryl took two photos of the bleeding man, thinking, *this is evidence for tomorrow when I'll wonder if this really happened.*

Within eight minutes of Beryl's call, an ambulance, a fire truck, and a police vehicle pulled into her side yard. The drive area had a stoned access section adjacent to the rear yard. The whirling lights created such angst in Beryl, her nerve endings vibrated. Tears flowed and she wiped her eyes with her sleeve and unknowingly got blood on her face. *Why am*

I crying? I don't know this man. So much hoopla creates agita. It's bad enough, please don't make it worse. Please let him live. Please let him live. We shouldn't die all alone on a stranger's grass. But then, I am here and I can pray. That's really all anyone can do. He does not look well, not well at all.

Beryl was directed aside after she explained the situation to the first officer who questioned her. The officer was polite, but told Beryl to wait inside her home. Further, he said a detective would be taking a written statement insisting, "Ma'am, you look bad. I think you need a coffee or something and some space to quiet down."

Actually, he insisted she go inside her house for the waiting period, but she refused. Officer Shaughnessy suggested she stay out of their way. "You really would be better off not seeing all of this, it may not be good for you. Lady, you may want to reconsider going inside to wipe the blood off your face., and maybe get a mask on for your own safety. Never mind, leave it that way, the detectives will want the scene left as we found it."

Beryl answered with a brittle response. "What would blood on my face from wiping my eyes with my sleeve have to do with preserving the site. And it's a little late for me if this man had COVID-19, then I'll have it. I sincerely hope, Officer, you are not inferring something here. I'm not that old, Officer Shaughnessy, to put up with such nonsense even from the police. You think I'm put off by blood when I've seen more of death close to me than you could ever have imagine."

"Oh, you're a nurse. I guess it's okay for you to stay close by."

"No, Officer, I am not a nurse, just a survivor of life."

"You're not old, Ms. Kent."

Fortunately, and timely for Officer Shaughnessy, West Side detectives pulled their car further over on the stone side area near the ambulance. They drove over the edge of the stones hitting the grass. Beryl flinched, loudly whispering, "Like all my visitors they have no sense of the difficulty in re-grassing a damaged turf. They're detectives, they should be smarter."

She laughed at her short-sightedness, thinking, *Christmas, my kids, in-laws, and friends, many who have doctorate degrees, drive right over the boundary. Only construction workers respect it.*

MCU detectives, Lieutenant Petra Aylewood-Locke and Sergeant Juan Flores left their car on the grass with no apologies. Point of fact in Beryl's mind was, *they don't even know they've parked improperly. Tells me they don't do yard maintenance at home.*

Since the two detectives did not approach her first, she waited as they discussed the situation with the officers and then went over to the ambulance. The man by this time had been loaded onto a stretcher and was ready to be taken to the hospital. *He must be alive. They didn't cover his face. Thanks, angels out there. Protect him.*

The male detective glanced over at Beryl and she felt certain Officer Shaughnessy was discussing her with him. Beryl could not hide a glimmer of distrust on her face just as the woman detective also gazed in her direction. She immediately felt a meeting of the minds reinforced by the woman detective's walking towards her with a greeting of, "You must be Ms. Beryl Kent. I understand you found the man in your yard. I'm Lieutenant Petra Aylewood-Locke and my partner is Sergeant Juan Flores. Could you tell us about it?"

Beryl straightened her form, as her father would insist should happen in the event one was under the auspices of authority figures. She thought, *I'm fifty-seven years old and I still do what my dad told me to do, not always what my mom desired. She'd want me to play the poor little girl needing rescue game when with police of any kind. I guess we are forever our parents' children, whether we're going along with or rejecting their suggestions.*

In an attempt to relay all the information, she had, Beryl gave a non-emotional response addressing the rather shocking tale. She felt quite proud of herself for not sharing her first emotional reactions to seeing the bleeding man as he fell on her. Sergeant Flores asked, "Tell me again how this man fell on you. You have a great deal of blood on you and your face, Ms. Kent."

Beryl described the man's condition and the moment of impact when he reached out to her with what she suggested was a motion for her to help him. The Lieutenant asked why would he come to her house. Had he been there before? Beryl was testy in her response, saying, "Lieutenant, why would you ask me that when I said I didn't know him. If he'd been here before I would have known him. As far as I'm concerned it is a strange situation. He came across from the D'allasandro's yard direction. They've been in Florida for the duration of this virus scare. No one but workmen have been at his home for months. Further, if you looked at the man, he was not a workman unless they're dressing in eight-hundred dollars suits and four-hundred-dollar shoes now."

Sergeant Flores asked, "How did the man get in your back yard? There is a fence between the two houses for what looks to me like a hundred feet. Would he have come through your neighbor's house to get in the rear yard? Is there a fence on the other side? Could he have come in as we came in?"

Beryl Kent showed a distinct displeasure at their questions saying, "Sergeant, you cannot get blood out of a stone. I saw what I saw and only what I saw. The man walked from the direction of the D'allasandro's when I saw him, not from any other direction. If he came in through my access area in the condition he was in, you should be able to find blood drippings. As to a fence on the other side of my neighbor's home, there is one and you should check it out. The next home after Charlie D'allasandro's is a quarter mile away. The fence does not extend all the way between the two properties.

"A better question is, why didn't this man stay on the paved road when a car going by could stop to help? Why choose to go over grassy areas and avoid all the circular gardens my neighbor has and work around my out buildings. There is not a direct route here. He would have had to walk quite a ways. If you had a look at him you must have noticed he has extra weight on him. I don't see him as an exercise freak."

Juan laughed and said, "You're a detective, now, Ms. Kent."

Clearly annoyed, Beryl said, "Sergeant, I am simply stating the obvious. I observe and try to remember what I've seen and what it could mean. If that's being a detective, I will add it to my accomplishments."

Petra Aylewood-Locke glanced at Juan wondering the why behind his attitude toward the lady thinking, *even I know Beryl Kent is not to be taken lightly. I'll bet my bars, she was an English teacher, but must be a wealthy one to afford this home.*

Petra asked, "Do you have a dog? An officer noticed animal footprints near the woods. Did you hear barking before you saw the man?"

Beryl said, "Do you know the man's name? I saw you checking his pockets and taking some paper out?"

Juan said, "You didn't answer the lieutenant's question, Ms. Kent."

"No, I didn't and you didn't answer mine. Detectives, this is a two-way street. I'm perfectly willing to give you answers if I have them. Is it too much to ask for the name of a man who almost died in my backyard?"

Preventing Juan from giving a flip answer, Petra said, "We don't know his name. The paperwork in his pocket relates to a printout on some stocks with no identification. Now, do you have a dog?"

Beryl Kent answered, "No, I'm waiting for a rescue from Tennessee. My dog 'Eureka' crossed the rainbow bridge two months ago. I've only lived in this house for nine months. And no, there are no dogs close by other than a fenced in pair of greyhounds in a house half mile up the road. All the houses were built on enormous acreage for a suburban setting. As to my neighbor, Frank, when he is at home, he never is dressed formally like this bleeding man. I've never seen 'suits' like this around his home. I heard no barking to answer your other question. I was first attracted by the rustling of shrubs and branches thinking there was a baby deer who has been visiting my acreage for the last week."

Juan responded, "Could the man have come from the woods? You didn't actually see him coming from your neighbor's area, did you?"

Beryl said, "I did not say the man came from my neighbor's yard, I said I saw him coming from that direction. How could I know where he was coming from? I saw him for ten or fifteen seconds before he fell on me."

Petra intervened commenting, "Sergeant Flores is just trying to pin down exactly what you said. Often, witnesses know more than what they say. Not in your case, I'm guessing. Can you think of any other unusual happening today before the man came into your view, such as a noise?"

A calmer Beryl appeared to consider the question and nodded in the affirmative. "Yes, twenty minutes before, I heard a helicopter overhead. I've never heard one during my time in this house. Further, we are not in the airpath for planes here. Maybe it was going to Baystate Hospital with an accident victim, they have a helicopter pad on their roof."

The detectives asked if they could take pictures of her. Beryl was accommodating. Without their asking she said, "I suppose you want my clothes, I'll go in and take them off. Lieutenant, I imagine you'll want to accompany me. Do you have an evidence bag for them?"

Juan thought, *this lady must watch forensic files on some TV show. Talk about knowing a bit too much. Maybe she's practicing to be a female Sherlock Holmes.*

Later, after the excitement died down in Beryl's meditation area and the uniforms left after taping off the area, Beryl entered her yard and attempted to reclaim it for herself. Wandering through the existing opening in the rear, she walked to the woods. She found scuff marks in the soil about four or five feet in behind a large bush. There'd been a light rain during the night, just enough moisture to allow a tread mark from a shoe. She took a photo and tied her scarf to the bush. She thought, *I will call Lieutenant Aylewood-Locke and forward her this find. There is no blood, but someone was here. She said her name was Petra. My father always liked that name as his dad was named Peter.*

Beryl looked at the photo of the bleeding man she'd taken. Unfortunately, she only had a side view in the photo as he was lying on his belly with his head to the side, but it helped her reconstruct the facial features she saw for an instant when he came into view. *He had a good face, strong, but with extra weight that would take him out of the GQ profile for wealthy available businessmen. He is handsome in my mind, but I think it's because he has a solid and reliable look I have always valued in a man. Even when he looked at me and fell on me, he was afraid but was continuing to strive for life. I hope he lives. I don't know what he was into, but I like him. He may have been robbed since his wallet and cell were missing. The police will tell me nothing. I'll ask around. I feel obligated. He chose my land to collapse.*

2
The Area Search

MCU Captain Rudy Beauregard listened to the report from Lieutenant Aylewood-Lock on the bleeding man on his cell. Rudy had been incommunicado while suffering the indignities of a scope exam. He escaped the careful eye of the receptionist after telling her he was waiting for a ride, but didn't wait. The woman would call his wife Mona and he'd get hell later for this little fib. He never told Mona he had this medical appointment. It would just jar her nerves. *Hell, that's a lie, nothing jars Mona's nerves.*

Needing a strong coffee, he stopped at the village coffee shop called 'the Village Coffee Shop' thinking, *it's why I call it the village coffee shop. We don't have a village, I don't even think there was a village here two hundred years ago. The Versed they knocked me out with must be affecting my brain cells. I told Petra and Juan to stay with the victim. Lilly and Bill will organize the search. Bobby and Mason will take uniforms and visit the neighbors. It's probably an accident. Could be they'll find a car against a tree. Wallet and cell are missing so it's an auto accident and he leaves everything on the car seat or it's something else. Strange, he wouldn't stay on the road. Juan thought this lady, whose garden the body landed on, was off. Petra says Juan is uncomfortable with literalists like Beryl Kent. She couldn't understand why, since he's engaged to Sergeant Lilly Tagliano who heads the outspoken list of ladies.*

Meanwhile, Beauregard inhaled the shop's intoxicating aroma sighing with delight before his tongue tasted any brew. His choice for a restart to his day was a double latte. When his nerve endings signaled his body to come into alignment with his brain as if they were tin soldiers set up by kids, he was ready for action. He left the shop heading over to Yellow Brook Dingle. It was a short drive when he entered large columns with an overhead arch labeled, Yellow Brook. He drove for two miles before he hit number 24 and the home took his breath away. He thought, *I knew this was a ritzy area, and we have quite a few of them in West Side. This is not a neighborhood! You really can't see one house from the next-door neighbor's window. And we don't have movie stars here.*

Beauregard pulled into a paved area to the right of the home, carefully staying on the pavement. He saw marks in the grass where a vehicle had gone beyond it. He shook his head in disappointment muttering, "Juan and Petra, neither one has ever done lawn work. It surely is their car that did the damage, way over here to the right of where the ambulance would have parked."

A uniform, who was parked in front of the home, approached him and informed him the detectives were canvassing the area on this Dingle road, crossing over to the road behind called Yellow Brook Trail. "Silly name, 'Trail' Captain, the road's as wide as a highway."

The Captain asked if the owner of the home was inside. He was disappointed to discover she had left in her Volvo SUV. The officer explained, "While I was out front with the detectives, I could see her walking all over the rear of the property as if she was looking for something. She took some pictures. Next thing I know, Captain, she said she needed groceries. With this kind of house, I thought a housekeeper would do that. She's a cool one."

Rudy reclaimed his sedan, and went searching the area for his detectives. Within a few minutes, he saw their car on the parallel street called 'Trail.' Waiting for his detectives on the edge of a half-mile driveway to a practically hidden mansion, Rudy sat back and enjoyed the beautiful weather. He found himself dozing off until there was a knock on his window. A woman was saying, "Are you all right, Sir? Do you want me to call someone?"

The Captain appeared totally flustered and took a few seconds to scroll down his window. "No, Ma'am, I've had a bit of a day so far and I'm embarrassed to say I just caught a few winks."

The two took a measure of each other and the woman grabbed the floor first. "I didn't mean to interrupt your sleep, but no one sits outside these houses and naps other than a few landscapers. Go back to sleep. I'm so sorry for interrupting your nap."

She said this with a smile he decided was breathtaking. Rudy thought, *what's she doing here, walking on a street with houses no less than a three-quarters of a mile apart? If she's been strolling, maybe she has seen someone who doesn't belong in the area. If she'd seen the bleeding man, she surely would have done something about it, unless she's involved.*

After getting out of his car, Beauregard questioned, "I appreciate your community service and watch, let me introduce myself. I'm Captain Rudy Beauregard with the West Side Police. I wonder if you could help me by answering a few questions? For instance, have you seen any unusual activity in this area today?"

"Captain Beauregard, I've read about you. Let me introduce myself. I'm Beryl Kent and I live on the next street over. Perhaps the happening in my yard has brought you here, although it did not put me to sleep, I can tell you."

Jolted by her statement, Beauregard felt compelled to explain himself, something he did not ordinarily feel was part of his role as police. "Ms. Kent, I was waiting for my detectives to return from their interview in the home connected to this long driveway. But, I am interested in the event you spoke about. As I said before, have you seen anything untoward as you walked over here after the event?"

"No, I did not. The only 'untoward' as you say event was in my yard.

This neighborhood is quiet as I'm certain you have noticed. Earlier today, I did hear a helicopter which I thought was unusual, perhaps odd. I don't remember ever hearing one before. I told your detectives about it. What I did not tell your detectives was I found evidence of someone in the shrubs at the edge of the wood in my yard after they left it. I marked it for the police and was going to call the station later today."

The Captain asked, "Why didn't you tell the uniform stationed there, before you left for your groceries? Where is your car, Ms. Kent?"

Beryl laughed. "You've already read the reports, I see. Have you been to my home?"

"Yes. Where is your car? If your car is near, why are you walking?"

"Captain, and please call me Beryl, I'm investigating other possible routes the man might have taken to end up in my backyard or others may have taken. As one of your detectives so diligently pointed out I could be wrong about my determining the direction the bleeding man came from, particularly since I saw him before acting for less than thirty seconds. Do I have to explain any of my other actions? Am I under scrutiny?"

"No, not at all. I'm most interested in how to get to your yard from here. Especially since you've pointed out there may be an alternate route to your place. Let's walk. You can show me what you have seen or if not yet, what you were interested in viewing?"

Beryl quipped, "My, you are quick. I was given to understand you were slow to comment or move."

Grumbling, Beauregard said, "At times maybe, but not when it's important to move fast."

The two cut across the street to the large woods backing Beryl's home. They walked horizontally for about fifteen feet before discovering an old narrow path into the greens. The further they went in, the wider it became. A small clearing had a bunch of rocks in a surround. They discussed its possible use by kids. There was evidence of drug paraphernalia. They continued until the path stopped at an old stone wall. Beryl laughed saying, "I just love New Englanders with their history everywhere, just like in England, just not as much history. You see, Captain, all these houses were developed on farmland, often having stone walls to define the fields. The building contractors tend to leave them intact. I know this wall. It marks the edge of my property. If we climb over and head toward the left a little, there is another pathway. It ends about ten feet from my tended yard."

And so, it did. The two followed the pathway taking a few steps to the right when they saw Beryl's yard edge. There was the space located behind a holly bush invisible to those in the yard. Beryl showed the marking of the space and her photos on her camera. She said, "Captain, I am certain someone was watching while I awaited the ambulance. I had that feeling and looked around. I couldn't see anyone. Later I walked the wood edge and found this area. You can see what I saw."

"So, Ms. Kent, what are your conclusions related to your 'bleeding man.'"

Beryl inspected the Captain for insincerity in his manner. Finding none, she answered, "He could not have come down this path. There would be blood. There isn't. Therefore, we must find his path. But someone else came down this path and watched us. My conclusion is he was interested in the fate of the 'bleeding man.' I don't think it's unreasonable to think so, do you, Captain?"

Without giving her an answer, Beauregard insisted they walk the area to look for blood. He seemed surprised when she suggested they spread out at arms-length to ensure good coverage of the ground. It took a while before they spotted blood on a bush halfway onto the neighbor's grounds at the edge of the woods. There behind the bush was another short trail leading up to the road where they had met. Beryl asked, "Why no blood on my yard, but ample amounts on that bush and just a few on bushes on the path? I saw none on the path itself."

Beauregard queried, "Beryl, do you remember where most of the blood was on the man's body? Was it higher up?"

Thinking his words over, he thought, *I have never called a witness by first name unless previously known to me. This Beryl does have a way of ingratiating herself. I'll have to be more careful, but for now, I'm stuck with calling her by her first name.*

Beryl was thoughtful for a short time, finally saying, "I've forgotten most of the anatomy course I took in college, but he bled from the neck and chest, I think. At first, I thought he had a knife through his heart, there was so much bleeding. I thought more about it and decided he had a puncture injury that bled and stopped. The injury was disturbed and bled again. If he had what I learned in science, a hemothorax, he'd bleed and die within two hours. Either way, I think the injury was less than an hour before he ended in my yard."

"And you think he came from the area where I was parked, Beryl?"

Her nod was enough. He told her thank you and headed back to the trail to his car. Surprisingly to him, she followed him. When questioned, she said, "Captain, together we've come up with some ideas. It's logical for me to help you search grounds on the 'Trail' where you parked. I think I'm entitled to follow my nose in a case where a man almost died bleeding in my arms. Also, I have to retrieve my car."

Beauregard did not look at her as he quickly moved through the path asserting, "Ms. Kent, this is an investigation for professionals, not for amateurs. We don't know yet who's involved. It could be an accident. Please go home. If I learn anything, I will call you."

"Captain Beauregard, what kind of detective are you and do you think I'm stupid? First, you refer to me in a formal manner after using my first name, as you try to exorcise me from your diligent inquiry into the cause of the 'bleeding man's' injuries. You will never call me, you would have a subordinate call me with nothing important to say. I can join you or I can work on my own. I have an interest in why this man would fall on my property and I will pursue it."

Detectives Aylewood-Locke and Flores waved to them, forcing a disruption in their conversation. Beauregard thought, *I'm kind of stuck with her now. I'll go along and after today won't deal with Ms. Kent or Beryl or whatever. She is way too interested in this; what is her background?*

Petra and Juan asked to speak with Beauregard alone. Beryl did not challenge and the Captain moved fifteen feet away to assure privacy. Sergeant Flores went first. "What's she doing tagging along, Captain? Did she capture you at the scene? She is one intrusive lady."

Petra laughed. "Anytime someone doesn't stay in her place, and notice, Captain, I said 'her,' Juan has a problem, but I don't think 'intrusive' is a bad word. She is intrusive. I just don't know enough about this Ms. Kent to know if intrusive is good or bad."

Beauregard impatiently responded, "Enough about the intrusive lady. Who lives here and what, if anything, has gone on in this area today?"

Petra insisted on describing their interview with Monsieur Rene DesCartes. "If you can believe that name. I'm always distrustful of famous names used by people living in oversized, glamorous homes. He does have what sounds like a legitimate French accent, but he sure doesn't look like a mathematician like DesCartes. He claims he lives here half a year, but this is October. I'd move back to the South of France at this time If I were him. Another thing, Captain, he saw us with masks and didn't put one on. When I asked him to, he said, 'You should not worry. I have fresh air cycled in with returns and filters. They constantly clean the air. It is like being outside. You do not need masks in here, detectives from the police.' Juan asked him why he would call us detectives from the police and what other kinds of detectives would be here asking questions about a local accident. He gave us a smile and told us some bull about there being all kinds of detectives in local, provincial, and federal areas in all countries. And he just wanted us to know what he understood about us being local police. I had to step on Juan's toes to prevent him from divulging more."

"Lieutenant, enough. What have you learned about him or anything related going on today?"

"Mr. DesCartes has not heard anything unusual today. He said he had some business conducted in his home with visitors and perhaps wasn't paying attention to what was going on around the area. We did have rain last night, Captain, and his driveway is cleaner than my mother's kitchen floor and you know my mother. I asked him how his visitors came, whether by Uber or their own cars. He said they were flown in by helicopter and directed us to a pad in the back. Since Ms. Kent said she heard a helicopter before she saw the man, but did not remember hearing one frequently or maybe ever, I asked about the frequency of the use of his pad. He got a bit squirrely and asked why it was important. When I didn't respond, he said, 'It's there for my convenience for when I need it. How often is not important.' I don't like the man, Captain."

Beauregard caught Beryl leaning forward and wondered if perhaps she'd heard Petra's conversation, given Petra's animation concerning her dislike for Mr. DesCartes. *That woman is very interested in every aspect of this case, defies convention at every corner. She's going to run with this information if she's heard it. I hope she's not a publicity junkie and will call in news reporters. I don't think so. I think she can't help herself. She is just plain intrusive.*

Beauregard suggested the detectives look for blood spatter related to what Beryl and he had uncovered. He caught Juan smiling and said, "She is dogged and difficult to separate from, Sergeant."

Juan laughed. "I believe you. She's going nowhere. What do you think, Captain, we start at the helicopter pad and work backwards? You think maybe the man was attacked when he got off the helicopter and was able to flee?"

"No, Sergeant, I actually think he may have jumped out of the helicopter when it was flying low to land and landed on some hard bushes that pierced his chest. Hell, I don't know. It's just a thought. If it has value you'll find a mess in some bushes within two hundred feet of the pad. In which direction I don't know. Try this side first and maybe in a part of the wood near where Ms. Kent and I traveled."

3
Who is the Man?

Back at the station, Sergeant Lilly Tagliano joined Lieutenant Mason Smith in the search for the 'bleeding man's' identity. Automated Fingerprinting Identification System (AFIS) did not give out a matching print. Lilly said, "The man is in his late fifties or early sixties. AFIS only has military prints for after 2000, he'd have had to be a career man to have his prints. We rolled it over to Next Generation Identification Photo System (NGI). Mason, he's not a known offender. He didn't look like an offender from the photos. Looks more like a wealthy businessman, high end clothes and a little girth, although not too much. He lives the good life. I have calls out on the clothes, but have to hit an appointment at the dentist in ten minutes. Will you take the calls on my line for a couple of hours?"

"I'm not Juan, Lilly. I can say no to you. I just happen to be a nice guy today, go ahead."

Mason worked the phones for Lilly for two hours. All the man's labels were from various high-end Florida, Atlanta, and New York menswear stores. He searched the internet and found most of the stores had free direct ship for all, but custom fitted suits were picked up. Mason growled to himself and thought, *hell, with the prices listed on some of this stuff, it's a wonder they don't hand deliver. Socks are listed as $30 - $50. Monique gets my socks at COSTCO. And the price of ties in these places. I'd never wear one if I had to pay that much, then again, I rarely wear a tie. I don't have to impress anyone with what I wear. Am I getting sloppy? I was a cool dude in high school. My mom had the best clothes for me and now I don't even look at* *what I throw on. I'll have a talk with Monique. She'll set me straight if I'm becoming a bum with my dress.*

Mason received fruitful calls from Canali's Boutique in NYC and Moda 404 Men's Boutique in Atlanta. The 'bleeding man's tie was unique and identified as sold to twenty-five men from the NYC store. The shirt in its stated size was more common, and had been sold to eighty customers. The stores gave the names and contact numbers of the purchasers. Mason thought, *I hope his wife or girlfriend didn't buy them or if so, she bought both. I'm looking for a common purchaser.*

Later in the day, Mason had two lists in front of him and it took no time at all to see a common name, Jed Mattias of Atlanta, Georgia. They had no residence on him, but did have an office number. He called and the receptionist announced, "Mattias and Leonard, Attorneys-at-law." He asked if Mr. Mattias was in today. When the receptionist responded in the negative, he identified himself and asked to speak with the other partner, Mr. Leonard or a managing partner. She was quiet for a moment, then she sadly related that Mr. Leonard had been killed in an accident three weeks before, but she could connect him to Attorney Grace Grantley.

A strong woman's voice answered. When informed of the reason for his call, she was hesitant stating, "It just can't be Jed. He is a conservative and careful man. He did have a business appointment in New Jersey yesterday, and is expected to be back today or tomorrow. He often shops in NYC when he is out in the shops' area."

When asked to describe Jed, her profile was right on the money. He confirmed it. Grace answered, "It just can't be. We have such a great firm here and now one partner is dead and the other injured."

He gave her his hospitalization details after she explained his wife had died five years before from bone cancer. He had one daughter living the dream in Austin, Texas. Grace would contact her. She also gave the detective contact numbers. When asked if there was a lady friend, she laughed and said, "Many, but he wanted what he had before. It was a high standard set and so far, no one had met it."

Mason informed the Captain of Jed Mattias as the 'bleeding man' after he'd retracted a scan of Jed's studio photo from his legal firm web page. Sergeant Bobby Barr offered to do a study of Jed's law practice from the web, and social media. He said it probably would be ready in an hour. He would also contact Attorney Grace Grantley for more information on Jed's schedule during the last week.

Beauregard thought Mattias may have had business in Springfield and asked for a check with the doctors on info on the cause of Jed's chest and other injuries. They would decide which way this investigation was trending by tomorrow's staff meeting.

———

Beauregard sometimes felt overwhelmed when visiting Baystate Hospital's ER, and especially so, now with its COVID-19 restrictions on visitors. Despite being a police captain with legitimate interests in a patient, the rigamarole he obeyed was annoying and, in his mind, a waste of his time. A familiar face greeted him. He'd met Dr. Fisher, an emergency room stalwart noted for his ability to make quick and good decisions without extensive and unavailable immediate testing. Dr. Fisher asked him a question before Beauregard could give his planned statement insisting, "Captain, do you know what happened to this patient? He received an injury from some hell of an impact. I can't see it coming from just falling over. He had multiple contusions all over the front of his body with several what look-like pieces of branches embedded in his chest. Nothing on his back or on his head with the exception of an egg on the middle of his forehead which is as good a place as any to get a bad bump. I was told he was walking before he fell over. He shows evidence of heavy sweating. His clothes were drenched. I don't understand really how he could walk with those injuries. He just missed cutting major arteries. His spleen and kidneys are damaged, but I think they'll heal. He is in fair condition, so I think he'll survive. Other than a little bit of extra weight, the man is in good condition."

"I don't know what happened, Doctor. How far could he have fallen to sustain serious damage and live, say, fall from a second story window?"

"Second story fallers are normally jumpers. We'd see breaks in legs, ankles, knees, or if they went forward on the head, arms and shoulders. His injuries are different, but he did fall from some height onto shrubs or trees of some kind. I've saved the bits and pieces for you to take a look at. He isn't conscious yet, but we have him in an induced coma because he'd be in such pain if we let him come out yet. I want the spleen and kidneys injuries to calm down first. Give me your card, Captain. I know I have it someplace from before, but everything gets lost here. I'll call you."

Rudy said his good-byes and headed out of the ER, only to see Ms. Beryl Kent entering and getting her temperature taken. She saw him and immediately went out the entrance and waited for him to exit. He thought, *how did she know I'd be here. I didn't tell her. This Beryl is a buttinsky and I see a difficult future with her. She may be bothering me often. Ah, why do I have to be nice to citizens who don't know their place?*

"Captain Beauregard, how is Mr. Mattias? I've heard he's in a coma for now. It looks like he'll live for which I am so grateful, not to have a man dying in my backyard. Wouldn't be good karma, now would it? When will you be able to talk to him? I heard he's from Atlanta and is a lawyer. He must have a client in my neighborhood."

If Beryl Kent knew Captain Beauregard better, she would have been warned by the dark blaze of his eyes. "How do you know Mr. Mattias' name, Ms. Kent? You didn't know it an hour ago. And where he lives? I want an answer."

Beryl did not seem at all disturbed and answered, "Captain, as I told you before, I don't know him, but I called this friend of mine who works here, and whose name you will never get out of me even if you torture me, who found a note in his pants small pocket written on his firm's letterhead."

"And do you have that piece of evidence in case we have a crime here, Ms. Kent? You simply cannot, I say again, cannot, withhold evidence from the police in an investigation."

"Of course, I don't have it. The clothes were handed over to the police. You have it. You just didn't know yet you had it. I must say you did well to get his name so quickly. I commend you. And, Captain, there is a probable crime here. I don't think it's attempted suicide; it's more likely an attempted murder, I don't know, but it is one or the other. Mark my words. Now I really do have to grocery shop. I'll say good-bye. Don't hesitate to call me, Captain, I'm going to do some neighborly searching. Could be, there is something we've missed."

Beryl Kent walked off using a long stride capturing some looks from bystanders. Beauregard grumbled to himself, "Don't hesitate to call, Captain. Who's doing the investigating? And I thought you were entering the hospital." *I do believe she's telling the truth, but she is a most difficult woman and, what's that word, 'intrusive.' She doesn't know when not to butt in. Well, the hell with her, maybe it'll be the last I'll see of Beryl Kent. I hope so. How'd she know someone at the hospital? It must be one of the nurses. It won't hurt for me to ask about her and her connections here. See who they are and where they're from. When we do Beryl's background check, I can look for matches, just to ensure Beryl is truthful.*

Rudy did not leave the hospital. He was surprised by the surplus of new information. Beryl Kent volunteered at the hospital one day every two weeks, a whole day. She was welcomed by the nurses, staff, and patients. It didn't matter which unit she worked in, there was praise. One nurse said, "Captain, Beryl is one of those people who can walk in your kitchen and know what to do without alienating your wife. She sees everything. We want her more, but with this COVID-19 thing, we think it's best to lessen exposure to the public, and she is older in her late fifties, close in age to the danger category for catching a serious case of the virus."

The Captain felt aggrieved. *I don't like this woman inferring 'sixty years' intimated a danger zone. Beryl is a smart kiss-ass is what she is, and I'm quite certain she won't let this go. Why can't citizens stay in their place. I shouldn't think like this. Little boys and girls have helped me in the past. I didn't like it either. Mona says I'm an individualist and she thinks it's funny that I am required to work with a team and be beholden to the citizens for my job. She says it saves me from my natural inclination of trying to control. Who's more controlling than Mona. She runs me and the boys and her classes. I'm a novice next to her.*

4
Car Crash

MCU detectives were waiting for him when he reached the station. Lilly said, "Didn't you hear your phone buzzer active, Captain? Ash called from traffic. He wants to speak with you about an accident and said it was important."

"Sergeant, did he say 'important' or 'urgent?'"

"Just important, Captain, but Ash never over speaks, you get my drift?"

Beauregard headed toward his office to call Lieutenant Ashton Lent, a former and highly-regarded MCU detective now serving in the department's traffic division unit after receiving his lieutenant's stripes and was sadly missed in MCU. Ash said, "Thanks for calling back so quickly, Captain. There was an accident case over by the heavily traveled road parallel to West Street. Two people died in the crash. There were witnesses, but there is something funny about it and my detective sensitivities are crawling.

"Look, the driver was going at a high rate of speed for the road, maybe at seventy miles an hour with a Land Rover following him at the same rate. The driver of a large refrigerated truck coming from the opposite direction insists the second car was following the first car. The first car was over on the wrong side of the road when the truck came around the corner. The car, instead of going back to his travel lane pulled over to the left and hit a very large tree. The second car did not stop at the scene. The trucker insists the first car was trying to escape the second car. A man and woman were DOA when the medics arrived. Do you want to meet me at the scene or if you're coming back here, I'll drive?"

Lieutenant Lent drove and Beauregard noticed they were not far from the 'bleeding man' scene over on Yellow Brook Dingle and the Trail. He asked Ash if he was familiar with the area. "Yeah, Captain, there are lots of complaints coming from several of the parallel and perpendicular roads lately. Shouldn't be much traffic on those roads, but must be some kids from the big houses over there. The complaints are about late-night speeding in big fancy cars. One neighbor said he would hear three or four cars in a row speeding. He'd look out and they were sportscars and big SUVs. He figured it was just spoiled college kids bored with staying home doing computer work because of COVID."

"Ash, it doesn't appear to be a densely populated area. I am surprised. What about traffic on 'The Trail?' It's parallel to Yellow Brook Dingle and a few other streets in the same almost gated community."

"You mean the ritzy area? We had a couple of complaints about the Trail, but it was only on two nights and it stopped, yesterday and the day before. I don't know about calls today."

When the men reached the accident site, they walked a quarter of a mile up from the site in the direction the cars originated. Ash said, "This is why I wanted you here, Captain. Take a look."

They could see a car skidded further back and had gone over to the other lane at least once before the trucker even caught sight of the car. They both agreed there may have been a car chase or a cat and mouse game as played by kids, except Ash said the victims were not kids. They continued to the accident site. The car hit the massive tree trunk head-on. The impact would have been severe. This accident could not have left a living soul. Beauregard studied the area and upon inspecting the 2020 Chevrolet Tahoe said, "Ash, this car has damage on the rear. When accident reconstruction takes it, have them examine the back carefully. I believe this damage happened just before the accident. Look at this car.

It's built high, but the bumper that hit it was big enough to go past the fender and make a dent. There are paint chips not from this car. What color was the car following the first car, Ash?"

"An off-white Land Rover, not the black of this Tahoe. I'll have Cyrus Jones take a look at this. You used him in the elderly men murder cases and you told me he was the best accident reconstructionist the state police had working for them."

Beauregard asked Ash to follow his logic. "Two cars were racing each other. The second car wanted to get the first car off the road for whatever reason, could be a case of playing chicken, but I doubt it. Too much money invested in these vehicles to play chicken unless the drivers were teenagers. How old, do you guess, are the victims, Ash?"

"Marlene Green, age forty-nine and David Spencer, age fifty-six are too old to play chicken, Captain. Further, they were dressed in business attire."

"You have just taken it out of the accident or stupidity area, Ash. It was a deliberate running off the road by another vehicle. The driver of the second car could not have anticipated the truck coming down this street. This is not a highway. The truck was delivering to the country club. This is a shorter route from the main road. What was the reason for trying to run this car off the road? Road rage is always a reason. Drivers go berserk when someone cuts them off. Could have happened. There is a four-way stop about a mile back. Should have some uniforms do interviewing down there. Another reason is domestic. Maybe the man and woman were involved and a partner was following them. It is one way to get rid of a cheating spouse. Then, it may just be a case of business being done, funny business. Backgrounds on the two victims are critical here, Ash, but your nose is accurate. This was not an accident."

Suddenly a large truck came barreling around the curve forcing the two men to jump back onto the crime scene. Ash said, "Traffic had better monitor this road. I never knew truckers took this shortcut and the truck is heading over to the mall. There are better ways to get there, but they all have traffic lights. And where were they coming from? Check the car's memory and their cell phones. There is a story to be told and the cell towers, GPS, and phones will start the story for us."

Milli met Beauregard at the door to his office. "Get home, Captain. Mona called to remind you about your virtual appointment with you primary, Dr. Johnson. She has it set up already. You have twenty minutes."

Grumbling about overprotective wives, Rudy turned around and obeyed his admin's instructions. He did for a couple of reasons. Mona would kill him if he missed his appointment and Millie took no prisoners. She took Mona's word as gospel, over and above any instructions from her boss. By the time he reached home, there was no time left to chat with his wife. Dr. Johnson was too young to be his doctor. He replaced Rudy's previous PCP who was a silver-haired angel who would spend all his appointment time shooting the breeze before he gave the usual medical lecture about his potential for diabetes and heart disease. Dr. Johnson had no time for chatter, which really did not bother Rudy. What bothered Rudy was this doctor was too direct. He knew he was being a hypocrite, since his favorite complaint about most people was they were not direct enough.

The first few minutes with the doctor went well enough, until he said he did not like some of the test results, inferring his A1C and sodium levels were too high. The doctor continued, "Look, Rudy, you live under constant stress from your job and deny it. I know your wife and kids from the playing fields. They like you. They want you to live and live well. You're at an age, when it's important to learn to take care of yourself, kind of measure how much energy to put into your daily efforts. I can tell you right now, get out of your police car and office and start walking, or go to the gym, or play racket ball. Now I'm going to order some tests for you to give us a baseline for your heart and health."

"I'm not old enough to go down that road now, Dr. Johnson. Hold off."

"Oh, you are, you are. And I'll order them and you'll take them because you are not a foolish man. I want a nuclear stress test and an echocardiogram, along with a full blood panel. Your last A1C was high and your blood-pressure's been elevated twice in the last six months. You know. You promised you'd watch it. Rudy, you're too young to go down the adult onset diabetes trail if you can prevent it. Your weight was up today five pounds. So, we check you out and if changes are needed, you must embrace them, not make Mona the gatekeeper. It is not her responsibility. Further, Rudy, it is not fair to her for you to abdicate your self-care responsibility."

Rudy was unable to hold back his displeasure at being given a guilt trip. He said, "You're my doctor, not my mother or wife. I don't need the guilt, but I probably did need the eye-opener. Another MCU detective's wife has had heart surgery and she's younger than me, she had no signs I could see, before it was bad enough to get her on the table for surgery. I can't go there. I'm not that brave. I will take the tests, and I guess, thank you after all for taking an interest."

Dr. Johnson laughed and said, "What would West Side do without our noted solver of serial murder crimes?"

"Harrumph, my detectives could take right over for me. Not to worry, Doctor Johnson, no one is indispensable in life."

What Rudy didn't know was there were two ears listening from the adjacent room. Mona was a happy camper. Her previous conversation with Dr. Johnson brought the right results saving her from a testy conversation on health with Rudy.

Rudy left for the station, stopping first for some lunch. It was later than usual for him and he was ready for a juicy double cheeseburger and some fries. The angel on one shoulder told him no, and for once he listened. He called and placed an order for a salad with grilled chicken and vinaigrette dressing at Auntie Kathie's Kitchen in Agawam. The restaurant was not far away. He'd be there by the time it was ready.

On the way, he would stop by a friend's house. Jack Robinson was retired as a captain from the Springfield Police Department. Jack was particularly knowledgeable in researching people and their backgrounds. He had a flair for intuition. One fact could lead him in more directions than Mona at a women's clothing store sale. He knew Jack would be home in his workshop. He'd suffered a bad fall while on the force in an altercation with a young drug dealer who was six foot five inches tall. Jack was at best five foot seven.

Jack would not accept early retirement at first and especially disability, but after several years of desk duty and back operations, he was forced to reconsider. Since then, he was the most attentive Springfield citizen. If he heard about neighborhood drug problems he was on community policing, if rumors of severe domestic violence reached him, DYS or DSS was called, and he continued to this day his policing skills helping the blue with general info about neighborhoods, hoods in general, kids looking for trouble, drag racing dates, fireworks planned dates, and unusual goings on. He was the person who pointed the finger on a major meth lab in the area.

Rudy entered his shop/office to find Jack at his desk going through a pile of old folders. His first thought was the department was letting him peruse old unclosed cases looking for details missed for reinvestigation. Rudy noticed the cases were stamped with court stamps and there were papers from Defense Attorney Norberto Cull. Rudy said, "Well, Jack, I thought you could help with some research, but I can't compete with

Norbie Cull's pricing. I'm government and have nothing to offer."

"Ha, the little 'suck me in' with humility routine. You think I'm going to fall for that. Just tell me about the 'Cabal' killings you solved, we all want to know more. The biggest joke is you having to deal with sadomasochism practitioners. You gave us all a laugh. What do you want, Rudy? I know you wouldn't be here if there wasn't something interesting."

Beauregard detailed yesterday's events including his discomfort with Ms. Beryl Kent, the pushy lady, saying, "I don't think I'll be able to get rid of her easily. She's smart, but nosy. Given the 'bleeding man' almost died on her property, she has lots of reasons to continue to ask police questions. The other accident is not an accident. In my mind, Jack, without real evidence, it'd be easy to convince they may be connected."

Jack smiled. "When were your detectives unable to do searches on people? What's your hunch? You've got business people possibly being chased and both cars each cost over seventy-five thousand dollars, so, they're on the wealthy side. Speaks of a business deal. You've got a lady who's smart and interfering and your cops probably treated her like a doer and she didn't like that, so now she's working to ensure her name's cleared. What do you want from me?"

Rudy groaned. "There was noise thought to be from a helicopter not long before the 'bleeding man' fell on Ms. Kent. A neighbor has a pad on his property but said it's rarely used and was squirrelly about it. I want to know about Beryl Kent. I think she's free of involvement, but she got info before me and I need to understand her. She will be butting in. Also, I thought you'd know all about air traffic. You know the right people. I know you have a plane and were a pilot in the service. Can you tell if a flight plan or pattern, whichever it's called now, was filed for the address here on 'The Trail,' West Side, yesterday morning?"

Jack responded, "Maybe! You know there is a great deal of monitoring of drones. Lots of construction companies and other industries use them. They are so plentiful now they are regulated. Low Altitude and Notification Capability (LAANC), a collaboration between FAA and Industry has registration for them. I have a friend who will tell me who is over in your area operating regularly. I can have some info on the helicopter that flew over. They'll have everything. Drone fliers are the nosiest people in the world. Sometimes I think they're all spies for someone. I'll get you some answers. I'll do rigorous background work on your live and dead victims. Don't worry, Rudy. You're thinking straight."

The two men talked personally for a bit. Their wives actually knew each other from their teaching positions over twenty years before. Western Massachusetts was a close community where friendships often lasted a lifetime. Jack's son was playing soccer on one of the league's teams with one of Rudy's sons. Their attitudes showed their respect for each other. Jack ended the conversation by saying, "I will call when I have something, but it'll have to wait until tomorrow. Norbie Cull has me working on a case for a client where he feels the client had poor representation and is in the slammer when he shouldn't have even been charged. He thinks there's something funny with the case going all the way up. And he may be right. I will call my drone guy once you leave and get him started."

———

"Well, our illustrious Captain will love this, Lilly."

"What have you got, Juan?"

"The lady Kent has been married three times. One husband disappeared for seven years and was found in Florida in a home for people with dementia. He died later not long after she found him. The other two died and I'm waiting for the death certificates. Her work history is interesting. She took over one husband's business, increased its market, and sold it to a national company CBW Retail. She carries licenses and certifications in several fields. Looks like she doesn't know what she wants."

Lilly was disgusted. "Juan, there you go again disparaging women with goals and aspirations. This Beryl is probably very intelligent and finds lots of career fields interesting. Could be she hasn't found work that moves her soul. Me, I never wanted anything but policing. I'm a people person. I love culture. I'm confounded by our society. I like to help. Policing is it."

"Lilly, you're right and I like your focus. I hope you are a one-man woman, that you find me 'it' like policing."

Lilly laughed. "Trouble with you, Juan, is you want constant validation. Tell me what is she licensed in, this 'Lady Kent' as you call her?"

"Something called SHTM® in human resources, Licensed Project Manager (construction) in two states, CPSM® in Supply Change Management. She's also been an auctioneer specializing in American furniture. She graduated from Yale and has a Master's in Fine Arts in photography from University of Mass at Dartmouth."

"Get it all for the Captain, Juan. He has interest in her aside from her annoying him."

Millie walked in to ask which of the two wished to speak with a concerned citizen who was at the Sergeant's Duty Desk. Juan, normally the easiest mark, agreed. He asked the citizen's name as he walked towards the door. Millie said, "Ms. Beryl Kent. She says she met the Captain and he's aware of her concerns. Who is she?"

Lilly answered, "Juan and I will both meet with her, Millie. She may be the Captain's Moriarty, you know like in Sherlock Holmes' nemesis. I can't wait to speak with her."

The Lady Kent smiled brilliantly as she greeted the two detectives.

As they moved into the conference room she said, "I've not met you before, Sergeant Tagliano. I did meet Lieutenant Aylewood-Locke with you, Sergeant Flores. I did ask to speak with Captain Beauregard, but I was told he was not at the station. Thank you for taking your time to see me."

Lilly was far more impressed with Ms. Kent's good manners than Juan who believed she was laying a trap for them in some way. Given his discomfort, he took charge with a brisk, "How can we help you, Ms. Kent?"

"Hmmm. I did promise the Captain, I would bring new information to him when and if there was any. He also agreed to tell me what he would learn about the man who was found almost dead on my property. I believe we've been calling him the 'bleeding man,' who is now identified as Jed Mattias."

Juan interrupted. "How did you know his name, Ms. Kent?"

"Well, it is his name, Detective. The Captain knows I know."

Lilly thought, *she doesn't answer the question, but she is not fresh. She won't tell Juan how she discovered the name of the victim. She'll just refer to the Captain. I hope Juan doesn't pursue this. It's a waste of time. I want to know what she wants today.*

To cut Juan off at the pass as her father would say, Lilly asked, "What is the new information you have for us, Ms. Kent? We need all the help we can get from citizens."

Beryl smiled and said, "Why thank you, Detective. I don't want to be a bother, but the why's and who's and what's of this man delivering his body to my grounds make me a most interested party in this investigation."

Trying not to be impatient, Juan responded, "What have you learned?"

"I've tracked through the property on the Trail which the Captain and I walked through yesterday. I think Mr. Mattias jumped from the helicopter and I have found the exact spot. There is blood on the bushes on which he landed and more on the ground where he must have fallen on after landing on the branches. He was not thrown out. There is no logical reason to think he was thrown. There were no marks of a fight on him and the way he landed tells me he planned it as best he could. His jump on the landing site, as I call it, is not far from the DesCartes house. The question I had from viewing this landing site, is why didn't Mr. Mattias go right to the DesCartes house?"

Lilly questioned back, "Why didn't he, Ms. Kent? It was closer. There are more questions to be answered first. Was he conscious enough in his condition to allow logical decision-making? Could he actually see the house from where he landed? Our officers were out by the pad looking for a trail he may have traveled. They found no evidence. Just how did you find his landing site? Did he tell you something you've not shared with us?"

Beryl Kent smiled. She said, "Please call me Beryl. I'm uncomfortable with the Ms. salutation, since I've been Miss, Mrs., Ma'am, Professor, in Italy Senora, and in France Madame. I told the officers at the scene and you, Sergeant Flores and your partner later, Lieutenant Aylewood-Locke, what Mr. Mattias said. I'll repeat it for you. He said or I heard, 'Help me. I don't deserve to die…' It is all I heard. You do raise a good point, Detective Tagliano and it's not to be put aside, but he went a long way to reach my property, through a treed area, crossing the road, and going through woods first through to my neighbor's house and turning to head toward my back area when I saw him. The question is why didn't he go further to my next-door neighbor's yard? At first, I couldn't figure the question out. I walked over to Mr. D'allasandro's property and discovered there was evidence he was not there. The back porch had been shuddered completely. I think it plausible Mr. Mattias heard a dog barking and thought it came from my house. When he saw me, he rushed toward me."

Juan asked, "How'd you find his landing spot? You haven't really told us your logic for your discovery, Beryl?"

"Sergeant, I simply made two assumptions. One was he arrived at his expected destination by helicopter. Somewhere during his flight, he decided he was in jeopardy. Secondly, it was obvious if he did not want to go where he was being taken, and since I assume there were probably at least two and maybe more in the helicopter, he realized escape after landing was not feasible. Think about how copters go in for a landing, I see them circling in horizontally. I don't see the doors open. He could only jump if the doors were open. I don't know where the bathroom is on the copter. I don't know if Mr. Mattias was a pilot or someone knowledgeable in helicopters. I do know copter pilots and was told the most knowledgeable of flying occupants are the most likely to be invited to sit up front with the pilot. So, how could he even jump if the doors weren't open? Many questions when you use assumptions."

Lilly and Juan both shook their heads. Juan said, "Beryl, how did you know where to look for the trail? Our officers did not find Mr. Mattias' fall site, but you easily did? How did you know where to look?"

Beryl sighed. "I feel like Sherlock Holmes right now. Logic, I used logic. I followed my assumptions. If I was wrong, then I wouldn't have found the site. I believed Mr. Mattias jumped from the copter which meant he had to be able to jump from the copter. To do that, the copter door must have been open. I thought if I were he and thought I was at death's door, either from the other occupants in the copter or from those waiting for us, I would chance a jump. Jumping infers he had intense and reasonable fear unless he was crazy. His web page and legal history from the state of Georgia tell me his history does not warrant a conclusion he was nuts. So, I extrapolated from a guess, because I have no knowledge of copters. I assumed he would jump the minute the door opened and the copter was less than one hundred feet from the ground.

"There still is the big question of why the door would be open. Could be they were getting ready to throw him out, but I don't think so. Perhaps, he was a copter pilot or generally knowledgeable about aircraft. He could have opened the door. I understand second seating in the cockpit is reserved for the most flight knowledgeable occupant. He could have been second seating and heard something in flight that scared him. Where are the controls for opening the door? Can a passenger get access if he knows where the controls are? Is there a restroom in a copter? You need to answer these questions."

Lilly thought, *she makes us look foolish. If she is an innocent in this, she is one hell of a smart one. Juan must feel foolish. We'll have to answer her questions. Beauregard would have loved all these assumptions and questions if we, his detectives, came up with them, but he won't like Beryl's involvement. I better help Juan do some nicey-nicey and get her out of here.*

"Thank you, Beryl. You have been most helpful. We'll share your questions for answers to our IT specialist, Lieutenant Smith. He is a wonderful resource and will research their plausibility. Juan, we do have a call and we must leave."

Beryl did not find the abrupt ending disconcerting at all. Her good-bye included, "I will see you or Captain Beauregard soon. I do hope you have some technical answers for me. I'll talk to some of my friends in the military just to satisfy myself."

Juan instantly replied, "Beryl, our conversations, or any conversations about an open case is confidential. That applies to you too."

"Of course, Sergeant. No need to state the obvious."

5

Big Time Financiers and Lawyers

There were more questions to be answered by the police including those relevant to the accident death cases. Beauregard was holding a meeting this morning at ten and the detectives were to be caught up on the two cases' specifics by then. Mason, who typically was early for any meeting, yelled for the others to join him at the conference table before the Captain walked in. Petra complained, "I just walk in, grab a coffee, and Mason, you're louder than my baby Carlotta. Cool down. These cases won't be solved sitting down and don't think they're serial murder cases that need rushing to stop more murders. They're probably not connected."

The detectives waited and waited until it was twenty past when Sergeant Bobby Barr insisted it was time to worry about Beauregard. "He's never more than five minutes late. I'm calling him."

The call was fortuitous. The illustrious Captain's car had been hit by a speeding car running a red light. Beauregard answered his cell apologizing immediately for not being there. He explained he was forcibly put in an ambulance and was headed for Baystate Hospital. Ash, who was attending the meeting on the accident issue, grabbed the phone. "Where were you hit, Captain?"

The cell clicked off. Sergeant Bill Border insisted they choose someone to go in because the hospital would not let all of them in despite being police. Petra asked, "What about Mona?"

Juan said, "Beauregard would have called her immediately."

Lilly contradicted, "If he is really hurt, he'd call her last. It's not a matter of trust, it's just he's trying to protect his wife. I know him. He's got a macho side coming out. I'll put money on it."

Mason said, "Ash, you go over to the hospital and explain you have an emergency signature required from the Captain. It should get you in there, call Mona on the way. I think they let in only one family member or friend. This COVID business sucks for families with health problems. You'll have an opportunity to assess his condition to give some assurances to Mona."

After Ash left, the detectives clucked for a while, a term Lilly coined to replace the put-down of gossip. She insisted the group when it was gossiping looked like chickens clucking with no direction. In the end they all settled down sharing their efforts on the 'bleeding man.' Lilly described Beryl Kent, her assumptions and conclusions. Sergeant Bill Border mused, "Her logic is good, but we need to know more about helicopters. There's an officer who just came on after me when I was at the Holyoke PD. He was a pilot. I'll contact him, unless you know someone here."

Sergeant Ted Torrington, who had been on vacation for the past few days and was just catching up, said, "That's the technical question to be answered, but the real question is the legitimacy of Beryl Kent. The Captain does not like interference in his investigations and she appears to be one step ahead of us. How can she beat the Captain?"

Mason answered, "She has had a most interesting life with no time gaps. Three husbands, careers, and two kids. She's only lived in Western Massachusetts for the last nine months. What brought her here at this time in her life, we don't know. It's going to take some work to trace her many addresses and work situations. The obituary for her first husband lists two children, a boy named Oliver and a girl named Jocelyn. They'd be in their thirties today. Maybe one of them lives here. I checked for Oliver Kent locally, but no luck. Same for Jocelyn Kent, then I realized she'd probably be married. More work is needed now. Beryl did register to vote as unenrolled. She's also been active in the arts in West Side. Ted, can your wife Charlotte ask around about her? Charlotte's in all the activities in West Side, aside from her job as the mayor's sister. She know everything going on. If Jocelyn Kent is living in or near West Side, Charlotte will know."

"Yup, my Charlotte knows everything meaning I can't get away with stuff. If there is a daughter, I can tell you mothers talk about their daughters all the time. She'll get the scuttlebutt."

Bobby Barr presented an analysis of Jed Mattias' web page. "He and his recently deceased partner's practice is in Personal Injury, Criminal Defense, Civil Litigation, and Business Law. The web page lists some cases in many areas but leans to commercial business law. They were good. Mattias was the lead litigator while the partner managed the firm and seemed to have second seated him a few times. There were big wins in Civil Litigation and Criminal Defense. It didn't list the personal injury case wins. They were too numerous, which means this firm tried lots of cases. Unlike most in our county where the PI cases are settled early. The settled cases are not listed, just the tried cases. The page shows several large corporate national companies including Digital National, Farming Vertical, Inc., Financial Aid Resources, Equity Insurers, and Se Espera Justicia. Org. They were or are a formidable legal firm. I think we should look at what clients they were currently working cases on, but we don't have a death here. We have to be political. Ted would be the one, he's low key and non-threatening and would give Grace, the managing attorney another go, and make it productive."

There was unanimous agreement. Then, Petra insisted there had been enough talk about Beryl Kent and started on the accident case saying, "Ash is gone, but we've all read the facts. This was not an accident. Beauregard knows it's not an accident. Did you interview the truck driver, Bill?"

"He was accompanied by his lawyer and guess who?"

"No way. Of course, Cull. Who else? Was the driver from this area? How'd he find Cull?"

Bill said, "Turns out he saw and liked Cull's billboard for accident cases which is on 291 coming in from the Pike. I don't think of Cull's firm doing accident work as mainstays. Although the ad says personal injury. In this case, it would be a defense case. I heard Mattias' firm is paying for Cull."

Petra asked, "Did he let the driver talk?"

Border smiled insisting, "Yes. You know what that means? He believes the guy and thinks he's got all the facts. The trucking company has a camera installed on it. I've looked at the video, it completely supports his story. It also gives a partial plate on the second car. Good news for us. We're looking for its registration now."

There had been a problem notifying the victims' families. There was enough identification to know their addresses, but their cell phones were missing. Lilly said, "Nah, something big is up here. Professionals keep their cells close. Why would they go anywhere without one. Funny business. Do we have cell tower activity yet? Mason, we'll have to know what their numbers are, to get their activity."

Mason informed them the two came from two different areas outside of West Side. Marlene Green's address was in Stamford, Connecticut and David Spencer was from Providence, Rhode Island. He googled for telephone numbers and made the calls. Voice mail answered both numbers and there were no call backs. "The numbers were cell numbers and we're getting the data," he said. "Google will also let us know public info on them that I won't find. They did not show up as big users in social media. There is an M. Green on Linked-in. Could be the same lady and there are several David Spencer's. I'm working on it."

Ted said there was no word from the Medical Examiner's office. The forensics teams and accident investigation reports were not yet received. Lilly wondered aloud, if while the Captain was at the hospital, perhaps any of them visiting, or the Captain himself, could get inside to see Mattias. Juan remarked, "Lilly, the Captain is not Superman. He's injured. Today is not a day for him to be investigating."

Contrary to Juan's assumption, Beauregard decided, while fighting the groans of pain from his leg, that his closeness to Jed Mattias could give him an opportunity to access him, or at least access the nurses caring for him. He was grateful when Ash arrived. He hoped Ash could talk the doctors out of several nights of hospitalization. Actually, he was surprised they let Ash in, but Beauregard signed the bogus papers Ashe presented chuckling to himself. Rudy explained to Ash his job was to prevent Mona from over dramatizing his injury. To which, Ash answered, "You are badly injured, Captain. It looks like you need surgery. They found all kinds of bruises on your chest as well, so they've scheduled tests. You know you're not out of hot water yet. Good thing your head wasn't injured. I know that because you're still manipulating."

"I don't manipulate, I plan."

Rudy said this giving Ash a most disgusting grimace. Further discussion was prevented by the orthopedic surgeon who upon entering Rudy's room informed him that an immediate operation was needed to save the leg. Beauregard now paid attention to his condition, which the doctor said was a comminuted open fracture of the femur shaft and would require a long recovery. There were several pieces requiring surgery to put back together. He explained the femur is one of the largest bones in the body. There may also be some muscle and nerve damage. Rudy peppered him with questions, but in the end, signed some permissions.

The doctor said, "Good thing you're in peak condition, Captain."

Rudy laughed and told him about waiting for test appointments because his doctor did not like his weight gain and blood pressure. He was told he was fortunate his doctor monitored his health so carefully.

Rudy, before he was brought into surgery, asked Ash to wait for Mona and explained, "Tell her not to worry and I love her."

Ash was invited to wait upstairs in the surgical waiting room. Instead he waited for Mona.

Two hours later, Mona and Ash were greeted by Rudy's surgeon with good news. The leg was reset. It was a complicated surgery and the surgeon described the potential lengthy recovery. After he left the room, Mona said, "He will go back to work with a full cast on. I know him. Do you think he'll be okay, Ash? I am so worried. My life will be quite difficult. Rudy is not an easy patient."

Ash said, "It's COVID time. I'll ask Mason to set up a big screen on his computer and all the gadgets for him to function. It'll be all right. One of the guys will go to appointments with you and carry him in and out on wheelchairs. We can get you an electric one for at home so you're not running to his room every second. You know Rudy will need to have some control."

At the moment they were about to leave, Attorney Norberto Cull walked into the room. They all showed surprise. Norbie was apprised of Rudy's accident and condition. He asked for the facts and insisted he take over the case. "Mona, don't let this go by. The other driver is at fault and Rudy may have some permanent damage. I'll start Sheila investigating the facts."

Mona protested, but listened to Ash's advice to proceed. It took a minute before Mona asked why Norbie was in the waiting room. He said he had an appointment with a client's doctor, the client almost died in a bad accident. His law firm hired him to investigate what had happened.

Ash thought, *it just couldn't be Attorney Jed Mattias he's representing, could it?*

And he asked the question, receiving a questioning look from Norbie. "How the hell could you know that? He wasn't in an auto accident. Is he in some kind of trouble, Ash? If so, I do need to know before I speak with him."

"How can you speak with him? He is in a coma."

"He came out of the coma a short time ago. The hospital has instructions to let me visit in place of next of kin."

"Hell, they were supposed to call us first."

"Why is he on Beauregard's most wanted list? My client talks to me first, then maybe you with me there. If he did nothing, you have no right nor duty to interrogate him, especially in his fragile condition."

"Wait a minute, I don't have to tell you about police business with Mr. Mattias. Beauregard would reject you in the first instance and you know so."

"Calm yourself, Ash, you're in front of Mona. She doesn't have to listen to this rubbing of egos."

Mona interjected, "Both of you calm down. Rudy would have you come to an agreement, I know he would. Is this Mr. Mattias in trouble, Ash? I mean, has he committed a felony? If not, why can't you two work together? I heard Norbie say he was in some sort of an accident. Doesn't that make him a victim? Both of you know how to treat a victim."

The two men looked embarrassed. Norbie was the first to speak. "Okay, the lady wins. I'll talk with the nurse. If she'll only let one person in, then I apologize, but I'll be that person. It's all up to hospital protocol."

"Don't worry, Norbie. She'll let me in."

A nurse Mariah Stetson introduced herself and asked who, here, was Attorney Cull. Norbie listened to her instructions for following her to Mr. Mattias' room before he stated Lieutenant Lent would be joining him. Ash was pleased with the conversation until Mariah balked at the idea of police interviewing Mr. Mattias who was still exhausted from his injuries. She questioned whether Ash could wait until the next day. Ash explained he was there to listen to Mr. Mattias' story, not to question or create stress. Mariah nodded and led the way leaving Mona in the waiting room alone.

Cull whispered as they walked, "Smooth, Ash, you know when to back down."

"No, I know when to exhaust a situation for information in any open avenue, that's all."

Mariah opened the door to Mr. Mattias' room and left. Cull said, "If he appears to be in any risk for some phantom prosecution by you guys, you're out of here. It's just normal information we're here for today."

Jed Mattias looked over at them and said, "Who the hell are you? Tell me. If I don't like your answer I have my finger on the buzzer and out you go."

Norbie introduced himself and Ash. He then showed Jed a letter of engagement signed by Attorney Grace Grantley, Managing Partner of his law firm. Jed had difficulty focusing and asked Lieutenant Lent to read the letter aloud to him. "I trust you, Lieutenant. I've learned not to trust lawyers. Don't take it personally, Mr. Cull. As you're aware, I'm also an attorney and we are not all of the same ilk. I don't know you. I suppose if Grace hired you, she researched your background. You just need to convince me you're not in business with some of my clients."

Norbie presented his credentials with a summary of business clients he represented whose names could be made public. Jed asked how he could be certain Cull didn't represent his clients in some fashion. The answer was 'typical Cull,' at least Ash thought so. "I can't, Jed, be certain myself. I did a review on your website of your listed clients and I don't represent any of them. Be specific. Ask me. I'll tell you if there could be a conflict. That aside, what have your clients to do with you almost bleeding to death in West Side?"

"I don't know. I don't know. You see, I'm having dreams, really dark dreams. I wake up knowing someone tried to kill me and I escaped. The problem is I remember none of it with the exception of falling into a beautiful lady's arms and knocking her over. That's it."

Ash asked Jed if he had any memory of the last few days before his accident. He was quickly told, "No accident, it was no accident. How could I be found on the ground in a town I've never been to? The last thing I remember is taking a limo to a small airport expecting to settle a client's situation. I don't remember which airport and if I actually got there. I don't remember which client."

The nurse entered the room and asked them to leave. Jed did look tired. Jed said, "Norbie, I want you on this case. I don't know what I'm mixed up in, but I run an honest law firm and my friend, my partner, was recently killed in an auto accident. Check the accident out for me. Strange, I think, for both of us to almost leave this earth in such a short time. I'll try to remember. And, Detective, can you give me protection please while I'm in here?"

"Give me a reason, Jed. I can't just put a man on you because you can't remember."

Norbie turned to Ash with an idea. "Rudy's in here for a while. Maybe you could have a watch on Jed using any of the detectives visiting Rudy."

"Maybe! If the Captain okays it."

They were swooshed out by the nurse who told them, "There is tomorrow, gentlemen. I'll take good care of Mr. Mattias. By the way, Ms. Kent was in here twice today waiting for him to waken, she'll be happy to watch over him for you."

Ash grimaced and the facial expression was caught by Norbie. As they walked away, Norbie asked, "What's going on here. Kent is not under suspicion and if so, suspicion for what? Jed thinks something's wrong but he can't remember. He wants protection for what? You don't like Ms. Kent. How does she have access to his room when I, the patient's counsellor, had to wait twenty minutes to be brought in accompanied by the police? Who is this Ms. Kent?"

"The Captain says she is a most intrusive citizen. She's all over this investigation claiming she wants to know why someone almost died in her yard."

Cull laughed. "She's in Beauregard's way. I love it. Do you think she's to be trusted to be around Jed?"

"We haven't found criminal stuff, but she has lived an interesting life. She is educated in many areas, been married several times, and recently moved to West Side. Kent lives in high rent real estate, I can tell you. Whether she can be trusted, I don't know. Jed seems to believe he is in danger. Don't know how he knows this, if he's telling the truth and doesn't know how he got here. Questionable for sure!"

Cull said, "Could be, he was chasing a woman, got in trouble over it and is trying to hide from his foolishness. Problem with this theory is he is unmarried and is not responsible to anyone unless he has a serious girlfriend back home. Could be he's an attorney for a cartel. Could be anything. I've got to be in court shortly, Ash. Please keep me posted. I'll be back to visit Rudy. Being laid up for him is a horror show, even more so for Mona and you guys."

6
Confusion

Which way could he have gone? Which way would have been easier, aside from the DesCartes home? No way was easier than the DesCartes home. This line of discussion was followed by Mason and Petra back at the station. Petra insisted, "No matter which way you look at it, he would have seen the DesCartes home from where he landed. The trees were near the open cared for lawn. True, it was a wooded area but the trees did not have undergrowth to prevent a view of the very big house. I think we should start with Mr. DesCartes. Ted was to speak with Jed's firm's managing partner to choke out Jed's most recent cases and contacts, focusing especially on the appointment in New Jersey the day before his accident. I think we should cross reference any of DesCartes' companies with Jed's legal or business activities. We need a trail of players, until or if Jed ever has memory recovery."

Ash called for an update on the Captain and for details on Attorney Cull representing Attorney Jed Mattias. To say Petra thought this was an interesting development would be an understatement and Mason totally agreed. They pulled Ted Torrington into the conference room and after discussing Ash's call, Ted said, "This Attorney Jed Mattias' law firm is a Southern powerhouse as the go to firm if a corporation wished to close a deal, be protected from some serious civil litigation, and occasionally have corporate officers given defense counsel for big business-related felony infractions. There could be many reasons to put the firm out of business from a corporate perspective. Just sayin', don't say I'm imagining. I don't imagine. One partner is dead and the other is left for dead in circumstances appearing not to be related to his personal or business life. A sham! He was marked, but unless he remembers, we'll need boots on the ground."

Petra answered, "Not like you to step out from the crowd, Ted, without specific details. How do we go about this, Master?"

"I like the 'we,' Petra, not sure about the 'how.' Has Bobby finished speaking with Grace Grantley? Her interview may be interesting if she was willing to give up his schedule for the past couple of weeks and his client list with contact info."

Mason shared that Bobby would have a report the next morning, meanwhile stating there was the question of whether Jed Mattias needed protection. Petra said she was certain Lilly was willing to do some babysitting at the hospital. "We could do it under the guise of checking on the Captain and whether he was safe enough there. We could tell the hospital there are some serious open cases, cases with perpetrators not interested in the Captain's well-being. It is the truth or somewhat the truth."

"Great idea, Petra. Mona will be in and out of the hospital during the day and maybe she can just keep an eye on Mr. Mattias' room. You know watch for the ins-and-outs. They will both be on the post-surgical floor."

Mason said, "We won't know. Depends on type of surgery. Jed just reached stabilization. Ash can tell us the fine points. Lilly can cover 11:00 to 7:00 shift. I think it's going to be difficult for anyone to access Jed's room during COVID. A watch may be foolish."

Ted commented, "Mason, never underestimate a criminal mind. If Jed Mattias is a marked man, there will be some nurse or doctor or staff or admin who will allow an opening. Maybe they would be unwilling accomplices. Money buys a lot."

Mason agreed to using Juan for watch when Lilly was needed elsewhere. "We can all cover at times," he said. "We'll be into the Captain with paperwork. They don't know he puts off most paperwork requiring a signature that's not an emergency for just two dates a month. It's the only ploy we have for entry, so we won't tell them. Meanwhile, visiting Jed does allow us access purpose. This will only be for a couple of days. We'll have more information on Jed and his accident later."

Detective Bobby Barr, while intending to drive to the station after picking up some lunch, received a surprising call. Grace Grantley said, "Sergeant Barr, I've just landed at Bradley Airport. I've been informed by Lieutenant Mason Smith to call you when I got into the city. I plan to catch an Uber to the Casino Hotel in Springfield.

"Before I visit Jed, would you meet me someplace? I need an update on his health and your investigation. I have the willies about this. I've brought along a list of cases, Jed's itinerary for the past few weeks, and a record of his emails on the firm's email for him. I don't have his cell phone.

"This afternoon at four o'clock works for me. I just don't know where to meet. I don't know what's open up here."

"Attorney Grantley, right near your hotel, if you walk north on Main Street, is a restaurant I know is open called 'Nadim's Mediterranean Grill.' I'll meet you inside."

Bobby chose a table with the help of the owner near the back. He'd met the owner through Ash, who had played violin at many Middle Eastern events. While waiting and settling in with his coffee, he thought, *there's no interrupting this lady when she's talking. She takes over not leaving space for any comment.*

He looked up and got a vision of a smartly-dressed woman heading toward him. She had the 'Margaret Thatcher' air of importance as she moved. There was no sashaying, but you had to notice her good looks. Grace Grantley did not wait for him to rise. She practically slid into her chair with a graceful movement, all the while introducing herself to Bobby and thanking him for his selection for the meet. They spoke in short sentences as they ordered.

Decisive was the word Ash would use later to describe Grace Grantley to the other detectives. Grace described Jed Mattias as a spectacular business attorney who rarely called attention to himself. His work was valued by most other attorneys, the courts, and his clients. He was by nature a cautious man. He would take risks, but when he did, they were based on his passion for his legal objective. He had amassed a fortune from his practice, lived carefully, and apart from his daughter, had no personal weak spots.

When asked about Jed's daughter, Grace said, "I have tried to get hold of her, but I've not been successful. She normally calls him twice a week. I called her cell, with no return call from her. Further, she left suddenly for a three-week vacation in the islands surprising her colleagues. I called a couple of her friends and they didn't even know she'd gone. This is a weird situation. I don't like it. You see, Lieutenant, Marthea Mattias would never go anywhere without speaking with Jed first. They were extraordinarily close. She may be a free spirit involved in the music industry in Austin, but she's a kind woman. She would not worry him."

Bobby and Grace pored over Jed's itinerary for the past three weeks. Grace connected every meeting to his clients with the exception of two. They were listed discretely under the names of 'March' and a 'federal finance' case. She had looked up new matters on their computer and found no listing for a Mr./s. March. She'd questioned his secretary who said he took both calls after closing his door. It was at that time Jed scheduled his plans for travel to New Jersey. His travel was for a client named Arrow Management, LLC. The company was listed on the firm's travel allowance form. Mr. Leonard, before he passed, had managed daily business for the firm. He was adamant all attorneys keep records, including himself and Jed.

Grace said, "I called Harry Leonard's secretary Joyce and questioned whether she had ever heard of Harry meeting with a client named March or with Arrow Management, LLC., or a special federal finance case. Joyce found a record for Harry meeting with President Raleigh from Arrow Management whom she was told was only in town for a few days. A note said Raleigh was Jed's client. This meeting occurred two days before Harry died. Joyce found nothing else, but this alone concerns me. Jed was not secretive within the firm about business. He and Harry had the best of relations. I don't like this. Harry was the more outgoing of the two partners and truly a 'good ole boy' from the Southern tradition."

Bobby said, "We'll look for Marthea. Her disappearing is odd given her relationship with her dad. Did he help with her support in Austin, Grace?"

"He'd buy her a car every two years, but she was careful with her money and liked to rely on herself. She does some kind of music videos and is a songwriter/performer. I've heard a few albums sung by others and liked the melodies and words. She does both. Jed told me recently she was on her way. She recently broke up a two-year romance, but the breakup was amicable and there is a new guy Jed liked."

"I imagine you've already tried to research Arrow Management, LLC. If so, what did you find?"

"Sergeant, there are so many Arrow Management, LLCs in many states. I assumed it would be in New Jersey and there is one, but they've never heard of our firm. I called Joyce and asked her if the name was just

Arrow Management, LLC. She double checked and found two letters in front of the word 'arrow.' She thought it was a scribble from his pen. It could be an 'ff or fyy.'

They finished their lunch. Grace said she would head to the hospital as soon as possible. He questioned how she would gain entry, and with a big dimpled smile she simply said, "Well, Sergeant, I am an attorney in a law firm with a big reach. You know, a client knows another client who is in with the hospital admin or one of the top physicians. I already have a pass. So far, I understand he has not been allowed to wake from an induced coma. I'm still going there, but perhaps tomorrow."

Grace would be in town for several days. She thought she could do most of her work on her computer and by ZOOM or other conference methods. She would not be able to stay too much longer, as she was needed in Atlanta on the next Tuesday. Grace said while they were leaving, "Sergeant, please let me know on your progress. I will tell you all I know. If I feel anything Jed tells me is in your domain, I will share the info. Jed's life is important to me and not just for business reasons. I'm hopeful he will tell me about any reservations he might have about holding back. I can't believe he has no memory. The doctor told me when I called, there was no head trauma. His feeling was the memory loss was from fright, but Jed got restless when he couldn't remember, so they put him back into an induced sleep. Jed does not frighten easily. He is a man always on his toes when things get really bad."

7

The Lady is Dogged

Beryl Kent's fingers were flying on the computer as she scanned Attorney Jed Mattias' life's work to the extent Google would allow. Not pleased with the results, she pulled up one of her three paid for search services she had used for many years. Always helpful, they had not helped her in finding her first husband when he went missing. No, her husband finally found her. She could not blame the search programs as their services were not available for non-professionals at that time nor were their programs easy to access back then. She knew she had professional research skills. One program could get info on a person, another on business to business, one for criminal records, and another for other than the US.

Beryl thought, *this Jed is a stand-up guy. No bar complaints other than one whacked-out lady who said he wouldn't take her case. She apparently tried to knife a cop for sitting in her favorite place in a diner. It was dismissed. She was mentally ill. Wonder how many written statements he had to make to have it go away. He was married just once and is now a widower. There is a daughter. I'll check on her. Maybe she's involved in something. Social media hasn't much to say about him. Never ran for public office or it'd be out there. Some negative press from his representation of clients wanting to build in what was considered conservation land, but it wasn't. Neighbors abutting the land didn't want new building. Represented a client in a big tax avoidance case. Client was found not guilty. Still no evidence he did a lot of those cases. Maybe the government didn't like the press he got and put a squash on public exposure on future cases he won. There's posted photos at big dinners, often with a good-looking lady at his side, but never the same lady. Despite the frequency, there were no ladies writing trash about him. He is not a bounder.*

The doorbell rang surprising her to talk aloud to no one. "Eureka always barked ahead of time to warn me of visitors and now Eureka is living the life in dog heaven. Who could be bothering me? It's 9:30 in the morning and I'm not expecting company nor vendors."

She looked through a sidelight and there, big as life, was her neighbor Monsieur DesCartes dressed in a dark print shirt with contrasting ascot. She thought, *debonair he may be but with this outfit, it's clear he does not want to fit into the New England suburban culture. He's never visited me before, I can't wait to hear what he's up to. I don't believe his visit is unrelated to the Mr. Mattias accident. Lordy, I just love serendipitous events.*

"Welcome, Mr. DesCartes. How kind of you to visit so early in the day. Please come in. I'll make some latte or espresso or whatever you like. I don't imagine you're a tea drinker."

"Madame Kent, thank you. I'll have whatever you are drinking but a nice espresso with a twist would be lovely."

Beryl thought for an instant, *just love his arrogance. I need a twist — not waiting for me to ask if he would like one. So European of him and masculine. Even a European woman would wait to be asked and say something like, 'please, if it's no trouble.' Oh Beryl, you are disparaging a Frenchman. Shame on you. I'm getting grouchy in my dotage, but this visit is if nothing suspicious.*

Contrary to her normal custom of bringing friends back to the oversized space she called kitchen, Beryl directed him to the small room off the enormous front hall thinking, *I don't want this man to see too much of my life. Although having won an award for design, this room tells nothing about me. I don't feel the trust about him and I do trust my feelings.*

In a matter of minutes, and all the while she watched Mr. DesCartes' actions on camera, Beryl entered with a tray of espresso, tea, and coffee cake. Setting the stand-up table of goodies directly in front of the man,

Beryl took her ginger tea in hand and sat directly across from him. If her action were viewed by another, it may have appeared to be intimidating. Perhaps that's what she wished, for Mr. DesCartes almost fumbled with his coffee causing a slight grin on Beryl's face. "Mr. DesCartes, much as I enjoy visiting with my neighbors, mornings for me are for work. I am on a tight schedule for turning in a project. It would help if we eliminated small talk and get to the point of your visit."

His demeanor darkened slightly and Beryl thought, *good, I have you angry and uncomfortable. Perhaps you'll not come again without calling first. I do not want your company when I am alone. My sixth sense says you are dangerous. Some think you should keep your enemies close, but I have learned by doing that, the enemy can see the cracks in my armor. No, I don't want you close, Mr. DesCartes.*

"Please call me Rene and I will call you Beryl." Further annoyed by this unwarranted social advance from a European, but choosing to look at least somewhat friendly and aware she had already laid down some social rules, Beryl replied, "I do like the economy of using first names, Rene. Thank you.'

"I know you are aware the police have visited me based on a situation originating at your home recently. I saw you in front of my house talking with the West Side Major Crimes Unit Captain. Beauregard is his name, I think. I have not met him yet, but I think I have every reason to complain about the high-handed inquisition in which his detectives treated me, that's how you say arrogance here, I think. Some strange man arrives on your property injured and they think I have knowledge of this man. Absurd, absolutely absurd!"

Beryl saw Rene's face puff up in anger and redden. She said, "Why do you think the detectives thought you knew this man, Rene? Strange, don't you think? Was there some evidence he came from your street or property?"

Rene appeared to be assessing Beryl's intentions. He quietly answered, "Well, it's not important. Of course, they were just checking the whole area. I called my neighbors, but I was the only house where they questioned the owner."

"Rene, yours is only one of three houses on a mile of road. Your house is directly behind my home after a trek through the woods. Seems a reasonable assumption to me for them to check in all directions from my home."

"Beryl, you are right. I have overreacted. I have been concerned about the health of the poor man. The detectives would not share any information about his health status. I don't know his name. I called the hospital and asked about the man brought into the emergency room from West Side with serious injuries. The operator transferred me over to a doctor who wanted to know if I knew him. Of course, I don't. I was refused any further information. My housekeeper said you have done some volunteer work at the hospital and you would be able to help me. Another friend, who is a nurse, said you were at the hospital that same day. How is he doing?"

Beryl thought, *I'm going to need all my drama skills from my acting days to convince him I know nothing. He must think I just came out of the cabbage patch to believe his story. He is connected. I don't know how, but he is connected. I must keep him ignorant without letting him know I'm on to him.*

"Rene, I did check on him. Pretty certain, he's not going to make it. At that time, they did not have his identity. There was no cell found and no info on him. I'm having a most difficult time, myself, processing how a man would collapse on me and probably will die. He is in a coma."

Beryl cried and shook, eliciting the gentleman to react in a consoling manner. In less than ten minutes Rene left the house. She thought, *once he knew the man was going to die, he was out of here, but not before asking me if he said anything before collapsing. I mentioned he mumbled some words, but I couldn't understand him. I will speak with Beauregard and no one else. I think it is important to share info with him when I get it, I don't want to be on the dark side of the Captain. He is already uncomfortable with my style of speaking out. I can't change. Honesty in all my actions will eventually persuade him I can be of help.*

If someone were to assess Beryl's actions, they might find them much too aggressive for the circumstances, which Beryl acknowledged to herself, but she was not persuaded to slow down. She went immediately to the police station where she discovered Beauregard would not be in for at least a week. She did not assume as most folks would have, that he was on vacation. Beryl thought, *Beauregard is not the kind of man to leave on vacation with a question like this attempted murder unresolved. I would not leave, he is much like me; he is determined.*

She queried, and looked innocent, as she said, "Oh dear, he said I was only to talk to him about this issue. Its secrecy was important. I was to talk to no one else."

An observer would probably think the officer at the desk was quite taken with Beryl. He bent forward and said, "The Captain was in a car accident and is laid up. Give me your name. I'll put it in an envelope and one of the detectives will bring it to him."

Taking a chance, Beryl said, "Oh, in that case, I'll visit him at home while he's recuperating. You said he'll be out for at least a week. I'm sure he'd love some company."

The officer said, "He's not at home, but if you can call Mona, she'll give you all the details."

Beryl thanked the officer and told him not to bother Captain Beauregard with her name. She explained if he were still in the hospital, then it would be wrong for her to add more stress at this time; she could wait a week until he came home. Smiling brilliantly, she thanked him again, adding, "I will call Mona later when she's back from the hospital.

It's a good thing I didn't hear about his accident from gossip. I would have been worried sick. You have so reassured me."

The desk officer was certain he had just done a favor for the Captain and for the handsome lady. Beryl took control not to rush out of the station. She thought, *I hope he never figures out he's been had. Now I know Beauregard's in the hospital. A good thing for me as long as he is in recovery. I have access to him at the hospital, I would never have at the station.*

Beryl phoned the chief of volunteers at the hospital, Alva Nunes, and asked if she could be of help. After a long discussion on why she had chosen not to volunteer during the last two months, and now was pleased to help out, Beryl said, "I believed I'd been exposed before and took three tests in two weeks. They were negative. After which I took the anti-body test which is positive. I'll bring my test results in, but I feel comfortable I won't be a source of patient infection. I have never been sick. They tell me some people do not feel the virus. Does that gel with the hospital's requirements?"

Ms. Nunes was pleased to have her back. Beryl was then almost joyous when Alva said, "Beryl, the police from your city have been in to visit one patient and their Major Crimes Unit captain is in here with a bad leg from an accident. The floor nurses say they're concerned with police coming in and out. I think they are exaggerating. Only two or three officers have been in and at different times, but you could do all the tough calls over there. Just tell the head nurse to throw them out. They'll blame you and be happy to do it."

Beryl asked for a later shift reminding Ms. Nunes that police tend to make their visits in the afternoon after taking care of regular police work first. Alva agreed and wondered if Beryl could start this day, which of course was exactly what Beryl had in mind.

Decked out to look anonymous, Beryl responded to her shift duties. Within an hour she was on the hospital floor covering two patients of interest to her. She determined to visit Mr. Mattias first, thinking, *I'll see what I can get out of him if he is conscious. After, I'll visit the Captain. He will most likely not be pleased to see me, but I have information for him. Information is the currency to access his good will.*

Upon entering the Jed Mattias room, Beryl found the patient sitting upright staring out the window. Turning toward the noise she made Jed said, "You are the lady I fell on. You have the one face here I can trust. You could have killed me when I was down. No one would know the difference. You didn't."

"Mr. Mattias, I didn't, wouldn't, couldn't and why would you think it was possible? I don't know you. I want an answer for both our sakes. Am I at risk because I saw you? Do you remember what you said to me before you passed out? You and I both know you are in some serious trouble. Let me help you."

"What can you do? You are just a nice lady who saved a stranger who dropped in, literally dropped in, from death. I thank you, but you can't help."

"Mr. Mattias, I can. I will help with or without your permission. If you wanted secrecy, you should not have chosen my home. I know you chose my home over Mr. Rene DesCartes' home. You will do well not to deny it."

Jed said, "What is your name?"

"Beryl Roisin Arabella Kent."

"Arabella, are you from Atlanta?"

"No, and no, I knew nothing about you nor your business when you dropped in. Now, I do."

"What do you know, Beryl? It is easier for me to use your first name if it's alright with you?"

"I know Mr. DesCartes is too interested in your state of health. I know your law partner was recently killed in an unexplainable auto accident. I know you have a daughter living in Austin. I know you are single and take complicated litigation cases in business, big business. I know you are worried about whoever did this will renew their efforts. I know you fell out of a helicopter, it's the only explanation for your injuries. I know more, but just can't remember it all now."

Mr. Mattias answered, "It's all conjecture, some good guessing going on in your mind. I'm fine."

"Your fear is overwhelming you, Mr. Mattias. Consider your situation. You know I can be trusted. I believe the police can be trusted because they have no history on you, but there will be many people who may reach out to the police and share a story which will perhaps not be true, thus coloring your attempt to protect yourself. It's important for you to spill the beans."

"Who have you spoken to aside from the police, and how do you have the ability to visit my room? It's COVID time and I'm told strict restrictions apply. I have reason to be suspicious. I don't know how I got here. Maybe you should leave."

Beryl thought, *don't rush this man. He has reason to question me. If I can stay in this room with him long enough, he'll adjust to me. He'll consider I saved his life. He's already said that but his fear is overwhelming. I suppose when I think about it, he's a famous attorney who is used to being in charge and having all the answers. He has some answers, but he is not in a state to properly analyze all the facts. I've got to get him thinking as he would have if he were his own client. I hope I have long enough time with him before a nurse comes in to take some stats on him.*

Beryl waited fussing with the sink counter putting things in order. Jed watched her carefully. He said, "You're not going to leave, are you? Just why are you so interested in me and the why of my accident? Beryl, it is inconceivable you would go to such efforts to see me when you don't know me."

"Ah, Mr. Mattias, that's because I'm a woman and you're a man. I don't think you had an accident. I've said that before, so don't insist it was one. You were marked as a victim and you somehow got away. You have some knowledge about your escape or your occasional memory of your fears. I think you know DesCartes or someone likely to have used that name. Don't think it all won't come out. The police know it is not an accident from their forensics results. Help me. I want to protect you, and I can hang around here. You are my current good social work project, to keep you alive in spite of yourself. Help me."

Jed answered, "It is a mess in my brain. I normally have no trouble with memory, but I just have glimpses of being in a plane or helicopter and being very fearful. I remember a gun pointed at me. I remember looking at this huge modern home and deciding not to go in that direction. I don't know why, because the other direction was all woods and I was uncertain I would be able to get through them and find a live person to help. I remember not going down the road in front of the house. I was certain, then, I would be followed. I don't know why I knew this. I cannot put a name on my pursuers or why I was being pursued. Grace Grantley, my firm's managing partner is scheduled to see me today. She'll bring my calendar and client lists and records from my cell phone. Until I see them, I can't tell you anything more. However, I do stand corrected, Beryl. I trust you. I have years of dealing with people who lie. You don't lie. You do manipulate, but you have some smarts. Please do what you can to protect me until I'm out of here. I am grateful to you."

Beryl looked at her watch, startled by the time. She knew it was nursing rounds time. "I don't think you should see your friend, Grace Grantley. She should be turned away for the time being. She would have to tell those concerned about you that you are well. The gossip should be you are near death and won't survive. Jed, I'm going to disappear for a bit. I'll monitor your room as best as I can. As long as they think you are near death, you are safe. If someone unknown to you enters, pretend you are almost dead. I can't give you a gun, but here is a carving knife from the kitchen if there is a problem. I'm certain the police will be here. You'll know more later and I will know more later."

"Beryl, thank you for the weapon, now how will you know more later? I totally trust Grace Grantley. How can you keep her away?"

"Just know I will, Jed, I will."

Beryl waltzed silently out of Jed Mattias' room. Catching a nurse headed in her direction, she entered the next room which was a double. Two men occupied the room and both had recently undergone surgery on their legs, one on the left leg and one on the right. She asked them if they were identical twins with perfect opposing injuries. There was laughter. Beryl had left her cart of newspapers and other items for the patients in the corridor including some flower arrangements. The hospital no longer let florists in to deliver or other people. In fact, all items, when allowed did a couple of hours of storage with the idea the virus could be timed out; she thought there was some nonsense in COVID practices. She was surprised the hospital allowed any additional accoutrements at all for the patients during this virus time. The cart allowed her a reason to hang around the corridor. Her role in general was one of good will. She would report to her supervisor any patient complaints.

The two gentlemen in this room wanted gum and candy and had nothing negative to say about the nursing. They were both unable to get out of their beds given the weight of the thigh length casts they supported. She spent ten minutes with them when a nurse entered for stats. She smiled and greeted Beryl, who quickly exited the room. She rolled her cart down the corridor and entered several rooms before coming to Captain Beauregard's room. Her timing was impeccable. There were no visitors nor nurses around. She walked in without knocking. Beauregard heard her quiet footsteps and turned his head immediately. Given his having recent surgery, Beryl was shocked at his ability to pay immediate attention to her. He said, "I'm not rid of you yet, Ms. Kent. How did you find your way here? Now I'm in fear. At the station I could avoid you. Here you have an immovable detective unable to escape. Not fair, Ms. Kent."

"Since you are unable to be ambulatory, Captain, please call me Beryl, or else I'll move your tray out of reach."

Beauregard laughed. "What are you here for anyway? I don't think you're conducting a mercy visit."

"I am mercy for your mental health. I did promise you I would share with you anything I discovered. Especially information you would not be able to learn on your own."

Beauregard's ears perked and he sat with some difficulty a little straighter in his bed. "Tell me, Beryl, what news do we have for me."

Beryl collected her thoughts before answering. *So now he'll call me Beryl. By itself the act shows improvement. I can work with this man. He is just difficult. No more difficult than husband one and two.*

She shared with the Captain her visit from Mr. DesCartes and their conversation. Specifically, Beryl described her instinctive feeling about Mr. DesCartes when she shared Jed's condition. DesCartes was pleased to hear Attorney Jed Mattias was close to death. She said, "It is not my imagination, Captain. Jed Mattias is in jeopardy and Rene DesCartes knows him. He does not want him to live a long life with memory revival. He wanted to know what Jed told me before collapsing. How did he know something was said to me? Did he just throw it out to see if I would bite or did your detectives tell him what Jed said. I told him I could not understand Mr. Mattias, and to me, what was said was just gibberish. He is a dangerous man. My instinct is Mr. Mattias is on the wrong side of some big business or political deal."

Beauregard answered, "You simply cannot, Beryl, jump to conclusions based on limited information. Although I agree his visit and behavior are suspicious, one cannot conclude it is based on business or politics. It could be personal. Some competitor of his firm could be deranged. We will investigate."

"Captain, Jed Mattias didn't look like he was a sucker for some wacko lady or friend in his personal life. He's widowed, doesn't have a record of being a philanderer, and is a most well-respected attorney. It is in his work, I just know it. Or if it's personal, he doesn't know it. He does not refer to anyone particularly right now. If he were involved personally, he'd be worried about a particular person and would be calling. What about the daughter? Did your detectives call her? Is she coming here?"

Ignoring Beryl's fishing for information, but not ignoring the fact she knew too much, he said, "How do you know he doesn't know if it's personal? Have you spoken to him? I told you to stay away from him, Beryl."

"No, Captain, you specifically told me to share with you any information I discovered, which is what I have just done. I am free to visit this man who I saved from dying. He knows I can be trusted and I think it's important for him to have an honest friend until he recovers, don't you?"

Practically sputtering and ignoring her question, Beauregard said, "Beryl, do not interfere with police investigations. You'll cause harm. We have not determined as yet there is a crime here."

"Captain, you may not have determined if there is a crime, but I have. Further, protect this man, until his memory has recovered, because it will. The best protection is to keep up the façade he is at death's door. Communicate that information to all visitors, whether they appear to be friend or foe. He is at risk from someone who wants him dead. His firm's managing partner is coming to visit, she should be held off from visiting. He knows something he shouldn't know or he is in a position to interfere in someone else's plans. I'm going now. Before I leave, I apologize for upsetting you. It is not kind of me not to not have considered your condition first. I must say you look quite well for a person who had such serious leg surgery two days ago."

"It's not so bad. I'll be walking without a cast in four weeks. I'll also be at least ten pounds lighter from eating hospital food. Mona, my wife, will not supplement with her home cooking. She thinks this is an opportunity for me to diet. She is bringing some health food supplements. You are not causing me to suffer, Mona is."

Beryl laughed. "You are like all husbands, and I have experience in the husband area. Blame the wife who is looking out for your interests. I must meet Mona. I'm certain we would get along, Captain. I'm quite certain."

A quick good-bye from Beryl, and Beauregard was left alone to wonder just how much Beryl Kent would interfere, thinking, *I can't complain she is not logical. She is. The problem is she goes where she shouldn't. I know she visited Mattias. I hope she told me all. I will take her warning about Mattias' safety. His law firm's managing partner is visiting. His colleagues may be involved. And where is the daughter, she's supposed to be close to him. Is she in jeopardy? I'll call Mason.*

Two minutes later when his call connected to Mason, Beauregard's neck hairs prickled when he realized Sergeant Barr was with Attorney Grace Grantley. He then called Bobby and asked him to take the call privately. When alone, Bobby told the Captain he assured Grace that Mattias was doing well and would recover. Beauregard charged Bobby with covering the story of Mattias' health with news of a downgrade in his condition. He was to ensure Grace Grantley be informed Mattias' life was in jeopardy and he was not now available for a visit. Beauregard insisted Bobby get in there before Grace could possibly bypass his instructions to medical personnel. And he was to tell Mattias of the plan. "Insist he go along with it. I think he will, Bobby. He is frightened, as well he should be."

Bobby Barr was always comfortable pursuing action and very quickly implemented Beauregard's plan.

8
Accident - No

Beauregard, confined to bed, presented a dangerous situation. He could sit up. He'd limited pain pills to when they would be moving him. He did this for a reason, thinking, *'make hay while the sun shines' was one of his mother Lizette's favorite sayings for pushing him out of bed or for inviting him to do the lawn, take out the trash, or whatever else was needed. Well if it was good enough for Lizette, it's good enough for me.*

He spent some time calling his detectives for reports, but was told there were too many to discuss verbally. Petra or Ash would be in later with a summary. Beauregard showed his disgust with this news saying aloud, "Who're you kidding? Mona or Ash must have said not to bother me for a day or two. Probably they want to wait until I'm home. They leave me only one avenue for information, check that, two avenues. The intrusive Beryl Kent and Jack for now, no there is also Norbie Cull. I can ask him about his file, and mention I know he's representing the truck driver. Mona has him representing me. She wants me to sign some papers. Hell, I'm not looking for a windfall, just Cull's protection to ensure my driving was not at cause. I do need reimbursement of my medical co-pays and my service vehicle. I better get him in here to keep me informed."

Beauregard called Jack and asked for an update on drones reporting on helicopters in the air around the time of Mattias' injuries. He was not surprised when he was told, "Rudy, not only was there a helicopter that flew in the area in question about twenty minutes before your man collapsed, but I learned pilots don't necessarily have to have flight plans when they fly for leisure. There is a flight plan here that shows the pilot making a short stop to an East Windsor, Connecticut heliport before returning. It never arrived in East Windsor. Further, I checked on the pilot and he did not fly on this day. His wife was having surgery. The description of the helicopter belongs to one already in use in Massachusetts on this day. Why, since it's obvious the pilot was trying to mislead using a fake name for flying the helicopter, is the question. The drones saw it in the area. Their description is detailed and I'm trying to discover who owns similar helicopters. If it's flown in these airways we should find it. Finding the pilot is the problem, but don't worry I've initiated a question on its illicit flight pattern form application. Since one was filed and didn't have to be filed, I found it strange. It said he was flying businessmen to the areas listed, except the pilot did not land in all the areas listed."

"Jack, although I appreciate your work, it'll take forever to find the helicopter and when and if we do, the owner may know nothing about a short flight. Keep going and you can put in your search for remuneration. The helicopter is under police investigation for use in a felony. They'll think it's drug use and get serious. Direct all questions to me and use my cell. I'm in the hospital with a broken leg, don't tell them. This goes no further than you and me, okay?"

Beauregard concluded his call with Jack and mused, *well it is not only attempted murder but it is a planned attempted murder. No one hires a helicopter and a pilot and lies on the flight plan for no reason. Maybe drugs are involved.*

Interrupting his musings, Attorney Norberto Cull entered his room without knocking, which allowed Rudy to comment on his lack of good manners. Norbie was not embarrassed. Instead, the counsellor said, "I'm now your personal attorney, Rudy. It's like having a second wife. I need to know all about your injury, your suffering, your financial setback, and your memory of the accident to fill out my new client sheet for my para-legal who will kill me if anything's missing. I'm here for you, Rudy Beauregard, as your personal injury lawyer giving, you, personal service, just as I advertise."

Rudy snickered, "How the hell did you talk Mona into this. She is adamant I not be put in a negative financial position from being on the job. You know how to hurt a guy. I would have gotten my injuries covered from insurance and the department would fight for the car. You must have told her my pain and suffering was worth something. She's probably dreaming about adding a porch on the house."

"And you have a problem with good financing? Did you cause the accident? No! I have a sketch done by traffic. You are a victim of a speeding driver who, by the way, was drunk out of his mind. Good thing he broke his arm. They got blood and urine. It's not his first rodeo. You are a victim, get used to it, Rudy."

Norbie went through the data sheet painstakingly which appeared to annoy Rudy. He said, "Norbie, you've never taken so many notes on a defense trial. I'm tired of answering you."

"Okay, I'm finished. You don't understand, when I do personal injury defense, Rudy, all this work is done ahead of time by my staff. You are special. You get me with all the mistakes in data taking I can make."

Rudy cut in on Norbie's joke and questioned him about his defending the truck driver in the two-victim accident. Norbie answered, "He's in the clear. There is camera support, his stellar record, and other details to corroborate his story. He insists the second car was following the first car and had hit it to push it over in the other lane. There is damage on the rear of the first car noted after the accident which could not be attributed to the accident; it was a head on into the tree. He reports the second car then sped away as fast as it could with no mind to the victims. This was no accident. It was murder perpetrated by the driver of the second car. I'll help you investigate while you're held up in here. I have an interest in this case. The trucking company is paying me well."

"Norbie, it's an open case. You know I can't bring an interested party into it. I've told you a hundred times before this."

"True, you have, but I can investigate my legal case and if you're nice to me, I'll fill you in on what I've found. I expect the same from you unless we end up on opposite sides of the issue."

Rudy asked, "Let's talk about your other case, Jed Mattias' almost death. What have you learned there? You were in there before the police, I don't like it."

"Correction, you haven't kept up, Rudy. You must be hurt. I was in the interview with the police. I allowed the police to listen while I spoke with my client. Quite generous of me, if you were to ask. This is a case of attempted murder, Rudy, and not a murder of passion. I think there was planning involved. Mattias may be in additional danger."

"You think I don't know. We have it covered. He'll be watched. Just what have you discovered from the conversation? He must have told you something we don't know. Every bit of info is important. Did he mention his daughter or the managing partner of his firm, Norbie?"

"I can be certain of only two things, but both are conclusions from my carefully watching him as he detailed what he supposedly knows. He is lying. He never mentioned his daughter, but you asked about her. His eyes quivered when I asked about personal history as a basis for his problems. His denial about how he got hurt may be partially true. I do believe he doesn't remember everything, but he remembers things he's not telling us. He is an attorney. He'll never answer a question until he is assured it fits into his choice of stories. Much like fiction writers, we have to see where the action and suspense is going. He is very frightened.

"One other thing, Rudy, you don't like coincidences, I know you don't. The fatal non-accident occurred two streets over from Ms. Kent's yard. Bothers me some. What about you?"

Rudy laughed. "Norbie, Chief Coyne will kill me if I get involved in another serial case. Get out of here."

"Just a thought. It would not be a serial murder case, if the focus was on one personal or business problem, would it? It would just be a case of multiple murders. If you won't see if they're connected because you're worried about attention from Chief Coyne and the press, well, that surprises me."

Jocelyn Kent discussed her mother's surprise visitor on a very long phone conversation. Jocelyn was exasperated with Beryl. "Mother, leave it alone. It all sounds suspicious. You're alone. I can't come until, at the earliest, next week. I'm almost finished curating a big project for MOMA. God knows when they'll exhibit it. I'm pleased I did not contract for more than choosing works and getting loans from owners and support from big patrons. I'll be there as soon as possible. But… Mother…how many times have you gotten into dangerous situations by not minding your own business?"

Beryl appeared bored with Jocelyn's chastising her. "I am a generalist in life, my darling. You are always too focused on what is in front of you. You could meet Prince Charming and not know, if at the time you were curating a project. This man almost died in my yard and in my arms. I did not ask for him to fall into my arms. Apparently, karma has brought us together. I never question when the universe presents me presents or difficulties. I simply address them, and I won't and I can't leave it alone. I'll see you next week."

"Don't hang up on me, or I'll call Oliver. He'll talk sense into you."

"Darling, forget any Christmas present, if you call Oliver. You know he would like me to live with him so he won't have to worry about my, what he calls, thorny personality hurting the people of the world. He's an engineer, Jocelyn, do not bother him."

Ignoring Jocelyn's last words, Beryl went to work. She decided to call an old friend who now lived in Austin, Texas. The woman, Armel Lobel, was a guitarist and songwriter. Beryl had searched Marthea Mattias on Google. She was pleased to learn Marthea was known in music circles. Her hunch was Armel would and could get contact info on Marthea, maybe even more than that. She thought, *I need to know more about this man. Why hasn't his daughter called me, unless the police didn't tell her. Although the paper had my address listed. They loved the story of a man with no memory.*

About to make a call, Beryl's phone rang, and it showed Oliver calling. "Oliver, you must stop listening to Jocelyn's fears. I am fine."

"What are you talking about, Mom. I haven't spoken to Jocelyn in a week. She's in a snit from too much work and has no time for me. You must be up to something not subject to her approval or she'd never threaten to call me. She did threaten, didn't she? Tell me what evil deed is in your mind. I love the problems you get in. They are always interesting. You're not involved in another friend's domestic abuse problem, are you? You do know the last time you were, the boyfriend threatened to burn down your house."

Hoping to put Oliver off track, Beryl replied, "No. Just the inconvenience of a man collapsing and almost dying in my arms in my back yard. It required the police and ambulance. Now the police think it's suspicious. That's all."

"Wait a minute, Mom, that's big. A potential murder victim fell on you on your property, why on your property? Where did he come from? You said your yard. You call your back acreages, your yard. Why was he back there? If he needed help, wouldn't he come in from the street to your front door? This is big."

Ignoring his question on the importance of the event, Beryl did not answer. She asked, "How would you know enough to think it was a potential murder? I said he collapsed. I did not say there was an event beyond the falling into my arms. He could have been just plain old sick, Oliver."

"You said the police were there. You are also quite excited. It tells me the event was more than just sickness. I know you!"

"You would think like that, wouldn't you? Now, dear, what do you need? Are you calling about Christmas planning? You know we're only supposed to have six or eight to dinner under Governor Baker's orders. I don't think I can abide such limitation. I've contacted your uncle who's a medical statistician and is in on all the rules. He says to just use the six feet apart, masks, no collective sharing of food, etc. He should know, don't you think?"

"Mom, he's my step-uncle and he's nuts; he breaks every rule. I'm not sure I'd rely on his advice. That's not why I'm calling. I just took advantage of COVID-19 and its impact on the real estate market in Boston. I've bought a house and I can't get into it until late January. Problem is I sub-let my condo. They want to move in today or no go. Can I bunk with you? Most of my work is by computer right now. I'll be traveling no more than two days a week, Mom. Okay?"

"I'll love to have you for a roommate, my darling, with one caveat."

"What?"

"Anything that goes on here is not for Jocelyn's ears. You know how nosy she is and she'll then think she can get an edge on directing my life. I am not in my dotage. Cripes, I'm only fifty-eight years old, but to her I am on the brink of entering an old-age home. Hell, my health is probably better than hers. Promise to keep your mouth shut and I welcome you with open arms. Don't think for a minute she won't be calling you to get a scoop on my activities. She has never approved of my involvement in the world. She is not generally interested in the world and likes total focus on a project until she moves on to the next one. Jocelyn doesn't even know I'm alive until she is about to make her required weekly phone calls."

"I got it, but Mom, remember, it is who she is."

The doorbell rang forcing an end to the call.

A well-known news reporter greeted Beryl. With a million-dollar television personality grin, Samantha Griggs said, "Ms. Kent, I am Samantha Griggs. My station with its evening news interpretive show is interested in your experience now noted by the public as, 'The Bleeding Man' incident. May I come in and interview you, my audience is most interested in unusual situations our citizens face in their daily lives. I can't think of a more appropriate subject for our program. I understand he fell on you and bled all over you. Please share…"

Samantha Griggs spoke so quickly, Beryl couldn't completely process her words, but when she did, she interrupted, "Samantha, I am not interested in discussing this event. Thank you. I am going to close the door now."

As Beryl attempted to do so, Samantha kept talking. Beryl never liked leaving a conversation with a lack of minimum politeness, but Samantha showed great dedication into getting her story. With her back to the front door, Beryl sighed thinking, *this is a story. The press has already sniffed it out. I wonder if they've had help. Who would gain by having the story go public? I don't think it's good for the police with the Captain incapacitated, but there is always a mole in any organization. The people who did this, would they want the facts to come out in the light of day? Generally, not, but if they can't discover his health condition, the reporters will. Not good for me, Attorney Mattias, his family, or the police.*

Beryl connected to Armel. Delighted to hear from her, Armel ran on for several minutes about her life, the music industry, and her new man saying, "I didn't give up on men after the awful divorce, Beryl. I had faith like you told me. I'm getting married in March. Just a small affair with this COVID stuff, but I'm happy. If you are able to come to Austin, you can stand up for me. What do you say about it?"

"Armel, I've stood up for you twice. Bad idea, I am not a lucky charm for you. Besides, who knows who can leave or enter states in March. I am pleased for you, Armel, you don't like living alone."

A disappointed Armel said, "Tell me how I can help you, Beryl. You don't call often. There must be a reason and I know it's not related to travel. Have you an exhibition or a signing or podcast or what?"

"None of these, I am looking for information for someone in the music industry known down there. Her name is Marthea Mattias. She's called "The Lady MM.""

"I know her, Beryl, hell, I've played some of her music for demos for big names; two took them and now want me to do demos of some of her new work. What do you need? You do know Marthea is younger, early thirties I think. She's out of our age league. Just what do you want with her?"

"I know her dad. He's been trying to reach her with no luck. Do you have her number or if there's a boyfriend, his number?"

"Sure, I have both. I'm now confused, Beryl. Her friend Scott called me looking to reach her. She left him a message she was going on a two-week vacation climbing some mountains in the Dakotas. She left him no hotel or hostel number and is not answering her cell. I just thought she may want to have a breather. Guys can get under your skin sometimes. If her dad can't contact her, I'm now worried. She is a people person. I know she has a good relationship with her father. I've met him and for a big-time lawyer, I still like him; although I generally don't feel fuzzy-wuzzy about lawyers."

"Give me both cell numbers and her address. Do you know anyone who could let me into her apartment? I'd like to check on her safety for her dad."

"Beryl, I don't know if you should. Her boyfriend could let you in, but I'd have to vouch for you. I trust you. Get her dad to write a letter to let you in. That would work. I heard her dad likes Scott."

Beryl, not bothered by legal issues typed a letter of permission for herself to search Marthea's home. She looked at the photo she'd taken of his signature on some papers she saw in the hospital, thinking, *hmmm, I haven't been in Austin in a bit. I'll call Scott and have him pick me up from the airport. He'll even help me know what's important. It's not something the police will do. It would take ages for them to get a warrant. They'd wait the two weeks and if she didn't return, they'd do a wellness search. Daughter missing and dad almost dead are one too many events. I'll let Oliver know I'm gone to a teaching assignment. He won't have time to ask me too many questions. I'll call Scott now. I simply can't abide waiting for answers when a little action will give me background if not answers. I better call Alva Nunez and tell her I won't be in for a couple of days.*

Beryl was tired after her well over six-hour flight from Bradley Airport in Connecticut to Austin, Texas. She thought the stop at Charlotte was way too long for loading passengers. Traveling light, as always, she was one of the first to get out of the secured area. She recognized Scott, Marthea's boyfriend immediately, thinking, *just what I would have expected. Despite her ties to the music industry, she's chosen a classy type, in dress, at least. He is handsome; impressive.*

When Beryl greeted Scott by name, he was surprised and asked if she'd seen his picture. She said yes, but it was a fib, a fib that fit her narrative. He insisted they stop for something to eat. "Look, Beryl, it's late and you've had a long flight. I appreciate your caring about Marthea, but searching her condo will take time. I am happy to spend all the time in the world looking through her home. Marthea would not want me to worry. Let's eat something and you can hear her call to me. It is a strange call, almost as if she wanted me to question her. I'm mad about her. I thought maybe she was testing me, but she's always been straight forward in the past; so why not now?"

Over a Spanish but new American influenced cuisine of huevos rancheros, the two spoke about Marthea, her career, her dad, and her relationship with Scott. He owned a marketing firm specializing in music and was also an attorney specializing in the music industry. He explained there was synergy from both endeavors making his efforts easier. He represented Marthea in a copyright infringement case. "Beryl, it was an easy case. She'd submitted the work for play to a group and before they made a cut, a local group used the song. Marthea had her ear to the ground and caught it early. She didn't hesitate hiring me. Her father told her she must be aggressive in protecting her work. She had evidence. It was easy for me to look like a hero to her, I wanted to be her hero. She is special. Not just talented and nice, she is gorgeous. I am worried."

They finished their eggs and left for the condo. Beryl wondered aloud to Scott about the New England aesthetic Beryl now enjoyed vs the Atlanta in which Marthea was raised and now this sunny and open life she found slightly lacking in tree cover. His answer was succinct. "It's music. We love the access to music. Music controls some of our lives. Detroit for R&B, Nashville or Memphis for rock and country and on and on. I suppose big cities are for classical and Hollywood for movie music with New York for stage musicals. You go where you can create and be appreciated. If I were a lumberjack, I'd be in the Northwest or Canada. All the same, where is the work and where it is, is where we live."

I love getting these words of wisdom from this newer generation, but Scott is correct. I've lived in foreign countries with my diplomat husband and in my first husband's hometown where he developed his business. I was always happy in each place, although I do like West Mass and will stay there. How did I decide to live in Western Massachusetts? Ha, not brilliance on my part, just looked at a map. Oliver is in Boston and Jocelyn is in New York. West Mass is in between the two and it is beautiful and comfortable and gives me the feeling of home. Until Jed Mattias dropped into my lap.

Marthea's condo was distinctly modern with a Southwestern flair. Beryl told Scott, "This will be easy. Marthea keeps a clean space."

"Not in the music room, Beryl, it's a mess. Although she has a system. She can find a song from that enormous pile in an instant. What are you looking for? Before we start, listen to her message to me. I forgot to play it for you at the restaurant. Also, can I see the permission from Marthea's dad? I might need to explain later, if nothing is wrong, why we searched her space. She may not like it."

Beryl showed Scott the forged letter and was surprised he had not asked for it earlier. He scanned it and said thanks. Together they started their search with Beryl keeping an eye on her partner in crime. She listened to some calls on Marthea's home phone, decidedly surprised to find one. When she questioned Scott about someone so young keeping a house phone, he said it was devoted to messages from her dad and from him. She listened to the last week in messages. Scott had called her repeatedly the last eight days in a row. The first of the repeated calls coincided with his story of trying to reach her for a dinner they were scheduled to attend. Calls from her dad coincided with the day he left New Jersey for an unknown destination. There was one call from a man, who said he was a friend of her dad's. It was on the last day Beryl could place Mattias in New Jersey. Whether she called him back or not was unavailable for her. There was a pad of paper next to the phone with the name, Josh, and an address listed. She copied it and asked Scott if he knew a Josh who may have been doing some work with Marthea. His answer was not helpful with just the knowledge that 'Josh' was a common name in the industry but that Marthea had never mentioned a 'Josh.' Beryl next asked about the address, to which Scott laughed, saying, "Marthea doesn't regularly go to Dirty Sixth Street. It's the old music part of town."

They rummaged through her personal effects forming only one conclusion. Marthea did not take either of the two large pieces of luggage and did not wear her comfortable boots. A business outfit and favorite pair of sandals were missing along with her normally used shoulder bag. Her cosmetics were as Scott remembered them. Her computer had no password and showed no internet dating or questionable emails. There were notes on music, appointments, dates for meeting friends, music classes, etc. Beryl thought her visit to Austin did not look like it was bearing fruit.

Disgusted with her thoughts, she asked if Scott would take her to the address listed. They left the condo looking untouched. Beryl said, "You've searched apartments before, Scott. You were a downright specialist in searching. How'd you come by such experience?"

"I served as Military Police in the Army as a Criminal Investigation Warrant Officer. I learned a lot, mostly it wasn't my field for the future."

It was not a long drive to the address listed which was two streets down from Dirty Sixth. Beryl thought it was quite run down, not like in New York City, but for this clean city. Perhaps it appeared worse at this late hour. The address was a dirty door and doorway with a sign indicating no entry. She took a photo.

Later at her hotel she made arrangements to return home to West Side.

9

The Dead Victims and More

Data on the dead victims was decidedly lacking in suspicion. Both Marlene and David were divorced. David had two children living with his ex-wife in East Greenwich, Rhode Island. There was no evidence of an other than a business relationship between the two victims. David's ex-wife said she would know if there were. "I still had feelings for David, but business was his life. I can't believe he'd be having an affair. It's possible I know, but not likely. He is a great father and has not denied me financial support. If someone was after David, it was a business person. He was willing, always, to try new financial arrangements to get innovative businesses off the ground. I did not like some of his colleagues. They looked aggressive as wolves to me. I met Marlene. She was no less a risk taker than David. Marlene was quite handsome, but she was not into romance. Talking to her was akin to speaking to the Sphinx. You got nothing out of her because she wasn't human. I actually told David what I thought about her. He laughed and said, 'She's a great partner. I can trust her not to let on in any situation. She's got stones.'

"I did not think I would want to be described in such a manner. Have you talked to her ex? David told me Marlene's ex did not want to end the marriage."

Mason called Marlene's ex who was seriously distraught about her death. He wanted answers from the police. He questioned Mason, imploring him, "Lieutenant, is there a case against the trucker? The papers said a car was following them. Did the car cause the accident?

Marlene was a really good woman and should not have died this way. I want to know who caused this accident. She seemed distant but she was loving. I feel so guilty. I told her she'd have to find another line of work if our marriage could be saved. She told me to walk and I did. I regret pushing it. You simply couldn't push Marlene. I knew I shouldn't have, but I did. We were only just recently divorced. I wanted children and a normal home life. Wrong wife for that kind of life. I was warned. I didn't listen. Maybe she'd be alive if I didn't leave. She died on my birthday. If we were still married, she'd be home celebrating, she never missed my birthday."

Mason queried if there were lifestyle problems in the marriage. "Was Marlene a party girl, maybe a quiet life would never have worked for her."

The reply saddened Mason. "No. Marlene grew up poor. When we first married, she felt my way of living was heaven. Later, she saw it as just ordinary. When she got into finance, her brilliant mind caught onto the making big money fast goal. I remember when she scored her first big fee. It was two-hundred thousand dollars for two weeks work. Marlene set her sights on living in the lap of luxury. It also was personally important. Her mother and sister are both addicted to many things. Their minds are gone. Marlene pays for their nursing home care and I couldn't do it on what I make, and I make well over six figures. Those numbers are nothing compared to Marlene's earnings. She was not heartless, just money goal directed. She'd do anything to help me; not, however, give me what I wanted."

And he cried. Mason thought, *even on the phone I can hear his pain. It's not a phony act. Why do people throw good people out of their lives, when there aren't many who would love them like this guy?*

When Mason visited the Captain with his report, he was surprised at his response. Beauregard normally took Mason at his word, but this day, he didn't. "There is something here. These two were involved in some monkey business. David's ex didn't like his colleagues but liked her ex, and isn't jealous he died in a car with another woman. Marlene's ex still loves her and is grieving. Weird set of human condition, Mason. Marlene's greed is a signal and David's sinking into the abyss of the deal is also important. Has Ash investigated their offices? Do they have offices? Ask the exes if they know and request an okay for searching, sounds as if they'd be amenable to one. Let Ash know what you know. See if you are able to get access to their offices at home. Take Ash with you. Have the families scheduled services? This COVID really restricts us from the opportunity to view the families' interactions with victims' associations. Another negative of this virus and the nation's reaction to it. It interferes with police business."

Mason answered, "Don't go there, Captain. You're lucky they're letting us visit. No complaining, we're all waiting for you to act up."

Beauregard ended the call without a so long and wondered, *Mason's the second one to tell me to be nice. Mona insists she is not going to put up with any complaining from me now that she knows I'm on the recovery road. Who were these two victims? Do they run some sort of private equity scam? Maybe! Ted Torrington needs to look into their reputations. Although an engineer by training and previous work, he knows all the accountants in town. He also does tax returns on the side. He'll know who to call.*

Sergeant Ted Torrington, without calling in advance, entered the door of the local headquarters of a large equity firm. He knew the managing partner and his ability to resource portfolios, professionals active in the industry, current hot issues, and hopefully what was happening locally. Two hours later, with his head spinning with new information, he called the Captain. "There is too much for me to report over the phone, Captain, but I have a list of local professionals active on the big stage. Alex, my go through guy, says there are great opportunities locally for those who don't ask too many questions. Locally means the whole Northeast with less emphasis on NYC. I think he's talking about washed money. He would not be specific but listed several firms dealing with companies, When other respected firms choose not to do business with them. I have a list of thirteen firms, two have locals running them. I've heard of these two. He passed the name of our dead victims through and both have had dealings with six of the thirteen firms. He checked their backgrounds with all those firms.

"They get rave reviews for closing deals and they aren't lawyers. I asked Alex what he meant by 'closing deals.' He explained they got money for new ventures. They went through with no hitch. Both our victims are well thought of by these companies. It is just Alex who doesn't respect their opinions. I'll send a list of recent known deals and the names of the six firms to your email."

Beauregard, mentally excited by Ted's information, wondered, *I don't think of the Springfield area as a source for big-time funding of new business, but I would not be surprised if drug business money is being laundered. I know we shut down a big operation recently, but it was run by a Russian immigrant and discovered because of a Latino fight over territory and a crazy son. It involved a great deal of money by my standard of living, but Ted has inferred this money laundering situation is really big-time. If legitimate business equity funders get tempted to money launder, it involves numbers too big for me to get my head around. I'll call Jerry. Maybe he can direct me.*

Beauregard regarded Jerry LaRatelle, his close friend from his days working retail while in high school. Jerry went the police route ending with a job working for ICE. He would know about national problems with drugs, money laundering, and schemes used to cover for criminal proceeds. Beauregard thought he must understand, how money is moved from the illicit to the legal.

His conversation with Jerry left his brain whirling in circles. He would not discuss current investigations with Rudy, but if Rudy named a company he would let him know if he thought there may be a problem. Jerry agreed to go over Rudy's list with him later. Rudy called his office and asked Millie to take his email and organize it and give a list to Jerry saying, "Send the file to me when you're done. I am the only one Jerry will talk with."

Rudy, who now had to get help with personal services as he called them, was exhausted. He actually asked for pain medication. His nurse kidded him comparing his present likeness to one of a human being vs his previous insistence of acting like Superman. She said, "Captain Beauregard, take it easy or you won't be back in action quickly. You've been on the phone for well over an hour. Brain work takes a toll. You need to address your physical recovery. The work will wait."

Beauregard wanted to be annoyed by this motherly advice. Yet, he could not but smile at her sincerity.

<hr>

Beryl Kent felt exhausted from her trip to Austin. Oliver's peppering her with questions fueled a foul mood until she gave in and answered. She thought, *I would never tell Jocelyn. I tell Oliver. I love them both immensely. What is it about parenting? The children we get from the good Lord are different. Don't tell me siblings are the same. Oliver and Jocelyn are from different planets. Oliver, once I told him the reasons for my trip, was okay with it. Jocelyn's reactions would have been different with why on earth are you involving yourself, or don't you have enough to do in life and on and on. Jocelyn sometimes exhausts me. On the other hand, when I am in big trouble, which has happened, she is a born rescuer. She doesn't want me to rescue myself. She thinks she's my parent. Oliver thinks he's my friend. I can't complain, but I do treat each differently.*

Laying out her plans for the day took a few minutes. She decided a visit to Beauregard was a must saying aloud, "I'll visit early when Mona is there. I'll get to know her. If she trusts me, I'll have access to the Captain through her. Without her help, I'll be toast."

Beryl enjoyed some lunch with Oliver and found him quite helpful. He examined her options and gave her a list of questions to be answered first. The essentials were: how did Mattias get to the proximity of her home, what business deal could be involved, what kind of business deals had he recently played a role in, what role did DesCartes have in all of this, did Mattias ever have dealings with DesCartes' related operations, ask for a list of DesCartes' businesses, talk to neighbors about DesCartes' comings and goings, drain as much info as possible from the police, particularly in regards to Mattias' daughter and his associates, and finally, "Mom, accept it if you cannot produce the results you want."

"Oliver, you exhaust me with your list, but I will follow this list to the end. Whispers will become louder. DesCartes has three neighbors behind him. People always watch the goings on in their area. His home has an enormous open front but the back has a wire fence with major landscaped shrubbery. The houses back there are on a hill. There must be a view of the back of his house. The helipad is camouflaged, so it would not be visible. I do think the driveways and garages are visible from those buildings. It's worth a visit, don't you think, Oliver?"

"Mom, or shall I call you, Arabella? Isn't that what Poppop called you when you went off the rails. Like now, you take what you want to follow out of my list's sequence."

"Go on, I asked for your contribution, Oliver, it doesn't mean I'll follow it verbatim. Thankfully, I don't think like an engineer. I'm quite creative, I'll have you know."

"Not new information for me, Mom. Your creativity got me in more trouble as a kid than I myself could think of. Thank God, your choice in men has always been pretty decent, at least for husbands. Some of your men friends are whacked out."

The two finished the dishes leaving Beryl free to visit some neighbors before heading over to the hospital. She thought, *Oliver has given direction. It's up to me to find connections, but his list will prevent me from going on tangents before I fill in the facts. What do I really think now? I think someone has blackmailed Mattias and has the daughter Marthea captive. Jed will tell us nothing until Marthea is found safe. It's what I would do. How do I convince the Captain to search for Marthea? I have little evidence. I must look at players close to Jed, those who know about his personal life and could get Marthea in a position, alone, to be abducted or isolated. The abductors would need an understanding of what's important to her, what issue could cause her to go out at night to a chancy neighborhood. Her car has not been found. The Austin police will look for it now. She's been gone too long and Scott has filed a missing person's order. The car will be found if it's been left on the street or airport or shopping center. With this COVID stuff, it will be easier for them to locate the car unless it's garaged.*

Three hours later found Beryl slightly frustrated. She'd only had access to two of DesCartes' rear neighbors. The third abutter, the one with the best view, was working and normally came home at six in the evening. The other two neighbors were quite clear about the third neighbor's schedule, fueling hope in Beryl's heart there were more insights to be garnered. However, the two she spoke with did not like Mr. DesCartes and she wondered about their veracity. She thought, *they dislike him. It's difficult to know if they aren't adding a little to their stories because of their distrust. Raymond Lucasian was the most loquacious of the two couples. He regaled complaints of DesCartes planting enormous trees in his rear yard. Despite their enormous cost, three did not take. Lucasian still had a good view. He said fancy cars were always visiting after nine o'clock in the evening. Nothing interesting normally happened over there before late night. He had seen her visiting and the police visiting.*

She took notes. *So, for all her nosiness, she only discovered he had late night company. Lucasian said there were no wild parties. DesCartes occasionally had some female company earlier in the evenings on Thursdays. He thought one lady looked like DesCartes and may be a relative.*

Beryl decided to use her time wisely and sped off to visit Beauregard at the hospital before going back to visit the third neighbor. She called her supervisor explaining she would be returning to duty for a couple of hours this day and four hours the next day. There was no problem other than the time for medical inspection to enter the hospital, receive a cart, and get up to the floor. She did not mention her trip to Austin and felt a little guilt, but was confident she had no exposure to COVID and certainly no symptoms. The planes had few passengers. Beryl did not initially go to the Captain's room, instead she parked her cart about three doorways from Jed Mattias' room. Looking about in an off-hand way, she was assured her entry into his room would go unnoticed. And it did. She found Jed napping. Impatiently she made a few noises. He woke and immediately knew her. "When you didn't come back to see me, I thought, perhaps, I bored you, Beryl."

"Not at all, you are of great interest to me. Now tell me, Mr. Mattias, who has abducted your daughter Marthea? Don't say you don't know. You do. I have just come back from a short trip to Austin for business. I looked for her. Her boyfriend nor any friends know where she is. A missing person's complaint has been filed. You can't keep this a secret any more. Stop interrupting me. There is one really important question you must answer. Who, just who, in your life knows how important your relationship to Marthea is to you?"

Mattias' face turned quite ruddy, as if he were healthy, but it was more fear bringing out the color. In anger, he answered, "What right do you have to interfere in my life? My daughter is fine. She's on holiday and now you've brought her into a police matter. Call it off. Do you understand? Call this off. Tell the police I've heard from her. If you don't, I'll call them."

Beryl did not respond. Pulling up a chair she sat quietly waiting for Jed to calm himself. In time, perhaps a good three minutes, he said, "You're not going to do that, are you?"

"How can I? Someone is trying to kill you? A person has abducted your daughter or somehow has her convinced she doesn't need her phone. They will be looking for her cell, the police I mean. If the phone is in a river this becomes a serious police investigation. Tell me what you know. I'll help you."

"Beryl, I am extremely sorry I collapsed on your property. If I'd known you were the kind of woman who butts in, I would have fallen elsewhere. You are putting her in danger."

"How so? You knew she was missing - you did know! Did you remember a threat? When did you remember?"

Jed Mattias searched for some words, settling on, "There were two notes in the inside pocket of my pants. My pants are custom made with a small unnoticeable pocket inside the regular pocket. When I gained my senses lying on some extremely hard and uncomfortable bushes, I couldn't remember anything. I fell off the bushes and the first thing I did was search my clothes for identification. There was a handkerchief, but nothing else until I tried the secret pocket. There were two notes, one bigger and the other smaller. A note with cutouts said, "Do as you're told, or you won't ever see Marthea again" and I think the other had a date and time.

"The note did not stimulate my memory, just gave me an overwhelming fear for my girl and as to the other note I don't remember the name of the client connected to the date and time. Why do you think, despite the pain of my injuries, I was able to get as far as your home? I had to know she was safe. Don't tell me not to worry. Look at the condition I found myself in, Beryl. I escaped from something. I'm certain of it. I agree with you. Someone wants me dead. I kept the knife, and then you show up while I'm nodding off. If you were trying to kill me, you would have been successful. I cannot protect myself, nor my girl."

"Where are the notes now, Jed?"

Jed told her he hid one note, the date and time note, while the other note should still be in the pocket. He was not certain where or why he hid one note over the other, but he knew he hid it. "I won't give it to you even if I remember where I put it. I know you'd take it to the police. You would have to cover yourself legally."

Beryl said, "It is difficult for me to believe without evidence, but I do believe you. Who else knows, Jed, how close you and Marthea are to each other? No, who amongst your colleagues even knows about Marthea? Do you brag about her? Who would know Marthea was so important to you? Think about it. I have been. I want you to write down everything you remember in the order of its occurrence. Tomorrow, see if just one more item can be added to your list. Each day, re-edit. Your life and perhaps Marthea's depends on it. Any memory is important, but... I'm a puzzle master. I'll put your small clips of memory as you get them into an organized scenario. Help me, Jed."

Beryl left Jed's room feeling slightly uncomfortable after pressuring a recovering patient. She was content though in the overall direction she was taking. Beryl knocked on the Captain's door for admittance. She heard voices discussing two murders. She thought, *what murders? There have been none in West Side, although I've not listened to the news or read a paper in three days.*

Beryl scrolled to local news on her cell and scanned quickly the news about a truck accident with the driver being questioned in two deaths.

Entering, Beryl said a breezy hello to the Captain, to a woman whom Beryl was certain was Mona, and to the infamous defense Attorney Norberto Cull. She had read about Cull's defense skills and appreciated the honors given him by the state bar association and private groups. In general, Beryl applauded talent put to good use. Introductions were made. Mona greeted Beryl as if she were an old friend. "Beryl, I've heard all about you."

Confused and hesitant, Beryl asked, "Mona, I hope the Captain hasn't been complaining about my being a nosey neighbor. He has to me, but I'd hoped he kept those complaints to himself."

Beauregard looked quite uncomfortable until Mona answered, "Oh no, Beryl, Rudy doesn't tell the left hand what the right had is doing with the exception of discussions with his merry band of detectives. Augusta Milford lives way down from you on Yellow Brook Dingle. She's on the Library Board with you and says you are a wonderfully sensible business board member."

Beryl laughed, replying, "Sensible is not the first word normally used for describing me, Mona, but I do like hearing it. I do remember Augusta exclaiming about you and Charlotte Torrington working together on a project to help the middle school with an art support program. Let me know if you need more help, I'll join you. There are simply not enough programs of interest for some age groups. I particularly like kids of that age. They may still be unpolished, but they are so honest. It's a joy to work with them."

Norbie had had enough. Listening to the ladies' good works was of lesser importance to him than any of Beryl's investigations. Just watching her self-control and monitoring her conversation informed him she had much to share. Why could or would she just walk into Jed's room and he knew she had? He noticed her immediate attention to Mona. He thought, *is it just a woman's thing? Speak to the woman in the room first?*

Maybe, but I think she's setting Mona up so she can visit the house when Rudy gets home. I'll bet I'm right.

Norbie asked, "Beryl, have you visited Jed yet?"

Beryl turned to face him, gave him a brilliant smile, and responded, "Of course, I am most interested in Jed's continued good health. I was disturbed to see how easily I could enter his room. He was nodding off. If I had the desire to harm him, believe me, today, I had opportunity. No one was in the hallway. I spoke with him at length and not one medical or police personnel entered while I was there. Jed needs protection."

Taking advantage of Rudy's condition slowing him down, Norbie quickly said, "Why so, Beryl? Why do you think he needs protection? You don't believe his landing in your lap in your backyard was accidental?"

Rudy was not so infirmed not to intervene. "Norbie, my investigation, not yours, stay with your truck driver."

Mona was now interested. She'd not had time to hear about Rudy's cases given the last few days of trauma. She decided she was now interested in the broader world and said, "Beryl, tell me about Jed Mattias. I read about it in the news, but they said he probably wouldn't make it. Yet, you had a conversation with him. What did he say, poor man?"

Before Beryl could answer, Rudy blustered, "Mona, this is police business. I'll talk to Beryl alone if you all don't mind."

They did mind. They took what was later reviewed by Rudy as 'their own sweet time' before leaving. Beryl said, "I would not have told any details to them, Captain. You should not worry about my discretion – experience has taught me discretion."

Blustering, Beauregard quipped, "Then why did you say you visited and spoke with Jed. Even Mona knows he's supposed to be almost dead. Now she knows he can talk. You let her and Cull know he is in danger and his room is easily accessible; not discrete, Beryl, not discrete."

If Beauregard for a minute thought Beryl Kent would be apologetic he was wrong. Instead, she said, "Don't you trust Mona and Mr. Cull to keep their mouths shut? I do. Now let's get to what I have learned, unless you are not interested."

Grumpy, but motioning for her to go ahead, Beryl discussed her travel to Austin and related info. Beauregard, while she was relaying her story, couldn't decide what bothered him more: her success or her gall. He thought, *she flies on her own ticket to Austin based on knowledge from some past association, speaks with the boyfriend, breaks into the daughter's house, finds the girl's last known destination, gets the boyfriend to file a missing person's complaint, talks to Jed about it, and thinks this is normal behavior just because she's a witness.*

Aloud, he said, "Do you have the second note? If not, have you seen it?"

"No and No! But I believe him. It was not found on him, therefore, it's in some alcove of a tree or buried near a rock. Despite his condition, Captain, Jed is always the wily lawyer. It is there somewhere. Hopefully it's not in a place where the rain will erase it. It's been dry for days. Your uniforms should get on it."

Rudy believed she was right, but was still annoyed with this investigator newbie and he told her so. Beryl did not take offense, answering, "You don't strike me, Captain, as someone who would refuse assistance just because you don't like the person giving assistance. By the way, I will continue to assist."

Beryl walked out of the room leaving Rudy quite ticked off, not just at her but at himself and his foolish reactions to her good work.

Outside the room, Mona and Norbie waited for her, questioning whether it was safe to reenter or had she so enraged the dragon they should wait. A nurse moving down the hall reminded them they could not stay in the hall, masked or not. Mona decided to leave and finish some

Christmas shopping, mentioning, "I will have to do all the Christmas work this year since Rudy is out of commission. It will be better when I'm home. I'm at home teaching and my mom or Rudy's mom will keep his crazy side in check while I get ready for the holidays. I hope to see you both at our home. Thank you, Beryl, for giving Rudy something to mentally chew on. And Norbie, don't stay away. I know you will help him with his cases as will his detectives. Thank you."

Norbie asked Beryl if she had time for a coffee. Not at all surprised, she agreed. Thinking of a restaurant nearby allowing inside seating took a minute when they settled on The Munich Haus in Chicopee. Although it was located in the next town, it was less than a mile away. Once settled after ordering potato pancakes, fried cheese, and German ale, Norbie asked, "What's your take on Jed? Do you think he's holding back?"

Surprised he did not ask her why she was so interested as to investigate on her own, she thought, *this Mr. Cull doesn't appear to think I'm odd. He's all about business. I like his focus on the problem. No fuss! Just business. Now should I tell him anything? Will he run right back to Beauregard? Is there a conflict here? My only obligation to Beauregard is to tell him what I know and I've already broken that obligation. I didn't tell him about the visits I made to the neighbors up on the hill. His detectives will get there soon and find I've been around. I have to speak with that third neighbor before they get there, then I'll tell Beauregard. I don't think my actions are interfering with a police investigation, if they are, then it is problematic.*

But, can I trust this Cull? I'll ask him about himself. He'll reveal enough for me to decide. It's obvious, despite their often being on opposite sides of the criminal justice line, Beauregard trusts this guy.

"Tell me, Mr. Cull, your interest in Jed Mattias."

"I'll call you Beryl, if you don't mind."

Beryl nodded in agreement and waited for Cull to continue. He said, "I represent Mr. Mattias through his law firm."

"That was fast. How did they find you, did you know Jed before? And why does the firm feel it needs an attorney? Are they questioning the quality of their cases or of Jed's life?"

Cull smiled and said, "Beryl, I am their attorney. There is the concept of privacy. I told you I was acting as the firm's attorney, because I am aware you are involved in this case. Our goals are most likely similar with one exception. You are free to share and I am not."

"Mr. Cull, when I entered the Captain's room, I overheard you two speaking about an accident death case in West Mass that may be two murders. You represent the truck driver. You also represent Mr. Mattias. Is there a connection?"

"Beryl, I don't think you heard all that. I think you have made some assumptions. I will answer anyway. I had not thought of a connection before you brought up the issue. There has been no evidence I have seen connecting the two events. Why would you think there is a connection?"

"Mr. Cull, I am relatively new to West Side, but I know one thing, it is a mainly suburban community. Lots of soccer moms, health clubs, cute local places to grab a coffee, ethnic restaurants and other than two areas of the city, we residents don't come across business types during the day. Two business people, not from this area, were killed on a quasi-two-lane road by a trucker. The road was not a normal trucker's route. Not good for your client's defense. Who were the other people? What were they doing on a more rural section of town squeezed between two gated communities? It seems reasonable to me to connect two events that are just weird and uncommon in their nature. You and I both know someone tried to kill Jed. Your truck driver said someone was following the accident victims' vehicle and didn't stop after the accident. Two pieces of information bothering my brain. I'd like your opinion."

Cull thought, *she is quick. It was only recently, when Sheila commented there was a lot of negative activity in West Side that I even considered a possible connection. Now, Beryl comes up with the same insight. I will have to consider this. Has the thought passed through Beauregard's brain? Maybe not, since he's in a certain amount of pain now, but it will.*

"Beryl, I hadn't thought about it until you mentioned it. I would need some evidence to even entertain a connection. Yes, West Side is not the normal location for settling in by big-time business folks, but we are not without our wealthier residents as you well know. Those residents have associates and it is quite the norm in Western Massachusetts for us to entertain our business associates in our homes. I don't do it often. My clients frequently are in trouble with the police or I'm dealing with business deals where my services have been solicited and there is no personal interaction. I don't look for clients now. My attorneys do, to increase their practices and their revenue share. We do advertise our firm through me. To pursue your theory, you need something more."

"Mr. Cull, I don't believe you hadn't previously wondered if there was a connection. I have just learned about the accident and I can assure you I will know more about those people by the end of the day. In my glancing at the news article, I could not absorb it all in a few seconds. What make of cars were the two involved autos, the one with the victims inside and the one following it? Do you know? If it's public information, you certainly could tell me."

"Yes, it was in the news. The victims' car was a dark 2020 Ford Tahoe and the car following it was a white Land Rover."

Beryl asked if the police had been able to find the Land Rover on cameras in the time frame. She was told defense attorneys would get reports later after they had been written, but there was often a time gap between police knowledge of details and reports written and when such reports were discoverable by defense. She asked why, in a good relationship which she perceived Beauregard and Cull enjoyed, Cull hadn't yet been informed. Cull didn't respond other than to remind her of the line, which is normally not crossed between police investigations and defense attorneys' strategies for gleaning evidence in support of their client. Beryl then questioned Cull about Mattias' firm. Who there had hired Cull? And why wasn't it his daughter who hired Cull? Was it because she doesn't know he's been injured and why hasn't she been informed? Cull decided then he'd had enough of Beryl's fishing but not sharing and said, "Beryl, you are being disingenuous with me. You question as if you don't know the answers, but the questions themselves infer you have information you haven't shared with me. Believe me, it must be a two-way street for me to work with you. You decide."

With some heightened color flushing Beryl's face, she said, "Just let's say we're getting to know each other, Mr. Cull. What do you think I know that you don't know?"

"Well, for starters, answer your own questions. You asked them so I would correct you and fill some added info for you. You can start with the daughter. You know the daughter doesn't know about her dad's injuries, which tells me you know why the daughter, being his only relative, was not told or even could be told."

Beryl laughed. "I should be more careful in trying to outfox a fox of the law, Mr. Cull. I generally believe my gift in investigating is one of looking at a bigger picture than most investigators do. Your and the Captain's specialties are in putting the details together. Yes, the daughter has disappeared. No, I don't know where. Her cell phone is not available, nor does she answer it. She, Marthea, is noted as being quite close to her father and would normally tell him if she were to go on a trip. I'm told, she told no one. I personally think she's being held as blackmail to ensure silence from the father or to force him to do something. Just some assumptions."

Cull answered, "If her father was almost done away with, why hold the daughter now?"

"I guess this idea does not compute with my assumptions, does it? What does compute is the daughter's gone, Jed was almost killed, and his partner recently died in an auto accident. Who from the firm hired you, Mr. Cull?"

Cull responded, "Have you spoken with anyone from the firm, Beryl? If so, what was the story?"

Beryl sighed. "You're not telling me. Does it mean your contact is protected? Okay, I know from the police, Jed's partner was killed in an accident. I know there is a managing partner taking over. I've gone over the firm's website. That's it, not enough."

Cull attempted to explain to Beryl, "Look, some of this you will not be able to discover without getting in the way of the police. I commend you, Beryl, for your civic actions, but you can't interfere in a police investigation. I cannot share my case details with you. You, as I'm sure you know, are able to share with me. It is not a two-way street, but it is what it is. If you're interested in pursuing justice, I'll chase down every lead you give me as will Beauregard."

"I don't like being closed out of the inner circle. It has happened often in my life, but I understand legalese. If I find a lead, I will tell you. I promise. I won't stop. Do you have a card with your cell number on it?"

Cull gave Beryl his card noting on it his personal cell, said good-bye, and thought, *this is not the last of her. She knows even more than what she has said. She has a path to follow or she would still be with me trying to suck more info from me. Rudy's got his work cut out for him with this lady.*

10

Grace, Mona, and Beryl

Grace Grantley received a call from her contact at the hospital. She was not happy. "What do you mean, his condition is downgraded. I was told he was well enough to speak. He has no memory of recent events? How did it happen? He had no head injury."

The caller had no further information to share other than, "Grace, they had to restart his heart and maybe there was blood loss. I don't know. He's in trouble and in an induced coma."

Given her propensity for action, Grace called Detective Barr. He did not pick up. She used some time to google what she thought were Jed's injuries. She thought, *it is possible the heart was traumatized, but previously I was told there was no heart damage. Why would there be a need to restart the heart days after he'd been kept at a recovery level? Was there a medical error in meds made? Did he suddenly just give up? Not likely, Jed never gives up. It's the trait behind his success and also behind his problems. He'd want to live for Marthea, if not for anything or anyone else. If he is at all awake, I must speak to him about Harry's client. Jed always thought he could keep Harry in line, but how many times did we have to retrace Harry's steps to protect the firm. Harry, you idiot, you got us into a mess this time?*

Grace tried the highest level of hospital administrator she could get, and received the same party line, "You simply cannot visit Mr. Mattias, Attorney Grantley. We'll call you when he is awake."

She thought, *not a word about his health. I gave him all kinds of legalese about the absence of Jed's daughter, and the fact I had the right to know his condition. Did this guy debate me, no, he just referred me to their lawyer. There's no pushing them.*

Grace was shaking with repressed anger when Sergeant Barr returned her call. They discussed the case for an hour. The Sergeant said he could not counter the medical experts. Grace questioned if Jed were safe and was told there was a watch on him. When she questioned why, the Sergeant dripped with sarcasm. "You may know the reason for his need for safety more than I would."

Realizing she needed to be less vitriolic, Grace asked if she would be able to conference with MCU Captain Beauregard. Again, the Sergeant stalled her with some excuse about the Captain being out from his duties for at least a month and informed her Lieutenant Petra Aylewood-Locke was acting unit head for day to day ordinary problems until the Captain's return to work. She said, "Well, I could continue to speak with you on a daily basis or would it be better if I called the acting head?"

She could almost hear Detective Barr smiling when he said, "Whatever is most convenient for you. I guess we will both get the same information. You have access to hospital administrators. You may know if he is better before we do. Please keep us informed if you hear from his daughter."

"I will, or course. Thank you for your assistance, Sergeant."

Grace seethed as she mused, *closed out… They've closed me out. Why? They must know something more than they are sharing. After all, I am Jed's partner and the closest to him other than Marthea. Why close me out? I could, upon calling the list of recent clients, come up with helpful information the police would not as easily recover. So, why shut me out? Unless, they were able to speak with Jed, what could Jed have said? I couldn't possibly be listed as under suspicion, could I? Would Jed have said anything about my attempt at a more personal relationship? Hell, it didn't work. He stopped with just one sentence, 'Grace, I don't play where I work.' Like I wanted to play. I wanted marriage. No, he couldn't get over the dead wife. Christmas, you'd think she was a walking saint.*

Mona Beauregard was in and out of several strip malls visiting their small retailers. She was Christmas shopping before Rudy would be brought home. She thought, *the shopping must be completed today and tomorrow morning. I don't need this additional pressure. One guy coming home from college and bringing his girlfriend for the holidays under the excuse she can't get back into Oregon because of COVID-19. Jeremiah and Lucas are thrilled to meet Roland's special girl. This is important. It will be six in the immediate family and our parents which makes ten. We'd be breaking the rules, but I'm going for it. I told Roland to have himself and his girlfriend tested for COVID before they come home. It probably won't make a difference. They have it or they don't have it. I hope Rudy won't complain. I can write my cards when he's home and wrap gifts and make calls and cookies, I just can't go out whenever I want to shop. Jeremiah will food shop for me and our parents. Hell, he's better at it than me. Where did his skills in shopping originate? Not from Rudy, for sure.*

Mona studied several woolen cardigans before purchasing them for Rudy's mom, Lizette. Lizette needed short to the waist sweaters which on her, because she was quite petite, reached her hips. About to choose a sage green one, she was tapped on the shoulder by her friend Bernice. No hugging allowed during COVID time, the two giggled as they touched elbows in a most ungraceful manner. Mona said, "It's been suggested we bow like the Japanese do to acknowledge each other, but I'd be just as self-conscious as I am doing the elbow greet."

"I know, Mona. How is Rudy? You missed our book club meeting. Janice said Rudy was in a car accident and has been in the hospital for a few days. Is he doing better?"

Mona detailed the story explaining how the additional stress was driving her bonkers. After a few minutes of catching up and a moment before Bernice was about to leave, Mona asked, "You live over near Yellow Brook Dingle, Bernice, do you know a Beryl Kent? She recently moved there. I've met her and liked her immediately. She is already on the Library Board."

Bernice replied, "You met her through the police investigation into some man who collapsed against her bleeding and who almost died. I was trying to find out about it without calling her and directly asking. It must have been frightening for Beryl, although, I don't think she's the type to be easily put off. I am nosey, but try to do the appropriate thing. I heard she's now not answering her home phone. The Frenchman, do you know him, Monsieur DesCartes? He lives in the oversized contemporary home on the Trail settled in the midst of wooded land. Well, he talked to Beryl's neighbors questioning about the incident. The neighbor, Mr. Johnson, doesn't like DesCartes and shut him right off with, 'In the States, we don't gossip about these things, Rene.' I could never say such a remark directly, although I find 'Rene' insufferable. I was at the Healthy Cafe in town and heard Monsieur DesCartes commenting on the limited types of pate carried. He gave our Lance some garbage about refined palates needing more variety. He is a snob."

Mona did respond she had heard Rene speak at an art show. He had invested in a showing of a local artist. "The show was in a private space in downtown Springfield and I saw all the museum folks there and lots of others I've never seen in arts related work before. They were definitely money types. The art was by Suzette Bjorn and it's good, but I saw some of the pieces going for full price and not local pricing. I was pleased we could have such a show in our area."

Bernice stated she still did not like Rene and it didn't matter if he was a supporter of the arts. "After all, Mona, he only lives here half a year and he's not a Florida snowbird."

"Bernice, don't be so judgmental. Florida or France, what's the difference?"

They said their good-byes and Mona mused, *she likes Beryl, and Bernice does have good insight into people. I'll encourage Rudy. Strong men must deal with strong women to balance them. I like Beryl. I'll welcome her to our home.*

Mona continued her shopping with a bounce in her step. *COVID and an auto accident will not put a damper on our Christmas. Neither will our son Roland's lady guest.*

Beryl Kent was laughing with Oliver as they decorated the Christmas tree. Oliver had surprised her. She arrived home from her visit with Rudy to find the tree set up. "How could you pick a tree without me? I always made the final choice. This thing is enormous and you haven't let the branches droop before decorating. You know better, Oliver."

"You talk about Jocelyn with control issues, Mom. After all these years, I can't pick a tree without you. You would have picked a miniscule one. You've started playing it safe in your dotage."

"If you say 'dotage' to me one more time, Oliver, you are dead! Besides, I ordered this beautiful artificial tree. What will I do now?"

"Not to worry, it arrived and I put it in the basement for next year, or maybe the year after or even later."

Oliver smirked and Beryl found herself annoyed. *I've lived through the deaths of three husbands and I'm now angry with Oliver when I normally wait breathlessly for his calls. I am an idiot, but Oliver does need some limits. I am the mother, he is the child. Just when did he think our relationship changed?*

"Oliver, what makes you think you can make decisions for me when you are staying in my home? Now I have this gorgeous artificial tree in storage. It would have worked. Did it arrive before you bought this humongous tree? Just answer me, please?"

Oliver with his light coloring turned beet red, mumbled something to the effect of 'maybe.' Beryl was certain it must be 'maybe' and acted upon her assumption. "See, you countered my wishes deliberately. Not right, Oliver, you are no longer a naughty boy, you are an adult."

"In my defense, Mom, that artificial tree is five feet high. Your room has a fourteen-foot ceiling. It wouldn't work and I saved you from an occasional bad judgment on your part. We can put the fake tree in the little sitting room if you like. I'll do it all."

"Oliver, it is not the point. Never mind."

Beryl's cell rang. Detective Bobby Barr was calling to invite her to the station for a conference at five in the afternoon, this afternoon. She explained she was busy for the early evening, but could be there in the morning. His reply was simple. He would call her tomorrow. Beryl was annoyed and could not compute why, thinking, *he agreed to what I wanted but did not state what time tomorrow. He'll make me wait all day long for a phone call. Waiting disrupts my focus. It's as if I'm waiting for a doctor's call. It can come anytime of the day. Oops, Oliver is staring at me.*

"Mom, is there a problem, you look irritated? Frankly, you've been intense since I came home. I know you, what is going on?"

"I apologize, Oliver. I've been overwhelmed by this incident with Jed Mattias. The police will not keep me informed. I can't leave this one alone. Detective Barr called to speak with me, but I know he won't be truly informative. He's going to give me minimal information if he gives me any information at all. Ticks me off."

A slightly heated discussion ensued. Oliver reminded his mom about several past incidences where her nosiness created situations of risk for her and the family. Beryl pointed out the resolutions in all those incidences solved mysteries for the common good. He laughed and said, "Mother, dear Beryl, as Dad would say if he had lived, sometimes we should not be the architects of perfect solutions."

They laughed at the memory with Beryl thanking him for the reminder. She said, "It's almost time for me to leave you alone to finish this tree. I have to get up to one of Monsieur DesCartes' neighbors for an interview."

Oliver groaned in resignation threatening to tell Jocelyn about Beryl's antics, but smiled and wished her good luck in her investigations. He said, "I'll keep my phone on in case you get into trouble, Mom."

Honestly, he thinks I'm a child, both of them do. What is this about adult children today? I'd never have treated my parents as children despite the fact my mother, my hippie mother, never embraced responsibility as a necessity. She would do the minimal of what she had to do, but every action of mine or anybody's was okay, maybe even wonderful. She danced through life and never felt the need to investigate or question anyone. Her favorite mantra was 'Like the breeze in the air, I wish to float through life.' And she did. I don't know how Dad put up with it. He was sensible and structured. He was lucky if Mom made him a breakfast once a week. I'm certain he was my caretaker when I was small. The relatives, who all dearly loved Mom, how could they not, said Dad was very involved with me. That's a euphemism for 'your mom was too busy being her.' Mom was a siren for people with problems. She listened to everyone, but felt no need to suggest solutions. Maybe that's what's wrong with mental health agencies. Maybe they should hire people who will just listen without commenting. Well, here I am at the Nathan Connault home and the view is better than I previously thought.

Beryl knocked on the door and Nathan Connault answered. She knew it was he from her review of his Facebook account. She introduced herself but Nathan interrupted with, "I expected you, Ms. Kent. My neighbors cannot keep to themselves. Welcome, come inside please."

Nathan took care of the niceties, coffee and pastries, insisting on calling Beryl, Beryl, and himself, Nathan, as well as spelling out in a very soft intro his view of Monsieur DesCartes. "Beryl, I understand your interest in DesCartes. I have friends on the force and the reports are the police searched DesCartes' property and had interviewed him related to the man found in your backyard. Please tell me what happened that day."

"Nathan, you first, please. What did you see that day, if anything? Were you at home? You have a clear view from up here."

Nathan smiled brilliantly causing Beryl to reassess him, thinking, *he is handsome but not in the classical manner. He is charming, affable, totally at home in his shoes. These are qualities of only the righteously self-assured. I must be careful around him, he is a turn-on.*

"Beryl, I was home working over there at my desk which as you can see faces the French doors to the large patio. The man was at the edge of the wood when I caught sight of him. He appeared to have stumbled against a humongous column holding an oversized birdfeeder.

"Everything DesCartes does is extravagant. He loves attention, actually, he waits for his neighbors to notice additions he makes to his property. The helipad caused a constant flutter amongst our neighbors including a City Council meeting. DesCartes loved it, didn't mind paying for representation that evening. Don't get me wrong, Beryl, I understand men who need to show off their success and excess. He also believes we Americans are generally not sophisticated. I think he will never accept our desire to connect with society despite individuals' roots. On the good side, he does not think money makes a man, although he'll entertain anyone with bucks."

"Nathan, why do you say that? Do you see who he entertains from up here?"

"We are like the old ladies, you and me, sitting here describing what I see out my window. I have to admit, DesCartes' visitors have held my interest. Several of them are money men, men who loan funds at higher than normal business interest rates. Not Mafia types, but they are blue suit types, though just as cutthroat. I have multiple businesses, mostly in the financial and manufacturing sectors, no public relations or retail. Along the way I've seen business vultures loan funds and when the borrower was late and couldn't find alternate financing, their normal process was to take over the businesses. They'd tie the borrower up with paperwork, the best lawyer in town couldn't break down."

Beryl asked, "Is there more to this? Are these vultures going after businesses for another reason?"

"Like what, Beryl? Money laundering, could be. Here in the Northeast we think of money laundering as a mob or drug king operation, but the suits are the backbone. There must be techniques for moving the money into the financial world to make it legitimate, then separating the criminal proceeds from their origin (this is called layering), and integration, or using what looks like legitimate transactions to disguise money's original source."

Beryl laughingly asked, "You know a lot about money laundering, Nathan, is there a lot going on in this area I'm not aware of? How would I tell?"

He smiled and did not quite answer with, "Whenever lots of money goes into a business that shows success in comparison to other businesses of the same type not doing well, there could be a question. It's difficult to know, because a good entrepreneur with sweat equity can make a great business in a field where most would not be successful. Auditors, bankers, and financial analysts often pick up a smell of laundering by observing money movements. The federal government often has to be directed to a smelly situation before investigation starts. If the launderers get an inkling they are under the government's radar, they change course to another business or area of dumping."

"How would you report any suspicion of money laundering and who would you report to?"

Nathan appeared uncomfortable with her question and said, "Beryl, you just don't report someone because you don't like them or because they have alienated their neighbors. You need to have some evidence of wrongdoing."

"Nathan, I'm not reporting anyone. I would like to know what the process is in doing so. Do you have a problem with it? If so, I'll google it. I've never thought about this before today. My brain is reeling at possibilities related to folks I've known in the past who may have been involved in funny money."

"In some countries it's called Black Money and money laundering is a world-wide financial problem often blamed for the lack of economic health in some Third World countries."

"Nathan, where would I report suspicious activities?"

With a sigh, Nathan answered, "National Crimes Agency, NCA. You would make a Suspicious Activity Report, SAR. Money laundering is a federal crime The US Department of the Treasury is charged with enforcement. You can make a report, but you won't necessarily be able to see how it is followed up. For someone like you, Beryl, so naturally nosey, that will be a disappointment."

Beryl crunched on her pastry, thinking, *he thinks I'm too inquisitive, probably thinks I have no controls. What do I care what he thinks? I do care. Why do I care, just because he's attractive? Jocelyn says I've had enough relationships for a lifetime. I did not end them. Life took my partners from me.*

"Nathan, I am not reporting anyone. I do not have evidence of suspicious activity which as you kindly stated would be proper. Thank you for answering my question. One other thing, do you know the name of the biggest drug cartel?"

"There are lots of them, Beryl. I think the Sinaloa Cartel may currently be top dog. Don't think drugs are the only cash being laundered. All kinds of illegal activity profits from prostitution, illicit trade, art and jewelry theft, and avoidance of taxes on legal activities are points for use in laundering. I think we should go back to why you are here visiting me. What else do you need to know?"

"I am certain as of now you have an eye for trouble. I wonder if you've ever been in military or other governmental investigation agencies. Aside from my invasion of your privacy, tell me about any cars you've seen in the vicinity of DesCartes' home on the day of my incident and before and after, maybe the day after."

"You drop a bomb on me, Beryl, and then ask a legitimate question. I have to say I admire your chutzpah. I won't answer your first question. I'll wait for another time when perhaps over drinks we can both do background checks on each other. We may astound each other with new knowledge.

"And, yes to the second questions. There was some activity the night of the event after the police left. Several large SUVs visited and only one was a relative or a lady. On the day after, and I find it strange you would ask about that day, there were several SUVs there for what I thought was maybe a long business conference. One car left after an hour and returned several hours later. A second car left after two hours in a hurry, with the third car delayed by ten minutes, but with a single well-built man rushing to leave. He rushed so much he fell on the mud near the paved driveway. Instead of going back inside to clean himself off, because his pants were quite muddy, he left quickly. I thought at the time it was odd, but figured he may have had a confrontation with Rene.

Rene DesCartes could raise the blood pressure in most folks.

"What make of cars did you see? Was there commonality between the car you saw on the night of the event and any of the cars on the day after? And I would be pleased to have drinks with you this weekend if there is a decent place open before four o'clock. We must obey the Governor's new mandates, you know!"

"Saturday at six at B'Napoli's in West Springfield sound okay for you?"

"Yes, I'll meet you there, but not unless you describe the cars."

"Beryl, it is my pleasure to tell you the auto I saw after the police left that night is the auto I saw the next day, the one whose driver fell and muddied his pants. It was an ivory colored Land Rover. The other two cars were a dark blue Mercedes SUV and a black Chevrolet Tahoe. Is there any other query you have for me?"

Pausing to remember something said earlier, Beryl asked, "Two things, Nathan, just two more things for now. I don't want to lose track of my thoughts, so remember there are two questions. In what order, did the first two cars leave and do you think there was a place on the birdfeeder to hide paper?"

He laughed. "You know something. Do the police know that something? Should I be answering them and not you?"

"I promise you, Nathan, I will tell the police everything in a very short while. You may have them visiting you in the next few days and you can tell them about this visit."

"The Mercedes left first and the black Chevrolet left next and then of course the Land Rover. To your other question, there is a slinky hanging down below the feeder held with nails all around it, maybe to keep squirrels off the post. If that's the reason, it's not working. Could be a place to hold some paper, it would stick to the spikes, but if it rained, not safe for paper hiding. I don't know."

Nathan and Beryl discussed her situation with the bleeding man. He truly was interested in how she felt when she was knocked over. With quiet respect, he carefully advised her to talk to a professional about the day's event mentioning the possibility she may have emotional repercussions later. She pooh-poohed his caretaking interests with, "Nathan, I've spoken with the police, my son Oliver, and now you, a Special Forces veteran. It's all the help I require."

She rose to leave with his words following her, "I never said I was in Special Forces and be there, please, on Saturday night."

11

Disruption and Displeasure

Beauregard was cranky. His displeasure was evident when he insisted he not be banned to his bedroom. His sons were invited by Mona to move his lounge chair to the living room, not the den or family room. He asked his wife why he couldn't recover in his den and her answer humbled him. "Rudy, you're the cop. All our personal papers are in there. You'll have visitors and I don't know who they'll be. You've always been so secretive about privacy and now you want the public to relax in your space."

"No one's going to come here except my detectives. They're okay."

"I don't believe that for a minute. You'll be getting reports from people, the Chief will come to show his support, and probably Mayor Fischler will show."

With a slight growl, Rudy signaled to Mona he agreed. If he had not, he'd have insisted on lounging in the den. She thought, *I don't know how long this recuperation will take, but, I sure hope he'll insist on going back to the station soon. Rudy is not meant for this quiet life. He may be slow moving, but he can't stand being prevented from moving, and I know it is a direct result from the damage he suffered in his childhood.*

His walker and crutch, both of which Rudy insisted he didn't need but would use to head for the bathroom if no one was in the room, lay next to him. He expressed his displeasure at the table set next to him with water and coffee carafes, Kleenex, pen and ink, and his laptop. He insisted it already smelled like a hospital room to which Mona said, "If there are odors, dearest, they are yours. There are no bedpans in here."

Rudy told google to play Christmas music, perhaps hoping to lighten his mood, and the ring doorbell chimed. He looked pleased at the possibility of a visitor. When he heard Norbie's voice, he yelled, "Welcome, Norbie. I need to talk to someone. Come in."

"Ah! King Rudy set up on his throne. You'll never go back to work if Mona keeps treating you like this. Although, she's now in charge of your diet. Right? It's too difficult for you to move with a full cast."

"Yes, about her controlling my food intake, but you're wrong about the cast. This isn't even a cast. It may look like one to you, but I don't get the full cast until my stitches are removed next week. This thing is awkward and difficult to move with. I can't bend my leg even with this brace or whatever they call it. Forget this, tell me what's going on outside."

"For starters, Ms. Kent, or Beryl as I call her now, is busy investigating."

"Damn, Norbie, did you speak to her?"

"Yeah. Told her about the line between you and me and the line between me and her and you and her. Beryl is not interested in borders, Rudy. She's on a mission. She'll be in soon to tell you all about whatever she has discovered. I explained the whole interfering in a police investigation. She'll share, perhaps not always timely. Be patient."

"This Beryl Kent is one nosey lady for an ordinary citizen."

"Beryl is anything but ordinary. Intrusive yes, ordinary no."

Rudy asked, "Just what did you get out of her?"

"She knows all about Jed's daughter Marthea and says she's missing. Sheila had already suspected she was missing. She spoke with the boyfriend. Beryl wouldn't tell me more, but there is a story there. I believe she wonders if Marthea is a captive of someone. Apparently, Marthea is close with her dad, and wouldn't not be in contact with him. She knows more about this."

Norbie appraised the look on Rudy's face. "You know all this, don't you?"

"Norbie, we're working on it. Why would she be held captive once the dad was out of the way? I suppose now he might live, it's blackmail to keep him from talking. The day she went missing, was the day before Jed was found in Beryl's yard. Could be they got him here in West Side to agree on something using the daughter as the blackmail. How did he get out of the helicopter? Why doesn't he tell us the story? I don't believe he doesn't remember."

Cull nodded in agreement. He said, "One other issue came up. Beryl thinks it's possible your accident case could be connected to the murder attempt on Jed. She has no reason to believe in a nexus between the two cases. She is simply uncomfortable with coincidences and pointed out the business type accident victims driving on a back road, both victims were not from this town, less than a mile and a half from Beryl's home is odd. You and I have both discussed this possibility. Strange Beryl could see it too."

"I am investigating both cases. If I find the slightest inkling they should be joined, I will pursue a joint investigation. I don't like coincidences either, but sometimes there are coincidences. What do you think, Norbie?"

"Beryl is inquisitive, and maybe really intuitive. She's also driven. Go along with her and let her do her thing. I think you gain in your police investigation if you don't miss any of her details. Think of Beryl's work as insurance. No different, Rudy, than in the big drug case with the boys' artwork which directed your solving it."

Not looking put out, but thoughtful, Rudy replied, "I have to speak with Jack, my drone guy. In addition to looking for helicopters, I want what cars were in the vicinity for two days before and after. Can the drones see plate numbers and do they record what they see? I don't know anything about this stuff."

Cull surmised, "The government has high level drones with GPS. Whether drones flown in the area are of that caliber is questionable. You may not get license plates numbers, but it's probable you can get make of car and color in the daylight. Remember, Rudy, it's early December. Daytime ends at four-thirty."

"Well I'll call Jack, see if he's located drones and their owners. It's one avenue Beryl has no close friends."

"Don't be certain. She might have an old boyfriend in the service. Have you checked out her husbands yet?"

"Cull, how do you know she's had plural husbands? Oh, I get it, you googled her."

"Rudy, my sources are always mine. Have you finished with my truck driver? You know he was not at fault and had no connection to the victims. I know it is now a murder investigation. He knows that, too. He's taken a leave from driving. His wife says he's having a difficult time coping. Will your guys talk to him, Rudy? They would be able to tell him he is not a person of interest. Help him out. He is a good guy, a family man."

"I'll have Ted Torrington do it. He's Mayor Fischler's brother-in-law."

"Just when I think you're not political, Captain, you show your true colors. Nice move. Why didn't I think of it. The mayor will prevent scrutiny, but, you know, he'll throw it back on you if there are citizens or press complaints. I suppose it's better if police are sharing info and not the mayor's office."

———

Lieutenant Aylewood-Locke was playing mommy today with her Carlotta. She called any time she spent with her baby, playing mommy. Jim did not like that phrase. He'd say, "Just because you are a working mommy, doesn't mean you're not mommy when you are not with her. I work and I'm always daddy."

Petra would laugh, telling him, "My mom was a stay at home mom, Jim. It does seem as if I'm not a mom when I'm working. Police work involves my body, mind, and soul. I don't know I'm married when I'm chasing a felon on paper or literally."

"Petra, you'd better never forget you're married, you hear."

She often thought, *I'm not so good with language sometimes. What I think is cute or funny gets reinterpreted by others. The Captain corrected me on this same issue. He said, "Petra, when a felon has a gun to your head, all you will think about is Jim and Carlotta." I know that. How else can I refer to the complete focus I have on my job when I'm there and my baby when I with her.*

She'd spent the morning doing research. The other detectives often commented that Mason and she were often a tag team on research. Mason could take a lead and follow it forever. Petra was the generalist who could take a detail and build more out of it. Her work seemed contrary to the other detectives who often said it was not logical to jump from the specific to the universal. Not noted for any serious artistic inklings, Petra would still answer, "It's an art form. I infer possibilities, follow them, and often I find a new investigative inquiry to follow."

The response was always the same, "Inquiry, you think you're in a British mystery police show?"

Today, Petra was loaded with reports from other police departments on their referrals to the Feds on money transfers after investigation of drug cases or any case where a lot of dough was questionable. There were many. She had a problem at first with too much data. Just how or what direction she could take to find any sort of commonality was the problem. Drugs as a commonality did not really fit the direction of the suits involved in the accident. So, street info would not be telling. The next step up, where names were dropped on big money injections or any exchange of money for another service was more difficult to discover. The independent street criminal, unless working for a larger organization, would take the money and run. She was not interested in them today.

Meanwhile, Mason was spending time with connections he had with bankers. Little known to outsiders, Mason belonged to a group of Afro-American businessmen and women who had developed their own mentors and friends in all walks of business. Mason was the only member from the police, and for good reason. He was discrete and was trusted. There were several attorneys in the group, mostly doing civil legal work. And for today, his interest was with the banking members. He suggested lunch at the Fort, but was referred instead to a Caribbean restaurant in Springfield. It was new to him and surprisingly, it was not far from his home. The restaurant had a large backroom for such meetings and let only a few members book it. He told Petra to continue her work, for he was about to do his favorite occupation, eat. She laughed and said, "You better get something other than a full belly from this deal, Mason, while I'm loaded with paperwork. I might bring Ted or Bill to assist. They both are analytical about data organization. I think I need some assistance."

"Ted is OCD and Bill works info with the best. Either would work! Use Ted. Bill is working with some friend on helicopter activity, who had knowledge of who and how under the radar transporting of drugs by air may have happened."

Petra called Ted and asked him to join her when he came in to the station. His reply was, "Great, I'll be there today. I've been on the phone following up on Charlotte's thoughts about Beryl Kent's background. Petra, it's going to be a couple of hours before I hit the station, but I'll work with you as long as it takes. I have to check with the Captain about a report he has. If he okays it, it may help us."

An excited Petra answered, "The Captain comes first. I do understand. Now, tell me about Beryl. From what I hear, she may be a multi-faceted lady with three dead husbands. When I met her, she looked really gorgeous despite her disappointments."

"Petra, what makes you think her three husbands' deaths were a disappointment? The lady may wallow in the theatre of being a widow, you know like the 'Black Widow.'"

"I met her when she was recovering from the man falling on her. There was no drama there, Ted. Do you think she's killed her husbands? Three is not a lot of husbands today, can't indict her on just three. It's not even suspicious these days."

———

Mona welcomed Ted with open arms, actually hugging him which was now a no-no with COVID guilt hanging out all over. "Rudy will be oh so happy to see you, Sergeant. He is bored. Sitting in a chair all day is killing him. He does his chair exercise for his legs multiple times, and then tells me how frustrated he is."

The Captain greeted his sergeant with a what have you got for me look. Ted, confused, said, "You were supposed to have something for me, Captain. Some guy you know named Jerry was going to take my lists and connect them with activity."

The Captain's face clouded as he recalled what he had not remembered to do. "Did I break my freakin' brain or my leg? I didn't tell Millie to send Jerry my list. I planned to, but didn't."

Ted said, "Captain, it's nice for you to be making the mistake this time and not me. Now do not get excited or Mona will remove me. What instructions do you have for Millie? I'll call her in front of you and tell her it got lost in the confusion."

The Captain nodded, and Ted's response was from the Captain's view, quite elegant. "Millie, it's Sergeant Torrington here. I'm with the Captain and there was some misdirection in the troops. The Captain asked me to send some lists over to you. I had them, but you were to organize my report and send it over to him. We can't seem to find it on his computer. Could you see if you can find your editing of it and forward it?"

"Sergeant, he asked me to forward it to him and then said never mind, to just leave it on his desk. He didn't want a record of it on his email. The poor dear man, must have hit his head. He never forgets details. Do you want me to forward my work to him now?"

"Millie, you are a living saint. Could you do so? We are both waiting."

Reviewing the file including the Captain's notes took some time, but the reward of agreement between the two detectives was worth it. Beauregard said, "I love working alone but normally I don't make decisions singularly, Ted. Do you know why?"

Ted said he didn't, could probably hazard a guess, but he was more interested in the Captain's personal reason and said so. Beauregard commented, "Always in the beginning of an investigation, we are overwhelmed with possible directions. If we, and I say we, because we never work alone, choose a direction too soon, we make mistakes. Think about this case or cases. Are we looking for drug business funding, money washing from cash businesses on a grand scale, or the disguising of theft proceeds? If we choose one over the others and we're wrong, we waste time and assets. Always remember, Ted, we work for the public interest. So where does this list leave us? I need your honest opinion?"

Normally, Ted would easily give an opinion based on his work. He was hesitant. It was general knowledge the Captain always had an idea of a direction to head before he asked others' thoughts. Despite any pressure Ted may have felt, he said, "Captain, if you connect the two murders and the attempted murder case, I'd say it is not drug related. I'd go for the other two. Deciding between those, money laundering to cover cash businesses specifically vs illegal proceeds from theft, I can't answer; but outright theft is there too. The victims were suits, one was a well-known almost famous attorney who dealt mainly in civil cases, giving me to think it's not drug related. Add to that, the majority of names on the list we've gone through just now, well, they don't ring negatively from a criminal investigative perspective. Call Ash. Wasn't he going to attend the funerals and ask the families for access? Did he connect with the police in Providence and Stamford yet?"

Ted's answer drew a slew of epithets from the Captain, not recently heard. He realized Beauregard felt hamstrung by his immobility, but said, "Captain, it's of no use to the case for you to get upset, besides which Mona will throw me out if she hears that language. She'll blame me. No one has given direction to each of us since your accident. There have been no unit meetings to catch us up. I don't know who's doing what. Petra could run the meetings until you return to the station, or you could have ZOOM meetings. Mona would know how to do it or Millie. We need you involved. We're hanging out like cowboys here, Captain."

Rudy looked disturbed, pushing Ted to wonder if he'd gone too far. *I'm normally careful with my verbiage, but we need the Captain. If he's to be out of the office for a month, there must be a management of the investigation. Petra could do it, but the Captain is already in the midst of it. Sometimes, people, even the Captain, can't see what's right in front of them.*

Beauregard answered, "Ted, sometimes I can't see what's right in front of me."

Ted choked and the solicitous Captain asked him what was wrong with a 'nada' for an answer. Beauregard said, "I think ZOOM would work. Have Mason set it up for tomorrow afternoon. Thank you, Sergeant, for your honesty and vision. You have just done me a huge favor, I must be dense not to have recognized this problem before you did."

"Captain, are you insulting me?"

"No, I'm thinking I'm right in not making decisions in a vacuum."

The two men laughed at Beauregard's faulty but unintentional insult.

Jed Mattias was moving in and out of bed more easily, but still was confined to his room. He sat in his chair staring at the blank grayish colored wall thinking, *why can't I remember where I put the note? Why can't I remember? There was little trauma to my head. There must have been a loss of blood to the brain. Hell, I'll be a candidate for dementia later on. It was my mom's greatest fear when I played football. Where is the note and why did I feel the need to hide one and not the other? Beryl is going to tell the police. If they investigate, it may hurt Marthea. Hell, just the thought scares me that police investigating me will bring deadly action against her. What brought this on? The date and time on one note means nothing to me except it is in the time range of my trip north, but it must mean something for me to hide it. Why am I here in West Side? I do remember fighting two men in an enclosed space, fighting for my life. I remember thinking I must get out of here to get Marthea. I remember thinking I can't trust anyone. Since Harry's accident, I've been hyper-vigilant. I remember going through his files right afterward. Something was wrong. I recall thinking and getting uptight, but what file and what was wrong? Why can't I remember the important details? Are they lost forever? Where is Marthea?*

Jed now talked aloud. "Keep it up. I know more than yesterday. What did I add to my memories today. Beryl told me to keep a journal. I remember being afraid, and being on an airplane or helicopter which would explain the enclosed space I recall. I remember the gun, just not who held it on me. I remember fighting two men. How did I get away from two men? Now I remember the fear I felt when Harry was killed. I think I called an investigator to look into it. Which one did I call, not a firm investigator. I wouldn't have done that, would I? No, I wouldn't want anyone in the firm to think I was off my rocker. I would have called an investigator sophisticated in car crashes. Who would it be? Let me think. Do I really recall these thoughts or am I making them up? How normal is my brain functioning and can I trust any of these recalled memories."

A light knock on his door interrupted. He pulled the knife from the bedside table placing it under his blanket. The silhouette was distinctive causing him to pull the extra folded pillow from the bottom of the bed to lay on top of him. He did not speak, but waited. There was a long pause when the person he didn't know entered the room. Blinking, slightly, he caught a sight of a man dressed in blue scrubs. The man approached the bed saying, "Are you Jared Mattias?"

Jed's fear heightened by the formal use of his name. The hospital all called him Jed. He did not answer. The man approached his bed, wiggled Jed's toes, and when Jed did not react, he whispered, "You make it easy on me, Mr. Mattias, thank you."

The next Jed knew was the feel of a pillow over his face. He could not breathe. He thought, *this answers the age-old question: could I kill? I'm going to kill you, you motherfucker. His arms are up with the pillow, I'll go for the crotch.*

The man screamed bloody murder, and lessened his hold on the pillow, allowing Jed room to ring the buzzer. There was blood all over one side of his bed. The man was holding his junk screaming. All hell broke loose. A nurse rang a code blue or whatever because ten people entered his room along with security.

Detective Lilly Tagliano's stint for some security for the evening was just beginning. She knew the minute she got off the elevator holding her lunch and some goodies for the patient, something big was up. She was not in uniform and security attempted to push her away. She dropped her two bags and fished out her ID from under her jacket and said, "If this relates to patient Jed Mattias I'm on the job."

She was assured Jed was okay, but the man in his room was bleeding profusely. She watched while they tried to sedate the bleeding man and was astonished by the blood, thinking, *must have hit his John Thomas head on.*

Security let her in the room. "Talk to him. He won't even give a report until his attorney is here. He says nothing. I thought he was in a coma."

Lilly spent some time talking with security, actually laying the charm on the young man. "Look, I've been a detective for over twelve years and I'll tell you one thing. I don't care in what state you're in, someone tries to smother you with a pillow, you'll come alive for the moment and fight for your life. It's in our DNA."

"No shit, Detective. I never knew that."

The security officer had his back to Jed allowing Lilly to take the opportunity to say, "Look at the patient now. He's out like a light. I hope this trauma doesn't set him back. You'll get nothing out of him now."

"Yeah, he looks almost dead, but he was able to say, 'Lawyer, lawyer, I want my lawyer.' You sure he's not a criminal playing us?"

"No, he's a famous trial attorney from Atlanta."

"Same thing, I guess. I'll make a report but who's going to believe it. You better get his attorney in here. This guy might not make it."

The guard said he would have to stay until the police told him he could go. He added, "I don't want to insult you, Detective, but you're not Springfield blue. I've got to wait for them. How did you get in here? We're all but closed down. There's nothing on this chart of his about you. It says no visitors."

"And well it should, Duncan. We're doing some protection here. He's here recovering from an intent to kill him in West Side."

Duncan smiled slowly. "I know he's the bleeding man that fell and knocked Beryl over. She was upset when I asked her about it and wouldn't even talk about her experience. I heard she saved his life and now, if it's the way it looks, he may have saved his own life. Someone must want him gone, that's all I have to say."

Again, they were deluged by Springfield Police who removed her to a chair in an open room stating they would take her statement in a few minutes. Appearing to be solicitous of her rank, they promised not to take too long.

Her first call was to the Captain, who was furious he hadn't had coverage on Jed's room in the daytime. He asked what time did she get there. Her answer, "At four, Captain, but I was not to arrive until five. I came early because it just happened. I was near the hospital, picked up some take-out and came off the elevator to the tune of a code blue and a crowd. I don't have the story but I signaled Jed to go comatose until we know what's up. I called Norbie. Jed told the cops just one thing before going into a deep sleep. He wanted his attorney. All hell's going to break loose when Springfield police realize we were concerned about his life. Hospital admin won't lie to them."

12
Political Placating

Beauregard was energized by anger and regret. He thought, *why the hell didn't I put someone on him formally. Stupid of me! I'm thankful I didn't totally ignore protocol. I told the Chief to inform Springfield's Chief we weren't telling the public about the true nature of Mattias' health condition pending further investigation on what we thought was attempted murder. I don't think the hospital would have gone along with us anyway until contact was made to Springfield's police. They're pretty careful over there. One thing's for certain is this guy got in and I hope he lives to tell us how. Hell, to get my police in to see me when I was there took great storytelling. Petra will have to handle this one.*

He called Petra to smooth over why Lilly called him first because she was acting director until he came back to the station, which he now promised himself would be soon. She answered and said, "Don't worry, Captain, Lilly told me all about it. Her going to you first was brilliant. I sincerely hope you took care of a smooth road for me with the Springfield police. The last thing I need is a problem of who's in charge. I know it's their attempted murder, but we have the attempted murder of the victim which should allow for cross information. At least I'm hoping for a nice relationship. I'll get over there right away and keep you in the loop."

"Do that, Lieutenant. It would not be in our best interests to mention the missing daughter, the potential for big-time financial folks being involved, or anything about the intrepid Beryl Kent who volunteers at the hospital. Have Bobby contact Beryl and meet with her. He might keep her out of your hair and also keep the relationship going. He has a line on her. I don't want her interviewing Norbie who will be there for his client. I hope he's not off somewhere for the day. He escapes the law some days to have a daytrip with his wife, Sheri. Although, COVID makes it tough to find a venue worth the effort now."

"I'll put my husband Jim on finding him quickly, Captain. His private investigation work often includes cases for Norbie. He'll get Sheila, Norbie's paralegal, on the trail."

Beauregard called Mason. After giving a detailed explanation of the happenings, already known at the station, he charged him with calling the Chief in Springfield about the need for round the clock security on Jed, promising to use West Side officers if needed. He should have a detailed discussion with the Captain in the Chief's office.

Mason made the call. The Captain said he would speak with the Chief and call back, but assured Mason there already was an officer outside the patient's room for protection until a plan could be ironed out. He did request some answers on who might want to kill the patient and why. Mason suggested it may be a client of Mattias' firm and the thought was accepted. He finished his call with some regret. *I don't like fibbing like this, but we don't know who is after him. I can't send out some theories. If they are leaked out, the news will follow the worst idea. Better to fib! I think Beauregard would have said the same.*

13

A Meeting, Interrogation, and A Date

Beryl's route today while on her volunteer position was planned to bring her to Mattias' room at five in the afternoon. She noted several Springfield Police cars when she came in and wondered if there'd been a major accident. She took the staff elevator and found herself entering the normally quiet floor to one with an inordinate amount of medical traffic. When she saw the officer outside Mattias' room, she was at first not concerned until two detectives walked out with Sergeant Tagliano. Beryl did not go towards the room, but found a lady she knew delivering dinners on the floor. She asked Sally what was going on. The answer, although it offered her validation for her previous warning about Mattias' safety, surprised her. Beryl next asked how the patient protected himself from the attacker. "Beryl, he had a knife and somehow woke up and stabbed the attacker. That's what one of the transporters said. He said it was a large sharp kitchen knife typical of what's used in the hospital. I don't know how it found its way up to his room, unless the attacker had it. He couldn't get out of bed. The police will be checking our kitchens. I thought the patient was out of it. He must have felt the loss of breathing and came to consciousness. I've seen stranger things here."

Beryl thought, *how will Jed explain the knife? He's an attorney. He may have killed his attacker. If he did, there will be serious scrutiny and my participation in giving him the knife is a problem. I'd best get an attorney. Mr. Cull is Mattias' attorney. He won't be able to help me, his client's needs are counter to mine. Having the knife there already makes it look like he planned to harm. Although, if someone tries to smother you, you're entitled to fight for your life. That's if what Sally thinks happened, happened. This is serious. I was smart enough to wipe my prints off the knife before I gave it to him, but his story is what's important. For instance, did I deliberately wipe my prints knowingly because I knew he would use the knife to kill. It would point to me as assisting in the assault, maybe, maybe not. Where did I get the knife? Jed doesn't know. Why didn't I let the police take care of security? And the big question is, was the man whom Jed stabbed really trying to hurt him? It looks that way, but I don't know.*

Beryl went into several rooms while she waited for things to quiet down. Patients in two of those rooms had their doors open when the hullabaloo started. They had much to say about the man who was removed from the room. She was told he must be almost dead. She stood in the hallway for a bit and was pleased to see Attorney Cull exit an elevator. Approaching him, she asked if he knew of a good criminal attorney. Smiling, he suggested, "Moi."

"Mr. Cull, you may have a conflict, or you would be my first choice."

"Beryl, does this have something to do with Jed Mattias and the knifing of the assailant?"

"Maybe, you should speak with him before I say anything."

"It's imperative I see my client now, but if you can wait, I'll see you at my office at six thirty. I'll call Sheila. She'll wait for us."

Norbie gave Beryl his card. She finished her routine early and left thinking, *it's a good thing this position is not a job. I don't know what Jed will tell Cull, but if he doesn't tell him who gave him the knife, then I don't know what to do. I'll have to share the problem, my defense needs are involved with Mattias' needs. He'll guess. If Jed tells him, then he'll for sure have to get me an attorney. Does he have to disclose what I tell him to the police? What his client says is protected, not what I say.*

<hr>

Beryl was treated with the utmost respect by Sheila. There were two women leaving when she entered Cull's law offices. The waiting room seemed oversized to her until she read the ten attorneys listed and realized there were probably twenty support staff, making it a bigger operation than she'd previously understood. Cull was well-known but she had more or less assumed he may be a Perry Mason type with a few support staff; not now, *bizarre for me to think he wouldn't have a large office. When I researched him the bulk of his work is in business which is not normally advertised.*

Beryl's thoughts were interrupted when Cull entered the office from an inside door and welcomed her. Once settled in the conference room he asked why she needed an attorney's services. She said, "You may have a conflict, Mr. Cull, which, if I told you something related to a case you're involved in, would be evidence in the case. The evidence could place me in some jeopardy. I know you have privilege with your client, but you would have to tell the police what I know. Is it possible for me to give a hypothetical example, because it's not reality, you would not have to share it?"

"Beryl, I'm not certain what client's case you are referencing, but I have a colleague who would happily represent you. I can't say more. There is a particular reason I can't say anything more to you, Beryl. You are way too smart and inquisitive. If you pop up as a witness in any of my cases beyond being downed by the bleeding man, I know you'll act as you are doing in this case. I don't need a headache. Any hypothetical should not reference my clients' situations."

Beryl, not surprisingly for her, made a quick decision. "Let's say, Mr. Cull, someone was worried about their safety and a friend happened to give the person a borrowed weapon for protection. Later, the weapon was used against an attacker for self-defense. It's possible the person could have been confused and attacked someone mistaking him for an attempted assault."

"Say no more, Beryl."

Beryl laughed. "A one-way street all the way, Mr. Cull, all going your way. One rule I have is I must tell Captain Beauregard what I find. He will ask if I've told you."

"Beryl, Captain Beauregard does not like anyone in his way but he loves assistance from everyone. Never lie to him. That's my advice. Remember, you said you want to help my client. I believe you do, but what you tell me is your decision."

Beryl made a decision. "Mr. Cull, may I call you Norbie?"

"Not too professional, Beryl, but if you are more comfortable, go ahead."

"Now my friend has a problem. He gave a weapon to a friend of his who is infirmed. The weapon was not one needing registration or under government control. His friend was in potential danger. The friend may or may not have had reason to use the weapon. He doesn't know if his friend was using it in self-defense or if he misinterpreted a potential threat. He did use it and someone was hurt badly, he doesn't know if the victim will live. Does he have a problem with the law? And, by the way, the weapon was very common but was pilfered."

"Pilfered from where, Beryl? For example, taken from an institution where your friend was residing?"

"Probably. Norbie, would my friend be required to go to the police?"

"The last question should be answered by his own attorney. I'll give you a card for a lawyer who is trustworthy. He'll give a free consultation and your friend should retain him. He'll ask for a pittance, maybe one hundred dollars. Don't call until tomorrow, because I want to contact him before your friend calls to be assured he's available. Have him mention my name. He is quite busy, but talking with him will put your friend at some ease. Do nothing until your friend speaks with him. He'll guide him. Thank you, Beryl, you are a lesson in action and discretion."

The two spoke about other things. Beryl knew further conversation about the knife was not to be, and she did not try to force any, thinking, *three husbands and several careers and two children have trained me in knowing when to shut up.*

Norbie had much to consider from his consultation with his client Jed. And he reviewed his thoughts on the interview quietly for over an hour. He'd told his wife Sheri he needed some time alone. *Having a smart attorney for a client is not easy. And Jed is intelligent, but he is a very frightened client, one who clearly is not giving me the whole picture as he knows it. Beryl has filled in for one item held back by Jed. When I asked him how he got a sharp knife in the hospital when he had nothing, not even a cell phone or wallet when he was admitted, Jed insisted it was just there, it was on his food tray. Food trays in the hallway showed plastic utensils. Certainly, a knife sharp enough to pierce the attacker with such damage meant a very sharp knife. If Beryl had pilfered it from the institution her friend was staying in, then the knife came from the kitchen or dining area. I don't know if hospital dining was open to hospital volunteers during COVID or if she had access to the kitchen, but the description of the weapon which I hope won't be unique could place its source. I know Jed is not giving Beryl up as the source which tells me he trusts her. That may be important later.*

What Jed did tell me was he kept the knife under the covers because he has been in fear since his accident and his partial loss of memory. He'd been told to pretend he was comatose whenever someone other than the police, me, or Beryl entered the room. If it was medical personnel, they always identified themselves when they entered after knocking. This man was dressed in blue hospital garb, but entered without knocking. Jed could barely hear his footsteps. He waited for what seemed a long time feeling the man looking over him. He suspected quickly he was in jeopardy because the man approached his bed, wiggled Jed's toes, and when Jed did not react, he whispered, "You make it easy on me, Mr. Mattias, thank you."

Jed Mattias felt very strong pressure from a pillow over his head. He struggled and managed to grasp the knife in his right hand. The knife was hidden under a small towel he kept under his bed covers. The pillow forced his body towards the man leaving his right arm off the bed. He said he was certain he could not have been able to stab the man if his arm was on the bed.

Jed said, *"Cull, do you know how difficult it is to stab someone when you're lying down? I stabbed him once and pulled the knife out. The pressure on the pillow lessened slightly. I wildly stabbed again further up but did not have the strength to pull the knife out again. He fell on my injured gut and chest causing serious pain and I felt the imprint of the knife's handle on my leg and have a serious lump there. I know I screamed. The pain was excruciating. I pressed the nurse's button pinned to my bed just as the pressure on the pillow was released somewhat and as a nurse was knocking at the door to enter. I screamed again and then I passed out. I don't know how long."*

When Mattias awoke, he explained he became aware of his actions. A policeman was attempting to question him. He remembered saying, "I want my lawyer." He gave my name.

How long was he out? There was much activity in the room. They had to take the guy physically off him. It would not have been easy. And then the ensuing chaos of medicals doing their work on the attacker to keep him alive and on Mattias who was a mess. Did he really sleep through all the noise? He even denied Beryl had warned him to be careful. I was there with him when he asked for security. The guy is a fox. He knew he was a mark, but must know more about why he's a mark and is not telling me. Jed says the knife looked to him like a long steak knife of good quality. I don't think Beryl will have a problem if the police believe Jed's statement. I've held the police off until questioning tomorrow. I hope the attacker doesn't die. It'd be easier for us all if we have someone to question.

Norbie made his notes and joined his wife and mother-in-law in the great room.

———

Lieutenant Joe Stellato of Springfield's MCU entered Jed Mattias' hospital room. Mattias and Attorney Cull noticed he was ten minutes late for their meeting. Norbie knew it was one of Joe's practices to make witnesses wait a few, thinking it made them stressed and more likely to slip up if they intended to lie. Norbie himself had been heard criticizing the practice, saying, "If they're pros, they won't change their practice; if they're novices they would slip up anyway if they're lying; I see no reason to heighten the temperature in the room."

Stellato initiated the conversation with the usual soft approach. He asked how Jed was doing and if he felt comfortable reviewing his event. Mattias and Cull, as attorneys knew the game. Cull said, "Do you want to ask Jed questions, Joe, or just give a statement?"

"I'll ask the questions."

And he did for over an hour and a half. Norbie could see Jed was getting tired and stepped in. "Look, Joe, his injuries, as they were just healing yesterday, were re-traumatized. He's in no condition for further questioning. You can send me further questions for him and he'll answer them in writing. It's obvious what happened here and Jed is not holding back. I think you can see he is quite fearful now. Perhaps you can tell us something about the attacker. Do you know who he is and why he would attack a helpless patient? Is he known to you, maybe someone with mental illness? How did he get in here, it's locked tighter than a drum?"

"You know I can't give you any information while we're investigating. I'll tell you he is from out of town and a known enforcer working independently. So, your client here must know why he is a target and I'd like him to tell me why."

"Wrong, Joe. First, he's not saying another word. Secondly, he has some amnesia about recent events and you will have to wait along with us for resolution."

A smiling Stellato left with, "We'll see, Cull, what he's hiding, it's just a matter of time as you have inferred."

Mattias asked, "Does he think I'm a criminal, Cull? I've always been careful in my choice of clients, even in my choice of clients I've defended in serious matters. I could not have done something so nefarious in the last three weeks to bring about this terror. My life's been in jeopardy once and only once. It was a domestic matter and the guy tried to shoot me outside the courthouse after the divorce. He was a known felon and the sheriff serving the warrant was waiting to do service. He couldn't get into the courtroom, but saw the guy on the steps of the courthouse pulling his weapon and tackled him. That's it, the only time."

"Work on your memory. Captain Beauregard is a fair man. I believe you are hiding some facts. You have your reasons. You're an attorney, but attorneys are pretty bad clients. Don't forget that fact. Trust me, Jed. They know about your daughter. I know you are afraid for her, but you were the target here. No one sent you a message from her begging for something. She may be safe somewhere. You don't know. I don't know, but I do know you are not safe."

———

It was six in the evening on Saturday and despite COVID, the restaurant had a buzz. Nathan was there before her and when she entered he arose from his seat and walked over to greet her. She thought, *I like politeness in a man, but good manners aren't everything. I remember my husband Joel's partner. He was so charming and a perfect example of the gentleman who knew how to handle himself. Except he wasn't. He was a cad, a thief, a birddog, an all-out criminal who would have murdered an enemy if there were no other alternatives. He was the epitome of a sociopath and because he did nothing but evil, probably was also a psychopath.*

"I wondered if you'd know me with the mask and my wearing a hat. We don't even have snow and I'm dressed for Alaska."

They sat along the wall. He took the outside chair helping her slide in on the cushioned bench and said after she removed her coat, "Of course you would be cold, Beryl, your blouse doesn't have a lot of fabric."

And he smiled broadly while she thought, *so much for the idea he is too perfect. He may be normal after all.*

Beryl laughed and said, "You noticed?"

Nathan smiled while motioning to the waiter, who was standing judiciously a six-foot distance away, although within hearing. The waiter was grinning from ear to ear. They settled on drinks. Nathan said, "No prosecco or white wine for you, Beryl. You surprise me."

"Why? Do you think every woman in Western Massachusetts drinks the same beverage?"

"I haven't been paying attention, but most of my friends' wives do. I do not have drinks with ladies on a regular basis. Perhaps it's why I'm bungling this a bit."

Beryl told him his humility was an asset and they both laughed. The menu selections were enticing, so much so they both had a bit of difficulty choosing. In the end, although their choices were different, they both liked the other's choice. They agreed to share a salad, negating an appetizer. The conversation was easy, until Beryl started with her pointed questions on Nathan's background. His silence stopped her in her tracks. Since it was a noticeable pause, Beryl did not break the silence. She waited for Nathan. He said, "Look, Beryl, I wanted to enjoy this evening with you. My background, professionally, is complicated and I don't wish to share it nor am I able to share it. I know you'll make a lot out of it. Don't, please. The important items to remember are, I am single, do not play around, am fiscally sound, and willing to discuss our neighbors, Mattias, and any other local news related to these events. I'll let you pursue money laundering questions until I can go no further. I don't wish to sound secretive. I have no personal secrets."

She let the silence sit before speaking. "I was right the other night. You've been involved in the government. Clearances have implications. I understand. However, I hope you are telling me the truth, I don't know if you are, but I will eventually sniff out any untruths. Nathan, if you are untruthful, you won't be able to keep me in the dark forever. I will eventually know."

Beryl thought for a moment, *he's either a sociopath playing a good game or a government related guy or a spy. I'll know. I'll do a check on him. Blanks in a person's story say a lot.*

"What do you want to know, that I know. Then I'll pepper you with my questions."

And she shared the attempt on Jed's life, his missing daughter, and his questionable lapses in memory. Beryl said, "I know you know all this already and more I don't know. Not from the police, but from the hospital administration. It leaves me one question."

"And how do I know this, Ms. Know-it-all?"

"Whoever the man is who tried to kill Jed, he found his way in through the medical or admin of the hospital or he works there. I don't know his identity yet. You are, shall we say, in the helpful government investigative services. Don't deny it. I wouldn't believe you. Just where you fit in is your business. I don't want to know which service or in what capacity. You won't tell me and it's not important, but my instincts are good. I'm satisfied I understand how you and I can get to know each other, which I would like, and yet not have me step on your toes. Who is the attacker, Nathan?"

"The attacker's name is Larue Bastionne."

Beryl smiled. "And?"

"How much more do you want from me. Rudy Beauregard probably knows now, so it's not a state secret. Larue is a Southern dude from Louisiana and is a well-known independent in the silencing game. I'm shocked Jed was able to kill him. From what I hear, he shoved the knife in Larue's gut from a lying down position. Very difficult to do while you're fighting for air and being smothered to death. Jed Mattias has the will to live."

"Not quite from a lying down position, Nathan. Jed has insisted his bed be slanted about thirty-five degrees. The position may have helped."

"If so, it would have. It also would have made smothering Jed more difficult and the knife would have gone in a more sensitive spot. Larue is a long rangy guy."

"You know him, Nathan?"

"I've dealt with families who lost loved ones from Larue's work. I wouldn't say I know him personally. I do know this is his sloppiest work."

"This attempt on Jed's life looks daring to me, not sloppy. If Jed did not have a knife, and no normal person would expect him to have a knife, Jed would be dead."

"And why, Beryl, did Jed have a kitchen knife under his bed covers?"

"Why would I know the answer?"

She smiled and Nathan smiled back answering, "Hmmm, because the police would not tell him to have a knife stashed, nor would his lawyer tell him. He's just a little discombobulated. I choose you, Beryl. You don't like seeing the handicapped at a loss for a weapon. Don't tell me. Plausible deniability is being thrown around as a term today. It's a good defense term."

"Well, it is one possible theory. I'm more interested in whether you think there will be more attempts on Jed's life and how to stop them. I'm interested in finding his daughter Marthea who has disappeared. I want to discover what was going on in his law firm and the cases he and his partner handled. Did they lead to the attempts on his life. I'd like to know if the partner's accident was legitimately an accident. I want to understand the issue of money laundering taking place in Western Massachusetts."

Nathan answered, "And, Beryl, I'm more interested in you, but I see there may be a cost to my interest. My help will be better if you share what you find out and I'll fill you in on probabilities of other avenues to search."

"Nathan, you are not a lawyer. I know Norbie Cull is defending Jed on Larue's knifing. And with attorneys, it's always a one-way street. I'd hoped for more from you."

"I'm certain you do expect more from me. I make no promises. But be assured, I have the same interest in Jed Mattias' assault as you do. Trust me. I want he and Marthea alive. They are the key to some important justice issues, despite the fact Jed did not know he was important. Now I think he does know. His memory may be spotty, but the guy is a wonderful lawyer. His instincts are enough to make him wonder, without any current memories, what has happened. Stay with him, Beryl. You are the key. If he remembers he'll tell you because he trusts you. He won't tell Rudy until he has evidence. He may trust his attorney eventually, but he'll need to be certain Cull is a straight arrow and not a talker. He knows he's a good attorney, but it won't be enough for him. What do you know about Jed's managing partner at the law firm, Attorney Grace Grantley, Beryl? And why has she not been let in to visit him? His cover is now blown. A comatose man cannot stab another man. So, to answer you, I think Jed is at risk. You are at risk too. I will attempt to protect you, but you must be careful."

Beryl was confused. "Why do you think I'm at risk. Few people know of my interest other than Jed fell into my arms quite accidently."

"Beryl, as we discussed before, Rene DesCartes knows and tried to intimidate you looking for answers. What else do you need to know?"

"Nathan, how did you know DesCartes visited me?"

"I saw him go to your home."

"You never told me."

Nathan didn't answer her. Instead he called the waiter over for a dessert menu. They ordered one affogato to split and enjoyed the homemade gelato with espresso. Nathan spent some time questioning Beryl. She thought, *I do believe he knows all the answers. Is he testing me as to whether I'll lie? I suppose if I knew more about him I'd do the same. I have had three husbands. Oliver says any guy interested in me would wonder about my domestic history. Jocelyn says I should stay away from romance. With my history she insists I can't go through another loss. And she says she refuses to feel anything for the next guy I should love. They're right. It's just, life happens.*

"Look, Nathan, are you aware, your questions are all pointed? They leave me to believe you've done an excellent job of background checking on me, but I don't want to answer questions. Public information is one thing. More than that, I have to have a reason to share."

"Agreed. However, your second husband was government and his death is still being investigated. When you're ready, maybe we can solve one together, if you are interested."

She was and she told him so, but after Jed Mattias' case. She remembered, *my dad always insisted on working one case at a time. I recall one of his few criticisms of Mom. He mentioned, "Your mom's mind is terribly creative, Beryl, but it goes too fast for her at times. The speed interferes with getting things done."*

Beryl and Nathan left the restaurant and walked along the small common area, then crossed over to the larger common brightly lit for

Christmas. They talked of Christmas, politics, music, and cities vs towns. The night ended with Nathan walking her to her car and saying, "Next night out, I'll pick you up. Seems foolish to have two cars driving back to the same area."

She did not reject the suggestion.

14

Grace Grantley and Jed Mattias

Grace Grantley was not satisfied by Bobby Barr's answers to her continued insistence on visiting Jed. She heard through the grapevine there had been an attack on a patient in the hospital. Naturally suspicious, she asked her friends in the hospital. They would not identify the patient, but did say the incident was remarkable. The patient was almost comatose but defended himself with a knife, severely wounding the attacker. Grace called the on-call Lieutenant Aylewood-Locke. She insisted she be brought into visiting Jed saying, "Lieutenant, Jed is awake enough to stab his attacker. I wonder why Sergeant Barr didn't call me to inform me. I am Jed's partner. We have important business issues to discuss. I insist on seeing him. I've called Attorney Norberto Cull today whose firm is authorized to represent him. He has not called back yet."

If Grace was looking for resistance to her request, she didn't get it. Petra called the hospital and requested allowance for Attorney Grace Grantley to be put on the list for allowable visitors for Jed Mattias. Petra told Grace to give the hospital an hour to implement the change. She warned Grace she would see a police officer outside the room at all times for security. Grace said, "Lieutenant, am I to believe you are inferring there may be another attempt on Jed's live?"

"We are being prudent. There are no facts as of this date to lead us to such a conclusion. Still, Mr. Mattias was attacked by someone intending to kill him. He certainly didn't provoke the attack. We wonder. Perhaps you know a reason for the attack."

Grace did not seem to be perturbed by Petra's question, answering, "If I did, I would share my suspicions with you, Lieutenant. I care deeply for Jed and want him to live for both business and personal reasons."

Petra offered to take Grace to see Jed, insisting she was going there at this time with some questions about the incident in West Mass, the one which put him in the hospital in the first place. She mentioned Springfield police would be there later with Jed's attorney for additional questions. His condition was upgraded but the doctors would be monitoring Jed for any stress suffered from visitations and would intervene if necessary. Grace took the news with more than a little disdain. "Captain, I will know immediately if Jed is well. I do wonder if I shouldn't have been there earlier. Perhaps Jed was previously non-talkative because he didn't trust his environment. He would have trusted me, I can assure you. If you don't mind, I'll go it alone."

———

Grace waited longer than an hour to visit the hospital. She found the masking and facility entrance requirements annoying and complained to the entry personnel. She was surprised to hear the woman say softly, "I understand, but it is for all our sakes, we do this. If you've ever seen a patient on a ventilator you would gladly wear your mask."

Grace's face softened. She thought, *she is so compliant and I fight all orders from others. I do feel some shame sometimes, but it's still a pain complying. Being an outsider in a city like this leaves me eating in the same place, because I simply can't walk into any restaurant. It might be take-out only or reservations required, or a situation where until I get in a facility, I don't realize if it's even clean enough for my safety requirements. I don't know the area. And I don't have tons of folks who I know in this hospital allowing me special privileges for Jed. Normally I'd be great at helping. Jed wouldn't look to be catered, but I do. Hell, he's probably eating hospital food. Ugg!*

Grace was stopped at the nurse's station. After her license was inspected and matched to a list of names, she received her pass. She was then instructed to leave her name with the officer outside Jed's room. Grace thought, *they are serious about his protection. What do they know? Jed will tell me.*

Finally, she was admitted to Jed's room and found him sitting up in his bed reading the local newspaper and drinking coffee. She rushed to his side only to find him holding back from his usual greeting. She said, "It's me, Jed, Grace. You haven't lost all memory, have you?"

"Grace, how good it is to see you. Thankfully, I remember you. I don't remember much, I can tell you. This experience and the attempt on my life have me a bit nervous. I know you understand. I am hopeful you can jog my memory some."

Grace thought, *I didn't expect him to be so cold to me. He must have had a heck of an injury. Doesn't he remember when I asked him to marry me and he said no and I cried? Well, it's best he doesn't remember. We'll see how much he remembers from the cases I've brought. He never forgot a fact in any case.*

And for the next hour Grace played a game with Jed of what she would later explain to a colleague as 'cat and mouse.' She would go through the facts on a case; in many of the cases she had worked with him. He would remember some clients, but his memory was inconsistent. Later she would wonder if he was completely honest with her. She had previous experience in two cases with clients who had memory loss from an accident. In both those cases, they remembered almost nothing about their accident and a few days before or after, but they did remember their work. Jed would flounder on cases he had taken over for Harry Leonard after his death. He appeared to be asking her to fill in some of the facts. She said, "Jed, when you took over most of Harry's open cases, you would not allow me to assist you. I thought it was strange, but was perhaps part of your grieving process for Harry. I can't help you. Why is your memory on his cases so spotty? Do you remember something in them related to your problems? It's almost as if you're asking me to supply facts about which I have no knowledge."

Jed said, "Give it up, Grace, you have always looked at every case of every lawyer in the firm. You are nosey and intuitive. You're not helping me here by holding back and I wonder why."

Grace moved in the uncomfortable hospital chair. She drew her legs up on the chair and said, "I wish to protect you, Jed. You've been attacked once and maybe twice with the intent to kill you. I don't want you at further risk. It doesn't take an idiot to realize you must have been endangered by one of your clients' cases. Which one, I don't know, but it's only on Harry's cases you are giving me the run-around. Additionally, you went on a bogus trip to New Jersey on one of his cases, so let's look at the case. Tell me, what do you remember from that trip? Don't put me off, Jed? I know you."

"Look, Grace, you're giving me a headache like you always do. You can't control this situation. I don't remember the case bringing me to New Jersey. I don't remember a lot about all of Harry's cases. I'm not bullshitting you. I don't have the energy nor the temperament right now to bother."

As the two lawyers almost hissed at each other as recalled later by Jed, Lieutenant Joe Stellato from Springfield's MCU entered with Attorney Norberto Cull. Three other detectives joined them. Jed said, "Sorry, guys, COVID won't allow a gathering of more than six people. Grace, you'll have to leave."

Smarting at the slur of 'guys,' Grace argued, "I am a lawyer from Jed's firm which hired Mr. Cull. I have a right to be here."

Jed said, "This is not the time, Grace, please leave."

Grace left saying she'd return the next day. Lieutenant Stellato questioned, "Jed, you didn't have to do get rid of her. I'm more than happy to get Attorney Grantley's thoughts on your situation."

Cull stopped the Lieutenant. "I'm the attorney of record, Joe. No nonsense. My client as the senior, and now the only full, partner in the firm is the only one able to make a decision on the firm's cases and their availability. Don't play games. Ms. Grantley is not a part of this investigation, unless you've held back on some information."

Stellato smoothly continued his conversation focusing on changes in Jed's memory. "What is new in the memory bank, Jed? Do you remember how you got the knife you used?"

Before Jed could answer, Norbie said, "Lieutenant, you've asked the same question before. My client is interested in the attacker's health. How is his medical condition? Please give us an update? One source says he is dead or near dead. Or if he is conscious, did he give a reason for attacking my client who fortunately woke from his deep sleep when being smothered to grab a weapon nearby to defend himself?"

"So, we play it like this, Mr. Attorney. Alright, lucky for you, Mr. Mattias, Mr. Bastionne is recovering and will live. However, he has serious injuries which may affect his everyday living. It's certain he'll file a civil suit against you since he's ranting about taking every dollar you have."

An angry Cull said, "Enough, Joe. My client used the only defense available to defend himself. Where is Mr. Bastionne from, and why was he here in my client's room when no visitors were allowed? Does he work for the hospital in some capacity? Is he a long-term resident of this area or newly visiting from Louisiana? Does he say he knows my client? He is ranting about taking every dollar from my client, so he must know something about my client."

"How much of your work do you want me to do, Norbie? I don't try cases. And how did you know he was from Louisiana? Does this mean your client knows him?"

"The same way you found out, Joe. He's an outside enforcer for hire. You and I both know that. We both did the research. Stop being cute. What is the guy's story?"

Stellato said, "Need some details first. We did a reenactment of the scene. You and I both know your client wasn't comatose. Why didn't he yell for help or push the buzzer before there was a smothering attempt? It's a big question I have."

Neither answered as lawyers rarely answered questions quickly, if at all. Cull said, "I won't have Mr. Mattias answer that question. Joe, you're attempting to put words in his mouth. Logic would tell you some 'maybe' answers to that question. What is the attacker's story? Why was he there? The answers may help our client's memory if he was previously known to him. Without some additional info, how could he answer you?"

"C'mon, Cull, he should know who is after him, and who would know how to hire an enforcer."

Cull retorted, "I have many criminal clients who know how to hire an outside enforcer, because I do some criminal defense work. However, my client focus is on civil work. His firm does criminal work, but normally does not deal with that type of clientele. Further, Jed's professional life has been in upheaval. A couple of weeks before his injury his partner was killed in an accident. He has been busy trying to sort out those cases. I'm certain he was overwhelmed. Have you located his daughter Marthea yet?"

"What do you know about her, Cull? We just got the missing person's report from Austin. Who told you about Marthea Mattias?"

"Just the background check informed me. Sheila my paralegal chased her down and talked with the boyfriend who hasn't seen her since my client came north. What's with a missing person's report?"

"The boyfriend filed it."

Jed Mattias held his tongue until the discussion focused further on his daughter. Demonstrating some anxiety, he said, "Leave Marthea out of this. I'm certain she's not missing, just out for a week or two. She loves to travel, particularly in the West and Southwest. Probably on a ranch somewhere learning how to cook steak properly. She'll go nuts when she gets back about all this fuss."

Stellato retorted, "What kind of a father are you? You won't tell the truth so your daughter can be rescued. What type of clients do you have they would kidnap your girl?"

Before Cull could stop him, Jed tried to lunge from his inclined bed but showed immediate and serious pain as he screamed, "Don't try to intimidate me, Lieutenant. If I'm being investigated, tell Cull here or leave because I have nothing to tell you."

Before Cull could respond, Stellato smirked saying, "One thing's certain now, Cull. I believe your client could not have easily gotten out of bed and his story on the attacker now rings true."

Cull, nor his client, were amused by these antics. The conversation was now stilted and discussion on the whereabouts of Marthea was verboten. Cull allowed Jed to go through his remembrance on the sequence of the attack story event. He did not expect Jed to change the facts and Jed did not. Stellato thought, *damn attorneys, it's difficult to trip them up. Can be done, but with two of them, probably not going to happen. Where the hell is the daughter and does she play any role in this? Why is this guy here? His original injury is not my case and I don't think Beauregard will tell me much until he solves it. We both know that solving that story is the key to this attack. I think I'll have a sick room visit with Rudy and bring him some deli sandwiches to confound his very nice wife and win points with Rudy. I'll get nothing from these two.*

The lieutenant and the other detectives left quickly. Jed asked, "Cull, what's going on? Why didn't they press me more? I don't feel comfortable.

They're not acting like typical police, and Stellato is a wolf who would go all the way. I know. I can smell his energy. He is no slouch."

Cull agreed. His version was, "Jed, he saw he was moving up the wrong road with you. The reason he left is he didn't want to answer the questions we had about the attacker. I'll put my favorite PI, Jim Locke, on it. We'll know as much as Stellato by tomorrow afternoon. Get some sleep."

Cull spoke to the officer on duty outside Jed's room cautioning him to keep his client in the room and everyone outside of police and Beryl from entering saying, "And if an officer comes in who walks funny check his ID and call it in if you have the slightest suspicion he's not who he says he is. If there is another try on Mattias' life, your life won't matter either."

Grace Grantley, smarting from her ejection from her partner's room by her own partner, headed for Captain Rudy Beauregard's residence. She'd researched the location and with her GPS was there in no time. She thought, *I love these smaller cities and burbs. The traffic is not Atlanta's traffic. It takes over an hour to get cross town. Here, I'm at Beauregard's house in an adjourning city in twelve minutes. Nice house! The pay must be good here or the cost of living is really low. Probably is the second one. Now how will I get by the wife is the question I have. Her name from Google is 'Mona.' A cop's wife isn't always easy to push around. Google says she is a high school teacher or counselor. I guess she's done both. I better play it straight; after all, she is the sentry.*

The pretty red front door was opened quickly by a woman. Grace introduced herself. "Mrs. Beauregard, I apologize for bringing police business to your home, but I'm here from Atlanta for just a few days. I understand the Captain is recovering from a broken leg, but I just need a few minutes with him. My client is the man called 'the bleeding man' in the newspapers and I surely think the Captain may want to talk to me while I'm in town. Would you please ask him to give me an audience."

Mona laughed and said, "Attorney Grantley, do I have the name right? Rudy is not the pope and asking for an audience may tickle him. Please come in. If he's feeling well, he'll see you. If he says 'no,' Attorney, it is 'no.' Okay?"

Grace waited in the entry knowing Beauregard, if he were like any MCU detective, would want to know more about his victim, and she had keys to at least some gossip. Mona returned and with domestic kindness offered her coffee as they walked toward his den. Introductions made, Grace sat in a comfortable chair, and Mona placed a coffee and small tray of cookies remarking, "For you, Grace, they are not for my patient."

Captain Beauregard grimaced at Mona's caution. His denial from eating cookies interfered with any portrait of the Captain having the appearance of his reputation as a great sleuth and closer of cases to her. She thought, *all the brouhaha about him as the nemesis for serial murderers and he looks rather ordinary. I suppose the broken leg doesn't help. One never knows how smart or deceptive or ingenious another is. Actions tell the story not words. Compare Harry and Jed. Both were brilliant lawyers but on opposite sides of any established moral business prospective. Perhaps I should be very careful of Beauregard. I don't really know what my partners know or have done. Beauregard will suspect preservation of the reputation of the firm for myself and Jed as my reason for being here.*

"Captain, I've read a great deal about you and your detectives' ability to solve murder cases. I'm comfortable you will go the distance. My visit today is meant to share with you information from our recent cases, if I am able to, in order to assist you. I certainly will be able to direct you away from some less fruitful avenues of investigation."

Rudy told Grace to call him 'Rudy'. From what she had been told about his formal attitude towards witnesses and suspects, this informality in using her first name convinced her he was interested in her thoughts. She returned his offer and 'Grace' not Attorney was used. He said, "Grace, I would like your summary and opinion on the histories and attitudes of your partners. I know Harry has passed, but Jed has shared he was winding up some of Harry's cases. I thought it most unfortunate and coincidental to have both partners' lives at risk within two weeks of each other. Therefore, I felt compelled to explore their recent activities. I understand your restraints as an attorney, but just stop me if I go too far as I'm sure you will."

"Captain, Jed Mattias is the most honorable attorney I have ever worked with, so let's start there. If Jed suspected any of us in our firm to be less than honorable, he would stop us in our tracks. However, I do agree. Harry's untimely death two weeks before Jed's odd accident and later attack on his life makes me also wonder. Jed acted squirrelly after his interview with the chief of police in Atlanta on Harry's accident. A firm conference was held which included me and two paralegals who worked on Harry's cases. We honed the cases down, eliminating repetitive boring business cases with known clients, ordinary accident cases, normal although maybe contentious divorce cases, and chose fifteen cases to review. I have reviewed those cases and only two were with relatively new clients. Jed said he would further review those cases. Rudy, Jed claims he doesn't remember why he went to New Jersey."

Beauregard was very interested now, but he did not pursue which cases she reviewed immediately. Instead, he asked about Harry's personal lifestyle and attitude. "Was Harry a player either personally or professionally, Grace?"

"Harry was downright charming in every forum. The ladies loved him, and he loved the ladies. Somehow, he always kept control of his love situations. I think they mostly understood he was a 'good-time boy' and nothing more. The same loose attitude was visible at times with clients. He'd try to take on new clients without a firm review; not unusual in firms, but it happened too often with Harry. Sometimes we'd catch up to the new client because he wouldn't turn in a new matters sheet timely. Work would be done on the case and we were stuck with the client. Harry also invested heavily as a part of a group of business folks who lent money to entrepreneurs for new start-ups. When the group got aggressive about collections and would take over a few businesses, it hit the papers. We put a stop to those activities just three months ago. Harry's judgment was excellent on which cases to settle and which cases to move forward for trial, but his good judgment ended there. I think Harry always needed really firm limits. So, could one of his cases be causation for trouble, I'd say yes."

"What could the 'ff' or the 'fyy' before client Arrow Management, LLC possibly mean? Sergeant Barr indicated you could not find a client named Arrow Management, LLC. Isn't there a payment to the firm for work before you proceed? It does seem strange there is not one here. And Sergeant said you may have an outside PI hired by Jed before his accident. Are there any complaints on his work or any billing by him for the firm you can't tie back to other cases?"

"Rudy, the PI question is a good one. I'll call Joyce and have her trace reports on Jed's desk. I've been here over eight days, not what I planned. I'll have her look at billings. If a PI sends in a report, an invoice is often attached. As to the meaning of those letters, I haven't the foggiest. Jed, when frustrated often whispered the 'F' word. Perhaps those letters are written expressions of his frustration and nothing more. Jed wanted to explore the name, President Raleigh, and I suppose he would have charged the PI to follow this lead. I'll call Joyce now and see if she has a PI report."

The call took ten minutes testing Grace's patience, who appeared to take work ethic seriously. She said, "Joyce, keep track of new correspondence to both Jed and Harry; they are of the utmost importance. Why aren't you checking daily and reporting to me? Please give this work due diligence."

Joyce called back minutes afterward to say there was a report on Jed's desk. It was not emailed to Jed, but paper copy only with CONFIDENTIAL marked all over it. Joyce would email it to her as an attachment shortly, after Grace requested Joyce to do the work herself asking her to scan then erase the scan after scanning, saying, "I don't want anyone in the firm to read it."

Grace asked Rudy while they were waiting if he would ask Attorney Cull to visit. "He should be the deciding factor for sharable info from this work. I have not seen the info, and am not adverse to using it to help Jed, but it might have reference to clients not involved. I simply cannot allow access if that is the case."

Rudy looked annoyed, thinking, *I knew she was being too accommodating. Now she's being a typical lawyer. She says Jed is straight up, but worries if something may be in the PI's report that's not kosher. She's not so sure now.*

He asked Grace, "Are you really certain your partner has nothing to hide? No one knows another person completely, Grace. Why wouldn't you just share this report?"

With the most engaging smile fully showing on her dimpled face, Grace said, "Ethics, Captain. You know about ethics."

Rudy called Cull. He answered, "I'm outside your door, Rudy. I see Grace Grantley is here already."

While Mona and Rudy made small talk and more coffee was presented, Grace read the PI's report. Rudy and Norbie both thought she looked troubled. She asked to speak to Cull in private. Rudy answered, "Certainly, Grace, but you are not Mattias' attorney, just a witness.

Anything you know is discoverable. I know the existence of the PI's report and I will get it."

"I know, Rudy, but not before Attorney Cull and I understand it."

They were directed into the dining room and Mona closed the French doors to the family room and the swing door to the kitchen to give them privacy. Norbie asked, "How did you get into this mess with Rudy, Grace? You know better. Never mind, I know you thought you were being helpful and had nothing to hide. Just what in this report is so meaningful?"

Grace gave her laptop to him and he read the report. It did not take long to read. Both attorneys could read technical reports in minutes and absorb problematic details on the fly. He did not respond after reading the material. Minutes later he said, "Who is President Raleigh? Your detective says Harry took her on as a client and then tried to ditch her. How does the firm handle negating a case it initially took, but pretty quickly wanted to dump? It looks like a divorce case and she was president of the family business. It is not the name we were looking for, but close. The PI has copies of her check given to the firm for representation, a letter sent later returning the check claiming a conflict of interest, her return letter insisting her husband had bribed them and every other attorney in Atlanta not to represent her, documentation she met with Harry again the day before he died, and statements from several friends insisting she said her husband had killed Harry when he finally agreed to represent her. In addition, a divorce petition or complaint was filed the day he met with her for Alexia March Raleigh vs Donald Arrow.

"Oops! Now we know where the client named March came from. I hate domestic law, Grace. Folks get crazy but this is almost absurd. The PI did not give the name of Donald Arrow's company. Wait, he has the divorce petition filed attached. It could be mentioned in it."

They both scanned the petition, and the company was listed as "FFO

Arrow, Inc.," registered in New Jersey. They pulled up the company's page and found it to be non-helpful, documented only with obscure financial terms. The company's FFO in the name was explained as Financial Funds from Operations. They assumed the FFO was from the Arrow company work product, and wondered if investors sought a different kind of meaning. To them it appeared to be a shell investment company with no ability to purchase any product other than investing in the firm. Later they would pull up the stats on New Jersey companies, but for now they had little understanding of the firm. Cull said, "Jed looks clean here, Grace. He may have been investigating info the wife gave in her statement to Harry. Could be he discovered something, they didn't bargain for? None of this would rise to importance if Harry hadn't been killed in an accident the next day and if Jed had not been hurt after going to New Jersey. Also, you know most lawyers are particular about writing correct names of people and corporations. His notes tell us he was being deceptive about the firm. He was suspicious from day one. The final report says the PI could not find Alexis March Raleigh. She left a text with her friends the day after Harry died, she was taking a vacation for two months. Her friends say she needed to clear her head after filing for divorce. They thought it was slightly off, since Alexia needed friends and crowds and was not one to go on vacation without a big sendoff."

Grace said, "It sounds just like Harry. Alexia must be good looking. He took her on as a client without thinking it through. Notice the retainer check is for fifty thousand dollars. He saw money and good looks. Later he asked around and saw a difficult divorce and tried to get rid of her as a client. Our evaluation committee for new cases never saw this one. She must have created havoc for him or more likely talked sweet to him with promises. Harry wasn't the type to scare easily, but he was a romantic. It all makes sense and I'm afraid for Jed."

"I'm going to share this info with Rudy, Grace. Normally, I'd make him formally request but Jed needs protection, and this corporation needs eyes on its work. Rudy is Captain of MCU in a small city with decent public administration. I don't think the administration would hold back his investigation. I'm getting my PI, Jim Locke, to explore more on the husband and his business. Alexia was most likely looking for a good settlement using information she had on her husband's business as fodder. Alexia knew her husband was not one to be pushed around. She may have told Harry, giving him a reason why he filed the petition the same day as the meeting. He wanted to protect them both by having it filed in court, but it didn't work. Did anyone question the accident?"

"Jed and I reviewed the file. It was a single car accident. Harry had a few pops in him but below the limit. There was no citation, but wouldn't be for a single car accident. The accident stated Harry's car was going about seventy miles an hour on a fifty-five mile an hour road, skidded, and hit a jersey barrier flipping it over into a ditch. Harry would speed. I can't argue with part of the report, but he always had terrific control over any vehicle he drove. Even soused, he could find his way in the strangest of places and often did. I think it may be worth a look at the police file, Norbie. Harry deserves our investigation. I thought Jed was doing just that, but this report says nothing about Harry's accident."

Norbie replied, "Time to fess up to the Captain, Grace. You can trust him to get the accident case reviewed. Lieutenant Ash Lent formerly of MCU is now over in traffic and has tremendous associations all over the country. He was, I guess still is, a classical guitarist, but has played in all kinds of bands. He might know someone in Atlanta who could have the police review the accident file."

Rudy listened to Grace. Her PI report was of great interest; mostly he questioned what good angel sitting on her shoulder whispered to her to give up the report so easily. He thought, *first lawyer I've worked with to do this, actually two lawyers. Heaven is celebrating.*

Aloud, he thanked them both. "Your PI's report is helpful. The company's business supports one of our theories. A funny financial structure could be a money laundering scheme. I didn't, nor did my detectives, think of a divorce as a key to murder. We heard Harry's personal situation was stable. Grace, please tell me more about Harry. Would he knowingly be involved in a money scheme?"

The two men listened to Grace describe her former partner, Harry. She made no bones about his easy ways but insisted he was a fair player. She explained his personality differences from Jed. "Harry took chances, but never went too far. He would never be involved in money laundering. If he felt he was in over his head, he'd call on Jed to get him out. What's funny here is he didn't tell Jed about his concerns on this case. Not like Harry, unless he was doing some social work for the lady. He was a soft touch for a good heart throbbing story. But, Harry would never knowingly get involved with money laundering. He'd call business of that kind, 'the dark whole from which nobody exits whole.'

God, how I miss him and his little sayings. Harry wouldn't take any gang related cases, a contrast from his interest in helping the underdog. He wouldn't take those risks despite being a risk taker. He'd say, 'Risk taking is not gambling. You can estimate your risk. If it's an eighty percent shot on the positive, I'll take it. But working for the 'dark whole' the risk for trouble is far too great.' Notice I say 'whole' not 'hole.' He explained it as the whole inferred a much bigger group than in a hole. That's Harry logic. And now he's dead, and it could be only an accident, I thought; but now I'm uncertain in light of what's happened to Jed."

Rudy asked, "Jed appears quite conservative, at least according to you. His hiring a PI to research Harry's client vs just waiting it out tells me he thought there was something important or dangerous to him and the firm. I believe if we find questions in Harry's auto accident, then the only other avenue to pursue is the group of entrepreneurs and their funding, for which Jed stopped Harry's activities a couple of months before the accident. Can you tell me more about what happened?"

Grace tried to answer. "I never understood what happened. Jed said something to the effect some really savvy and honorable business folks, both men and women who had big bucks, created a fund to support new ventures with new entrepreneurs. It was not wholly for charitable purposes. There was a three-member board and a staff member charged with making directives for the money. The entrepreneur was not required to do a lot of paperwork. Just give the staff member financials for the last two years or a five-year pro forma if it were a new business. Banking reputations and credits were scoured by the staff person. It was her full-time job and she had a great resume for the position. Worked for three years with no problems until one member of the board heard some rumors about another member of the board having a personal relationship with the staffer. He told Jed he thought a review was necessary. A local CPA firm was hired to do a reconciliation and investigation of all moneys in and out. They found five of the recipients had given kickbacks to the board member for substantial amounts. At the same time the accountants found four bogus entrepreneurial companies. All in all, about seventy million dollars had been siphoned off. It hit the papers and the fund was dissolved. Since it was all personal money invested, only the investors would pursue collection. Two investors sued and the resulting suit got lots of press. Imagine, all these business gurus getting swindled. The firm has lists of all involved."

"Where is the suit now? Was Harry one of the investors?"

"Yes, Harry and Jed both were. They thought it was a good opportunity for mentoring new businesses, and the Fund received a small percentage of all the companies it supported along with interest on the loans. These entrepreneurs would not have access to such loans at the lower interest rate without the Fund. Jed and Harry were not on the board and had no board liability. Jed told me he didn't think it was worth the hassle to join the suit since most of the big money met the purpose of the board. The rest was just a business loss to him. Jed and Harry's investments were over three million dollars each."

Rudy thought such a large amount of loss would throw himself into a tizzy and told her. Grace stated, generally, Jed and Harry were big givers and loved the idea of helping entrepreneurs get a foothold to enable competing in the market. She mentioned Jed said it was his first time to get taken. Harry was more upset at the loss. Harry could spend money on a five-hundred-dollar bottle of wine, but being taken by a supposed friend was different. Jed had to keep Harry from confronting the staffer and his so-called friend on the board. Jed was not adverse to Harry joining the lawsuit, but Harry took Jed's advice about unwanted notoriety.

15
Details

Beauregard found himself quite able to move around and when Mona was busy distance-teaching her students, he, with amazing agility at moving his cast, left the house. Getting into his sedan required him to move the seat way back. The break was in the left leg which would allow him to drive. However, getting it in the car took enough effort to wind Rudy. He thought, *I wanted this oversized garage for storage. Never thought it would be necessary for a handicap. I'm all set for when we get old. It's level to the house. I would not have been able to open the driver side door if it were normal size. I have to get out of here before Mona notices me gone.*

In a flash, Beauregard was at the station with officers trying to assist him. He rejected all help, but smarting at his own discomfort, for the first time since the accident he took the elevator up to MCU. Finally, he was in his office with Millie fussing around bringing him a cup of the best java and insisting he not get overwhelmed by the pile of files on his desk. He said nothing. *I'm in charge again. It's not easy to work from home. They only give me some of the stuff. My eyes were killing me looking at a screen all day. I need to order those computer glare reducing glasses. I'll tell Mona. She's always looking to buy me something I need. I'm home here and now, finally.*

Beauregard called a meeting. Every detective attended including Petra who though off duty arrived bringing baby Carlotta. Millie happily took Carlotta, a talking machine, into her office for the duration of the meeting. Petra said, "Do not feed her sugar, Millie. I know you're a Southern gal, but Carlotta gets feisty on sugar."

Millie smiled and said, "We're going to cut out paper dolls and play and if there is a cookie given here or there, well not to worry, I'll handle the sugar fit."

Mason said, "Just when are you going to give up control? Millie's doing you a favor and you're telling her what she can't do. Jim has some issues to fight with you, Queen Petra. "

There was laughter and a comfortable sigh as they turned to the cases at hand. Lieutenant Ashton Lent of Traffic joined them and said, "Captain, does Mona know you escaped?"

No answer was his answer. Beauregard was an outlaw and all wondered when they would hear from his wife. A report on the two-fatality accident was first on the agenda. Ash went over some of the details for the squad. He had contacted the police in Stamford and Providence. They had no history on the two victims. Ash reported on his attendance at the funeral of each victim. "Captain, there was just family and a few friends attending the funerals and both were held in church. Some suits were there, but they looked legitimate and I couldn't question them. An officer from my unit took video, just in case a photo shows up later you may want to match."

Beauregard asked for a copy of the video. Ash agreed and said, "We found the helicopter at an airport in upper state New York. They don't know who brought it in and never saw it before. It's registered to a Delaware company called, 'Ralrow, LLC.' The company went belly-up this year and there're all kinds of liens on the helicopter."

Mason offered to do the investigation on Ralrow, LLC. He would check open investigations. Beauregard stopped them all, "Jed's partner Harry took a difficult divorce case with implications for suspect financial dealings. What just caught my ear was this corporation name of Ralrow. The parties in the divorce case are a wife named Raleigh and a husband named Arrow. You put the first three letters of wife's name and last three letters of husband's name and you get Ralrow. Strange, but quite the norm in the U.S. Consider all the kids with first names combining parents' first names. Look into a possible connection, Mason. If you find it, you've connected the two cases. Too many possible connections are one too many for me."

Bill Border verbalized some of the excitement in the air. "It feels like a movement forward for me, Captain. I like when there are puzzle pieces fitting together. Consider what we do know. Helicopter owned by a suspect corporation with a questionable name may be connected to the bleeding man. Two dead victims with good reputations recently connected to more secretive activities. A bizarre accident definitely precipitated by a car pushing another car off the road in front of an ongoing truck. If we agree it was no accident, then why were those victims chosen for death? It's got to be financial. They weren't the type of people to be involved in drug activity. Their families loved them and there was no ongoing domestic issues. They were generally stand-up human beings who perhaps unknowingly got into some financial transactions putting them at risk. Why they were together in the same car since they were both independents in their own financial investment businesses also makes me wonder. Why they were in West Mass is also a hint to, at the minimum, affiliations. These cases have commonality."

Petra thought, *one thing about Bill, when he makes up his mind, he is a bloodhound, a boots on the ground kind; whereas Mason and Ted chase records. I'm more like Bill and I do agree with this. Look at the Captain; silence. When he is silent, it means pending action.*

Lilly and Juan both tried to speak at once, but were interrupted by the Captain. "Bill has summarized the info to date quite well. Anyone in disagreement with his analysis?"

Not an answer from one person. No disagreement was a rare

occurrence. Lilly responded, "Captain, Jed Mattias has at least some of the answers. The daughter is missing or maybe not. Needs exploring. If she is safe, we'll get more from him. He knows something and maybe he shared info with Beryl Kent which she is holding back from us. I understand she is nosey to the point of maybe being obstructive. I saw her outside Mattias' room the day of the attack and she gracefully avoided me speaking to one of the attendants to get the scoop. She is a sharpie."

Juan agreed. "She is smart. Who else would go to Austin on her own ticket to follow a lead? Is she more involved in this investigation other than being a witness?"

The Captain, to everyone's surprise did not agree. "Beryl Kent is a pain you know where, but she's legitimate. I believe her and to a certain extent respect her doggedness. I've never been in a position beyond policing to follow my instincts. Well, I won't say never, but not usually; whereas, Mona would do as Beryl does. She just doesn't have the time or resources, but she would want to know. Have we found the note yet? Where are the interviews on the neighbors behind the big house? Bobby and Mason, weren't you scheduled to do their interviews?"

Bobby and Mason said the interviews were on hold. They would get to them today. As to the note, the directive for a more intensive search was not put out. The hospital attempt on Mattias' life took the energy out of the unit. Bobby said, "Look, Captain, there have been so many directions to work on and so little assistance. We had some regular cases needing our attention. I'll get right on the search."

Beauregard closed the meeting and thought, *how much work do I really do? My most successful efforts have to do with putting others' work product together. Maybe I'm not important; although I'm really happy to be back in my office. This is all I've ever wanted for my professional life and I've got it: a professional detective crew and little interference from above.*

Although Beryl Kent may end up my enemy if she goes too far. I'll do what they say, 'Keep my enemies and intrusive citizens close.'

Beauregard spent some time reviewing the video of the funerals of the two dead victims from the deliberate auto accident. He took his time. Both victims had families who were sorrowful. The funerals were held in churches and masks were worn, making identification difficult. He also had a copy of those who signed in. He noticed the process of signing in at Saint Raymond's church in Providence, where a member of the family walked around looking for signatures of family and friends. He knew how important it was for grieving families to have a member get addresses to allow thank you notes later. When a funeral was held in an official funeral home, the staff there took care of this type of business. What he did see from the video of David's funeral in Providence were two suits who carefully avoided signing. They did it well. When the guest directory holder came toward the pew, one suit appeared to be choking and moved to the back of the church with his friend assisting him. Beauregard noticed they then stayed near the back of the church viewing the attendants. They did not leave until the end of the service, but never once went to speak to family or friends. Because they were masked, he could not see their faces. He regretted his police did not take video of outside cars.

Excited he then viewed Marlene's service. The church in Stamford was an Episcopal Church. The video showed Ash in the midst of the small group there who appeared to be quite sociable to all attendees including Ash and two suits. There was again a person charged with signing in, but stayed to the side awaiting those who came to him and wrote their details. Two men in suits did not go and sign in nor did Ash. Beauregard went back and forth between the two videos looking at the body language of the suits. He thought, *they're the same guys. One's actually wearing the same suit and shoes on both days, while the other changed his suit but not his shoes. Both did not sign in on either funeral. Why would they be there? Did they expect someone to be there, and if so, who?*

―――――

Bobby and Mason interviewed two neighbors in the afternoon. Their efforts were frustrated by the neighbors reviewing with them all of Beryl's questions. Beryl made quite an impression on them. The trouble was their skills in interviewing did not reveal much new; just Beryl's questions, whose answers from the neighbors now were by rote and obviously discussed between the two neighbors. They had no information about 'the bleeding man event' but lots to say about Monsieur Rene DesCartes. They did not like him and proceeded to not hold back every bit of gossip they'd heard concerning the man. Bobby told Mason later, "With poisonous neighbors like them, if I were DesCartes, I'd move."

Mason said, "Bobby, I grew up in a crowded neighborhood in Springfield in the hood. Everyone knew everything about you, unless you had a mother like mine. Mama insisted we tell 'Nobody, Nothing.' The mailman, milkman in those days, and the old ladies on the street had a gossip network far better than the internet, because they caught all the nuances in language. These kids today don't know what a nuance is and can be easily fooled by someone cool. They know all the cool acronyms but can't read emotion in language; it confuses them. They are going to be screwed."

"Well, these interviewees, my friend, aren't kids, and the only nuances I got were distrust and dislike of DesCartes. They did say the other neighbor higher on the hill works late, but I saw a car in his drive. Let's try him. COVID maybe keeps him home most days."

Bobby knocked on Mr. Nathan Connault's door, realizing the house would make a great party pad looking out as it did on a wooded valley with roofs of few houses in the view. Nathan answered, completely shocking Bobby Barr. "Colonel, I didn't expect you. And your name was Ian, not Nathan when I knew you."

Nathan laughed. "Nor did I expect you. I thought you were in traffic, but it's obvious now you're a detective. Nathan is my middle name. I like it better. Come on in."

As they entered, Bobby introduced Mason who said, "I'd have known you were a Colonel or something. Why'd you retire, you're young and probably could have been a general."

They all laughed, but Nathan's answer was unexpected. "There's a lot more work out here for my talents than inside, Lieutenant. And tell me, if you please, how would you know I was military? I'm asking because another person told me the same thing recently. It'd be nice to know what signals I put out; I'll make changes."

Bobby snickered saying, "Colonel, was Beryl Kent the one who was on to you?"

"I'll tell you the answer, Sergeant, if you tell me what I need to change."

Bobby said, "I don't know how Ms. Kent knew, but did you ever compare yourself to the average joe, Colonel? You're at home working but your clothes are pressed. You're wearing a pressed sweatshirt. You're of a certain age and you stand at attention, despite the fact you have three computer screens large enough for TV screens. You should be bent over by now if that's your work. You're in stocking feet but your boots were left at the door. For all I know you were stationed in Japan for a while and learned some good habits, or you were stationed in Turkey. The Muslims often require shoes taken off at residences. Your eyes don't waver when you're talking, telling me you were trained to blink less than normal folks. Look at this room. Unless the cleaning service just left, you are a military neatnik. I had a Scottish mom and I was trained from the cradle in some of these practices, but you are a pro."

Nathan's reply caused them to relax. "I simply don't have the will to become a slob, but Sergeant you've given me hints to explain my habits to Ms. Kent who asked me if I was military or worked for the government. I'll tell her I was stationed in Turkey and had a Scots mother. She might go for that rationale."

Mason said, "Nope, she'll investigate you further if I know her and I think I do. But her observation is good. You're government now, somehow. Tell me to back off if it's for security reasons."

Nathan smiled as he told them he'd never tell the police to back off saying, "Why wouldn't I allow a complete invitation? Now sit down, guys, and I'll get coffee and if you're willing some good whiskey to sweeten it."

They were willing. The conversation was almost identical to Nathan's interview with Beryl. So much so, Mason observed aloud, "Sounds, uhm, Colonel, like a recording. Is this what you told Ms. Kent word for word? If so, you have a hell of a memory."

"I do, Lieutenant, I do."

Bobby asked, "You told Beryl about the pole with the birdfeeder and the slinky around it. Did you ever see anyone look in the birdfeeder?"

"Sergeant, believe it or not, I'm not like my other two neighbors. I don't look below all day long. In fact, most days I'm not here much of the time. I can't answer, but I do think you should check. I'm surprised Beryl hasn't been there searching."

Mason replied, "Easy, Colonel, it's private property and it's my guess Beryl doesn't want to go near Rene DesCartes, and as you know the bird feeder is on his property."

Nathan's answer was, "And you think Beryl would stop at a minor trespassing? What do you think is secreted in the feeder?"

Bobby's answer was meant to remind the Colonel he was the one being questioned; instead, Nathan appeared embarrassed and apologized for, as he put it, 'not staying in line.'

Mason used this lapse on Nathan's part stating, "Just what do you do in West Side, Colonel? Are you working or retired? I do wonder why you've chosen West Side to live. You've been here for eighteen months and it appears you have no relatives living in Western Massachusetts. Why locate here?"

"I do not have to satisfy your curiosity, Lieutenant, but I'm an easy-going guy. I'm happy to tell you the Pioneer Valley is a beauteous area, near Bradley Airport, almost centered midst Boston, New York, Hartford, and Providence. Vermont is practically next door.

"You couldn't possibly know if I have relatives nearby. I come from quite an extended family with non-matching surnames falling in several age groups. As to my work, it is basically service related and working from my computer with occasional corporate visits; which are now rarely held because of COVID-19."

Nathan rose letting them know it was exit time. They said their good-byes. Bobby told Mason as they were driving down toward the DesCartes residence, "Too cool, Mason, he was always too cool. It was rumored even when I knew him, he was way up in the investigative chain. Some said he left the service for the CIA or other kinds of work. He gave great 'no-answers' to our questions. I particularly like his 'service related and working from my computer with occasional corporate visits...' And his reference to a huge family. Probably has one kid."

Mason's answer was to charge Bobby with calling all their known connections and asking about good old Colonel Ian Nathan Connault. "He is in the area for a reason. Check how he bought his house, where the money came from, who was the real estate agent for the sale, and who previously owned it. He is government, Bobby. Is he investigating something related to our case? His memory is so well trained, it was as if we were reading the report the Captain wrote from questioning Beryl.

There were no differences at all. I think the guy knows something about this situation and is investigating DesCartes. It's all connected. Beryl Kent says it and I agree. I'm with nosey ladies. I grew up with them always in my business. They kept me honest, because they could see things I couldn't at the time. It was great training, I'll tell you."

Bobby said, "There you go again making believe I should have grown up in the Hood of Springfield."

They parked in front of DesCartes home, hung their badges outside their jackets and walked to the post. Both detectives were big guys but Mason clearly was too bulky in form to climb the post. Bobby was about to put his foot on Mason's hands to make the climb when they noticed a button on the pole. Bobby pushed it and the bird feeder slid down halfway making it reachable to an ordinary height person. Mason said, "How the hell would Jed Mattias know about the button? He was injured."

Bobby said, "I saw the cameras show Mattias leaning against the pole and he must have pushed the pole in. Nothing's showing but this bird house has pretty large holes for the birds; it must be feeding ravens or something."

From the largest of the three holes, Bobby pulled out a scrap of paper. It had a date and time on it and nothing more. They pushed the button again and the birdhouse rose to its normal place. They wondered who would design such a complicated access to a bird house. Mason said, "Creativity is everywhere, but who's going to pay for this design? I wouldn't."

<h1 style="text-align:center">16</h1>

Beryl on the Perils of Dating

Beryl and Oliver were wrapping packages for Christmas Day, when the Vienna Waltz on her phone played. She barely heard it but Oliver said, "Mom, can't you get a more modern ring. It's embarrassing. You're not old enough to be playing classical music as your ring tone."

When she swiped without looking she heard a deep baritone voice hit some emotional button, because she smiled immediately and said quietly, "Hello. Nathan, what can I do for you today? It is Sunday and my son Oliver and I are making presents pretty."

"Need my help, I'm a great wrapper up, if that phrase is a legitimate phrase."

She thought, *I'll just bet you are,* but said, "Nope, we've got it covered. We're actually just about through. You called when you were not needed."

"Beryl, I know it's last minute, but are you willing to take a ride out to Sturbridge area and have some dinner? Avellino's is still open for dinner and the food is decent. You might know I have some questions about Mr. Mattias which you can help me answer."

She didn't think about an answer, just said, "Sure. What time will you pick me up?"

Oliver made a quick remark as she clicked off. "All right, Beryl, play hard to get."

"Don't be wise, Oliver. He's just a friend."

"I hope not. You'd be better to marry him. Your husbands were nicer to you than your friends with special benefits."

Red-faced with anger, her response was not measured. "You think you know everything. I had wonderful husbands for a time and then time or illness or murderers took them from me. I would have been pleased to have just one of them for a lifetime. As to boyfriends, you have never seen me act inappropriately. How dare you presume anything else?"

Taken back, but willing to say more, Oliver replied. "Don't take offense, Mom. I don't want you hurt. You help everybody in trouble. You don't need more trouble. You told me, yourself, this new guy, Nathan, may be a government man. I know from your phrasing, you think he's undercover or a spy or CIA or in some other agency business. Be smart. Find out why he's living here in West Side. I googled him. Nothing sticks out. I mean nothing. He's been here less than two years. Two years is a long time and I don't see much of a footprint from him. You be careful and I want to meet him when he picks you up."

Still smarting, Beryl commented, "You are worse than Jocelyn. She'll be here in a week. I do not want you discussing my friends with her. Do you get me, Oliver."

"Yeah, yeah. She's a monster when she's on the prowl. I wouldn't want Jocelyn on my case. You know she has a new young man. If I know her, he'll be our guest for Christmas."

"Who is he? Are you guessing? You must know something; you're an engineer and always need a piece of evidence before you jump into a discussion."

"I don't know, nosey mother. What I heard was a male's voice in her apartment while I was speaking with her, and he asked her if she wanted more cheese on her fettucine. Jocelyn would not let a guy cook for her unless he's fueled some feeling of a domestic future. Jocelyn's idea of the perfect man would be a hunk with kitchen skills to keep him busy while she paints or designs or arranges or whatever she does."

Beryl gave Oliver a big forgiving smile. "You, my dear, are wonderful at investigation. You get that from me, not from your father. He was a bit like Jocelyn with his head in the books. Maybe not into art, but focused always focused. Thank you and we will welcome the hunk with kitchen skills with open arms and none of your snide snickers."

The doorbell rang and Oliver reacted. "Just change your shirt, Mom, the rest is okay. I'll get to know Nathan Connault while you make yourself beautiful."

Yelling as she headed for her bedroom, Beryl asked but did not get an answer to, "How did you know his full name? I didn't tell you."

Oliver and Nathan spent less than ten minutes together before Beryl appeared back in the great room. She could tell they got on and it made her nervous resulting ins her tripping on the area rug's edge. She was caught by both men. Oliver remarked, "Mom was always into a dramatic entrance."

Nathan laughed at the hateful look Beryl gave her son, saying, "You're a brave man Oliver to incur Beryl Kent's wrath. I myself am deadly afraid of her wrath."

"I'm safe, Nathan, we're blood."

After regaining her composure, Beryl and Nathan left the home with Oliver, always a wise guy, instructing, "Drive safely, kids. It's dangerous out there."

———

"You have a son, Beryl, who will be investigating me tomorrow. It's all good. I like he cares for his mom."

"Too late, your observation is too late, because Oliver has investigated you already."

"Hmmm! I suppose his results have led you to some questions. Fire away."

Beryl said she would rather wait until they were seated for dinner. They drove the old route to Sturbridge. The longer time allowed them to review what they both knew about Jed Mattias. Nathan dropped a bomb, saying, "Marthea Mattias is not missing, Beryl. She is teaching in a music camp for emotionally disabled children outside of Santa Barbara."

"How do you know? How could you have discovered her whereabouts? Her boyfriend didn't know."

"He didn't know because his social justice soul is not quite as refined as Marthea's. She never told him. As to how I discovered it, just know I have connections and leave it at that, if you can."

"I will get back to you with my answer. Why wouldn't she tell anyone about it?"

"She had a good reason. Marthea has an agent and he had signed her up for this gig, which paid quite well, without telling her until the last minute. When he did tell her, he explained the rumor would fly in the industry she wasn't up for serious work or even that she would take less money. He didn't want the onslaught of pecuniary jobs offered which would interfere with her commercial success and the rate level she had enjoyed. The position would pay her while the dearth of performance opportunities from COVID continued. The agent is a decent agent, as they go, but seems to have a fear of the music industry's snobbery about performing for certain audiences."

"You spoke with her agent. I never thought of contacting him. I assumed Marthea's boyfriend would connect me to the music world. I can't believe I missed this. Have you told the police? Captain Beauregard needs to know. This is important."

Beryl caught a strange look on Nathan's face leading her to wonder, *I've seen that look before. My husbands all had that look. I know what it means. It's the 'I can't get involved in this, Beryl. It's up to you. After all it's your baby.' But why can't you be involved, Nathan?*

"You will call him, won't you, Nathan?"

"We're here at Avellino's. I'll explain the situation over dinner."

It took a few minutes before they were seated and could remove their COVID masks. Beryl had not been here before and thought, *it's comfortable and the food smells wonderful. I must be careful with this man. Just why is he dragging his feet on telling Beauregard? I know he likes Beauregard. He let it slip in conversation the Captain is very well thought of in policing communities. I let that remark go then. Why didn't I follow up?*

She waited for their selection, or rather his selection of wine to be served. Beryl was about to start questioning Nathan when he apologized for directing the wine order to his favorite saying, "I'm sorry, Beryl. I should have asked for your choice, but this one is so very good. It's a Piedmont Barolo and I don't see it offered everywhere."

"Nathan, I am not a wine aficionado. In fact, a little prosecco or a bourbon would do me just fine, but I appreciate your ability to choose a wine to tempt my palate. May I add, don't let the outside world's answers to what's the right thing to do control your behavior. I never have."

"I don't know, Beryl. I think if I took control, you'd be out of here."

She answered, "It's all in the intention of the words for me, not the actual words. Actual words are unfortunately, a national problem, but not my problem."

They enjoyed their dinners, hers was Gnocchi Ala Vodka and Nathan chose the duck. They chatted amicably. Over a simple dessert of ice cream topped with espresso coffee liqueur and lots of whipped cream, an American version of affogato, Nathan said, "Let's get it over, Beryl. What do you want to know?"

She peppered him with questions without waiting for answers. He asked if she thought she would forget her questions, or was she ensuring he would give answer quickly preventing any prevarication. She answered yes to both. Nathan said, "I would like us to have a trusting relationship, Beryl, but there are parts of my work I simply can't share with you. I know you hate the term 'trust me' but I lay it before you to accept. If you find in the future I have been untrustworthy, I want just one thing from you. Give me a chance to explain.

"As to why I resist calling Beauregard about Marthea, well it is work related. I would have to share with him my source and methodology. It would just interfere with his investigation and if he knew, he would say, 'Why didn't you keep it under your hat?' The Captain understands compartmentalization better than anyone. Keep blocks of knowledge separate. But I'm not trying to keep this from him. I will give you the name of Marthea's agent. You can call and verify and then share it with the Captain. He does need to know how you knew this."

"Alright, Nathan, I can follow the lead and get the info independently, but I see the hanging thread here and I can't help but follow it every time. It brings me to ask another question. Why are Jed Mattias' life and his daughter important to you? You made a claim to me before that he had become important to you. Why?"

"Trust me, Beryl, I can't tell you. Ask another question. Maybe I can answer. What I am able to say is I'll try to help you. Although you don't know it, we have the same goals."

Beryl looked miffed, but quickly said, "Alright, you have secrets, but I do want to know why you have a 'life footprint' of about two years with no information beyond."

He laughed. "I thought Oliver was better than that. He didn't look on the dark web, did he? Look, it is important nobody local looks into my background now. In a few months it won't matter. I work in government, but not directly and my background has been deliberately, and mostly deleted. You can look at various organizations I have belonged to and find my name. There are several out there not hidden from the public.

This is my real name. I am sixty-one years old. I am a widower and you don't need to know about my marriage, other than my wife died of ovarian cancer when she was thirty-five years old. I regret I have no children. I do have several god-children. My personal life has been overshadowed by my professional life ever since my wife died. I'm not telling you this to make you feel sympathy for me. My life as stated is a fact. After her death, I had this opportunity to do work I liked. I did not realize I was short-sighted living this way. I've had a good life, not necessarily the life I wanted. I intend to make changes when I finish my current endeavor."

Beryl took a moment to digest this no information given response. Nodding her head, she said, "Okay, Nathan, I accept your offer to suspend judgment for three months. It means I'll be watching your every move."

"I don't doubt it, and hope you approve of my every move. Now I have questions. Has Jed given any more details or in any way remembered something? How is the accident investigation going? Do you still see the Captain?"

Beryl was so slow before answering, Nathan questioned her truthfulness, commenting, "You are aware, Beryl, your taking a long time before responding indicates the truth is troublesome. What's up? Are you and the Captain on the outs? I did hear he was back in his office, broken leg and all."

"I did not know. I was going to visit him at home. I find him much more communicative at home, if that's the right word. Mona just inspires sociability and she likes me. Do you and Beauregard meet? I mean how do you know he's back in his office?"

He laughed. "It's all over town. Beauregard is the man to talk about. It's like he's an old-time sheriff from the cowboy movies who's earned everyone's respect. Only one person I know doesn't like him and there's good reason. Beauregard caught him with his hand in the till of the non-profit where the guy was working. How Beauregard knew is a question. The guy was allowed to pay back the funds with no record. He stayed in town. He was near retirement age and had an income. I heard Beauregard just saw some spending while he was investigating a murder case. One witness mentioned her neighbor hitting the lottery, but it was not in the papers. I have heard he is the best at taking small tidbits and putting them together to make a bigger picture. Who knows? Maybe the wife squealed on the guy. The guy is always putting forward nasty thoughts about Beauregard. No one listens, because as my mother would say, 'The guy's got history.' She meant if you know what a guy's been like in the past, you can decide whether to listen to him or not. By the way, she meant that for women too, Beryl. My mom was into equality between the sexes."

"Are you kidding me? You heard around town he went into work at the station. You are reaching, Nathan, but I promised I'd suspend judgment for three months. You are walking on ice, you know."

He answered, "The cops found the note. It was in the birdhouse."

Beryl looked directly at him and giggled. "How did you know? I don't think the cops are around town talking about finding evidence."

"Nope. I discovered it the old-fashioned way. I was interviewed at my home. The cops knew about the birdfeeder, probably from your report to Beauregard, if you told him. I watched from my window as they retrieved it. It was shortly after they left my home. Nothing secretive there."

Beryl found herself beginning to like this game. "You watched them after they left thinking they would look for the note immediately. Surprising to me is the fact the police asked you about the note. Is it how you found out about it? I don't remember telling you."

"'Do you not believe me, Beryl? Why would I tell you about their finding the note? Don't you think we should be looking at what the note said. Do you know? Could you find out?"

"Nathan, whether I believe you or not isn't important. You know what is important is to find the meaning of the note."

"Beryl, you know what the note says, don't you? Give it up."

Beryl paused, longer than she should. "Nathan, it has a date and time. I don't know what it is or its meaning, but it must have a meaning. He did not hide the other note only this note. I'm thinking it is the date and time of when he met with someone. He said it was from before he left for his trip. I think his partner, Grace Grantley, would have his schedule. I doubt she would give it to me.

"The date and time had some meaning to Jed even when he was in fear of his life, but he can't remember the meaning now. Do I believe him? Do you believe him? Did he connect with a known bad dude or did he not connect? We have to discover the note's meaning. The other alternative is to help him recover his memory. I think his injuries by themselves would not create loss of memory. It's more likely, the loss is related to his absolute fear for his life. Do you think lawyers normally have to worry about dying on the job?"

Nathan responded, "No, their combat missions are conducted with words not guns. Jumping from a helicopter and avoiding gunshots and thinking his daughter is in captivity could create loss, but it will come back.

"Beryl, I think you should get back in there and tell Jed, his daughter is safe. Contact her host of the program's number and give it to Jed, so he can call her. He won't believe she's safe until he speaks with her. Contact the agent. He'll have no problem relaying her information. If he does, tell me; it would mean he knew he was to be silent. That's not the case, I'm certain."

"Nathan, you have lots of avenues for me to follow. You give yourself no assignments. Yet, you have a deep interest in my pursuits. You are involved in this mess, aren't you?"

Nathan smiled. He answered very slowly, "You know the old saying, Beryl, if I told you, I'd have to kill you."

Beryl's answer was not in the defensive at all. "Nathan, I am not afraid of you. I've assessed your character and if I'm wrong, well, it would be my mistake. I have made mistakes in my life, mainly when I've gone along with others' ideas. When I make an assessment based on my instincts or maybe experience or perhaps insight from some heavenly place, I do well."

"I am more than happy you will judge me by your instincts, Beryl. Thank you."

There was a moment of silence. It stretched out, but not uncomfortably. They finished their coffee and tea and left to travel home. He exited off 291 for Armory Street instead of home. Beryl asked where they were going. He questioned her in return, "Are you dressed warm enough to take a walk?"

Beryl answered yes. She did not question him further. She waited thinking, *in my younger days, I would not have fallen for the 'take a walk' scenario. Oh, no, I'd have been right on his case with a 'where to' and a 'why.' I don't want to go home. I like his company. I don't like that I like his company. I don't need complications in my life. As Jocelyn says, "No more love affairs, Mom. Get over it." Easy for her, she does not engage with the human race easily.*

When they reached Armory Street and passed the abandoned Our Lady of Hope Church. Beryl knew they were headed for Van Horn Park. "Nathan, I know the park. I've watched some games over there. The woods and pond are beautiful, but there aren't lights inside."

"Just wait."

They parked on Chapin Terrace and walked across Armory Street to the parking area. Nathan headed over to the closest playing field to an almost covered pathway. It was a shortcut to the pond and in the moonlight the water glistened. He said, "If you want to get in touch with your feelings, I've found silence and surrounding beauty as the road to my soul."

She did not contradict him. She tried to enter his idea for self-talking to her soul. She tried to repress her words. And she did for about fifteen minutes of sitting on the old log he knew was there and absorbing the feeling of the clean air and the smell of the water and woods. Still, she was Beryl. "I'm in touch now, Nathan, but why here? This place could be a drop for a spy to leave info."

"I'm not answering spy questions. How about you tell me if you feel more relaxed and could you do this before making rash decisions? This is a good therapy for someone like you. Someone who is often action oriented."

"Is that a criticism?"

"Nope. I think you are perfect. I do think people with warm thoughts for all those living life can get overly wrapped up in the ordinary, the quietude can be a good influence. I know I need it."

"Nathan, you live in a beautiful home on a high hill overlooking a valley halfway up a small mountain. Why would you come to an inner-city park for inspiration?"

"Probably because it's an inner-city park. It's close to downtown. Nobody's here at night; well, unless they're up to no good. I sometimes hear frogs in the summer. I lived near here as a child for just two years. It smells like home to me."

Beryl laughed. "I have new information on you. You lived in Springfield as a child. Oliver will make good use of that tidbit in researching you. Can't blame me, Nathan, you gave it up."

Nathan leaned toward her, took her face in his hands, came closer, but did not kiss her. He said, "I will have to watch you, but will enjoy every minute. Wait for me, please, until I finish this assignment."

She didn't answer. He didn't offer more explanation. They found their way out of the woods with his flashlight and the assistance of the moon, and headed home.

17
Busy Work

"Defunct corporation! Just how can a helicopter still fly when it's owned by a defunct corporation!" shouted a frustrated Mason Smith.

"Did you guys know that's not a problem? The problem is the pilot must be licensed. Don't they crack down on ownership? The pilot can fly any copter, as long as he or she is licensed and lands where a copter is allowed to land. The trouble is the pilot didn't leave his name when he parked the damn copter at the New York airport. We thought we could find him through ownership of the copter. No way, the corporate officers listed are all dead other than the President."

Petra challenged Mason, "No way. There must be a trail. Copters are used for carrying drugs. If this is a phantom copter with no trace, the DEA will know about it. Did the Captain call DEA? I'll check, but if not, contact Smitty over there and see what he has to say."

"Petra, you want me, Smith, to call Smitty? Sounds like some redundancy to me."

They laughed and Mason went back to his office to make the call while Petra read a new report just in on the double fatality accident case. There was no plate number picked up on cameras on the second car which was suspected in causing the accident. She thought, the time frame searched was too narrow. She looked at the cameras and their locations near Monsieur DesCartes' home and realized that one camera was located near the direction the cars had been going that day. There was no mention of cameras in the other direction. Problems with camera coverage were reported during two days before and after the accident. That alone raised the hackles on her back. She called Ash in traffic. He was available. "Ash, how come there is a camera near DesCartes' home and it doesn't pick up cars leaving his abode? And, further, what's up with no camera coverage on the day before, on, and day after in the area."

"Petra, I am just now reviewing the report I received. Camera coverage in the area used ALPRs or Automobile License Plate Readers and are part of a web controlled by a service. It is accessible on the web and can be hacked. I will report this. What's interesting to me is the report doesn't show camera footage from the other direction. The Land Rover could have come from that direction when coming to DesCartes' residence. I don't know if those cameras were also out during the time period, but we have to check for coverage."

"Ash, I want coverage days before and after, as many as are needed. I think the Land Rover's been there before. I may not be able to connect the owner to the day, time, or event, but I would like to discover his or her name. What about coverage of the accident scene?"

"We get into trouble there, Petra, with cameras on the accident, but they are not at an angle to capture the plate on the second car. They picked up the plate on the first car, but not the second and not the truck."

"What use are they then, Ash? All the money invested in cameras and nothing of value resulting from their use."

"In both those areas, the big problem is speeding cars, not generally crime or gangs. They're traffic cameras for speeding cars. Since there is little traffic, they're spaced far away and angled for capturing the car from a fixed distance. Another thing to remember is the high error rate in reading the plates, sometimes as high as 37%. I went to a seminar on the legal use in investigations using ALPRs. It's complicated and varies by area and state. Double whammies exist for us in both these cases. Coming from the DesCartes home, the cameras didn't work. At the accident scene, the second car's rear plate was covered by mud and the front plate was covered by the car that was hit. They enlarged the rear plate and recovered the third letter on the plate as a possible 'B' but not clear enough for evidence at trial. They are printing a list of all plates with that letter as the third letter. I don't hold out a lot of hope. If you have a suspect and the third letter of his or her vehicle is a 'B' it could be corroborative."

"Captain's going to love this, Ash. Thanks for your help. Please call my cell when you get reports on any Land Rover in the area. I'll chase them all down. Also find out about the cameras' outage. I think hacking was involved. There was no storm. Call me, don't wait to send the report. Thanks, Ash."

Petra moved across the room to Bobby Barr's desk and sat on the edge waiting to get his attention. He was on a call and gave her a 'wait' signal. It still took him three minutes to finish the call. "Sorry, Petra for the wait, but this is a call in from a resident who says her neighbor is a 'spy.' She is certain. I said I'd speak to the neighbor. Her rationale is he hides his car in a barn and it's an expensive car, some sort of new large SUV. She's watched some crime solving shows on television where illegal doings and cars involved in accidents or stolen cars, or cars used in drug deliveries were often hidden in barns. The owner looks foreign to her, maybe not Hispanic, but could be Muslim, like the two are both just suspect because they look foreign to her. I thinks she's a crazy, but I'll have to take a ride, because she's going to call all the Selectmen and the Mayor if I don't report back to her by tomorrow. So, what's up?"

"What kind and color is the SUV? Does she know?"

"A pretty ivory and she doesn't know types of cars. Says it is big and fancy like on television."

"Bobby, do you mind if I go with you on the interview?"

"Absolutely not, you can handle the interview. She is a nut you know?"

"Most of our leads are from nuts and that is something you should know already, Bobby."

Smirking, he asked, "What did you originally want from me, Petra? You didn't know about the crazy lady when you walked over."

"Nope, I didn't. Do you have an analysis of Jed Mattias' calendar for the few weeks before his accident with names possibly connected to the time and date we found on the note he hid?"

"I didn't get the calendar and details from Grace Grantley, Petra, although I asked for them. Attorney Grantley delivered it to the Captain and Attorney Cull. I'm low on the chain. She is not easy to deal with, although she can be charming. To me, she appears to have an actress's veneer hiding a devious mind. Let me show you what I do have on my report."

The two looked over every person listed. They checked the names against firm clients and only found the Alexia March Raleigh name. There was a list of Harry's fifteen cases and one was related to the suit they were not parties to except as witnesses. They were victims, but chose not to be party to the case. Interesting to the detectives was the fact there were victims listed by geographical area with initials, but not names. Two listed were a D. S. from Rhode Island and a M. G. from Stamford. Bobby commented, "Fishy, if you ask me. We have two murder victims with the same initials and both were in the finance business. The list of initials are for witnesses and not complainants. This is a law firm with a partner dying shortly after the lawsuit and the other partner hurt not long after. Both were also listed in the initial witness list along with the two dead victims. The Captain will love these links, but how the hell will we prove it. Surely, Grace Grantley will have the complete names of the witnesses."

"Bobby, financial crimes crossing state borders will be investigated by the Feds. We need to have the Captain connect on this one. For all we know, we're in the midst of a federal investigation. You know the Captain takes murder as his domain and will interfere if he has to. The trouble is, as we saw in past cases, they will want us out of it. We have Springfield police with duties on the murder attempt on Jed's life as well as us. It's getting messy. And the Ralrow company must be involved in this case too, or are we looking at just a coincidental divorce mess? Have they located Alexia March Raleigh yet?"

Petra said, "The Raleigh woman must have left a trail with credit cards or something. Let's pursue her history. Meanwhile, I'll talk to the Captain. He's not in today. Probably, yesterday was too much for him. I'll call Mona and see if I can visit. I won't call him; if I do he'll insist I come. Mona will know what condition he's in today."

Bobby laughed. "Won't she tell on you? The Captain will kill you if he thinks you're determining his health condition."

"Nah, Mona's the best. She'll tell me the truth without squealing to the Captain. She is good at selective truth telling."

The detectives called the crazy lady to schedule a visit. She answered their question with, "Well, it's about time the police earn their keep. I called patrol and they wouldn't take me seriously. Are you serious? I hope so, because I will call the Selectmen and the Mayor if you don't. Something is up with my neighbor. I can sniff it out. I have this instinct for troublesome people."

The name on the door was 'Bleeker' in blocked four-inch print. There was no initial and no bell. Bobby knocked with a forceful closed fist and yelled, "West Side Police."

Petra whispered, "Bobby, did you have to announce it to the world? She may be sensitive to her neighbors knowing she's the one calling on her."

"Lieutenant, no way. She is not sensitive. I know from just talking to her on the phone."

The oversized door opened and the detectives could see inside to a huge room, but the entrance was crowded with a wheelchair, walker, a metal umbrella stand holding four sizes of canes and two shillelaghs. Coarse crazy growing gray hair covered a multi-lined, but once handsome face. Marge Bleeker welcomed them with, "Come in. It's friggin' cold out there. There's a fox around too cold and too lazy to chase the four squirrels hiding in back. And this wimp of a dog of mine won't leave to do his duty; I have to throw him out."

Marge pointed them to an old Victorian high back couch which from Petra's limited interior décor knowledge, was at odds with all the old wooden boxes with cushions for seating. The furniture was a collage of nineteenth century odds and ends with the exception of the magnificent large holding cabinet and enormous pine trestle table with backed benches. The whole of the room was comforting, at least, that's what Bobby said. "Ms. Bleeker, with the fire going, I love this room."

"The name in Marge, Detective and I spit at the term Ms. I am a miss, a single lady, although I was not always. Now I have herb tea I make myself from my herb garden or 'godawful' coffee, take your choice. My muffins are the best. You can't go wrong with them."

Before Petra could say 'no' her colleague gratefully accepted explaining he was always hungry this time in the day. Marge Bleeker said, "Of course you are, you're a big guy. My husband was too. He ate us out of house and home, but then he keels over and dies on me at age fifty. Not fair to leave me to face life alone. You take care and cut back on those sirloins. They killed Eddie; food, and the beer."

They were directed to sit on the old-fashioned couch and could see into a kitchen, the size of Bobby's condo. It was a throwback also but with all the latest appliances. Petra thought, *people and houses, you never know what's inside. This place is worth a bundle. Just fix up the outside for some curbside appeal and it's a money maker. She grows all the herbs for her teas and I see orchards out back, but if there was a single bush and grass out front I didn't see it. Lots of pavers. I wonder what Eddie did before he died. I guess her to be about sixty-five making him gone for a while.*

Onto an old carpenter's chest, Marge placed a tray of luscious looking muffins and two teapots of blue and white crockery ensconced in printed blue and white tea cozies Napkins matched in blue, and Marge served them with grace. And then she spoke. Her husky, but audible voice, took away the adjective, grace, from any further description of Marge. "Did you see the ***** barn across the way? It is a wonderful barn, although the likes of those people would never appreciate its historic significance. They're too busy doing nefarious deeds. Don't laugh at me. My Eddie if he were alive would agree with me. He'd have been over there looking in windows for details before he would have called the police, but I don't trust them. They'd have me arrested for looking in their windows."

Petra asked, "How can you see what's going on, Marge? I can't see the barn from here."

"Look behind you on the left at those barn doors. I often open them. There is a window to match the one across from you, but I need some privacy so I open the doors at night and occasionally in the day. In the spring through fall seasons it's always open, but in the winter, I get a cold and unsafe feeling, so I keep the doors shut then."

Marge opened the barn doors and the view across the street was complete with barn and house both visible. She then gave a complete review of her neighbor's antics emphasizing he wouldn't put his name on the mailbox, just the number. Everybody on the street had their surname on the box or their house visible to all. She theorized he was hiding his name and not surprising to her, since there were several men all about the same age going in and out of the house on a regular basis. Only two of the men stayed over. She thought they were overdressed for West Side. They looked like the city slicker type, all designer suits and overcoats.

Bobby tried to explain to Petra's amusement the police could not investigate based on fancy clothes and putting a car in the barn in the winter. Marge's shackles rose. "Do you think I'm stupid; is that what you think, Detective?"

Bobby answered quickly. "No, but you appear to believe police have investigative powers we don't have. What can you tell me that makes your neighbors something other than 'outsiders' in this city?"

"What? I have to supply your evidence for you. Well, okay, what about the fact they have multiple cars and never put one of those fancy cars in the barn, just this one SUV? Seems suspicious to me. I think little variations in behavior speak volumes."

"Do you know what day they put the SUV in the barn? We can check for accidents."

"Helpful, Detective, I believe you're being helpful. Let me get my calendar."

Marge pulled out a wrinkled mess of a calendar. She caught him looking at it as if it were a diseased animal and said, "It is December and I have a busy life. It's all in here. Let me read some of my observations on my neighbors. Mind you, I can't capture everything, but if I'm sitting here, I get a lot. They've been here for about two years. You expect comings and goings when people move in, but a few months ago there were trucks going in and out of there every day with fancy cars."

Marge proceeded to state dates and times with short descriptions of men and a few women who were on scene. She could not match how long an individual stayed, with the exception of what she called two regulars. All work on the home outside was done by a national service including lawncare, cleaning, painting, etc. Not one vendor was from West Side. She said it showed too, since the place looked godawful for all the money they must have paid. The detectives closed their interview by telling her she was quite helpful and they would call her back after reviewing the case. Marge looked directly into Petra's eyes and said, "You do that, but take care. If I don't hear back from you, I will call the Selectmen and the Mayor and your boss, the serial murderer capturer."

Despite the tasty morning glory and orange cranberry home-made muffins, the two detectives were relieved to exit Marge's home. They looked at the home across the street. It was an older home built in the nineteen fifties, but built with some style and not in terrible shape. It did not look like a hideout or a place where criminal activity took place. The only oddity was a nineteen fifties home with an eighteen hundred's era barn. They both thought Marge's house would draw more attention to passers-by. Petra concluded, "If you're driving you don't even notice the house across from Marge. Good spot then for her speculative 'nefarious' activities, but Bobby, she is not a nutcase. Everything about her is organized and thought out. Maybe we should go back with some pictures of cars, all ivory or white, and see if she can ID one. Wouldn't take long and would keep her off our backs."

Beryl Kent giggled as she ate Oliver's creative attempt at making ranchero huevos eggs. She asked him if cooking with lots of spice was an antidote to the required confines of engineering work. His response was a yes, but this spice was to keep his mom directed to life, saying, "If it knocks your brain a little, I know you're not in dream land investigating our neighbors. Look, Mom, Jocelyn will be home tomorrow for

Christmas. If she gets wind of you flying around the countryside looking for evildoers, she'll be on you like maple syrup on pancakes."

"How old are you, Oliver? That is one very ole-time saying. I don't believe I've ever used it."

"Joel, your second husband, did, don't you remember?"

"Not until just now. You jarred my emotions using the phrase. That is the way it is with loss. Little things jump at you to remind you, even after a long time, I feel warm and loving thoughts when reminded of Joel. I've never accepted his death. We don't know the whole story."

"What's written in your notebook today? Better get your work out of the way. I'm telling you, Jocelyn's bringing the big guy home and she'll want you to be the sweet docile mother you are not. Start prepping your script."

"I should tell you, Oliver, you had better keep my confidence from your sister, you hear? I'm to see Jed Mattias before I tell the police his daughter is safe. Then we'll call from his hospital room. I've learned they are finally getting rid of him. They tried sending him to a nursing home for rehab and he refused, demanded he would recover at home and get services if he needed them. He's not ready to go back to Atlanta. I'll bet he'll go stay at Grace Grantley's hotel, which makes sense. If only I were certain she is trustworthy. I must get to know her more completely, Oliver. Women seem to hide their bad sides better."

"You're telling me, Mom. Remember the wacko girlfriend Jane I dated for six months. Came on like a milkmaid. In the end, I discovered she had three of us on the hook and was investigating my financial background. She discovered my trust from Cliff and was dumb enough to question me, whether it was just a trust for paying living expenses, or could I withdraw large amounts. I axed her fast. Women are devious, Mom, including you."

"The sweet looking brunette with braids tied on the top of her head like Heidi from the kid's book. No, I wouldn't have figured that one at first. Remember, Oliver, you need time to assess anyone's character. She did act too sweet for a woman of this generation."

"My other dates have been mixed. One woman wanted to use only non-gendered language. Do you know how disruptive it is to discuss important issues and replace he, she, it with they. Another would only discuss misogyny and racial divide in the nation. She insisted my engineering profession was problematic; that I think of people as numbers or robots and not as passionate activists. It gets old, this dating business."

"Darling, you'll just have to attempt to find your place to fit in."

"Ha, like you Mom. You've never fit in. You've acted as a producer and director of your life. It's only with your husbands and us you show the totally involved sensitive soul I know you to be. I get it. Protect yourself with outsiders. Express yourself with family, but I'm just me. I hope there is a woman out there who will appreciate just me. I'm like Dad. I like a continuum in life."

He hugged his mother hoping to do away with the concern showing on her face, knowing he was the one who created it.

Restrictions at the hospital were tighter. Beryl had been warned by the usual piece in the news of new rules for hospitals and nursing homes. She had to see her supervisor before entry, because she wasn't on the list for working this day. After some verbal discussion, Beryl was successful and entered Jed's room in time to interrupt his packing. He looked disturbed. "Jed, where are you going from here? I have some news for you, some good news."

"They wanted me to go to a nursing home, Beryl. I'd be incommunicado except by phone. I need to look for Marthea. Neither police nor Grace has been successful."

There was great anguish in his face as he tried to walk, leaning forward as if the pain did not allow his body to straighten. She touched his shoulder and told him to sit down. Sharing her info on Marthea's whereabouts brought relief to slide across his face allowing a broad smile. "How did you find out? Can we call now? I need to be certain."

Beryl noticed him almost collapsing down into his chair with tears running down his face. She called the number given by Nathan and spoke with the director of the program. He agreed to call Marthea at her training spot and have her call back on Beryl's phone. The wait was difficult. Jed did not want to talk. He just sat. She remembered being like that one time when the news was good for her, but she feared it would not be. In her case, it was twenty-four hours before her anxiety was lifted.

The phone rang. Beryl answered. "Is something wrong? Where is my dad? This is a Massachusetts area code."

Beryl handed the phone to Jed who said, "Marti, are you okay? No one knew where you were for weeks. Where are you? Can you come to Massachusetts for a couple of weeks, Honey? I was in an accident and lost some of my memory, but getting it back drip by drip. I need you. I can't go home yet. I still need treatment, but instead of going to a nursing home, I'll go to a hotel. How soon can you come? I love you."

Beryl was moved by Jed's honest display of emotion. She tried not to listen, more for herself than for Jed, but she heard every emotional nuance in the simple loving words spoken. Jed tearfully told his daughter to be very careful in traveling to Springfield and not to share her destination. She was to call him when she was enroute. He would have a service pick her up with a sign stating her name. She was to go with no one but that person, even if she recognized someone else there at the airport. Beryl heard one side of the lengthy discussion connected to what Marthea called his over-protective attitude. He ended with a, "Do what I ask, Marti; I can't take any more discussion. Just do this once for me."

Marti must have heard the urgency in her father's language because Beryl heard her say 'okay' and the call was over shortly afterward.

Beryl said, "Jed, I don't like your being in a hotel when you should be in rehab. The doctors don't want it. If it wasn't for COVID, you would never have been ejected. I read your chart. There may be the need for some pulmonary work if you have trouble breathing. Come stay at my home. Marthea is also welcome. It's Christmas and my home will be cheerier. My son Oliver is there and is quite funny. He would enjoy a break from trying to control me. My daughter Jocelyn will be in for Christmas holiday with her boyfriend. They're arriving just before Christmas, but will leave on Boxing Day. She's working on some installation, and the work can't wait.

"My house has five suites and a great air flow system that filters and cleans new air sending the old air out constantly. Helpful for breathing after your chest trauma and you can stay six feet apart and wear a mask. I do expect to own a dog shortly, but the air system should solve most problems you may have. You would be much more comfortable at my home with music of your choice and all the movies Netflix offers. Please? You'll be safer there than in a hotel and I'll call Captain Beauregard for some security."

"What more can I do to interfere in your life? Beryl, I'm sorry to intrude, but I am grateful. I have no protection in a hotel despite Grace's assurances. But to put you at risk is a burden for my conscience. I accept this offer with gratitude. I am frightened."

"Not to worry, Jed. We have good friends with the city's police. We have my son Oliver who doesn't trust anyone and then my daughter Jocelyn whose friend, I am told, is an extra special specimen of the male species. How much more safety do you need?

"Now, Jed, tell me what you have remembered. I am certain you have had new recalled memories."

"When Marthea arrives safely, then I'll tell you the bits and pieces I've recalled. They don't make sense to me. When Marthea is safely here, we can examine my thoughts."

Jed was nicely settled in his own suite on the second floor of Beryl's home, with only one wise remark made by Oliver, who said, "Welcome, Mr. Mattias. You are a sight better than Mom's usual rescues. We'll have a nice Christmas together. I think we're in keeping with the Governor's COVID mandate of six indoors; or is it for restaurants, Mom?"

Beryl gave Oliver the steely eye and told him to 'shush.' He did not shush.

18

Christmas Holiday and the Rescue Dog

Morning coffee, croissants, and Finnish pancakes with an array of fresh fruit were being enjoyed by all, when the house phone rang. Beryl seldom used the home phone, and its ringing caused her to run through her brain the catalogue of possible users. She realized the area code was from Tennessee and she happily grabbed the phone. She listened while Oliver and Jed watched her facial expression go from quizzical to happiness. "Today, today; that would be wonderful. What time? Why didn't you let me know before? You did. I apologize. I have been busy and have not checked my email lately."

When she clicked off, Beryl announced, "Puppy is coming. I'm so excited. He's only three months old so perhaps his situation was not long enough for his previous caretakers to ruin him. She said he is lovely, but then the rescue folks think all their animals are lovely. They took him off a farm with thirty dogs kept in all kinds of crates, but the smaller dogs appeared to have been better cared for. The owner was in her nineties and tried to keep everything going after her husband passed last year. She broke her leg and didn't tell anyone of the animals for three weeks. Sad, don't you think when you have the heart for the job but can no longer do it?"

Oliver smiled and trying with all his might not to appear as a distant unemotional engineer said, "Apparently it's a male. What breed? I assume he's got all his shots and is neutered, right?"

Beryl talked with passion about the raid that took place in a small farm near Kingsport, Tennessee. There was a rescue mission in Washington

County and she had discovered this animal advertised on Facebook. She actually didn't discover the dog, but her friend who lived in the area did. The picture of the animal with his big eyes melted her heart and she made an immediate decision he was to live in her home. She told her small audience this morning, "I named him immediately 'Amico.' I thought he looked as if he were a black labradoodle. The rescuers thought he had hair and for sure there was poodle in him, but they thought he'd be less than sixty pounds as an adult dog and maybe something else was in the mix. Mostly rescued dogs in the South have some coon or hound in the mix. They couldn't be certain. Amico means friend, and on that day, I felt I needed a friend. I so missed my dog 'Eureka.' Amico's on his way and could be delivered late today or tomorrow morning. I'm to have an early Christmas gift. God is in heaven helping me again."

Oliver, always the practical one commented on the complexity involved with having a houseful of guests, the holiday, and training a new puppy who may well be already behaviorally damaged. No one responded to his remarks. Jed just thought, *love these people. They're clearly nuts, but good nuts. I'll volunteer to put up those buckets of holly. Oliver does have a point. He complains. Beryl ignores. I like this. They may love each other, but they also like each other. Jocelyn may be a different story. I know from my marriage, my daughter has always felt she owned us.*

Jed grabbed a bucket of freshly cut stringed holly branches and said, "Where to? I need direction."

Two voices entered the discussion. Starting with completely divergent opinions, in moments they agreed. Inside gets decorated this morning and outside was held off until later when the sun warmed the front of the house for the afternoon décor work. Outside work demanded lots of lighting and brought Beryl to comment, "Jed, Oliver does outside. You are not to go there. Do you hear? You haven't recovered completely and it's way too cold for you in your condition to be out there. And…and, it is not safe and I won't have it."

To which, Oliver laughed, saying, "Jed, she's taken a stand. Don't argue, she'll win in the end. I get to do the grunt work outside with direction from Mom who will probably wrap herself in one of her gorgeous furs for warmth, which she doesn't wear now. The social consciousness, environmental, and PETA people have had a profound effect on suburban women. I think I read an article on it written by a Canadian furrier who was infuriated by this trend."

The morning was spent decorating the interior of the main rooms with real holly but cheating with extra artificial berries, ribbons, and small white lights. The three were delighted with their result. Jed said, "New Englanders can challenge us from Atlanta; I can see that now. Old kinds of real decorations with pizzazz. With the fire blazing in the fireplace, Beryl, you've created a haven for celebrating. I think even my Marthea will feel welcome."

They lunched on deli sandwiches created with style by a la Beryl, when a small truck pulled up by the front door. Beryl raced to the door saying, "It must be Amico. He has arrived."

A middle-aged man was about to knock when the door opened. His smile said it all. He was there to bring the puppy to his new home and was delighted with his reception. Beryl asked, "Where is my puppy?"

"Mrs. Kent, I have some paperwork here for you. My partner will bring in Amico. That is the name you told our agency you have given him. We try to use the name if we know it. It helps the animals adjust to their new homes."

Beryl signed the documents quickly as a woman brought in Amico. They all fell in love within minutes and Amico appeared to have assessed his situation and gave happy looks as much as a young puppy could to demonstrate his comfort. Oliver was annoyed to be expelled to the outdoors when the puppy was indoors being held by Beryl and Jed. He worked quickly hoping to get his chance at spoiling. He did notice a West Side police car drove slowly by the house twice every hour. He wondered about the police protection strategy, *how helpful is the protection detail. Any fool could see the timing of the detail and if they wanted to do their dirty work it would be between drive-bys. I can't tell Jed and Mom. They would just get nervous. Mom's got cameras out front, but are they shut off? Knowing her, she never worries about small details, especially her own security, but she'll worry about Jed's security*

His brain was busy. He did not see a large dark sedan pulling in the U-turn driveway. Colored by his thoughts, it was only the sound that made him spring to attention. Oliver tensed up until he realized it was a police vehicle. As a kid in three of the places the family lived, he'd early on learned to study police vehicles. He and his friend and Jocelyn had seen some friends picked up for shoplifting. He thought, *I never would shoplift, but their experience was enough to stop me. Know your surroundings. Identify the enemy. His first step-father had drilled it into his head. Why then did he die the way he did? Mom was certain he was killed. She never came right out and said it, but he knew she thought it.*

Oliver greeted the two men who exited the car. The driver was tall and friendly-looking for a cop. The passenger had a cast on his leg and Oliver knew immediately this must be the famous Captain Beauregard. He went to assist the Captain in his struggle to balance the heavy cast saying, "Allow me to assist, Captain. I am Oliver, Beryl's son. I've had a broken leg from skiing before. It's a bitch getting around isn't it?"

"Hi, Oliver, nice to meet you. I'm surprised I have a reputation; described now as the man with a broken leg."

"More than those words were said to describe you. My mom doesn't bother to discuss folks unless they've ticked her off or she likes them. Maybe you are in the latter category."

"Oliver, do you know if I am? I could easily be in the first grouping."

"Nice things, Captain, only nice things were said. Now before I let you in the house, I have to ask, do you like dogs?"

"Yeah, actually I do. Beryl didn't have one the last time I saw her and there was no mention of a dog on the incident report. Did she just buy one?"

"Amico was just delivered. He's a rescue and Mom's in love. We all are. He is a lovely animal, but he is a puppy. I can't guarantee he won't pee where he's not supposed to. This is my warning. We can't put him in isolation yet. He has just arrived and needs to know he is safe."

Beauregard laughed. "Let's go inside, Oliver, and meet Amico."

Before moving he introduced Detective Ashton Lent and asked Ash, "Are you ready to be peed on, Detective?"

Ash laughed, replying, "No end to what we see on this job, is there, Captain? Nice to meet you, Oliver. You have a lot of your mom's nice ways. Did anyone ever tell you?"

They entered the home. Beryl was chasing the puppy while Jed Mattias smiled and tried to keep up with them. Neither Beauregard nor Ash had ever seen Jed completely smile before. Beauregard thought, *well, I suppose relocating Jed to this house has at the very least improved his medical condition. I'd like to know the story about how this situation came about. I guarantee it was Beryl's idea. She acts based on her instincts and never asks permission. They were out of the hospital before I could say 'no.' I find it strange the Springfield police weren't notified before the hospital moved him. They had picked a nursing home for him. I suppose the hospital would eventually have let us know when Jed agreed on his new location.*

The puppy headed for the detectives and in so doing, announced to all he was socialized to people. One less worry for Beryl, who had announced earlier new puppies must be exposed to animals and people to be properly socialized. She greeted Beauregard and said, "Well, you've met Oliver and now a new member of the family, Amico. How are you, Captain? You are walking quite well now given the nature of your appendage. I have much to share with you, but was waiting to get Jed settled first. Let's move into the kitchen."

Beauregard and Ash appeared to like this room with Ash saying, "What a great space, Beryl. It's got great light but still captures New England."

Beryl's face colored a bit as she thanked him. Beauregard redirected the conversation to business. "You almost covered yourself, Beryl. I got your call at the station this morning. You called at eleven last evening. You have my cell phone. Why didn't you call me?"

Coloring slightly, Beryl answered without hesitation, "We were so busy getting Jed settled and to bed and with other business which we can discuss in a moment, I didn't even think about calling you until then. It was always on my mind, Captain, I assure you. I didn't call your cell because I was certain I would awaken you."

Beauregard took some time before answering, enough time to make Oliver appear uncomfortable. "Beryl, anything could have happened. We didn't start the increase in surveillance until this morning. Lieutenant Ayleward-Locke caught the call and ordered it. Jed's life is still in danger. What were you going to do if someone broke in here?"

Oliver, ever his mother's support, said, "Shoot him, Captain, or maybe her; I have to be politically correct now, or maybe a 'them' would work better."

Beauregard smiled. "I did notice, Beryl, you're licensed for a semi-automatic nine milli-meter gun. Actually, I'm surprised you don't have a collection."

Beryl did not explain herself. She smiled. "Why don't we sit down with Jed, if he's willing, but If he wants to wait for Attorney Cull, then I will tell you what I know to date."

Jed answered before Beauregard could get a word out. "Beryl, I'm tired. I'm going to take a nap. You and the Captain can talk in private."

The Captain thought, *smart attorney says he needs a nap, disallowing questioning without Cull. The nap routine says he was willing to speak with me but was too tired. I couldn't push him anyway. He has an attorney who's given notice his client is to speak with us only if he is present. Beryl and Jed have a partnership going here. I hate civilian involvement in my cases and Beryl is one pushy civilian. They interfere with my timing; civilian involvement always interferes with timing.*

It was slow moving Beauregard and Ash to the smaller office area. Beauregard was the one to compliment this room. "This is a nice office, Beryl. I feel comfortable in here."

She answered, "Of course you do, Captain. There's a humongous desk and recliner, lots of light, a big screen computer, a large television, Alexa for music, and it is soundproof."

Ash said, "Yup, I'm a musician and the acoustics in here are great. Do you play an instrument or sing to have invested in a room with this quality sound."

"I do a little of both, piano and singing, but the sound protection comes from some past negative experience, not worth discussing today when the Captain needs information I have."

Beauregard was grateful to get back to business. He said to Ash, "I know from the past your dissertations on music and sound baffling sometimes take hours."

He turned to Beryl. "And what don't I know you know, Beryl? And how long have you known what I don't know? And how did you discover what I don't know…"

Before he could finish his repetitive phrases, Beryl gave Beauregard, what had become obvious to Ash, a winning smile. "Just by accident, Captain, just by accident did I come upon Marthea Mattias' whereabouts. She will be here late tonight and I've invited her to stay with us."

Beauregard maintained a controlled facial expression which astonished Ash. Just in case it may be too difficult to manage for Beauregard to talk, Ash asked, "Mrs. Kent, how did you reach Marthea or know where to find her?"

Beryl spun her tale with not the slightest hint of subterfuge showing. When she explained her thinking to contact Marthea's agent, both detectives looked abashed. Ash thought, *how stupid of us. Not one of us pursued that avenue. The Austin police didn't either. No excuse. This citizen thought of it. It was that simple.*

Beryl worked diligently to lay down a line of investigation that looked simple enough for a layman to use. Her friend Nathan had assisted her in her story. She did wonder why she had to tell this fib to the police, and if in the future it could pose trouble for her. *I trust Nate. Should I? Well, I have. This is the road taken and I must follow it all the way.*

Beauregard bought her story. She felt momentarily relieved, but now had to hold them off. "Captain, when Marthea arrives and speaks with her father, I am quite certain he will be more open to us."

The Captain said, "We'll pick up the lady and bring her here. Do you have her ETA and flight number?"

Beryl sighed, responding with, "Her dad has already hired a service for the pick up at the airport. He instructed her not to go with any other person, just go with the man with the sign. I think it would work if your officers were there to follow the process. I don't know who Jed's relations or associates are. He has a new cell phone and maybe it's not monitored. What do you think?"

The Captain answered, "If his cell service is being monitored, we will have to be at the airport. It's too bad you didn't tell me earlier. We could have avoided the risk, however limited it may be."

Ash noticed Beryl's face fill with guilt; enough so he attempted to help her. "Mrs. Kent, I don't think you could have stopped Jed Mattias.

It's in an attorney's DNA to believe he can control events. Any risk assumed was not yours."

Beauregard wondered, *Ash, you have always been just too nice to be a detective. Instead of putting witnesses off their feet, you want to comfort them. Of all the witnesses I've ever met, Beryl is the one who least needs extra care. I guess it's who you are.*

The detectives left after getting all the relevant info for Marthea's entry to Bradley Airport. They promised to oversee the situation.

———

The flight from Chicago was packed. Marthea's connections from Southern California to Chicago to Hartford worked well for her. There was a one-hour layover in Chicago. Beauregard did worry about Marthea's safety in Chicago, but it was too late to assist. He thought, *even if the leakage of her coming to her father info were leaked, it would be too late for others as well as us to intervene, I hope.*

Bradley Airport's exit for passengers was a cattle call to the baggage section. It would be easy to pick her off, he thought. Detectives Lent and Tagliano stood and watched the travelers. They did notice a suit holding a sign saying 'Marthea'. Ash told Lilly, "Notice no last name here. I think that's good. The guy looks legit, but I'll put Detective Bobby Barr on him."

Ash, nor Bobby spotted Marthea, but Lilly did. She motioned to Bobby and they walked over to a girl dressed in jeans with so many rips, her shapely thighs caught the attention of all passers-by. Marthea was not playing at hiding her shape, and Bobby could not believe she was Mattias' daughter, saying, "She is a looker. What's with the funky scarf and hat covering her gorgeous hair? More coverage there than on her body. Cripes, she'll freeze outside."

Ash wanted her to remove her mask to be certain she was Marthea, but Lilly's certainty convinced him. Marthea attempted to avoid them heading for the suit with the sign. Lilly whispered loudly to Marthea, "We're the police here to protect you, Marthea. We know your dad told you to only go with the man with the sign. That's alright with us once we have a meet with him to assure he is who he says he is. So please just walk over to him and we'll have that conversation."

Without blinking, Marthea did as she was told. She asked the man with the sign who he was looking for. When he answered very quietly, 'Marthea Mattias,' she said, "Please speak with the police next to me and verify."

The man did, was very nervous, and seemed very pleased to leave Marthea in police custody, while Marthea was not as pleased. She said, "We could have stayed with Dad's plan, Detectives. Now anyone watching will know you are with me."

Ash introduced himself and said, "I'm certain they already know, Marthea. Our car outside took note of at least two suspicious cars waiting. We can't take a chance on an abduction, but we also can't move forward without any proof. Come with us as if you expected us. The cars outside will be followed."

The group continued to baggage. The young lady had two large canvas duffel bags. The detectives did not know how she had managed both until they saw her strength in lifting them off the carriage rolling rack. Ash went to help. She did accept his assistance, saying, "Thanks, it gets old after a while carrying them both, but it's what I had with me in Santa Barbara. I had to take it all with me because I'm not going back there."

They left for West Side while the police tracking the other cars followed their prey. Ash heard Detective Border call in from car A, "This one's not our guy. He was just marking time, went around, and picked up his wife and daughter." Flores in Car B said, "I've lost him. He did a run around through the airport and then hit the parking lot and exiting the other side. We got stopped by cars exiting. I'm calling in his plate now, but I'll bet it's stolen; it's a New Jersey plate number."

Ash said, "Call the Captain. He may want to double down based on your info. You're pretty sure this guy deliberately avoided you?"

"Lieutenant, the guy was a pro. I'd bet my life on it."

Marthea asked Lilly, "Sergeant Tagliano, are you going to tell me what's going on? I get these cryptic instructions from my dad; almost was an order, and he knows how poorly I do, taking orders. He sounded so different, almost as if he's not in charge. That's not my dad. I only saw him once like that and it was when mom was sick, and we knew she was dying."

Lilly replied, "You'll be with your dad in a few minutes, Marthea. I think he can explain it better. He's staying at the home of the woman who saved his life. You'll be staying there too. She's been very hospitable, and your dad is doing a lot better there than in the hospital."

"How old is this woman? Maybe my dad will like her. I've tried to get him meeting women. He is much too young to go it alone forever, but when I say something, he tells me to butt out."

"Marthea, you seem to assume your dad is fine. You do know he was seriously hurt and is recovering from his injuries? I don't think romance is on his mind. He has mainly been worried about you."

"Sergeant, from his words alone, I know he is doing well. Now he sounded in charge. Dad is back in business. If you think I wasn't worried, you're wrong. My relationship with Dad is special. We're different but alike, if you know what I mean? I love this man; he is a good man."

Lilly attempted to lessen the emotion expressed by Marthea while thinking, *if it were my dad, I'd be screaming for Mom or my brothers about taking care of Dad, but she feels just as deeply. I have some Mediterranean in me creating outbursts when Marthea does the same bit but quietly. I must learn not to judge so quickly.*

They pulled into Beryl's driveway. Marthea looked around remarking something to the effect Dad found the comforts of Atlanta in New England. She actually said, "Didn't think it possible. The house looks like a Hollywood version of New England. I thought there was a Puritan streak up here."

Ash laughed. "Marthea, for all its restraints, the citizens here commit just as many crimes and have the same vices. Never underestimate human nature. They also have a lot of goodness in them. Same everywhere from what I've seen in my travels, and I have traveled extensively with bands."

Beryl must have heard the car. She and Jed came out running to greet them. The reunion between father and daughter was moving enough that the detectives and Beryl turned their heads away to camouflage their tears. They hugged and whispered for what appeared to the onlookers as an interminably long time. Jed came to social awareness before anyone and said, "Let's move this joy inside, Baby."

Oliver easily hoisted Marthea's totes and coat upstairs to her room. Later, Beryl remembered to introduce Oliver to Marthea. The detectives left to be replaced by Captain Beauregard and Lieutenant Mason Smith followed by Attorney Norberto Cull, causing Beryl to comment quite loudly, "You could have waited for them to have a coffee and some family talk. Jed and Marthea have both been under much stress."

Cull in his usual sarcastic manner commented, "Not to worry, Beryl, maybe nothing will be said if I don't have a word with my client first."

Beauregard with a smile insisted, "Attorney Cull, your client is a victim. There's no need to be so concerned unless you think he's involved in something bigger. We've spoken about this before. You should have no concerns."

Marthea showed her warrior side. "Dad's not involved with anything criminal. Never has been and never will. What I do know from my law courses is having a lawyer does not imply guilt except in police minds who are attempting to entrap innocents."

Lieutenant Smith laughed and said, "Finally an education pays off. You are correct, Marthea, but we are looking at your dad's understanding of the crime. He was a victim and his interpretation is important. We need his help to find the perpetrators and your dad said he was willing to help once he knew you were found safely."

Beryl suggested Mr. Cull and Jed move to her den for a few minutes while she brought out some refreshments. Marthea wanted to stay with her dad but Oliver whispered, "Can't go in there with them, Marthea. You'd jeopardize any legal protections your dad would have."

He did not have to explain the reasons why. Marthea nodded she understood. Marthea said, "May I help you in the kitchen, Beryl?"

"Welcome, both you and Oliver. We'll set up in the kitchen. It'll be easier."

Amico followed them, already aware the kitchen may mean food droppings. Marthea said, "What a wondrous kitchen you have. It has everything I could ever want, a view of the woods from those large windows, an oversized fieldstone fireplace that looks natural and not designer icky, all the appliances anyone would want, an enormous serving center made from old distressed pine, and a big oak table with comfortable chairs. Are you a designer, Beryl?"

Ignoring her question, Beryl said, "I'm interested in all surroundings everywhere. This kitchen I could control, so I guess it's just me. Thank you for noticing. Also notice three or four people can operate in here. I was smart enough to plan for folks giving me assistance. Do you cook, Marthea?"

"I do and I'm really good at Southern, Mexican, and Southwestern style foods. Show me what you have, and I can do something quick with it. Just watch."

"You go, Marthea. I'll watch and learn."

A shocked Oliver remarked, "Marthea, this is quite a revelation for me. My mom never gives up the kitchen for me or anyone."

"Not true, Oliver, your dad and stepdads all helped me. Great chefs. Maybe that was the attraction, why I married. I never thought how important a chef in the kitchen was to me."

"Naw, that's not it, Mom. Laurencio was a great chef and you threw him right out."

"He was just a friend, Oliver. Marthea, Oliver is often outrageous in his assessment of me. Please don't listen. Just what are you going to do with those, Marthea?"

"I think I'm making a fried rice and some chili trimmed chicken with a side of guacamole and toasted cheese naan."

"You can't. It's mixed media. I'm more of an art purist."

"Leave it to me, Beryl, you like food, you'll love this. Nothing wrong with Chinese, Peruvian, Mexican, and Indian foods working in concert."

Oliver and Amico both appeared to be salivating at the scents produced by the artist Marthea in the kitchen.

***

"Alright, Jed, your vacation is over. Marthea is well. Let's keep you and her safe. I know you have more memories. Get them out now before Beauregard takes you into protective custody as a witness."

"Don't bullshit me, Norbie. It will never happen. It'd be newsworthy. Just think, 'Well-known Atlanta attorney victim of assault arrested as witness in his own case.'"

"Beauregard is not beyond a little press. Think about it, Jed. You want press. Go to it. Eventually, you'll have to fess up on what you think is going on. Do not tell me you don't know. Your memory is back; I can tell."

Norbie waited through thirty seconds of silence before Jed started on a long tale. "I don't remember everything, but know I was deeply suspicious of a corporation called 'Ralrow.' I did some investigation through a PI but the report wasn't in yet. Grace should have given it to me by now. She must have received it. My partner Harry accepted a client he should not have taken. Her case presented nothing but problems from the onset. I blame myself for not monitoring his activities more closely. He was looking quite nervous before his death and avoided the monthly partners' meeting, which he had never done before. Harry may have been a wild man, but he was a superior attorney. He said he was sick. He'd not been out sick in all the years we'd been together. Not Harry. He loved action and the good life. His death, in my mind, was questionable. I tried to investigate. I think I did. I formed some conclusions based on my gut and my interpretation of Harry's personality and potential for certain types of actions. I checked on his new cases when he didn't show up for the meeting. He put in a new case and then tried to take it out a few days later, but you cannot fuck with our program. You have to be IT specialists to completely erase something and I'm not really certain they can.

"I met with friends of the client in question, because I couldn't reach the client with the info in the file. There was an address. I went there and the house was in disarray. I didn't know if her husband had found her or if she had packed and left the place that way to get him in trouble. I questioned what I saw, because I called it in to the police and was told I was the second caller. She may have called the police herself to support a case of fear and abuse. Leaving her house, I found I picked up a tail. I'm not a novice, Norbie, I know when I'm being followed. I worked hard to duck him. Then I got a call. Word for word, he said, 'Do nothing on this case or you will be planted next to Harry.' I told him to 'fuck off,' but took a round-about route home. I called into the PI Harry had hired, but it was late. He may have gotten back to me, or maybe he was frightened off. I didn't get a call back before it all went off the rails."

"What do you mean, Jed?"

"Back at my home, a woman called me. Said she was the Marsh lady. I don't believe it now nor did I then. I have really good instincts for liars most of the time. She was not truthful; I just didn't know how untruthful. She arranged for me to fly to Newark for a conference with her husband Donald Arrow, who was willing to settle the financial arrangements for his divorce. I was given an address, a hotel known to me in New Jersey. I should not have gone, but I was on a trail to figure out what happened to Harry.

"I met with Arrow's attorney. He wore a two-thousand-dollar suit and gave me a glossy business card stating 'Attorney Bob Brown.' When I questioned him on the whereabouts of his client Donald Arrow, saying I expected to meet with them both, he insisted he was authorized to negotiate for Mr. Arrow. He had a letter from his client. I went along with it. He was generally professional and quite agreeable, not what I expected. We went to lunch. He was an interesting fellow with a great legal background. University of Virginia Law School with a previous graduate degree in finance from Wharton at the University of Pennsylvania, impressive throughout the conversation. He took a call from his client, or so he said. I listened to his side of the conversation. He paused putting the mute button on and asked if I was willing to meet his client at his home in Massachusetts saying it was not a long flight by helicopter. By this time, I'd been lulled into a false comfort zone. I completely dismissed the idea the woman's call was suspicious. I agreed to go, thinking I could get rid of this case and simultaneously ease my mind about Harry's accident; hoping it wasn't connected.

"A car came for me the next morning, but Bob was not a passenger, and I expected him to accompany me. The driver said he'd been driven to the airport the night before and would meet me in Massachusetts at the destination. I asked him if we were landing outside Boston. He replied closer to Connecticut. At the airport several men greeted me. The pilot was noncommittal which is not my experience as a business person passenger flying in a small craft. I thought he was bored. Two men introduced themselves as working for Mr. Donald Arrow. Other than their excellent physiques, they were quite professional; one said he was in marketing and the other in finance. I cannot for the life of me remember their names. We boarded and a third passenger entered. Then, I got nervous. He looked like a cleaned-up hitman. They asked me to sit in the co-pilot seat telling me Bob said I had history as a pilot. I never discussed flying with Bob. How did he know? They must have done a resume search on me.

"There had been a letter left for me at the hotel that morning. I didn't open it thinking it was from my office. I shut my phone and computer off in the evening. Otherwise, I'd never get any sleep. The morning before the limousine came to get me, I tried to get hold of Marthea. She always answers, but I thought she might be working in a sound studio or something. I'm not certain how all that stuff works. When we were in flight, I opened the envelope and found a scrap of paper with a note about Marthea. They all watched me open it. They knew what the note said. I took the note, ripped a section off it, and scribbled 'ff Arrow.' I put the ripped section in my small pocket. I knew then, and they knew I knew, this event was not going to end to my benefit. I said to the pilot, 'What the fuck gives with these three? Where are we going?' He told me we were headed towards Western Massachusetts and Northern Connecticut.

"He would receive a message on the destination shortly. The other three watched my every move. When I tried to make a call, the hood took my cell. He pushed me back in my seat, searched me and emptied my pockets. He must have been connected to my brain as I was trying to figure how I could take control of the flight. I realized I was the only other one, in addition to the pilot, to have flight experience. One of the men rightly said something to the effect helicopters were the last place to have a fight. The hood motioned me out of my seat to the interior. I was not unhappy with the change in seating. I knew for some reason they wanted me frightened or dead. I was already frightened for my daughter's safety and mine but did not want to die. I had to find Marthea. They'd gone too far."

Norbie said, "Just how did you get out of there? Look, I know a bit about helicopters, Jed. I don't know how you jumped out alive."

"I watched carefully the two suits, not the hood. I wanted him lulled into a sense of false security. I could see he thought I was a wimp. One of the suits was taking all the calls. He was the supposed marketing guy for Donald Arrow. As we got closer, they looked out the window and I could see we were going lower in a more rural area with big homes and lots of acreage. As we were landing, I waited for the pilot to open the door. I thought he may have been military collecting soldiers from bad situations, but I could see he wouldn't open the door until it landed. What no one noticed is, I had grabbed the remote opener when I was up front. It was easy for me. I knew what it looked like and the pilot left it out in the open. As we were low to the ground, I opened the door and threw everyone off balance. The hood took his gun out too late and he was off balance. Further, I'm certain he was uncertain as to the safety of firing in the enclosed space. I had undone my seatbelt and was in position to jump out and up to mitigate my potential injuries. Not that I did that well! I lost consciousness for a minute from the trauma. I'd landed on bushes, strong ones which helped break my fall. When I came to, I looked around, saw the big house, and knew not to go there. I climbed down and I was not doing well. I took my note from my pocket and hid them in the birdhouse pole thinking I was not going to make it, but there'd be a trail for the police. The rest is really quite hazy in my memory. I struggled walking away from the house and avoiding the road in front. When I entered another wood, I didn't know if I'd ever make it out of the wood I entered. I listened for dogs or people sounds. I fell against a tree and almost passed out, but thought of Marthea. I had to continue. I headed toward the back of a home when I realized it wasn't occupied and then headed over here and then I saw Beryl. I went to hug her in gratitude, but instead, collapsed on her."

19
Holiday Houseful

Beryl sat at her spy table seat, crunching on a toasted croissant splashed with sour cherry jam from Turkey. And she did spy a fox with the most lustrous furry tail strut through a corner of her property. She looked over to Amico who was still in his crate snoozing and hoped he'd stay that way. Amico did not bark often, but when he did, he did so with vengeance. She thought, *fox normally breed later. This one is a male. Why is it in the animal world the male is the showiest of all? Beautiful red cardinal birds are males, while the ladies are dressed in drab. This guy is a show-stopper, but if there are foxes out here, then there are coyotes. Amico would not be safe from coyotes. I'll have to expand my fenced yard portion to give Amico a good run. I have a houseful of guests, still it is so quiet. Jocelyn will be here with her friend by noon. Enjoy this quiet, Beryl, it's your last moment of peace.*

Beauregard and Ash spent a long time with Jed and Norbie last evening. By the time I got the full story, Jed was exhausted. I suppose Marthea and I made it difficult with all our questions. Jed said we asked more questions than Beauregard or Norbie. Oliver just listened. I need to be more like Oliver who is more careful about involvement. I do see his focus on Marthea and he is not steering clear of being involved with her. Is it a good thing? A musician and an engineer; talk about differences, but I like her. They are on their own. I will not interfere. Besides, it's time my kids made some commitments in life.

And the house guests started staggering in one at a time, leaving Beryl busy cooking up a storm. She said a good morning to Jed and, "You look much healthier this morning. I guess seeing Marthea was the best medicine for you. That and her cooking a wonderful, albeit unusual, dinner for us all. These omelets will look quite ordinary in comparison."

"I like ordinary, Beryl. I'm an ordinary guy. I have three calls from Grace Grantley, my law partner. She would like to come here to get the rest of the story. Do you mind?"

"Ordinarily it would not be a problem, Jed, but my daughter Jocelyn and her boyfriend are arriving. They will fill the room. You know what I mean. Could we wait until the day after Christmas?"

"Fine, actually, a lot better for me. Grace takes over and sometimes exhausts me. Another day or two before I have to answer her questions looks good to me."

Beryl served breakfast with Marthea and Oliver assisting. Beryl never witnessed Oliver setting the table before and placing napkins and utensils in perfect order. Before she had a chance to make a fresh comment to him, the bell rang. Jocelyn was here early.

Jocelyn entered with a big guy behind her carrying three bags at once compared to the one large bag she held. Kisses, introductions, and hugs followed. Beryl thought, *she looks wonderful and happy. I'll have to get to know more about Sam, her friend. He is not what I expected. What did I expect? Oliver gave me the impression he would be a page out of the local gym. This guy is good looking and in good shape, but he is just a nice guy with his own financial firm. Does he know what Jocelyn's like? She is pretty responsive to him. Hell, both my kids showing interest at the same time. God, why must the sun come out all at once after a dearth of years? Thank You. I didn't mean to question Your motives. I know better than to question.*

There was music and food and fun. Different ideas on Fauci, COVID vaccine, Russian and Chinese collusion, abortion and other issues were discussed without the fear of killing each other when views varied. Background stories were shared by all but Beryl, who felt her life was novel length, not short story limited. Laughter and gaiety abounded. Amico was held by all, as his people discussed the importance of socialization with humans for puppy training. They decided Jed and Marthea and Oliver would not attend Christmas Eve services, while the others would. Oliver explained, "Jed really must get some rest. He is not healthy enough to go out in the cold. I'll stay with him and Marthea. You all go ahead."

As they were leaving, Nathan showed up at the door, much to Beryl's surprise. He said, "You mentioned you'd be going for services later. I hope you don't mind if I join in, Beryl; I am alone. Christmas is not a time to be by oneself."

Oliver smirked. "Welcome, Nathan. Come for dinner tomorrow as well."

Beryl hesitated, then smiled. "Of course, Nathan, you are welcome."

She introduced Nathan to the others while thinking, *I want to kill Oliver. He thinks he's being funny. Hoping Nathan will keep me from watching his blooming relationship with Jed's daughter. I do not appreciate Oliver's sense of humor today.*

Christmas morning was filled with a blaze of tissue paper and wrappings strewn about the family room. Beryl was grateful for Oliver and Sam's presence. Two obsessive compulsive guys were truly her best present of the day. If it were up to Marthea and Jocelyn, the debris could stay there until all conversation was over. Beryl thought, *why can't there be more moderation in personalities? Just when did men become the neater of the sexes. My first husband was obsessive, but my second two were quite laid back. What is that noise? Why is Amico barking up a storm?*

Beryl walked from the family room to the kitchen to look out her window. No foxes came into view but there were two uniforms running into her woods. She paused for a moment, then shut the door to the kitchen aware her guests could not see the goings-on from the dining room. One problem existed, Amico barked incessantly. She brought him to Oliver and whispered, "Shut him up, and don't let anyone leave this room."

He did not question her and allowed her to return to the kitchen for dessert knowing something was up. Beryl thought, *I know he knows about Jed, but still, despite being so technically trained, he is intuitive, and knows something new is up. Now why today would the police be searching my woods? They saw something. We heard nothing. If what they saw is a danger, thank God they were here.*

From one corner of the room, she had a complete view of the area but could see nothing. She opened a side window and could hear tousling in the woods. She waited. She thought, *they are wrestling with someone. The voices are getting louder.*

The two officers were dragging a man from the woods. He was bleeding bringing déjà vu to Beryl. This man appeared seriously hurt and one officer had a long knife in his hand. She whispered loudly, "You guys don't carry knives as weapons, yet all three of you have blood on you. I can't call the police. They're here already. How do I keep this from my guests?"

All secrecy possibilities were gone when she heard sirens. She walked into the dining room and announced, "Dessert will be late. There has been a prowler outside. The police are on it, so please stay inside. I'll have a conversation with them, but a crowd would not be helpful."

All but Nathan stayed seated. He headed towards the back outside door as she moved to stop him. He quietly said, "I can't have Beauregard see me here. I invited myself today to protect you all. There was white noise out there. Jed could be removed easily on Christmas. I didn't think the police could stop it. I thought I could, but they're the ones who did. I'll quietly leave, Beryl, okay?"

"No way, Nathan. The police are not going to question us; I won't let them inside. Where's your car? They will take plate numbers."

"I am not worried. My car's parked a couple of blocks over. I walked. I knew they had a watch out on your home."

"Nathan, this trust thing is not easy for me. How did you know an attempt would be made today and who is doing it?"

"Beryl, I don't know who is doing it. I know it's bigger than you or Beauregard envision. I heard from sources someone had hired an out-of-town guy to put Jed down, not by name but by description. It could only have been Jed. My question is why? Why kill Jed now when they must know the police and his attorney have his story? You heard nothing unusual in Jed's story. It was not a good story but innocuous. The lawyer, 'Bob,' needs to be identified, if he is even a licensed attorney. The others are associated with your neighbor. The helicopter landed on DesCartes' property; that is enough to bring in DesCartes for serious questioning, but I think Beauregard is about to get a call telling him not to bring him in. He will be wild and is known for not taking 'no' well. I have to conclude, Beryl, either Jed is lying, or he doesn't remember something, or his file from Harry has something important in it he did not recognize. I think we should start with Jed later, if you can get him alone with us. Look, I'll tell our crowd I have a couple of calls to make. I'll make them upstairs, if it's okay with you?"

"We will together talk with Jed alone, once I get rid of the police. I don't think they will even try to enter on this holiday. I may be wrong, but don't think so."

Beryl motioned to one of the uniforms standing by her drive. He came over and apologized for the problem. She questioned the name and purpose of the intruder. "Officer, why on earth would someone try to break into my house when we were clearly all at home? Who is this foolish man and were, or are we in any danger?"

The officer appeared confused. "Ms. Kent, you do know we've been keeping an eye on your home because you have a houseguest who is at risk, don't you?"

Playing ignorance quite well, she answered, "It is Christmas. I am surprised. His name please, Officer, I saw he was badly hurt as were two of your men. I must be able to tell my company they are safe, that you have caught the culprit. Are you satisfied you have him? Do we have to worry any longer?"

"Here is Detective Smith. You had better address your concerns to him."

Mason Smith greeted Beryl. They spoke for ten minutes. He had no information for her, but promised the Captain would be by in the morning, saying, "I know you saw the skirmish in the woods, but I am certain you can't be a witness. Detective Lent says he was told you were looking out your kitchen window and you were alone. I don't think we have to involve any of you in this assault and maybe death. You could not see what happened and none of your guests were in your kitchen. Don't worry, we still have your back, but be careful."

"Detective Smith, can't you at least tell me the name of the man?"

"We don't have it yet. We're certain he's not local. Tomorrow, Ma'am, tomorrow."

"How can you know if you don't know his identity? Did you know something before he arrived informing you of the impending attack? Early info indicates outside perpetrators."

The Lieutenant smiled. "Don't know anything about early info; if you do, Ms. Kent, please share your source with the Captain tomorrow."

Beryl clinched her teeth in disappointment and thought, *who are you kidding, Lieutenant? You guys did nothing but drive-bys yesterday, but today you caught someone in my back woods. How'd you know enough to go there today? Were you up by DesCartes and saw him enter the woods there?*

How many were involved in this plan of attack? Why aren't we included in the info when we are the potential victims? How involved is Nathan and is his involvement in our favor? He is looking too good for an ordinary man. Be careful, Beryl. Take care of yourself.

Returning to her guests inside the home Beryl was forced to reinforce the bogus story about a prowler in the neighborhood. She reported a neighbor called them and because Jed was at her house, they were concerned. He gave the police a difficult time and was injured in the process. She fielded all the questions while noticing Nathan standing at the hallway door. He changed the conversation with skill fooling all but Jed and Oliver. With grace he raised a bottle of bourbon which was in his hand and said, "Over ice with a slice of orange, Beryl?"

Beryl gave a positive nod, thinking, *you got what you wanted, big man, I fielded the questions and you stayed hidden. Now you're all charm. Not certain what to think about this.*

More presents were opened. Jocelyn had brought a large assortment of art-related gifts which in Beryl's mind appeared to run the gamut from tacky to wondrous. The tacky ones apparently were quite in vogue. She knew because of loud cries yelling 'on point.' Nathan had naturally gravitated sitting next to her on the couch. He said, "What a great group you've assembled here, Beryl. You are easy and hospitable and your family and Jed and Marthea feel it. Me, not so much, because you question everything I say and do. I will explain my life shortly; I just can't now, but please hold back on determining judgment. You would be wrong."

"Nathan, you asked for three months. I'll do the three months, but you and I know we'll have ample information a lot sooner. This third attempt on Jed is all the data I need. He knows something about which you know something that I and Beauregard don't know. Beauregard and I are interested in his safety. Any additional mystery solving is a bonus. You and others, and I'm guessing governmental, are interested in solving a big criminal endeavor with Jed as the central bait. You could help me more, but your allegiance prevents you. I find it disappointing."

"I can't argue with your logic, Beryl, but life is not linear. Logic is sometimes flawed despite it having the look of truth. Just wait. Think about what Jed knows but doesn't know he knows. I'll go with the theory; I do not know what he knows, but I am certain it is relevant."

"Nathan, we have not seen the files Norbie Cull saw. He would listen to us, but he couldn't share with us and you don't want to interact with us. Grace Grantley may be willing to speak with me, not you."

"Beryl, be careful with Grace, she has sharp teeth. I am uncertain of her ethics. There is a case their firm was involved with, that hit the press. I heard through the grapevine she was furious with Harry. She thought he was a major player and should have seen the manager was a thief. She was behind the partners not joining the lawsuit against the managing partner. They then took their losses. Goes against Harry's normal practice. He was a street fighter. Jed always had more class. Could it be connected? Can you meet with Grace and see if any of the litigants or investors involved in the suit has a connection to something else?"

"Nathan, you want me to research for your interests. You tell me nothing, but I'm to do your work for you. You must know of a connection. Unlike me, I dream of a connection whereas you need evidence to proceed. I don't require evidence. If my gut and brain together feel a connection, I go with it. I will follow your evidence, despite you not sharing what you know. This is an unbalanced relationship. Maybe I won't share what I discover."

"Look, I'm here to protect you and Jed. I have also shared with you before. It's the best I can do now, Beryl."

"Do you think Grace will respond to me? She was not invited here. Jed did not want her here at Christmas. I thought it was inhospitable but honored his wishes. She could think I didn't want her."

"Beryl, Grace wants Jed as husband material. I don't think she loves him. I know he doesn't love her and has had several public arguments at firm meetings on business details with her. She would marry him to control the firm. This firm is successful, and despite the loss of Harry, will thrive at a high level."

Jocelyn interrupted their tete-a-tete. "Come on, join us. 'A Christmas Story' is on your awesomely capitalistic television. Just how big is it, Mom? Looks to me equal to the size of one wall of my condo living room."

"You do watch it, don't you? I don't need your socialist review of my purchases, darling. Just enjoy. We'll watch the movie; it is my favorite Christmas movie. It brings us back to what appears to me a simpler time when relationships were taken for granted. Maybe taking them for granted is an equivalent of enormous trust. I'd like to think so."

"Nathan," said Jocelyn, "watch out when my mom waxes philosophies of living. She can go on. The problem is we can't shut off her words of wisdom. They're like a song that goes on and on in your head. Can't get rid of it."

Beryl moved to her study and called Grace Grantley. When Grace answered her phone, there was a great deal of noise in the background. Beryl thought she may be in a bar, wondering why so much noise when gatherings had been limited by the Governor. She questioned what time Grace was available for a visit the next day. Her answer was curious. Grace said, "Everything's okay over there; you having a quiet Christmas dinner?"

"Lovely here, Grace. There was a prowler in the neighborhood, but a neighbor spotted him and police took care of the situation. Are you in the Casino? There is so much background noise."

"Not now, I'm at a house party. It's totally against the Governor's order, but no one including me is the slightest bit concerned."

"Oh, Grace, I don't think, given your exposure to so many people, I can allow your visit until you get tested. Jed is still not in great health and his lungs won't be completely healed for six months according to his doctor."

"That's ridiculous, Beryl. You have family there visiting and exposing him to who knows what."

"Not true, Grace, we've all been masked and staying apart at least three feet with no hugging. Get tested. You have enough juice to get a test. The turn-around for results is no more than two days. My request is prudent. Please get tested. I know Jed will want very much to see you."

Grace argued to no avail and in disgust clicked off her cell, leaving Beryl thinking, *just why did I take this stand? Because I am uncomfortable. This woman asking me if everything is okay here bothers me. Yes, it does. Why not a 'How're you all doing' or 'Is Jed enjoying himself' or whatever? She asks if it's all quiet here. Her saying that particular phrase was forced. She didn't use her free-flowing fast talk. Grace makes me feel uneasy. What is wrong with me? I question Nathan, despite his obvious complying with most of my wishes. Am I ever satisfied or always suspicious?*

Beryl watched her family and guests watching the famous good feeling movie which she was certain would eventually be cancelled by the new cancel culture movement. For now, she felt a sense of peace. She caught Nathan's glances, and motioned him to move to the kitchen. No one noticed their disappearance from the room. Pouring a coffee for them both, Beryl reviewed her conversation with Grace Grantley. "Beryl, did she say those exact words?"

"Yes, Nathan, and they did not ring true to me."

"It could be she has her ear to the ground in the finance world and heard something. Could also be, she's worried about involvement with a questionable client. Perhaps we have not asked Grace the right questions. By putting her off in that manner, we now can't ask."

"You think I made a big mistake. I do not feel she is being truthful. Further, I think she knew there was a potential action against him today. My gut says it."

"Beryl, don't worry. Your action may be good for us. What files does Grace have which are not available to us through Jed or his attorney?"

"None I know."

"Let's talk with Jed after the movie. I'll pull him aside. You tell everyone he is resting in your office, bring him some tea, and we'll go over them with you. He trusts you now."

"Nathan, can I trust you?"

There was no answer. He just stared at her, his face expressing sadness. Ignoring his emoting, she agreed to the plan but explained whatever they learned would be given to Captain Beauregard. He did not disagree.

Jed was not adverse to discussing his cases. He understood their concern, saying, "Look, I know there wasn't a prowler reported by the neighbors. I knew right away your story was bogus. It's difficult for me not to be in control, but Beryl, I trust you. Nathan, we've only met today. If Beryl says you are on my side, I believe it. Grace gave me the list of Harry's clients and they are as I remember them. I went over them last night when I had trouble sleeping. I felt much emotion working on these cases. If you think there's something in them, help me sort them out."

The three spent several hours going over Harry's cases. The divorce case was still the most interesting because it brought Jed to New Jersey. Beryl asked, "Where is the list of investors and litigants in the mentoring case?"

Jed said, "Beryl, I don't think there is a connection, but I have all the names here in one of the court filings. We tried to suppress publicity on the names, but couldn't. It's here. Give me a minute."

The three-hundred investors included national and Georgia local business types. Some were corporations and some were individuals. Harry and Jed were individuals listed. Beryl scanned the names first and handed the list to Nathan, saying, "See if you notice what I did?"

He did and nodded, while Jed grabbed the list. He practically sputtered, "It's all connected, isn't it? How could I not have seen this?"

20
Chicken or the Egg

Petra had spent Boxing Day morning returning gifts for Jim, her mother, and baby Carlotta. She felt guilty for being late at the station. She was on Saturday duty, but Mason told her he'd cover for her if she could finish in time to allow him an early exit. His mother was holding court for the holiday for friends and relatives who were unable to attend Christmas festivities. He remarked, "Petra, I don't know who was left to invite. Seems to me the whole world was there yesterday."

"Yeah, all but us. Our family gatherings are much smaller. I think we should join you next year. I'd have a lot less work to do."

"Listen, Petra, to be a domestic goddess, it takes time and energy."

"Never going to happen. I'm good at investigating, not searching for recipes and peeling vegetables. All the activities I like did not meet my mom's standards."

Petra's afternoon was spent fielding phone calls and making one house site visit when patrol had a domestic with the wife wielding a kitchen knife and chasing the husband outside the house to the entertainment of the neighbors. One neighbor called patrol and patrol called the detective unit. Petra took fifteen minutes to get the situation in order. Child services were called and an arrest made with the husband insisting it was not a big thing and arguing with the neighbors.

Returning to the station, Petra felt some relief doing paperwork. She thought, *this is not normal for me. I like being out in the field, but Christmas is not the time to witness domestic violence. I just was not ready for seeing three kids crying while the mom was on something and carrying on. She insisted her husband did not buy her the present she hinted all month she wanted. Hell, husbands don't hear hints with the exception of my Jim, who analyzes every word I say and never forgets. Wait a minute, lookee here. The Captain is going to love this.*

Petra tried to get hold of the Captain, but his phone was either turned off or he did not have it with him. Both possibilities in her mind were highly unlikely. She called the Captain's admin assistant Millie at home. Millie explained she thought Mona had dragged the Captain to her cousin's engagement luncheon, but he would be in the office by four to pick up some files. Petra waited impatiently while doing a whirlwind tour of cleaning her desk of debris some of which was three weeks old. She heard, as Mason was leaving, his greeting Beauregard.

Petra entered the Captain's office without knocking which, even for her, was unusual, saying, "Captain, wait until you see this."

She was waving papers at him. He surprised her, saying, "Lieutenant, is this the list of investors in the swindle our victim invested in?"

"You know already? Who told you?"

"Slow down, Lieutenant. We will find out in two minutes. Our interloper, Beryl Kent has the same list and certainly has some ideas about it. You and I should wait to hear hers first; maybe we'll learn something."

"Captain, it's pretty clear there's the connection you asked about before."

"Be patient, Petra, I agree with you, but which came first the chicken or the egg?"

"Huh!"

"It's time for a visit."

Beryl was expecting the Captain and greeted him and Lieutenant Aylewood-Locke warmly. The visitors refused coffee when offered.

Directed to her study, they found Jed there with his attorney, Norbie Cull. After the two asked about Jed's health and holiday, the usual banter between the Captain and Norbie played-out with Petra intercepting occasionally. Cull initiated a change in mood, saying, "Rudy, Jed and Beryl have some insights into the attacks on him, and you need to be in on the conversation."

"Jed, I'm interested in what you have to say. Please tell me."

Jed referred to Beryl, giving her credit for furthering the search into his legal records. Beryl made a grimace equal to the Captain's, while Norbie smirked at the pair's discomfort thinking, *what a match. She wanted to hide her input because Rudy would not approve. They had better learn to accept each other because they do work well together. I bet Beryl has never kept to rules in her whole life as she has with Rudy. It means she respects him. He's annoyed because she's not police and she doesn't know her place, but he has learned her insights are helpful and needed. I love watching this drama. I wonder how much Rudy knows of what Beryl and Jed have learned. I think Jed's legal and maybe physical health risks are over.*

"Captain, I don't know if Grace Grantley was shared Harry Leonard's itinerary by him before his death or his efforts in reviewing his current legal cases. Jed went through them and found some interesting links. There is a lawsuit pending based on what was originally considered to be a non-profit corporation involving a financially decent portfolio wherein investors would get a normal return on their invested money which was at risk, plus an equity position in the businesses invested. The money would support new entrepreneurial endeavors. The investor's piece of equity in the businesses developed could be a windfall if the businesses were successful. The staffer and a board member colluded in a scheme wherein about thirty million dollars was found unaccountable or missing. Harry and Jed were investors and victims of the embezzlement scheme. The board member involved in the scheme was a business friend. Some of the investors sued the board, and various government agencies became involved. Arrests were made and it hit the papers big time. What we noticed last night in the list of victims, perpetrators, and invested businesses were connections. Before I go any further and bore you, are you already aware of this?"

Petra said, "We have all those reports. What connections do you see?"

"Did you do correlations between the sets of names on all the lists?"

Petra nodded affirmatively but did not answer. Norbie said, "Then you don't need Jed and Beryl's assistance."

The Captain replied, "Stop the nonsense, Mr. Cull. Have your client tell us what you discerned. It's police business."

Beryl reported, "The date of the discovery of the embezzlement was almost two years ago. Publicity about it blew up just six months ago. Harry had a PI investigating. One of the results overlooked by Grace and Jed was the list of names of individual owners of corporations whose money was taken. There were three hundred investors and eighty percent were corporations. In the list of corporations, major owners were overlooked at first. Harry would have spotted the important names if he had lived. The PI was not discreet, and in his report, he states he informed all parties he was investigating for Harry Leonard, one of the victims. He also states Harry told him to use his name, because folks trusted him to do the right thing and would share information more easily. Jed will tell you he was surprised at Harry's instructions to the PI, because Harry had told Jed he'd keep out of the suit.

"Marlene Greene and David Spencer were listed as managing partners of corporations losing big time, to the tune of fifteen million. We can't believe your fatal accident case with their deaths is not connected. Those corporations were not connected to the Fund staffer or with the corporations getting money that was subverted. Jed does not believe they knew either of the two thieves. The next interesting fact is Ralrow, LLC was an entrepreneur applicant receiving sixteen million. If you remember, Ralrow is the company registered as owner of the Jed's event helicopter and has gone bankrupt. The husband of the wife in the big-time divorce case who brought Jed to West Mass was the president of Arrow Management. Who is Donald Arrow? Where is Alexia March Raleigh? Your cases are connected. Now the question is why? Ralrow received big money and went defunct. It is listed as one of the suspect companies receiving funds. Suspect because their going belly-up was suspicious. How are they connected to the two dead accident victims who appear to have lost a bundle in the Fund scam?"

The Captain responded, "Thank you, Beryl. The Lieutenant and I were on the same path, but missed Ralrow's receipt of such a large amount from the Fund. We do have further research on the companies losing the most and their connections as well as the companies who received the most and their current financial health. We'll get back to you. Jed, we will keep a patrol on this house."

Jed asked, "You think I'm still not safe? What else could I tell you?"

The Captain said, "The devil's in the details, Jed. You as an attorney understand this fact. This is big. I don't think my police department is the sole agency involved. Where did the money go? Was there a common receiver of lost funds? Why go to this much trouble when the Feds would eventually be involved?"

Attorney Norbie Cull mused aloud, "There was not supposed to be an obvious theft of funds, Rudy. The whole Fund was a source for money laundering, don't you think? No one would be the wiser. New businesses receiving dollars from a legitimate source to be paid back with the Fund as a new legitimate investor in each new company. It is a perfect scam."

Beryl's face lit up. "It makes sense to me. The staffer and the board member screwed up the plan by embezzling all the money and in such large amounts; thereby ensuring eventual discovery. How was the discovery first made? And my big question is why are the staffer and the board member still alive while Marlene, David, and Harry are dead and three attempts have been made on Jed's life?"

The Lieutenant said, "Since there is so much scrutiny on the case, they are temporarily protected, but, if I were them, I would not get too comfortable. The big question still is how were David, Marlene, and Harry at such risk? I think they were investigating into their losses and got too close; the same reason for chasing Jed. Someone was certain Jed knew what Harry knew. Foolish of them. Alexia Marsh Raleigh upset the applecart and Harry's pursuing her divorce led to Jed's involvement. I hope Alexia has a good hiding place."

Beauregard said, "They may have been investigating their losses, Lieutenant, or their companies could be a part of the laundering conspiracy. The question is DesCartes' involvement. They were there at his home before their deaths. Why were they there? Were they investigating together to discover who caused their losses? Or were they complaining about the investigation into the Fund and the potential for their personal risk. We don't have an answer."

Beryl asked the Captain, "Do you think the staffer and partner on the board are connected to murders? I don't think they know anything about them, but I do think they stole from some important actors, putting a magnifying glass on their criminal activities."

Rudy said, "I think you may be right, but it does not mean they won't pay a price for interfering in criminal business."

Under her breath, the Lieutenant said, "Criminals angry with other criminals for interfering with their criminal activities. There has to be some standard."

Captain Beauregard and the Lieutenant left, but not before the Captain thanked Beryl, Norbie, and Jed for their assistance. He did not say he would get back to them.

As Norbie Cull tried to reassure his client and Beryl the police would do everything within their power to protect Jed, Beryl interrupted. "You don't believe for a minute West Mass police are in this alone, or that they will not get assistance from others. The minute he starts vigilantly investigating the Fund embezzlement case, he'll be closed down."

"Hold on, Beryl, are you saying Rudy Beauregard could be closed down? If so, you're completely off. Rudy does not shut down for anyone. I know that from experience. Trust him. On another note, you appear to be well informed about the Fraud case. Who are you talking to?"

"Why would you think that?"

"Whoever your source is, watch yourself. Do not give away facts Beauregard does not want known now, and maybe you should stay away from further investigation. Multiple murders investigation by a layperson spells trouble."

Cull saw Beryl was infuriated by his statements, but he pursued his rationale. In the end, Beryl realized Cull was not trying to control her, but was concerned about her safety. She agreed to somewhat limit her future doings, as she called them, but had no intention of doing what she said.

After Cull left, Beryl and Jed reviewed the lists again. She asked Jed, "Does your firm have search programs for seeing complete data on folks, such as old friends, colleagues, employment, involvement in civil and criminal cases, from which we could scan for connections, Jed?"

"It does, but Grace would quickly discover what I was doing. I can ask Jodi, one of the paralegals, to do the work and keep it quiet. She doesn't particularly care for Grace."

"Why so, Jed?"

"Grace is notorious for being in everyone's business and Jodi thinks she interferes enough to create trouble with staff. Maybe she does, but Grace is such a worker, Harry and I would never correct her. Everything with Grace is an argument."

"Why was she not on top of Harry taking on Alexia Raleigh, Jed?"

"I wondered about her not seeing it, particularly when there was evidence of his meeting on the firm calendar. Grace loved to know what the two of us were doing day to day."

"Jed, I told Grace she could not visit you until she got tested for COVID. She was angry. It will delay her visit for a minimum of two days. Please support my action if she calls you."

"Dealing with Grace is always tiring. I'm not ready for her. I can wait a few days."

"What are the differences in general terms between Grace's renumeration as a partner compared to yours and Harry's?"

"Beryl, you have your finger on Grace's bone of contention with us as partners. It's not unusual. Harry and I developed the firm with most of the clients. Other attorneys and Grace also bring in clients, but we do the heavy lifting for big numbers. Our attorneys, don't get me wrong, do a great deal of work to earn their keep. They do good work on behalf of our clients as well as for their own. Grace is an attorney manager and good at it. Harry and I rebelled against doing the everyday managing of attorneys and staff. To be truthful, neither he nor I were particularly good at it. We got by, but Grace was better at keeping the noise down. I am a genius at creating workable systems, not so great at every day follow through. Grace received compensation for her work as manager at close to half a million a year, plus a percentage for clients she brought into the firm, and ten percent of our net. Grace makes good money and couldn't do as well elsewhere. We thought she was worth every penny on most days. Sometimes, her controlling trait got out of hand, but on the whole, it works. Right now, she is needed one hundred percent."

"Jed, did Grace want more money? Was there contention about her future?"

Jed was slow in his answer. "Grace will always want more. It is who she is. She'd marry me to get more and I know she doesn't love me. She thinks I'm suitable for a husband. She wants to be an equal partner in the firm, but has not made the necessary commitment to invest in the firm. Right now, if business goes down, she loses a little, but I pay all losses. I'd hate to deal with Grace if her money was at risk. Don't get me wrong, Beryl, she'd never hurt me."

Beauregard was in a dark mood. The detectives asked Millie if there was something wrong. Her answer: "They've given him a lighter contraption. He did too much too soon and is now angry with himself. He thought he'd be running by now."

They laughed at the thought of the Captain running, then remembered he placed high in his academy training only to be outdone by a woman who was now a captain of police in another town. They assembled at the conference table for a last-minute organized meeting awaiting their Captain. He was all business and started with, "I've been diddling around these cases making no decisions. Now's the time."

Lilly asked, "You know something, Captain, like who wants Jed dead?"

"Sergeant, we have three murders and maybe more and one assault. We know they're all connected. We have to move on DesCartes now. The Feds will be right behind us. Don't ask how I know; I just know. We have enough to bring him in now with Jed's statement. Before we had conjecture. The helicopter landing on his helipad was the one Jed jumped from and he was forced into the trip to DesCartes' house. The cars involved in Marlene and David's deaths were seen on that day at DesCartes' home by neighbors. Jed was brought to New Jersey by the lady looking for a divorce and now we discover her company was an entrepreneur receiver of thirteen million dollars from the Fund. She's disappeared. Harry's dead. All those moneys stolen by the staffer and board member left some hanging including Jed and Harry. I think Harry was looking for the money. I think Alexia Marsh Raleigh told him about how much her company received and it was siphoned off. I think she believes her husband took it. She wanted money from him. She was president of Ralrow and FFO Arrow and was the planned patsy. She decided to get out. I'm guessing she turned the Feds onto the Fund when she found all her money missing. But it's bigger than this. All this money gone and where did it come from? I want the sources of the money coming into the Fund. It will be difficult to get when the Feds have been all over it. Who else lost money in addition to Marlene, David, Harry, Jed, and Alexia's company? Alexia's company was a receiver while the other three were donors. What other folks were in David's and Marlene's separate corporations who lost from their investment in the Fund? Of those who lost money in addition to our known victims, just who are they? Were they hiding money laundering schemes in a perfect plot, of whose money is whose? Remember once dollars go into a common pot, it is called fungible, meaning the origin becomes unidentifiable."

Mason said, "Captain, I'll graph what came out and what went in. I can make a few calls. I've got some friends in the Atlanta area. They'll know how I can get info without opening up our need to know with the Feds. I'll work more on David and Marlene and Alexia. Folks who lose money are normally not like Harry and Jed. They talk about their losses to friends and mostly know who to blame. We may know the staffer and one board member responsible for a portion of lost funds, but as to the entrepreneurial investments that went south, their investor backgrounds need to be checked."

Beauregard said, "We don't know which came first, 'the chicken or the egg' or even who's the chicken or who's the egg or do we have a barnful of chickens. What if all the entrepreneurial investment companies going belly-up have a connection to a common source? And what if the source is a money launderer whose scheme was to drain part of the Fund making it look like normal bankruptcies from new business efforts and the embezzlement by others interfered with their plans. If they are not only criminal but powerful, this common source would not take the exposure lightly. Look for connections.

"Look for commonality. I think the source wants the Feds to find nothing other than to prosecute the staffer and her corporate accomplice and let the rest go unnoticed. It could happen that way if no one causes an uproar. The lawsuit is a problem for them. The group suing civilly had better have a weak attorney. Do we know anything about the suing group's representation? And frankly, what do they expect to get from the embezzlers. Do they have any money left?"

Ted Torrington offered to follow the lead, saying, "I want to follow this lead. I know many accountants down there and some political insiders. This, Captain, if you're on the right path, is big. The Feds are not going to like it."

"It's why you'll contact only those who love keeping secrets. Work fast before I'm stopped."

21

Conversations

Petra tried several times before reaching Rene DesCartes to schedule a home or station visit, which on contact, made timing a difficult task. DesCartes said he had visitors from Europe there for most of the week and wanted to put her visit off. When she invited him to come to the station instead, he thought perhaps he could find some time that afternoon. The Lieutenant and Sergeant Flores were led into a study in the back of the home decorated in a grand manner of fine eighteenth century furniture and what looked to Petra as original oils on the walls. It was a quite large room and she thought it beautiful. She told Mr. DesCartes so. He preened, saying, "You perhaps do not realize the value of these paintings. They are insured for a large sum and I have the best security when I leave for France."

Juan was about to jar his comfort with a remark about his security system, but stopped at Petra's slight kick on his leg. Instead he started the questioning. Since he was not the senior investigator his taking the lead was not the norm. Petra felt DesCartes did not need velvet glove questions. His arrogance in her mind deserved meat cleaver questions from Juan. DesCartes got the message and became quite defensive. "Just what is going on here? You act as if I have done something wrong. I don't know what you're talking about. I certainly don't know about those two accident victims. As to Mr. Mattias, I know nothing about him."

Petra listed some of the circumstantial evidence, leaving out Jed's latest contribution. DesCartes asked if he needed an attorney. Naturally their answer was, "Why, have you done something criminal?"

Instead of calling his attorney, which was what they expected, he acted like a novice and attempted to explain visitors to his home are a normal occurrence. Often, they are there to give him investment advice. He did not recall the names they had given him. He certainly didn't remember a David Spencer, but thought he recalled a good-looking woman named Marlene. She was a friend of a friend who suggested he meet with her and give her some business. The friend shared her portfolio and it was impressive. He did not realize she was killed in an accident that day. Petra asked, "How did you know it was an accident and if she died, didn't it jog your memory about David Spencer; they were both here and both were dead. If business acquaintances visiting my house were found dead shortly afterward, I would remember. I would so remember. I don't think you are being forthright with us. Who else was visiting you that day? You do remember what day I'm speaking about, don't you?"

"Of course, I remember, it was in the papers."

"Who else was here? Who was driving an ivory colored Land Rover?"

The question bothered DesCartes enough, he ended the interview. "You may reach my attorney. Here is his card. He is from New York. Call him and schedule an interview. Now I have to get back to my guests."

Juan stated, "Mr. DesCartes, please don't go out of town for now."

"I'm leaving for France in a few days. I'm sorry, but I have to go."

Petra replied, "No, Mr. DesCartes, do not test us. I'm certain you won't be comfortable as a protected witness in police custody, so stay around for now, please."

To say DesCartes was apoplectic was an understatement. The two detectives were practically excised by a big man who was standing outside the office door.

Back at the station, Petra shared the interview with the Captain. He thought Petra and Juan should have started in a softer vein, but after hearing the whole story, he said, "You've flushed him out, Lieutenant. You have done enough for now. Who is his attorney?"

Petra had not reviewed the card at DesCartes' home. She now did. "Captain, it is that lawyer Bob Brown. Jed said he met with him. This card says he has offices on Madison Avenue, NYC. Didn't Jed remember the card said offices someplace in New Jersey?"

"Petra, he could have offices in both places. This guy is our nexus. Does DesCartes remember Brown met with Jed?"

"He doesn't look careless, but it may be he thinks we are dumb and he also doesn't know Brown gave Jed his card. When they searched Jed in the helicopter they would have found the card if he had it on him. Let me look at the interview notes taken on the twenty-sixth. They could tell us whether Jed had possession of the card when he got on the helicopter."

Beauregard sighed. "Of course, they would have searched him and taken the card. They weren't worried about the lawyer's name because Jed would be dead. At least they thought he would be. They may worry about Jed's memory of the attorney's name now. We can hope they haven't thought that deeply, or it is a major worry for them."

"Captain, I'll do a search on Attorney Bob Brown in both NYC and New Jersey. Mason can assist. If he is a business attorney who goes to court when required, I'll follow the principals in those cases for connections. DesCartes gave him up as his attorney without thinking too much about it. Means to me he trusts the guy and has used him before. Brown has to have some knowledge about DesCartes' affairs. Why else would he be a front man for corralling Jed into the helicopter visit. When Jed disappeared, which is what we think would have happened, Brown would have been questioned."

"Yes and no, Lieutenant. DesCartes' associates would have buried him somewhere leaving the last trace in New Jersey. We have a dead end on the helicopter. We can't even find the pilot. Only DesCartes' men could squeal and we don't know who they are. Put Mason on it, and I'll call my guy Jack who knows about flying. I don't. Also connect with Bill Border about the pilot's description. He has a friend with the DEA who knows all the rogue pilots. Most have past arrests and lost licenses. Makes sense in this case because he used another pilot's name. Bill can contact him as well."

"I'm on it, Captain. It feels to me like a turning point in our cases."

Beauregard contacted his friend Jack. He questioned about rogue pilots out of the Northeast area. Jack asked if he had thought about using a police sketch artist with Jed since he was the only one who ever saw the pilot. "Rudy, I could pass the sketch around. Someone will know him."

Beauregard thanked Jack, thinking, *why didn't I do that? Have I lost my wits? Bill Border can show the sketch to his DEA friends. We'll get the guy before DesCartes can eliminate him. He would. DesCartes' first reaction when Petra and Juan pushed him was informing them he was leaving for France shortly. I'll make a call to put a stop on his passport. The problem is the Feds might stop me from the stop.*

Beauregard made a few phone calls. One was to a friend who had knowledge of federal and state investigations. He would not give Rudy names, but would talk generally about what was going on and where. A few minutes later, Rudy sat musing with a smile on his face, *I should have called him in the first instance, but, how could I? I wouldn't have recognized the investigation until recently. It's big and we are in the middle. Murder will not be big enough to consider as important in light of FEDS' quest for major laundering case perpetrators. I think DesCartes is important in our and their investigations. Unless I can figure out how to tie him to money laundering, we'll never get the murder solved. Laundering is, after all, the motive; nothing else makes sense.*

———

Unknown to Beryl, Oliver Kent had taken his mother's interest in her new friend Nathan to heart. He'd rented a small non-descript KIA and had set up near Nathan's home. He also used Nathan's visit to set up a remotely activated microphone on his cellular phone. It was only when Nathan ran out of the room and left the phone on the dining table he had the opportunity. Nathan said he was to make some calls without his phone? Only Oliver knew the phone was Nathan's. He wondered if Nathan checked his phone out for these bugs. Still it was worth a try. He thought, *I don't want Nathan to blame Mom. I'll fess up if I have to, but it's apparent Mom likes this guy. She doesn't need any more trouble; no more than she normally gets into by herself. Affairs of the heart are the worst. Besides, I don't have much to do. Marthea is writing music today or I'd be hanging with her.*

Oliver heard nothing but Mozart and Country music. He thought, *silence and music. Doesn't he have any friends or business? Must be thoroughly modern having everything done on the computer. He hasn't silenced his keystrokes. I hear them clacking away and his making trips to the kitchen. Speaking of which, this waiting is boring.*

Oliver heard some shuffling and then the opening of the garage door. A sporty black Mercedes Benz convertible pulled out. Oliver smarted when he realized it was not the car he'd driven the other night. He jotted the plate numbers and wondered, *single guy with two cars is not the norm out here, but then again, a convertible is not a go to car for grocery shopping or anything else. If he's investigating, a convertible is not a good surveillance car. It would be remembered. It does fit in this neighborhood which means it's important to him. Later on, I'll find what other cars are in his garage. Slick, you are slick, Nathan Connault.*

Oliver followed the convertible hoping Nathan was not grocery shopping or taking care of hum-drum errands. His first stop was for coffee at the local coffee shop. Oliver could see through the shop's large window Nathan shooting the breeze with the barrister who brewed the coffee order freshly. He returned to his car and headed into Springfield and was let into the parking garage of the federal building. *Got you now, Nathan. I know no one gets to park there unless they're government. Trouble is I can't get in there without my mask and identification. They'd probably not let me in without a known appointment. All this work and I learn what my Mom already suspected.*

Oliver parked his car not far from the parking garage's exit. It was the best he could do. Two hours later, Nathan exited the garage and headed over to the Massachusetts State Building. He did not park in their garage but in a lot nearby. Oliver decided, *he's a Fed not with the state, because the state wouldn't let him in without an appointment.*

This time he left the building in under an hour, and walked over to the Fort restaurant for lunch. Oliver waited ten minutes, pulled his baseball cap way down, parked in an adjacent lot, and entered the restaurant. He'd never been there before. He was taken back on entering, *booths right when I come in, a big dining room to the left and large bar to the right. If I were having quiet lunches, I'd want to sit in one of these booths in front of me. How do I see who's there?*

Oliver took a menu from the hostess and asked for a moment. Apparently, this was common and the woman sat the couple who came in after him. Holding the menu in front of his face, Oliver was able to see some people facing him and the tops of other patrons' heads. He spotted the back of Nathan's head and had a good view of the man sitting opposite to Nathan. Since Nathan could not see him, he took a chance. Putting his phone in front of his menu he waited until the man was looking straight at Nathan and took a photo. No one noticed.

Nathan turned and left the restaurant. *This guy looks familiar. I think I've seen him on television. He's definitely a professional. Well it's all I have today. I'll give it to Mom and tell her to use it for background material. In another day I'll go at this again. I have the car for two days, and two days for now is enough.*

———

Beryl found Detective Bill Border at her door. He'd called twenty minutes earlier to request some time with Jed Mattias alone. They'd all just finished lunch with Oliver noticeably absent without, in Beryl's mind, an excuse. The detective asked if Beryl would join him and said, "A sketch artist will be here in a minute. I'd like you there also. You may be able to help Jed accurately describe the pilot of the helicopter. I know you've asked Jed details about the pilot before. He may have forgotten some of those details now when the incident is not fresh in his mind. Do you mind helping?"

Beryl did not mind. The sketch artist was a woman in her early forties and was most attractive. They adjourned to Beryl's study. The artist, Josephine, set up her computer which had a large screen, and began questioning Jed. He said the pilot's face was from memory vague, but he would try. Josephine was patient in her pursuit of details and not at all discouraged by the necessity of showing many examples of foreheads, hair, nose, ears, cheeks, lips, dimples/no dimples, eyebrows, etc., repeatedly. Beryl said at one point, "Jed, didn't you say he had a look of an actor in the movie, 'Airplane'?"

Josephine asked Jed, "Which one, Jed, the lead guy? I loved that movie; it is really a comedy."

Jed said, "Yes, Josephine, but I don't remember his name. He played Striker, who was anti heroic. Funny as hell, you are right there. It was a long time ago when I saw it. Maybe I don't remember well."

Josephine answered, "His name was Robert Hays. It was a cult movie in our family. My uncle was a Navy pilot who thought it was a scream. I remember Hays' face. If it doesn't look like him, it's okay. I'll just erase. It's what I do every day. No problem."

Josephine drew a face within several minutes, while Beryl googled the movie. When Beryl saw the preliminary sketch, it displayed the essence of Robert Hays' photo in the movie graphic. She asked, "How could you remember the face, Josephine? I saw the movie. I remembered him, but I would not have been able to describe his features for a drawing."

Josephine laughed, simply replying, "We all have strengths. This is mine. Jed, are we getting closer?"

Jed was now excited. "Yeah, except my pilot's forehead is wider and the hair dips some in the middle. A couple of vertical ridges are needed on the side and I could barely see his ears. Flatten them a bit. The nose was wider at the bridge. His eyes were brown and his hair also brown and straight."

The two worked well together with Jed acting more certain of his memory of the pilot's face. A finished product pleasing Jed had enough detail in it to satisfy Josephine, Beryl, and Detective Border. Jed remarked, "Josephine, until you drew the first face similar to the actor I did not think I would be of any help, but this is the guy. I now remember he moved with a heaviness on one side, as if his knee hurt him. He had no tattoos. I could see that much. He did not wear glasses."

The detective and sketch artist were leaving when Jed asked Josephine if he could call her, saying, "I might recall something else. Do you mind?"

She told him no she didn't and gave her card after jotting her cell phone. Beryl smiled after noticing, *the third couple in a few days. I'm naming my home 'the romantic opportunity house.' Don't think, Josephine, I did not notice you slide your mask down. With such a smile, I guess I'd want the guy to see me. God, I'm not that old, am I? Like an old lady watching lovers is my occupation.*

Bill Border sent a copy of the drawing to his contact with the DEA with instructions for checking rogue pilots and licenses lost or recently regained and pilots suspected in drug runs; the same message was sent to Rudy to forward to his contact Jack, and to contacts he had in several small private airports in New Jersey. Jed had said the airport the helicopter flew out from had no signage making him think it was private. It was now waiting time. Bill did compose a list of pilots whose licenses were on hold for various reasons, mostly waiting for renewal applications and payment. He found photos of the pilot in each file. Scanning the files, he shortly felt numb thinking, *lots of them with similar stats. It's time for some coffee.*

Bill was joined in the break room by Mason, who appeared pleased with his work, saying, "The money trail tells a lot. The staffer and board member's theft is clearly there, but is small compared to the big losses from some of the Fund recipient corporations. My question is why weren't questions asked sooner? I built a calendar. Payments on loans were not sent for over a year from the recipient corporations. The other board members should have gotten at least a monthly review on each recipient corporation's payment back. It's how it normally works. I'm not an auditor, but I think the staffer covered payments of interest for a year to prevent discovery of the embezzlement moneys. Not unusual since embezzlers always think they can hide theft. But over time, it all comes out. She should have left the country about six months into her fraudulent activities. The other board member not involved must be dumb, lazy, or easily conned. If the Captain was able to interview him, we'd have a more complete picture, but the guy is a federal witness, and for sure, he's not going to speak with local police. Take a look at the graph. The flow of moneys in and out is clear."

Bill Border answered, "Ralrow, LLC received thirteen million. Do we know how her husband supposedly siphoned it off?"

Mason replied, "Ted is following the stolen moneys. He should have some answers from corporate reports, but not from the investigations. He said he would follow up with some of the other investors who were supposedly legitimate and see what they knew about investors and recipients."

22

Zero Sum Gaming

Beauregard had read most of the reports he'd requested. He still needed initial reports on the background on Attorney Bob Brown as well as info on the defense attorney in the Fund civil case. What he found unusual was the defense attorney was the same in both the civil and criminal cases. He thought, *different skills are required in each type of case. Certainly, the civil attorney would help in the criminal defense case, but I normally don't see one attorney being the lead in both such high-profile cases. He or she must have a hell of a background. How do I close these cases? I need the pilot. I need more on DesCartes. If we contact INTERPOL, the Feds will shut us down. They've been contacted, I'm sure, but I don't know what's in the file. They must have been contacted. Interest would be taken by their Organizational and Emergency Crimes Division. It reminds me of being tied and sitting with my brother Billie when I was a child. I couldn't move.*

Petra joined the Captain. "What's up, Captain, you look sad?"

"Thinking, Lieutenant, can make you sad sometimes. What's up with you? You are looking excited."

"Attorney Bob Brown is what's up. It's odd, don't you think, for an attorney to call himself Bob when his given name is Robert? I don't mean odd to use the shorter name, but he uses Bob on his credit cards, advertising, and correspondence, but his degrees all say Robert Brown, and his name isn't really Robert Brown anyway and not even Bob Brown. Like the New York City Mayor, his name was changed. But in this case changed by his mother. She changed it when he was eleven, hers as well to Brown and his to Robert Brown. Before his name was Luca Petronelli. And you know who Gino Petronelli was, Captain?"

"I do. He died in federal prison, and rightly so. He was mob connected and pretty high up in the northern New Jersey Mafia when Riggi was in charge. He served time along with Riggi. They were all part of the Cavalante family. Brown is his son? No wonder his mother changed their name. He becomes an attorney, but illegal money is so seductive he can't help himself. I'm jumping ahead. You did find his working on the wrong side, didn't you?"

"It's not perfectly direct, Captain. His bio claims he is a high-level criminal and civil lawyer. I don't see much civil other than representing businesses typically operating in the Mafia pattern, like massage parlors, uniform services, restaurants and bars with all their related permitting and legal problems. He doesn't defend them when they are in criminal trouble, but photos of criminal trials show him at the trials and speaking often to leading defense trial attorneys. He's written a book which is well thought of on the importance of being non-discriminatory when choosing clients. He's adjunct at several law schools and has received some great awards. He spends money easily and lives large. I have nothing directly connecting him, Captain, but he is connected. What can we do if we have no evidence of his wrongdoing, just his meeting with Mattias?"

"Go through his client list from public records and photos and assume if he was at a trial, he was retained for some purpose. Look for matches with anyone from the Fund investors to recipients from the Fund. My gut tells me you'll find a connection. If not, we'll meet with him after DesCartes meets with us. I want to know more about Bob Brown before meeting with him."

Beryl Kent raised her voice as she spoke which was not her norm. "Oliver, you're carrying your research too far. If Nathan is not what he says, I'll find out sooner or later, but for you to rent a car and follow him is a bit much. Don't you think, because I do?"

Oliver laughed. "Mother dear, it's okay for you to fly to Austin investigating Jed's daughter. This was far less effort. You know I picked up some of your habits over the years. Look, we now know he is government and federal at that. Also, despite your obvious feminine charms, Mom, he is looking for information from you. Make certain, you get more than you give."

"Did you say you have the car for two days? What were you going to do tomorrow?"

"I plan to give it one more day of surveillance and I can tell you there is nothing more boring than following a guy who's doing nothing interesting; no ladies or booze or odd behavior, just office visits to government buildings."

"Let me take your rental car tomorrow, Oliver? I have a gut feeling."

"Can't leave it alone, can you? You must like Nathan. Sure, but don't get into a chase scene. You are not a real detective, Mom. You're just a nosey lady."

———

Beryl was on Nathan's trail disguised in a pulled down canvas fisherman's hat and odd sunglasses. With her hair tied back, even her friends would not notice her. Her observations to date confirmed Oliver's. This was a boring job but she would stay with it until she returned the car before 6:00 p.m. thinking, *I should have gone last night but I was so tired and felt I must deliver dinner for my guests. Breakfast they can handle. I would love to know what Nathan does at night. Maybe he is seeing someone. Am I doing this because I feel a tickle of jealousy? I hope not.*

Nathan left the federal building, then drove down State Street, taking a left on Chestnut and then a right on Union and parked. As he left his car, he appeared to scan his setting, but couldn't see Beryl who had parked five spots behind his car. Next, he walked further into Springfield's South End. She went back to her car and drove guessing his destination. Sure enough, he entered AC Produce. She parked across the street which offered a good view. Lots of folks went into the market at lunch to get sandwiches. She thought the dining area would be closed. She was correct. Nathan came back in a few minutes with a large takeout and entered the front passenger side of a large black Mercedes sedan. The windows were darkened but she could see the other occupant was a man. She jotted down the New Jersey license plate number and waited.

Thirty-five minutes later, Nathan hopped out of the car and walked back to his own car. Beryl followed him for the rest of the day, but he busied himself grocery shopping, dropping off some cleaning, and then headed for home. Her hackles were raised, *is he working for two masters? If he's working for the Feds, why the surreptitious luncheon with a man in a car. What is the connection? Are you working on a private case?*

Beryl dropped off the rental car retrieving her own. With a determined look she phoned Lieutenant Petra Aylewood-Locke. "Lieutenant, I was just almost killed by a black Mercedes Sedan. I want to be certain I'm not being followed. Can you check the plates and reassure me. I felt as if he deliberately tried to push me over the side."

Petra fell for the story and ten minutes later called back. "Beryl, what cockamamie story are you trying to feed me? Fess up. You know lying to the police is a crime."

"I don't know what you mean. Who is it? Am I in danger? Is it connected to Jed Mattias?"

Petra calmed down and said, "If you are not lying, go home. I'll be there shortly."

A now distraught Beryl thought, *I have lied. They will never believe me again. Beauregard will believe even more than he does now that I'm a ditz. I do want his respect. Again, I've gone over the line. Why didn't I tell the truth? Will I fess up to her? No, no!*

Beryl invited the Lieutenant accompanied by the Captain into her office. Beauregard initiated the conversation. "Beryl, trust is a two-way avenue. How did you get this plate number and where?"

"I can't tell you, Captain. I want to, but I can't. Who has the plate number? It was a New Jersey plate."

"It belongs to Donald Arrow. You know who he is?"

"Yes. What is his background other than being the husband in the Alexia Raleigh divorce case? Isn't he supposed to have stolen the money from their corporation leaving Alexia to hold the bag of suspicion?"

Petra answered, "Yes, and your seeing the plate locally, which is what you said, says a lot. Who was he with?"

"All I can tell you is I followed one of the men to the federal building."

"How did you follow him? Did you get his car's plate?"

"No, it was covered in mud."

"What make and model, Beryl, was the car?"

"It was a black convertible and maybe a Mercedes too. It could be another make, I'm uncertain."

Beauregard said, "Did it have a black or white top?"

"Mmm, I think maybe black, but the top was down."

"Did he park his car and if so, didn't he raise the top to lock the car?"

"He wore a designer hoodie, and he didn't lock his car."

Beauregard took a pause before speaking, thinking, *You are lying to me, Beryl Kent and I don't know why. Whoever this second guy is, why are you protecting him? I remember two times you've had advanced info. You're playing with the Feds. Why haven't they closed us down if you've told them about our investigation. You haven't because you are playing both of us. I think you want the Perp even more than we do, but you will get your fingers burnt. I can't say you haven't given us your new information as you've learned it, but I don't like being played when I don't know who is with you on the other side. Scare tactics with you are not going to work; you'll just hunker down.*

"Beryl, you are not being completely honest with me. I'm letting it go, but I think whoever is advising you had better be as trustworthy as you believe. Think about telling me the complete truth. I can be an information source for you. While I'm here, I want to speak with Jed Mattias, without you present."

Feeling like a chastened and naughty child, Beryl brought Jed into the room and left them behind, thinking, *what does he want with Jed? He deliberately excluded me because I can't be trusted. I should have told Jed not to speak with him, but Jed's an attorney. He'll make his own decisions.*

Jed asked, "My attorney's not here, Captain. I can't tell you much without his presence."

The Captain asked, "Who had dinner with you on Christmas, Jed? Can you answer?"

"Of course, but you don't think anyone at our dinner table was a part of the potential attack on me, do you? What did your prisoner tell you?"

"Just tell me who was here. In this case, the person may have been the potential victim."

"You don't think they're after Marthea my daughter? No way. And Beryl and her family are not involved in all of this other than my choosing her to fall on. The other guy, Nathan, I tell you my gut tells me he is military. Is he who you're after?"

"Just give us his name, please."

"Nathan Connault is his name. He is a neighbor and very nice; he's probably military. He had the bearing. He was a good conversationalist. We all enjoyed him. Was the guy after him?"

The Captain explained he could not speak about an open case and thanked Jed while respectfully asking him to keep their conversation today off limits. Jed agreed.

The two detectives left the home with Beauregard thanking Beryl for meeting with him. On the one hand, Beryl looked confused, while on the other hand, the Captain left smiling. Beryl thought, *he's going to find out about Nathan. It won't hurt and may save me some heartache. I think he got something from Jed, and I can't imagine what it could be; unless Jed revealed Nathan was here on Christmas. What a sneaky fellow is the Captain. I think it's all to the good. I would have told him everything now. Why is he always pushing me? What does he know I don't know? It's time to tell Nathan what I suspect. His gig is up and he won't be happy.*

Beauregard was pleased with the conversations he had with both Beryl and Jed saying, "Lieutenant, you learn something new every day. What did Bobby and Mason say in their report, something about Bobby knowing Nathan Connault from the service as a colonel, but his name was Ian. Now we hear Donald Arrow's car is in town. Is there a connection here? The Feds are on the money trail and Donald Arrow's role in it is known to them. Why is Donald Arrow in Springfield unless he's a potential witness either identified by the Feds or maybe by Connault? Let's go back and review the reports and go after this divorce case. I don't think Harry would have stayed on the divorce case if he thought Alexia was a conspirator and actor in a money laundering scheme, do you?"

"Unless, Alexia fooled him. It wouldn't be the first time, Captain, a wife threw her husband under the bus, particularly if the marriage was rocky. Maybe she took the money and is blaming him. The Feds will have followed the money trail and if Donald is involved they would want him as a witness. The same would be true if Alexia was the thief and Donald could tell the story."

Beauregard said, "Petra, you are, for a feminist, quickly blaming the woman. You surprise me sometimes."

"You have it wrong, Captain. I go after the guilty ones regardless of gender, you know it."

At the station, Millie notified the detectives of an MCU meeting. Reports on all lists were on the agenda. The Captain asked Mason to answer some questions saying, "Lieutenant, I'm just skimming your first report on Ralrow, LLC and I wonder why nobody down there in Atlanta noticed what you've discovered? When did this happen?"

"I noticed from the first newspaper article on the Fund's loss of moneys after the civil lawsuit was made public about the corporate treasurer of the company committing suicide by hanging. At the time, it didn't seem implausible for the treasurer of the company which inexplicitly loses thirteen million dollars to go out before the trial. You know it happens. It was when you charged me with looking at all the officers of the Fund recipients who went belly-up, when dead officers appeared on my list, too many for natural causes. Ralrow's corporate secretary was fifty-two years old and crashed his car into a pole at three-thirty in the morning. His wife said he went to a late-night meeting for the company. Two of the other recipient companies lost one corporate officer each, corporate treasurers, from a drug overdose for one and another car accident for the other. The police reports on all these deaths did not show anything but accidental deaths. Stinks, Captain, don't you think?"

"Can we connect the victims' names to each other in some other business?"

"We have four of them dead and three of them are originally from New Jersey and have served on other boards in New York City and New Jersey. At least in two of those companies Bob Brown was the corporate attorney."

"Are attorneys' names on the financial statements of companies? Unless there is litigation, I'd not expect to see them mentioned. How'd you get this info?"

Mason said, "Captain, I called up the public relations contact in each case. In two of them, I got lucky. I made up a false resume, nothing in writing, but using a friend of mine as a contact. He's pretty important nationally and these folks wanted to be nice to me. I said I was interested in serving on the board and Leroy Haskins would write a letter of support. They're always looking for minority board members who can be trusted. I asked a few pointed questions about outstanding litigation saying I didn't want to be involved in situations with litigation going public; I'd always kept a private profile despite my successes. One woman called Leroy while I waited and then couldn't tell me enough."

"How in hell do you know Leroy Haskins, Mason? He is big."

"He's from the hood in Springfield where I grew up. Lot of locals made it big-time. You only hear about the actors and musicians and judges, not much about business scions."

"Bob Brown knew them. Interesting, but how do we connect him with their deaths? We don't. Have we connected Alexia with Bob Brown, or is our only connection Donald Arrow?"

"Even the connection of Bob Brown with Donald Arrow is tenuous, Captain."

"How so?"

"Bob Brown told Jed he was representing Donald Arrow. Nowhere do we have evidence outside of Jed's memory. Who is Donald Arrow? I checked the address connected with the license plate and it's a business, not a personal registration. The business address listed is a suite in the Empire State Building. When I called the number, it was a service. I was told it was the sales office for several corporations. I asked about the two companies having common board members and they were two of the companies with sales offices there. These are nothing offices, just a live contact messaging service center which is rare today when we have services without a live operator and therefore not in need of an office. I found no evidence of a Donald Arrow matching Alexia's description in New York or New Jersey. I don't know if he is real, Captain."

"He's real, we just don't know his real name. Chase all the corporations for common addresses and attorneys who filed the corporations, Lieutenant."

Mason said, "I have some reports on the ins and outs of moneys from each of the corporations who lost all the entrepreneurial investments from the Fund. Although each corporation had different businesses such as manufacturing, IT, Design, and Marketing, there were a few common vendors getting overly large contracts. Those common vendors all went bankrupt. They didn't do all the work contracted. I'm having a difficult time following the money from there because they were smaller businesses without public financial statements. We'd have to go through their banking and we don't now have a basis for a warrant."

Beauregard went on to Sergeant Bobby Barr's report on the pilot. "It says you found him, but not. Please explain."

"Captain, I think he is dead. His name is Martin McAuliffe or Marty. He's noted for a careless attitude for the rules but is or was a great air jockey. He hasn't been seen since the day of Jed's jump from the plane. I contacted his current girlfriend by phone. She lives in White Plains and was in the process of moving out of his house. He has not contacted her and the rent is due. He told her he was meeting her later after having made a big score. He never showed. He never did that before. She cried."

"Sergeant, did she call the police?"

"Yes, and they took a statement. They checked the house and neighbors. The two got along well or I think they did, because the police, after a couple of days, stopped calling."

"Sergeant, check her out. See if she has some money after she moves. She could be connected."

"Captain, she seemed totally overwhelmed with his absence. I did a preliminary on her. She works for a nursing home as a nurse and has for twelve years. She lived with Marty for three years with no reports of difficulties."

"Okay, Sergeant, for now we'll go with your hunch about her. I need you to help Mason chase money."

Beauregard greeted Lieutenant Lent who just arrived, saying, "Ash, thanks for coming. I appreciate your joining us. You said you had some names from the license plate with the number B as the third letter you thought may be connected."

"Captain, it was a Massachusetts plate and the first draft numbers were daunting. I honed the numbers down to Western Mass numbers and one was connected to a Ty Blanken from West Side. He has it garaged over in a barn where he lives…"

Petra and Bobby both interrupted with Petra talking faster. "Must be Marge Bleeker's evil neighbor across the street with the SUV hidden in the barn."

Bobby said, "We never got back there because we didn't have cause to search. You have basis for a warrant now, Captain."

Beauregard replied, "Get the warrant, but talk to me before enforcing. DesCartes will be in here with Attorney Bob Brown; enforce it at the same time. Bring two cars with police for the enforcement. If we are correct, they have guns and have murdered before. Hold on. Wait until DesCartes and Brown have left the station. Make contact with Bill and Ted who will follow them in two separate cars. Keep your eyes on the house and barn from afar while the others move on the warrant. I want to be there for the search. If either of them go in the direction of the barn being searched before I get there, call me."

Lilly said, "Finally there is some action on these cases. It didn't look good for a while."

Juan Flores harrumphed causing Lilly to throw her pencil at him. He mumbled, "Just saying, Lilly, not everything good is full of action. Footwork and slow paperwork allow a final action finish. You like the shine of the chase. You watch police chase scene reruns too often."

Petra laughed. "Juan, and you think you and Lilly are going to get married? So much for a tranquil married life, Juan."

Beauregard stopped the play with a request for Sergeant Barr's reports on Jed Mattias, Grace Grantley, and Beryl Kent. Petra asked, "I want more on Ms. Beryl Kent. She has had quite the life we know about; what else is there?"

Bobby said, "Beryl is what she says she is. What she doesn't say is interesting. She has connections everywhere and with the second bananas in many organizations. Folks love her."

Ted asked what it meant. "Well there are news photos of her with famous people because a couple of her husbands were connected. When I started to search, I found she had more associations with staffers of politicians and administrative assistants all the way over to business CEO's administrative assistants. She is a born communicator, but not one person I spoke with gave me any dirt. Her background from the point of view of catching her in lies is boring. Nada, nothing!

"Now when it comes to the other lady, Grace, she is formidable and generally not liked by most employees or vendors or neighbors in her condo. She has a couple of escorts on her arm at public events. One of them is a gay blade who likes to be seen at all the big events in Atlanta. With COVID, there aren't many. The other escort is a brother of her college roommate. I spoke with him about Grace. I told him we're concerned about her. He asked why, saying, 'You shouldn't be and I don't understand why the police would be. Grace is an anteater sucking up all the little ants, sometimes just for fun and not even for a business reason. I escort her because my sister's husband is an attorney in the firm. When she asked him to contact me, he said he couldn't say no to her. She doesn't take 'no' well. He also said she's a liar. She tells stories for self-aggrandizement and we should not take her seriously as a witness.' Get this, he was told by his brother-in-law she lost money investing in the Fund. I questioned how the guy knew this. He said Harry told him. Apparently, the brother-in-law did a lot of backup legal work for Harry. Everything I discovered tells me why Grace doesn't have a boyfriend. She is a miserable person."

The Captain asked, "Do we have any other source in support? Why does he escort her? I mean, would she can his brother-in-law if he wouldn't play the game?"

"Captain, this guy was adamant. Grace Grantley is not liked, but did she really invest in those companies?"

Beauregard said, "Find out. There has to be a financial trail in the court records on the civil suit."

Ted questioned, "Bobby, what about our lady Alexia? Can we connect her to Grace? I don't like two ladies in Atlanta connected somehow. Grace just may be a pushy and ambitious attorney wanting to lead her firm. If she is an investor and didn't tell us, real suspicion rears its head. What if she knew about Alexia and what I think is the phony divorce request. Could be Harry discovered more than we have seen or there is evidence in the court or firm's records we didn't recognize. I'd like to go through them. I'm good at that type of work."

"Ted, you looked through corporate records for me, and never said anything about Grace having an investment in the Fund or as a stockholder in any recipient's fund that went belly-up. What do you expect?'

"Think about it, Captain, every one of the investors in the Fund lost money. I haven't chased all of the connected corporate owners and officers of them all yet. And the recipients who did not go belly-up have not been looked at closely."

Beauregard said, "Well, we have thought there was the theft and then maybe money laundering. Alexia or her husband Donald Arrow, both of whom we can't find, is clearly a suspect in a theft conspiracy from a recipient corporation. Getting money and going belly-up requires a look-see. Or maybe not. Could be they are just part and parcel among a few investors and recipients seeking to wash cash, with either Alexia or Donald stealing from the money launderers. Harry was killed for his knowledge and what he was going to do with the knowledge. You go with it, Ted. Bobby, you okay with the change in plans?

"More importantly is the fact I can't get my head around how this money laundering works. Normally you invest black money into going businesses, propping them up beyond the pale and end up looking like a king of big finance with no one the wiser. Here, money goes in and disappears to various vendors. And they go bankrupt too. Find me the path."

Bobby was relieved. He said Ted was better at records. The Captain asked Bobby to join him and Petra for the meeting with DesCartes, saying, "I think this guy gets nervous around men and flutters around women. I don't know which one works better so we'll use both. Remember his attorney, Bob Brown, will be there. Be careful with body language. Attorneys are good at picking up signals from small tells."

Attorney Bob Brown was introduced to Captain Beauregard by Rene DesCartes as the group congregated in the large conference room. Petra and Bobby sat opposite the witness and his lawyer with the Captain sitting further away at the end of the table. Mr. Brown said, "Move closer, Captain. I want to be certain you hear everything my client explains."

Beauregard mentioned his seat was quite comfortable for both viewing and listening, while thinking, *son-of-a-bitch is trying to take control. He knows I love distance to see all the interactions. Sorry, man, no control today.*

Petra decided to play at a more helpful cop role starting the interview with a gracious thanks for coming to the station and explaining there would be a recording of the interview per policy. Brown interjected, "I think we could be more productive without recording the conversation. Recording makes a witness nervous."

Sergeant Barr looking innocuous which conflicted with his large frame answered, "Policy, Mr. Brown. You know how it is for policing today, we break policy, we have problems."

Brown looked over to the Captain and suggested then, "Perhaps this is a non-starter for us."

Beauregard softened his grimace and answered, "I hope not, for your client's sake, Mr. Brown."

Brown answered, "You don't have enough to bring him in as a protected witness. Please don't play with us."

The Captain said, "I'm not playing."

Silence soaked the room. Not one person moved for moments until Rene DesCartes said, "I'm not staying in jail, Bob, not for even one night; do you hear me?"

Sergeant Barr thought, *if this were poker and I guess it is, DesCartes just showed his hand.*

Mr. Brown retorted, "Shut up, Rene, you won't be kept as a witness. Now what do you want to know, Captain? I will stop my client from answering if I don't like your questions or your tone."

Beauregard nodded to Lieutenant Aylewood-Locke who continued the questioning. The first few questions were slow balls in Beauregard's mind, sort of introductory to relax the witness. The first question was partially answered before Brown could stop DesCartes. "Rene, I will tell you when to answer a question."

The Captain intervened. "Mr. Brown, we are not here without knowing certain information. The answer to the question is already known to us. Your interference tells me you either didn't know the answer because your client didn't tell you or you are not open to helping us find the truth in these investigations. If we can't go forward, I will have to take Mr. DesCartes into custody as a witness."

Petra thought, *we don't know the answer to the question. The Captain is bluffing or maybe not. He could know the answer. I haven't read every report.*

Brown agreed to move on. Question after question from did you know we found a note in your birdfeeder to what were two investors in an Atlanta entrepreneurial fund under federal government investigation doing leaving your premises just before being pushed into an oncoming truck? Brown stopped the questions saying, "Rene, it'll be good for your diet to spend a couple of days here."

"No way, it's a Friday. I'd be here until Monday. Bail me out."

Beauregard said, "Too late in the day for to happen."

DesCartes went ballistic swearing about what happens in American jails. "I'll be dead like Whitey Bulger and the pervert Epstein referring to some recent notorious deaths in American prisons."

There was a scene. Mr. Brown insisted DesCartes' doctor see his client. "Rene has some heart problems. He is certainly over excited. Before you arrest him, his doctor must attest to his health. He's only a witness."

"May be a witness with important answers. He'll be taken to a holding cell and your doctor may visit him in the company of our doctor."

Brown screamed in Beauregard's face, "This dinky town and you with your provincial attitudes. Don't worry, your Chief will hear from me as will every politician in this hellhole. Someone must hate you, Beauregard, and will assist with publicity against you."

Two officers took the emotional witness Rene DesCartes into custody. The detectives noticed he seemed subdued once he was out of sight of his attorney. Brown made his calls in their presence. They heard him repeat the explanation given him it was too late in the day to arrange a hearing. Beauregard wondered to whom his calls were made. He reminded Mr. Brown it is the duty of his client to disclose knowledge of a crime, and his client being vital enough may be detained in the absence of bail, as a material witness. Beauregard thought, *he knows this. It is a federal material witness law adopted in most states. Did he think we wouldn't know; perhaps he thinks it only works in federal crimes not murder? He apparently doesn't know this one may be both money laundering and possibly related murders. How much does he know?*

Brown asked the Captain what he was looking for from his client. Beauregard decided to play dumb saying, "He is a material witness. Mr. Mattias was dropped from a helicopter on your client's property and the copter landed on your client's pad and the pilot and others are known to your client. Use this as a starting point."

Brown left attempting to maintain his cool but Petra said later he appeared to her to be deeply disturbed. Beauregard asked Petra, "Lieutenant, I want Grace Grantley in here just as soon as Ted finishes his paper reviews on her and Alexia. In the reviews of Alexia, were there news reports of her and her husband together at any events? Hell, is he really her husband, and is Donald Arrow really his name? Finally, are they really married and when? I want a record of the marriage."

No detective wanted to point out to Beauregard, there had to be a marriage if Harry filed divorce papers. They would get the record for him.

The detectives connected with community policing who patrolled the barn area shortly before their planned warrant service. Two cars were in the driveway of the not well-cared for home across from Marge, the nosey neighbor. Bobby and Bill arranged for two squad cars to be behind them but to park not in sight of the windows of the home. A police car was to park in front of the barn's door while another one was to park sideways on the driveway to prohibit movement of the residents' cars. These were ordered to be in place a minute after the detectives and uniform walked to the door of the home.

The detectives followed by Officer Collins had the warrant to search in hand and were about to serve it when Juan said to Lilly, "Listen, when we ring the bell, the police cars will be by the barn and in front of the driveway shortly. Don't stand in front of the side glass panels on the door or the wooden door. These guys, if we have it right, are heavily armed."

Lilly hated to be reminded of danger, often telling the other detectives she was not their 'little lady' and hearing it from her soon to be wed set her off. "Listen, Juan, I'm from a family of cops and I'm a street cop. You don't own me. Now lay off with the Mexican protective stuff."

Juan sighed. They were ready to walk to the front door when he got a call from the Captain. "I'm on scene, but Attorney Bob Brown is headed this way. Back off. If you go down the street and turn left, it wraps around. Will take just a moment."

Juan gave the command to the others. They waited at the end of the U-street and saw a large Mercedes pull up into the search warrant home. Bob Brown was not driving and exited the car from the passenger side. The driver left. Lilly called in the New York registered plate. It was registered to Attorney Bob Brown's firm. Lilly said, "I thought the guy flew in for his conference with the Captain. He didn't. He drove in."

Brown entered the home and the two detectives implemented their plan. Juan said, "I feel safer now, Lilly. This guy Brown is not into police confrontation or any potential for crossfires. He'll call them off."

Juan rang the bell and stood back opposite Lilly. A large muscular man answered and his look told the detectives they were outed. Before they could serve the warrant, he said, "Get the hell off my doorstep. I don't give to the police."

The warrant was stuffed at him. Officer Collins captured the process on his cell. All hell broke loose as he ran in front of Lilly and headed for the barn only to be frustrated by the police car parked in front of the barn doors. By this time two other men exited the home, but not Brown. Lilly ran to the back of one side of the house while Juan ran to the other leaving Officer Collins on the front walk. Lilly saw the tall Mr. Brown making headway out the back door by walking swiftly through a garden gate to the neighbor's yard behind. She motioned to Juan who was ahead of her to stop him before he got to the gate. He said loudly, "Attorney Bob Brown, stop! We're the police. We have some questions for you."

Lilly thought, *this guy is wavering. He's thinking about not stopping. He's a fool. Why did he go here to begin with? He's going to run. Stupid.*

Juan tackled Brown on the other side of the garden gate to the entertainment of three boys playing basketball. Brown, now on the ground, complained vigorously about police abuse. Why were they following him? It was police harassment. Juan said, "Mr. Brown, please stand up. The only reason we chased you is because you ran out the back door of a home we were serving with a warrant. How well do you know these people and why are you here? Your driver dropped you off. Are you staying here?"

"I don't know anyone in this home. I was called with a request for my legal services. When all hell broke loose, I ran. I don't trust your police after what you did to my client Rene DesCartes. The poor man is despondent over his arrest as a material witness when he knows nothing."

Sergeant Tagliano gave him her badge number after he requested it. She thought, *he didn't ask for Juan's. He thinks I'm the easy one. No way! It ticks me off how these suits think they can intimidate women.*

Juan asked him where he was staying and some other information finishing with a request to come to the station for questioning. He refused. Juan turned away to make a call to the Captain, only to find Beauregard standing there big as life next to him.

The Captain addressed the disgruntled attorney. "Mr. Brown, you know I may hold you for running away from a police officer who asked you to stop. You know running away from police implies consciousness of guilt. I can hold you for questioning. I won't now, but don't think you're home free. My officer reported your driver is at the DesCartes home. He will tell him to come for you. Do not leave our little town, because we have unfinished business with your client and perhaps with you. You're an attorney. You know citizens shouldn't run away from a police officer. And don't tell me you were in fear of your life. No one will believe your story."

At the station the three men, who were arrested and read their rights, would not talk to the detectives until their attorneys came. Their efforts in calling for their attorneys were apparently not fruitful. Three hours later an attorney from New York entered the station saying he was the attorney for all three men.

Detectives Tagliano and Flores entered the conference room after knocking, backed up by two uniforms, and proceeded to read the men their rights. Their attorney asked what were the charges and appeared shocked when told they were for Vehicular Manslaughter. The three men were now noticeably defiant. One of them, named George Coderre, who matched the description of the man who had slipped in the mud outside of DesCartes' home said, "What the hell are you talking about?"

Lilly replied, "The ivory Land Rover in the barn was secreted by you three. We have witnesses who saw each of you at different times using and later moving the car into the barn after the auto accident. We have you, Mr. Coderre, leaving the scene of the accident and you Mr. Ty Blanken as registered owner of the car. Two people died in the accident. We have witnesses stating they saw you in your car leave Mr. DesCartes' home soon after the victims left the home. We have your plate on camera at the accident site. Once we match the damage on the Land Rover to the victims' vehicle, you'll be arraigned."

Noisy discussions and angry questions by the other two men created a situation out of control with an unhappy and frustrated attorney attempting to stop his clients from their verbosity. The other man insisted he knew nothing about an accident and just lived in the house. If he moved the auto it was at the request of George. And the angry protests continued. Their attorney left the room with instructions to his clients to stop talking to the police.

In another room he placed a call. Lilly overheard him say to the other caller, "Bob, get over here."

Lilly wondered, *how much trial experience does this guy have; he didn't inspire his clients enough to have them shut up. Why did he take on three clients at once? The answer is he has one goal and it's not the legal health of his clients, it's the common good of DesCartes and his crew. If Cull were the attorney, he would have had two other attorneys creating havoc here and none of these men would have said a word.*

We don't have the plate number; we have the third number in a plate of the same make vehicle. We actually don't have Mr. Coderre driving at the scene of the accident. We only have the auto, maybe, at the scene. Marge across the street most likely didn't see each of them drive the Land Rover and didn't see who returned the Land Rover that day. Still, the only admission we have is two of them agree they were not driving the Land Rover that day. We have Attorney Brown at their home which he says is because they are his clients. Brown cannot be DesCartes' attorney and their attorney. Too bad, we couldn't get each one alone to interrogate. I guess we can with this lawyer, but Bob Brown cannot be in the room with them.

23
Perp vs Victim

Beryl Kent received a call, one she was anticipating. Nathan agreed to meet her at Attorney Norberto Cull's office in an hour. He said the attorney was expecting him. He also informed her Attorney Bob Brown was in police custody but did not say for what. She attempted to ask him why, but he hung up. Frazzled by the call she thought, *what does Nathan know and why would he bring Norberto Cull into this? Cull was dying to know my early information source. So, he knows Nathan. How long has he known Nathan?*

Beryl was ushered quickly into Attorney Cull's conference room. Norbie was waiting for her, but not Nathan Connault. She asked, "Where is Nathan Connault?"

"He won't be with us, Beryl, and for good reason. Please be patient. I have some questions for you."

Beryl said, "I am losing patience, Norbie. Understand, please, I am not a chess piece to be moved around on someone else's game."

"Nathan asked me to meet with you. I do not know him, but have heard of him. He is an important character in some federal investigation activities. He testified against one of my clients in the past and unfortunately the case was lost, but it should have been. He wants to protect you and has asked me to assist in the process."

"Protect me, Norbie, when I don't need it? And if you think I do, tell me."

"You don't know it and I have just discovered Rudy and his team have arrested Rene DesCartes as a material witness in Jed's assault and the deaths of the two financial investors in the supposed car accident. He also found the Land Rover that forced the victims' car off the road. He met with the Attorney, Jed met with, who gave instructions for Jed to take the helicopter to West Mass. He has Attorney Bob Brown in custody."

"Great. He solved the cases. Tell me the why, behind these events. I mean, to prosecute them for murder, there must be a why. DesCartes may have ordered the assaults and murders, but he did not do them. Did Rudy find the perps and they talked?"

"Yes and no. He found them, but they aren't talking. Even if they do, they may not live to testify. As to the why, it is the salient question."

"Norbie, the other important question is why you think I'm in danger. You haven't told me."

"Nathan thinks you are, Beryl. He cannot tell me, but asked me to protect you. I told him I couldn't if I didn't know what the danger is and he said, you and I could figure it out. I was tempted not to do anything. Beryl, I can't ignore his words. I want to. I can't. He might think they'll try again to get Jed Mattias and you'll be in the way. DesCartes is a direct witness on the men involved in Jed's assault. All the dirty work location centered on DesCartes' estate. So, let's figure this out."

Beryl said, "Why not dump it on Beauregard? Why didn't Nathan tell him? Rudy is police with the duty to protect. This is bizarre. Why can't Rudy know?"

"If we can't figure out what Nathan's thinking, I will talk to Rudy, because I can't let you be at risk. And I expect Nathan doesn't want you at risk. First, let's try to figure this out. Tell me about Nathan."

"Before I tell you, have you seen or heard of Nathan or someone like him connected to this case?"

"I know the Feds are involved and combined with the state and federal task force, I expect some serious investigators to be out here undercover. I don't know who they are and you never told me about Nathan."

Beryl spent almost an hour reporting on all her interactions with Nathan Connault. The conversation was back and forth with Beryl stating what she remembered and Norbie interrupting her recital with questions. Beryl was getting flushed when Norbie noted the personal relationship developing between Beryl and Nathan and said so. He received cold and flip retorts and decided to eliminate any future social questions. They discussed the local site of Nathan's home at length. He asked her if the police had questioned his personal history. She did not know. Her statements on his directing her on the identity of Jed's attacker in the hospital, the direction to Marthea's agent in Austin and the music camp she was assigned , and Nathan's answers to questions on money laundering he found interesting. Norbie questioned Beryl at length when she described Nathan's behavior when the police were at her front door on Christmas arresting the intruder in her yard. He also observed Jed had not told Beauregard about meeting Nathan. If he had, Rudy would have insisted Beryl tell him about Nathan.

Why did Jed not tell him when Rudy questioned him on the Christmas Day incident? "There is much here to understand. Nathan's not wanting Rudy to know about him means they have met before. I remember Rudy catching the Spider Man in a national drug selling case. He could have met Nathan then. The Feds were all over the case. Two of Rudy's detectives were shot and he interfered with their drug case and pissed off everyone. Rudy is good at alienating anyone who gets in the way of his solving cases. I'm amazed he has not gotten rid of you, Beryl."

"Only because he suspects I have a source of information. I am certain he thinks it is a federal agent I met through one of my husband's questionable death. Why can't Nathan talk with Rudy and tell him things he knows directly?"

"Beryl, it would make him a witness. He's undercover and wants to stay undercover. I have to say your son Oliver has some chutzpah renting a car and taking a picture of the guy with Nathan. Do you have the photo with you, Beryl?"

When Norbie looked at the photo, he said, "I know him. He was in the Miami federal prosecutor's office handling the Noriega case. That was in the 1990s, thirty years ago. He was quite young then. Even with the passage of time I recognize him. He has the same face now. For sure this is a money laundering case and Nathan is undercover. Let's look at the Fund."

They worked the entrepreneurial firms receiving Fund moneys with Sheila, Norbie's assistant working the computer for research. A Donald Arrow, Arrow Marketing, and ARR-Finance were all vendors for three of the entrepreneurial firms who were recipients of moneys from the Fund. Norbie commented, "A Fund giving out big entrepreneurial dollars expects at least fifteen percent or more not to survive. Three firms going belly-up so soon would not normally be a sign of funding problems. The Fund would typically go after any assets left and attempt to find another opportunity business to take them over to remediate losses. The theft from the Fund by the staffer and cohort called unwanted attention and the launderers feared discovery. Bingo, the money launderers could now be seen. I still have trouble seeing the need for the murders. They didn't kill the staffer and partner, reassuring me they had nothing to do with money laundering."

At the station Mason and Beauregard were working lists again. The call from Norbie, in which he did not mention Beryl or Nathan, gave new energy to the Captain and Lieutenant. Beauregard directed

Mason to call the call center in NYC and ask about the three vendor corporations serving the bankrupt receivers of Fund moneys. There was excitement in the air when all three corporations with Arrow in their names used the same call center. Mason could not understand the stupidity of this, saying, "Captain, barely no corporations use call centers and now we have all these using the same center. Were they trying to save money when they were stealing millions?"

"No, Lieutenant, it is all about control. Someone wanted to monitor who was calling all the corporations to keep track. This info helps but just who is Donald Arrow. Check on original filings and his social security number. Can you get into one of these corporation's filings for a social security number?"

Mason was successful. At first, he wondered maybe it would be a wild goose chase if the social security number was stolen. His first success was the corporation ARR-Finance. It was formed in Massachusetts. The name associated with the account was Donald Grantley. Beauregard laughed. "Hell, right in front of us. We weren't comfortable with Grace Grantley. Her actions left questions. How is she related to Donald Grantley?'

"Captain, I'll start with all the Southern states with Georgia as number one and then on to New York and New Jersey. Grace's data for the firm did not list her as married. If Grantley is her maiden name then Donald may be a brother. I'll check marriage licenses using his social and his name with wife to be named 'Grace.' I'll get back to you. "Alexia's marriage showed her marrying Donald Arrow. I'll check his social security number on the license to make certain it's the same."

"Also check social security and see if it is the real name."

Mason checked the social security database and came up with 'Donald Arrow Grantley who was born in Newark, New Jersey in 1973.'

Using Donald's parents' names from his birth certificate, they found he was one of three sons born to the parents, the youngest of which was younger than Grace Grantley. The search now was for a marriage certificate for Donald and Grace. Mason expressed his hope Grace wasn't some cousin of Donald's making it more difficult to connect the two.

Mason used an early date of 1991 for marriage of Donald to the present. He searched New Jersey, New York, Massachusetts, and Georgia for starters. The search resulted in the marriage of Donald A. Grantley to Grace Bevois in Princeton, New Jersey in 1994. The bride's birthdate was 8/8/1974 and Donald's was listed as 5/12/1973. Grace's birthplace was Atlanta, Georgia. Mason thought, *I'll check Princeton University. They must both have been attending there. Also need to see if Grace had any other marriages but maybe kept her name.*

An hour later with several reports in his hand, Mason rushed into Beauregard's office. "Captain, Grace has been married and divorced twice." He explained she kept her Grantley name when she divorced her second husband Attorney Bob Brown. "She met him when he taught at Emory University Law School for a semester. She divorced him six months later. Her marriage to Donald Grantley lasted eight months. They had met at Princeton. This means there is a real Donald Grantley and Grace is connected to him and to Bob Brown. What is going on, Captain?"

"I don't know but you have some interesting results here, Lieutenant, some interesting results. It's so friggin' complicated, all these deaths and different players from several states being overseen by the Feds and nothing has been resolved. The Feds are waiting for a break. It has to be DesCartes. Why else would they have a former colonel undercover living in a home overlooking DesCartes' house? Those rumors about Grace investing in the Fund; are they true? Find out.

"Three companies were vendors to the bankrupt Fund money

receivers and have Grantley's name all over. I'll bet dollars to donuts Donald Grantley majored in finance in college. Go after his history at Princeton and what graduate school he attended. Shake the bushes. He had to have post graduate degrees to teach even for a semester at Emory Law School, possibly in law or finance. Shake the bushes and have Ted help you. Get Sergeant Border also help too. He has a way with the ladies on the phone. It's a gift. We have to find Grantley. Where did Jed Mattias go to undergraduate and law schools? If he crossed paths we need to know and the age span is not too different amongst the players. Damnit, I have to be certain Mattias is only a victim. As to Grace Bevois Grantley, why two such short marriages? Get a list of her friends at each of her academic endeavors. Someone must hate her. Is Bob Brown married now? Perhaps his wife has something to add to our story. Get Ted to help you."

Norbie Cull and his admin assistant searched Bob Brown's legal cases memorialized in news print. Norbie scanned all attorneys associated with Brown until he came up with two known to him. He was successful in his calls which took a long time weeding out Brown's personal information. One of the lawyers who knew Norbie in law school said, "Brown's an alright guy but is careful in his dress and in connections. He is a handsome dude. Says he was once married and the marriage soured him. Norbie, he lives like an old man in a fancy condo in NYC, goes to bed by ten, working out at six in the morning, eats the same breakfast and lunch each day, and absolutely becomes severely upset when surprised. It's why he acts only as a second in all the trials. He can't take the heat. Funny to me since he does a great deal of work with clients I wouldn't take. You know, clients related to businesses not always quite up and up. I know he never steps over the line. He is basically an honest guy with connected clients. I believe he is legitimate because he could never jeopardize his lifestyle. Did I tell you he is OCD?"

Brown now peaked Norbie's interest. He asked Sheila to trace his one supposedly disastrous marriage. The resulting listed wife brought a smile to Norbie's face. "Sheila, I was uncomfortable with Grace Grantley from the start. The license says she had one previous marriage ending in divorce. Check it out. I need to know more about Grace Grantley.

"Grace Bevois' history did not look unusual to Norbie for a high achiever other than her two marriages. The first marriage to Donald Arrow Grantley brought a smile to his face, as he thought, *you're in this deep, Grace, and I don't think it's with Jed Mattias. How many types of criminal endeavors are in this? Brown would not want to be involved in murder despite his connection as an attorney for DesCartes. Come to think about it, DesCartes is a money man or, if anything else is going on, he is laundering money through art. Beryl told me Beauregard's wife saw art going for high prices at a West Mass Art gallery sale and was surprised. Western Massachusetts is not the first choice of areas I would be selling art; maybe in the Lenox area in the summer. Brown's not talking to the police and knowing the guys' hiding the auto involved in the accident brings him right into murder. Sheila is searching for Donald Arrow Grantley now. I have friends who were undergraduates at Princeton at about the same time. When students marry so young, it used to be the talk at the school. Someone must know of the two of them.*

The stationhouse was busy with the normal everyday problems of policing. The desk Sergeant expressed his displeasure at the attorneys for MCU's arrestees and voiced it. "Arresting suits created havoc. Four lawyers in the last hour trying to push us around. Some of them I've never seen before, out of towners for sure. Beauregard is at it again. Lots of adjectives about him spewed in the last three hours. He made them wait for the processing of the witnesses. No arrests made for murder yet. Missing Norberto Cull today who is normally in on all of this stuff."

Meanwhile, Beauregard was waiting for the attorneys to conference. He also couldn't understand why his detectives could not find Grace Grantley. He thought, *I want her in here to see this mess. She knows what's up. Why can't they find her? We couldn't get rid of her before.*

His phone buzzed. The intrusive Beryl said hello. Impatiently, Rudy said, "I don't have a lot of time for you, Beryl. What do you want?"

"Grace Grantley showed up at my home a few minutes ago. Rudy, she makes me nervous. She asked a couple of pointed questions and I don't know why she would have the know-how unless you've contacted to inform her you've arrested Rene. She also questioned me about the arrests of men who were harboring a car involved in an accident. She said she heard Attorney Bob Brown has been arrested. Has he?"

"Thank you, Beryl. I'll send a squad car out to sit on your property. Don't let her in if she returns."

"I won't. I don't feel comfortable with her. She is quite cold when she's not being charming. Did you arrest Bob Brown?"

"Police business, Beryl, but no, not yet."

He finished Beryl's call, when the desk sergeant let him know a woman attorney Grace Grantley wished to speak with him. Beauregard said, "Get her up here now. Have her escorted and don't make her wait. I don't want her to leave."

Beauregard met Grace who brought with her excess charm and chutzpah. The Captain asked Petra to join him in the large conference room. He called Millie requesting refreshments who said, "I saw her, Captain. She gets refreshments when the other witnesses don't, just because she's a looker?"

Ignoring Millie, Beauregard told Grace, "Thanks for coming in. We thought you'd disappeared. My detectives have been calling, texting, and emailing you with no answers."

"Captain, when I have something to say, I generally don't speak with subordinates."

Petra tried with little success to hide her rankled feelings, and was about to question the witness when Grace said, "I'm here because I understand you've arrested Attorney Bob Brown. Now I do know him and I can say with great certainty, he is an honest man."

Petra, who had not previously prepared for this witness interview with the Captain, said, "What do you think we would arrest him for, Ms. Grantley? Arresting attorneys is not the norm around here."

"Well, I should hope not. He is just an attorney for Mr. DesCartes. I know you arrested him and I can't fathom why. Jed fell on his property. I have always wondered why Jed would get on the helicopter with people he didn't know. Do you have evidence of Mr. DesCartes association with the other men arrested?"

Before Petra could speak, Beauregard asked, "Grace, why didn't you tell me you were once married to both Donald Arrow and Bob Brown? It would have been helpful. You heard Jed say he was to meet Mr. Donald Arrow relative to the divorce, and yet you pretended you didn't know Mr. Arrow."

Grace laughed. "You think I would discuss my personal life with you; no way in hell. The fact I knew Donald doesn't matter. It was so many years ago. I may have been interested in who he married and the divorce case, but I would never have allowed the firm to take Donald's divorce case."

"Grace, when did you first arrive in Western Massachusetts? It was not when you learned of Jed's accident, was it?

Grace swished her pretty hair. The movement prevented the detectives from seeing her reaction to the question. She answered, "I don't remember. There's a great deal to see here. I'm sure I've been here a few times."

Petra said, "Ms. Grantley, were you an investor in any of the companies receiving funds from the Fund that went bankrupt?"

Rudy thought, *this is it. She'll lawyer up although she hates doing it. What a steely-eyed woman with no grace showing now, just extreme willfulness.*

And she did lawyer up. The first attorney she called was Norberto Cull, who turned her down. She finally got counsel with a noted criminal attorney from Boston. Beauregard left Grace and Petra and a uniform in the room. And he waited for one or any of the attorneys to meet with him on their clients' cases.

While he waited, he pondered whether to arrest Attorney Bob Brown. Instead he called him and asked him if he was available for an interview at DesCartes' home, the alternative being at the station. Confirming Beauregard's instinct, Mr. Brown was interested in being interviewed at the estate. Before Beauregard left the office, he instructed his detectives to take as long as possible in processing interviews with attorneys. If they left annoyed, it was okay with him. He did not think they would, saying, "There are big fees involved here. The lawyers will be patient."

Beryl was home and deeply disturbed by a conversation with Jocelyn, who said, "Mom, you are dealing with dangerous people. Oliver told me the French neighbor Rene DesCartes has been stalking you. Do you even know who he is? I have heard some serious gossip, not gossip, if it's true, about him."

"What are you talking about, Jocelyn; tell me what you've heard. How could you hear anything about DesCartes? You live in New York City. And Oliver should keep his mouth shut."

"Oliver only tells me about real dangers, not your love life. You are like a child, Mother, always into something you should not be investigating."

"Stop it, Jocelyn. Now what have you heard about Rene?"

"Oh, it's Rene, now. Mother, stay away from him. I think he's involved in art smuggling and theft. There are art dealers in New York who won't carry his paintings now. He normally sells European artists' works in the U.S. and American artists' works in Europe and Asia. He's your neighbor and he is coming around. Stay away, you hear."

"I do hear you and thank you, but Jocelyn, in your isolation with your small world of art you have become arrogant and disrespectful. I don't like it."

Silence prevailed while Beryl and Jocelyn both stewed until Sam coaxed Jocelyn to join him in a run. Left alone, Beryl considered the ramifications of Jocelyn's gossip, *money laundering is Rene's forte. I should have known from the local art sale with art going for greater than expected prices. Would he kill to cover up? He attempts to intimidate me, but I think it's because I'm a woman. Would he hire outsiders for murder? It may be possible. More likely someone in this with him would be in charge of dirty business, while he could pretend he didn't know.*

His lawyer is Brown. Brown coaxed Jed to fly out here. Jed was sent here to be murdered which means Rene knew about it. And what about the auto accident victims who were at Rene's shortly before being killed with the car involved noted as coming from Rene's home just before the accident. Who else could it be aside from Rene? Where is Alexia and her husband in all of this. They were the entry point for Jed to be in New Jersey with Attorney Bob Brown.

Beryl called the Captain and gave him a synopsis of her new conclusions. After telling him Rene DesCartes was most likely money laundering in the international art market, he thanked her. She said, "Captain, it must start in Atlanta or Jed would not have flown up to

New Jersey. Someone in Atlanta knew Jed loved Marthea and would do anything to protect her. Who knows Jed well? I think with Harry gone, only Grace would know so much about him. Jed came here because of Harry's divorce case for Alexia and Donald. Harry didn't at first want the case, but still pursued it. He dies. The other issue is the fraud from the Fund. Is it the start of this case? I wonder."

Beauregard thanked Beryl. She felt sincerity in his voice and told him so.

Beauregard met with three of his detectives in the conference room. He repeated Beryl's story saying, "We have everything to close this case with the exception where the hell are Alexia and Donald? Where are they?"

Mason walked into the room. Hearing the Captain, he said, "I'm here to save you, again, Captain."

There were groans and some laughter before they were hushed by an impatient Beauregard. Mason had traced Donald Arrow Grantley. He used both names, Donald Arrow and Donald Grantley, intermittently as circumstances required. Mason followed him to graduate school at Wharton. Mason asked, "Guess who else was there at the same time?"

The detectives went through every name in their files and got a yes for Bob Brown but were told to keep going. Lilly said, "Must be the Frenchman. Europeans like the prestige of schools like Wharton. I didn't think he had the smarts. Arrow fits in nicely with the art/money laundering. His field was finance, right?"

Mason nodded and the discussion moved on to Alexia Marsh Raleigh. He had news on her whereabouts. "She's in federal custody, Captain."

"Where the hell is Donald now, Mason? Do you know?"

"Yup. Remember the patrol car you ordered to babysit DesCartes' home. Patrolman Jackowicz noticed a man who kept walking a dog on the grounds, but he didn't look like hired help. He got a picture and sent it over. It's Donald Arrow Grantley sitting right under our noses."

"Mason, does Donald have any other marriages besides Grace and Alexia?"

"Nope, and the marriage to Alexia was a whirlwind marriage. They met at a seminar he gave on financing small business. She had a company she was starting and wanted help to apply for dollars from the Fund. I think he married her to use her business to drain money."

"I can't touch Alexia. We knew all along the possibility of her being held as a witness by the Feds. I'm one step away from closing this case before the Feds shut me out. I need Donald. And I need Grace."

Beauregard saw Donald as access to Grace, with Grace as the most important person. "Grace is the doer. I'm certain of it. Donald is an advisor on washing money in this international art scheme. And this scheme is bizarre. Descartes and Donald wanted the money from Alexia's company. How does that mean money laundering? I think there is separate thievery going on. The Feds must know Donald is the financial brain with Rene and the art front. They do not know about Grace as a potential murderer.

"I'm not sure Donald and Rene know what happened. They must suspect. Rene supposedly wanted to see Jed. If he did, it was to follow the trail of the entrepreneurial Fund. He'd gotten his money washed until the Fund manager and one board member became thieves. Rene was an investor. This brought the Feds in and threatened Rene. Why did Grace think she was in jeopardy? If she did not invest in the Fund or wasn't a player in one of the companies receiving funds from the Fund, she would not be in jeopardy. She must be a player and Harry discovered it and some others knew of her involvement. Why else would she murder?"

Juan asked, "Aren't you going out on a limb here, Captain? Do you think Donald will turn on Grace? Without connections to the Fund, Grace is clean."

"No, Sergeant. I have been watching her since she first arrived. I just couldn't figure out how she fit in the equation. The deaths of those corporations' secretaries are your starting point. Grace would have had her fingerprints on those corporations. Check our accident victims' corporations for any connection to Grace, as a client or an associate. The connections are there, somewhere. Meanwhile, arrest Donald Grantley for murder. Do it before I'm prevented from doing it. The Feds don't know he's at DesCartes' home. If they did, he would have been picked up as a witness."

After the Captain left the conference room, the detectives expressed problems with Donald Arrow Grantley's arrest. Petra didn't think Donald would talk. The other men arrested, when lawyered up, refused to speak. Rene DesCartes wasn't speaking either. Mason said, "It's the Captain's call. Our work is to somehow show what Grace's connection is to the Fund. We need her motive."

24

The Maze Unraveled

Sergeant Ted Torrington was enjoying his research. He'd not been in many of the meetings with the Captain, but he had all the reports in front of him. Beauregard's arrest of Donald Grantley was imminent. Torrington was aware of the risk in arresting Grantley. He understood Grantley could be put right in the middle of the murder plot, but like the Captain, he didn't think Donald Grantley had the cojones for murder, thinking, *the guy's a finance suit. He married Alexia to put her in place for the money laundering scam. It was simply a vehicle along with the art swindles for money. He's a sociopath who marries his potential victim for profit. I get it. His first wife, and it looks like he's not the marrying kind with so many years between the two marriages, is Grace. What happens when two sociopaths get together. One is going to prevail in personal desires. I think the more-evil one prevails.*

Ted scanned Grace's divorce from Donald Grantley and rushed into his boss's office. "Captain, it was right here in front of us. Donald Grantley divorced Grace and accused her of violence against him. He had a witness to her behavior. It was Attorney Bob Brown."

Beauregard answered, "How does it help other than to support a friendship between Brown and Grantley? And why would Brown marry Grace if he knew she were violent?"

"It's not a clean connection, but they are a trio, together years ago, and together today. Could be they understand each other. Could Donald and Bob be using Grace as the enforcer?"

Sergeants Lilly Tagliano and Bobby Barr arrested Donald Arrow

Grantley as he was walking his dog in the rear yard of the DesCartes estate. Grantley made only one statement: "How'd you know I was here?"

It took an hour before Donald Grantley was brought to the interview room. He was represented by a local attorney, Joseph Lassiter, who surprisingly had a slight drawl from his law school years in the South. Beauregard waited for answers to some initial questioning handled by Sergeant Aylewood-Locke before saying, "Did you know, Mr. Grantley, your wife Alexia is in federal custody?"

Donald could not hide his surprise. He asked for time with his attorney to speak. Beauregard said, "Of course, you may have time. You are in a fix, Donald. The first wife setting you up for murders and the second wife testifying against you for money laundering and giving you a motive for murder."

Not long after the detectives left the conference room, Mr. Lassiter asked to speak with the Captain. In a smaller room, Lassiter asked, "Why hasn't Donald been arrested by the FBI?"

"They'll be here once they learn of his arrest for murder. They have several agencies using FinCEN that allowed investigations into prosecuting Money Laundering Facilitators. Paperwork takes time. In addition, IRS will be all over it. Your client is in the catbird seat for multiple murders and attempts to murder. Good lawyering will help him on the federal level and he is stuck there, but does he want a murder conviction? Grace Grantley has set him up for a murder conviction."

"Captain, I don't see it. From what I know, Donald has done nothing to connect him with this murder. He says he's no different than Rene DesCartes. They may have been at the estate but know nothing about the murders."

Beauregard said softly, "Go that way if you think you can trust Grace Grantley. I don't believe Donald trusts her."

"Captain, you have Grace in custody as a witness? For what?"

"About a money laundering case? What else?"

Attorney Lassiter replied, "You're playing who talks first. What do you need to know? My client is not a murderer. Why would you arrest Rene DesCartes as a witness and my client as a murderer? The scant circumstantial evidence would be the same in both cases. Why not use my client as a witness?"

"Think of your client's connections to all the players, Mr. Lassiter, direct connections. He was married to Grace who was later married to Bob Brown. He knew Brown and DesCartes. He was arrested at DesCartes' residence where an assault action started. He has been in hiding. He has motive to get rid of witnesses based on his draining his wife's business assets. His wife is now a witness against him. And other circumstantial evidence exists. We have three men involved in the deliberate execution of two financial investors in the Funds who are waiting to talk to me. Prove Donald is not a murderer. Remember, Grace will testify against him."

Lassiter asked for some more time with his client. Not twenty minutes later he again asked to see the Captain. "Captain, my client is concerned his ex-wife Grace will say anything to protect herself. He wants you to know she was violent in their marriage and court records will support her violence. His current wife does not hate him. She is concerned about money for the divorce and he will allay those concerns. He insists he knows nothing about murder, but is willing to say what he does know about the goings on at the DesCartes residence. He stayed there during the time when the helicopter landed and thereafter. It is the limit on what he is willing to discuss."

They discussed protection from prosecution for Grantley as a witness for his statements related to the Fund. He was informed that Beauregard could not make promises. The Fund investigation was federal and he had no control. Grantley agreed to make a witness statement to his presence at the estate and his knowledge of the men who visited there. The essence of the statement included the following: he could identify Coderre as the man who left after Marlene Green and David Spencer left the estate; there had been a conference he was not invited to attend which angered him; Grace and DesCartes met with Green and Spencer, whose clients were investors in the Fund under the direction of DesCartes. The two wanted their money and were threatening to bring light on the Fund. Both sets of clients, who invested big money, now wanted their investments back; and DesCartes promised to back up their investments if they would not go forward in inviting trouble.

Donald Grantley heard all this from listening outside the study door at the house. According to him the staff was busy doing other work and thought he was to be trusted. DesCartes never told his staff to be careful of him. He said Grace was particularly gifted in persuading the two investors of her and DesCartes' their willingness to insure their clients' losses. Green and Spencer soon left. He did not hear about the accident until a week later when DesCartes told him the two were killed by a truck hitting them. Donald had met Coderre and the other two men the day before the accident when they helicoptered in. There was a lot of noise outside made them searching the area. He was told some piece of the copter fell and they were looking for the piece. Rene and Grace were tense. He never saw the police come to the estate. He'd often go into town out of boredom. DesCartes was, although a friend from way back, no fun as a companion. He did see Beryl visit the house. He wanted to meet her. DesCartes acted as if she was an old friend when he met her at the door. Instead of bringing her into the main room, he brought her into his office. She left soon afterward. According to Donald, Beryl did not see him.

Grace left for Atlanta the day of the car accident according to Donald's best memory. She had come to West Mass to see both Rene and him about Alexia's divorce and its implications. She was not a happy camper. Donald would not explain why his divorce was an issue with her and Rene. He said, "You're interested in murder. I did not murder anyone. I did not know about murders. As to Alexia and my divorce and the reasons why, that is my personal business."

Beauregard asked if Donald knew the three men who arrived in the helicopter. He said, "Captain, I met them in Atlanta. They came to my home before I left Alexia. She wasn't there that day. They looked like business types. I thought she knew them. I forgot to tell her. I was busy getting out of there. I knew there'd be too much attention on me."

Beauregard left Donald and his attorney in the room waiting to sign his statement. He said he would return later to make a decision. Lassiter said, "You can't believe Grace Grantley, Captain. She won't help him out. She's just as abusive today as she was in their marriage and he responds to it. Why he told her he was going to Rene's home I don't know. He claims he didn't tell her, so how did she know? Rene told her. They are in it together."

Lieutenant Aylewood-Locke and Sergeant Bill Border joined Beauregard in interviewing Grace Grantley with her attorney. Beauregard handed Sergeant Border the first opening question he was to use. She was willing to speak to them.

Sergeant Border started the questioning after he introduced himself to Grace and her lawyer. She interrupted the flow and said, "Sergeant, I'm here to support Rene, Bob, and Donald. Believe me, not one of those men is capable of murder. I don't understand how Bob or Donald could be witnesses in the assaults on Jed. I suppose you have a right to question Rene, who is a friend from way back. It was at his property on which you think Jed landed. I don't think he knows anything. The three men you arrested could be involved for all I know, but my friends could never murder."

"Miss Grantley, did you know those three men before you arrived at Rene DesCarte's home."

Grace appeared to think carefully, saying, "I really can't be certain, but I don't think so. They aren't my clients and not my type for social interaction."

Sergeant Border then questioned, "How much did you invest in the Fund through your relationship with David Spencer and Marlene Green's corporations?"

Grace said giving a hard smile, "Much as I would like to assist you, that's not a question I will answer."

Beauregard and Petra left the room leaving Bill Border to sit with the witness. Petra said, "Captain, when did you discover Grace actually invested funds in those corporations?"

"I didn't, Lieutenant. I guessed, and I guessed right. Now Mason must find evidence. And now I know Grace had a motive to kill and is a liar. It was all done to cover up her involvement in the money laundering. Harry got wise and bingo! He's dead. I do not know how she did it, but she did it. She thought and still thinks Jed has the paperwork in the divorce papers somewhere about her investment, making it necessary to remove him. The corporate secretaries who conveniently died probably witnessed her involvement directly. She was the only one close enough to Jed to pull the whole Marthea thing. She thought he would just disappear in New England, and the Feds would think Jed ran because of his involvement in the Fund's losses; after all, both he and Harry had directly and traceably invested some big money.

"Alexia's running created a problem. I think Donald would eventually be on Grace's murder list. He probably told Alexia about Grace being involved. If he's dead, without him Alexia can't support her claims. Grace cannot lose or let go. The whole situation was out of control. What looked easy at first became more difficult. She practically begged Harry and Jed not to join the civil suit under the pretense of the law firm's reputation. I'm certain we'll find she got the attorney for those investors who did file the civil suit by paying half the fee. He is a weak attorney and the money would look good. The civil case in the fund's losses will go nowhere in court with him as counsel. We have lots of holes in our case, but let's do it. Our goal is to arrest Grace Grantley for murder and conspiracy to murder for our three murders, Lieutenant. But I can't do that now. I'll ask the DA to impanel a grand jury and hear Donald Grantley, the three men, and Grace's testimonies. I'll inform Lieutenant Smith he is to contact police departments having jurisdiction on Harry's murder and the three corporate secretaries' murders today. The shit will hit the fan once Grace is charged for murder and it is made public. We'll change Donald's arrest to that of a material witness if he tells us more about Grace. And he will say more than he has now.

"Call Beryl Kent. Tell her she can inform the Feds. She'll know how. Just tell her I said to tell her friend. I have this feeling I'll be meeting Ms. Beryl Kent again. She may be intrusive, but she means to do good and she has."

Beryl Kent entertained her government colleague along with Jed, Marthea, and Oliver. Jed felt safe, but was particularly saddened by Grace Grantley's betrayal. "Beryl, I knew she went after the jugular in all her cases, but lots of lawyers do the same. I knew she loved money. I didn't know how much. I never, ever, thought she was a murderer. Grace is evil and I should have had some insight, but I didn't. Those closest to us can fool us because we don't really see them for what they are. They become an everyday colleague and thereby removed from suspicion."

Beryl's response was interrupted by the doorbell. She greeted the police artist Josephine who had been invited by Jed for supper. Beryl thought, *romance is in the air. Three couples arise from the ashes of murder. Then, there is me. My spy friend says he will tell all today. Maybe I'll believe him. I would like to believe him.*

Beryl's home was now safe, but West Mass citizens were shocked when all hell broke out. The grand jury rumors led citizens to believe that important people were to be arrested for murder and money laundering. One of those sure to be indicted was a French citizen, a resident of West Mass who supported the arts. Gossip prevailed despite masks and no groups larger than six people congregating under Massachusetts's mandate for COVID.

As to Captain Beauregard, he was happy. His light leg cast was off. He was now certain his murderer would be prosecuted and the players in the money laundering case would by the FEDS. The FEDS were pleased; they now had a basis to follow the money with its international implications. Moreover, Rudy mused, *the new year is almost here.*

The Feds had said nothing to the Captain when they claimed their prisoners and witnesses. Grace would be tried for murder in West Mass first, which was Beauregard's only goal. He did not welcome the invitation he received to meet with federal, state, and county prosecutors to discuss communications, but he thought, *what the heck, they know Grace should not walk the streets. Tried for murder is essential. Otherwise, she'd be a federal witness and make a deal. The murder charge would be put on the back burner and maybe never brought forward. She knows all the players both in the U. S. and internationally. Justice is somewhat appeased, never completely. The victims will always remain dead or traumatized. It's just the best I can do from my perch in life.*

Care to Review My Book?
(or "Honest Reviews Don't Kill")

Now that you've read the story to the end, I'd love to know what you think of it – and read your honest review about the book on Amazon, Goodreads or other major online book retailers where it is featured.

https://kbpellegrino.com/review-brothers-from-another-mother

Review some of my other books:

https://kbpellegrino.com/review-sunnyside-road
https://kbpellegrino.com/review-mary-lou
https://kbpellegrino.com/review-a-predatory-cabal
https://kbpellegrino.com/review-him-me-paulie
https://kbpellegrino.com/review-killing-the-venerable
https://kbpellegrino.com/review-beryl-kent

Thank you for your interest in my books!

Kathleen

More Books by K.B. Pellegrino

Evil Exists in West Side Trilogy:

–Sunnyside Road: Paradise Dissembling
(Livres-Ici Publishing) 2021, (Liferich Publishing) 2018

–Mary Lou: Oh! What Did She Do?
(Livres-Ici Publishing) 2021, (Liferich Publishing) 2018

–Brothers of Another Mother: All for One! Always?
(Livres-Ici Publishing) 2021, (Liferich Publishing) 2019

Other Books in the Captain Beauregard Mystery Series

–Him, Me and Paulie: Drugs, Murder and Undercover
(Livres-Ici Publishing) 2019

–A Predatory Cabal: Worm in the Apple
(Livres-Ici Publishing) 2020

–Killing the Venerable: It's Their Time!
(Livres-Ici Publishing) 2020

You can find K. B. Pellegrino's books on all major online Book Stores, such as Amazon, Barnes & Noble, kobo, and iBooks.

Bonuses, Giveaways, and Freebies

Free Chapters

"Sunnyside Road: Paradise Dissembling"

Download a free chapter of the first book in the Evil Exists in West Side Trilogy "Sunnyside Road: Paradise Dissembling" at www.kbpellegrino.com/sunnyside-road/FreeChapter

"Him, Me, and Paulie: Drugs, Murder and Undercover"

Download a free chapter of the Captain Beauregard Series book #4 "Him, Me, and Paulie: Drugs, Murder and Undercover" at www.kbpellegrino.com/him-me-paulie/FreeChapter

Join My Private Email List

To receive updates about books, new releases, upcoming events, or to simply keep in touch with me, join my private email list.

We do not release your information to any other vendors. www.kbpellegrino.com/join-list

To access more freebies, visit: www.kbpellegrino.com/bonus

Follow K. B. Pellegrino

On her website at www.kbpellegrino.com
On GoodReads at https://www.goodreads.com/author/K.B.Pellegrino
On Facebook: https://www.facebook.com/kbpellegrino
On Instagram: https://www.instagram.com/kbpellegrino_author/
On Twitter: https://twitter.com/kbpellegrino